The LaPorte Inheritance

By Deborah deBilly dit Courville

THE SAMOTHRACE PRESS

This is a work of fiction. All historical figures and places mentioned herein are represented as accurately as possible, except where reliable information was unavailable or conflicting to the extent that discernment of the facts was unable to be accomplished.

The author does not represent herself to know the actual feelings, motives, or opinions of any historical figures represented or referred to herein, unless such feelings, motives or opinions were discovered during the author's examination of primary source material while researching this book.

While most of the characters in this work were actual, living real people, others were not, and are purely the invention of the author's imagination. So too, while there are real places mentioned, there are others that have been contrived by the author for the purpose of advancing the narrative.

The author acknowledges the trademarked status of various items referenced herein, which have been used because such items and their names are in the public domain by dint of common use. The use of these trademarks is not associated with or sponsored by the trademark owners.

Any other interpretation of the matter contained in this book is beyond the scope of the author's intention.

About the Author

The author of THE LAPORTE INHERITANCE, Deborah deBilly dit Courville, is an historical interpreter at the LaPorte House at French Azilum, located near Towanda, Pennsylvania. As a member of the Board of Directors for Azilum, she volunteers as a tour guide, coordinates several special events at the site during its open season, curates the site's Period Clothing Exhibit, and helps maintain Azilum's herb garden and perennial beds. Since beginning her formal association with Azilum a few years ago, Courville has become fascinated with the characters who built the refuge more than two centuries in the past, and has now transformed that fascination into this historical novel.

Author of the popular 'Oldest House' series, set at another historic home in Northeastern Pennsylvania, Courville is known worldwide for her acclaimed mystery series, 'Reporting is Murder!'© penned under the name of a paternal great-great-grandmother, Eugénie D. West.

Courville holds a Ph.D. in Linguistics & English, enjoys history, languages, music and science, and is an intrepid and inveterate traveler. She is directly descended from Eleanor of Aquitaine, King Louis VII of France and Charlemagne.

Visit Courville on Twitter at @LadyCourville, on Facebook at Deborah de Billy dit Courville and her page, Deborah L. Courville, and on her blog, 'Lacing up a Modern Woman: Adventures in the 18th Century' at DLC18thcentury.blogspot.com

A Note From the Author

Historical fiction, if one cares about getting the details right, is not easy. It is harder when there are abundant sources from and concerning the time and people being written about. I feel that the author has a responsibility to be truthful whenever possible, but sometimes several sources can be contradictory, thus making this task more difficult.

This is the first work of fiction I have ever written for which I contemplated compiling a Bibliography. I chose not to, mostly because I had become so caught up in my research, I had neglected to write down all my sources, never thinking I might wish I had. And also, after all, this is *fiction*.

I was very fortunate while writing this book to have the endless and enthusiastic cooperation of French Azilum's Site Director, Lee Kleinsmith, as well as the opportunity to mine Azilum's Research Library with its collection of letters, accounts, memoirs and books. I am also glad that there are such excellent reference works available online in both English and French, which came in very handy for my research.

Still, there were some things—like the name of the ship that brought Talon and LaPorte to the United States—that it seemed no amount of research could uncover (although I did find some glaringly erroneous 'facts' in a few cases!). In situations like this, I have used what I call 'informed imagining' to fill in the details that I felt the narrative needed. At other junctures, there were two (or more!) conflicting accounts of events, dates, or the placement of various buildings at the original settlement. Confronted with this, I chose the one I either liked the best, felt made the most sense to me, or which fit with the story better than the others.

Similarly, although clues as to the characters' personalities and appearances can be gleaned from primary source material, including diaries, census records, sketches, and pictures, I have had to flesh out the rest, using logical deduction as well as my own instincts. I feel as though I have intuited my main characters' personalities pretty well, and I will confess, I became quite taken with my hero, Bartholomew LaPorte.

Despite fairly exhaustive research, it seems that almost every new source I encounter holds another tidbit of information I need to include. I could continue researching for several more years, but there comes a time when a compromise between research and publication must be struck, and this is that time.

I know that there will always be more to uncover and learn, and I am sure that, despite my efforts, I have recounted some details inaccurately. However, please remember that this is a novel, and therefore, fiction. Just as research and publication must reach an *entente*, so too must the plot and story line, with historical detail.

Although I have been as factual and accurate as possible within the scope of a fictional work, in a few cases I tweaked the truth to better fit with and further the story, or to be more pleasing to modern sensibilities. In other instances, I elided over details that I could not verify, particularly if they were not crucial to the action of the book.

And because every novel has to have a pivotal feature around which the rest of the story moves—otherwise it would be historical non-fiction—I invented the central thread that runs throughout this book and which forms its title: the LaPorte inheritance. There is absolutely no empirical evidence to suggest that anything like what I relate in this book actually happened. However, given other documented incidents around the time of the French Revolution, my fabrication is at least credible, if not factual. And, after more than 200 years, who's to say, really?

In any case, I hope readers will become as captivated as I have been by the LaPortes, the other families who sought refuge at this amazing colony, and the story of a mostly forgotten episode in history: French Azilum.

~DdeBditC, Doolittle Hill
 Summer, 2017

Also by Deborah L. Courville:

(The Oldest House Series)

A RIVER IN TIME

TREACHERY IN TIME

A CHRISTMAS IN TIME

A RESCUE IN TIME

§

RAPHAEL'S STORY

§

Writing as Eugénie D. West:

(The 'Reporting is Murder!'© Series)

BABY'S BREATH

COERCION

BLACK CARD

WHERE THERE'S SMOKE THERE'S MURDER

SPIN

TIDE'S REACH

NATURAL CAUSES

PRECIPICE

COUNTER MEASURES

CRIME & CRIMINI

APPLE OF MY EYE

NEARLY DEPARTED

Dedicated to all those who lived, worked, hoped and dreamed at French Azilum.

CONTEMPORARY (1795) SKETCH PLAN OF AZILUM

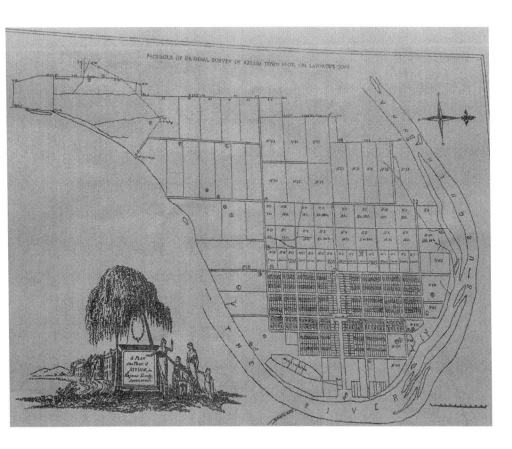

Courtesy of French Azilum, Inc.

Cover photo by Iris Associates©

Chapter One

Summer, 1857, the LaPorte House at French Azilum

"Charles?" Elizabeth, known to her family as 'Lisette,' turned in the big mahogany bed that had been her father's and felt only empty space along the soft cotton sheets. She felt the child inside her—he or she was nearing full term now—move. She sat up carefully, one hand on the delicate muslin chemise that cascaded over her belly, and then stood.

Through the window, the last quarter moon shone a faint silver, and the cool night breezes of mid June in the Pennsylvania countryside wafted scents of herbs and grasses. Elizabeth took a deep, contented breath.

But where was her husband? And what had awakened her?

She lifted a fringed silk shawl from the chair beside the bed and tiptoed the few feet towards the partially opened door. It creaked only slightly as she edged it wide and stepped into the upstairs hall.

It was more of a landing than a hall, really, as it was square: the doors to the attic and all the bedrooms opened onto it.

Everything was quiet. Elizabeth felt in the near darkness for the small box of matches and the candlesticks that were kept on the marble topped table here; finding them, she struck a match, and lit one of the beeswax stubs, then blew out the match and laid it carefully on the cool marble.

In the past several years, they'd had a whale oil lamp here lit all night, turned down low. But recent economies had meant that the expensive whale oil was only used on special occasions, not on a daily basis. And so, the candlesticks returned to favor. The ornamental whale oil lamp, however, still stood, dark, in the center of the table.

A soft rumbling came from behind the door that led to the house's attic. There, Nanny Moody had her little room, along with the most senior house maid. Crossing the landing, Elizabeth gained the partly open one of the children's room and peeked in.

Frederick and John were in their bunk beds against the inside wall, sleeping soundly. The boys loved the beds which they thought of as part of the United States' westward expansion and therefore very exciting. Sometimes, Elizabeth thought her sons liked coming from their main home in the nearby city of Athens to the family's summer home here at Azilum merely because it meant they got to sleep in those beds, and imagine themselves, like Daniel Boone, out on the wild frontier.

She smiled at them: Frederick was 12 and John nearly seven. She felt a sleepy kick from the baby she carried and put a soothing hand on her side. She wondered if it would join its brothers, if a boy, or find itself among the ranks of its sisters, if a girl.

Her daughter Louise, three, was in a crib between two of the room's three windows, all of which were open wide to the fresh air and dark, star-studded sky. The moon's beams touched the bare old floorboards faintly through the east-facing casement. Louise still sucked her thumb, and had thrown one plump leg out from under the covers Nanny Moody had no doubt tucked up carefully around her.

Elizabeth smiled again, and gave a quick glance around the room. When the new child came, it would sleep, for a while, in a cradle in the room she shared with her husband. By the time they returned to this house, however, next summer, it would be nearly a year old and Elizabeth wondered briefly if they might not better put

Louise in the other bed chamber, the one she had had herself, as a child. If the new baby were a girl, she could share with Louise. If it were a boy, it could share with its older brothers.

Well, they'd manage: they always did, she thought to herself with a soft smile, and then turned, and went to the head of the stair. Gripping the bannister firmly and holding up the hem of her chemise clear of her toes, she made her way carefully down the graceful stair until she reached the ground floor and the grand foyer.

A light shone dimly through the open door of her own little sitting room, and she knew her husband, Charles F. Welles, must be in the room beyond, which was the library, and which he used as his office.

"Charles?" she queried again, rounding the corner of the doorway between the two rooms and spying her husband. He was sitting in a leather and wood lounge chair in front of a low fire, its embers casting a reddish glow on the planes of his face. A tall, well made and not unattractive man who bore some resemblance in his presence and attitude to Elizabeth's father, Charles was normally quite a jovial man, with a positive can-do attitude and clear grey eyes that saw only opportunities.

But now, Elizabeth's husband was downcast: the ruddiness of his features was only due to the fire's light, for his complexion was pale. His head hung low as he stared into the fire, somber. He sighed.

"Charles—whatever is the matter?" Elizabeth asked quickly, and went to his side. Because of her bulk, bending was difficult, but she reached a hand out to clasp one of his and asked her question again.

Her husband sighed again, and gripped her hand tightly. Then, wordless, he rose and gestured for her to sit.

"I am sorry, Lisette, to have awakened you," he said softly as she sat down. Their hands were still clasped.

She shook her head, its long wavy brown hair cascading over her shoulders as she did so. "It is no matter, Charles: what is troubling you?" she asked, gazing up at him earnestly. She could see deep lines in his forehead and on either side of his mouth. Charles was 44, 13 years her senior, but tonight he looked far older than his years.

He gripped her hand again, and then bent down, lifting it to his lips, and kissed it in a gesture that reminded her of when they had first begun courting.

"Oh, my Lisette, I am so sorry..." he began in a low voice.

She waited. What had happened? What had he done? Had he been unfaithful to her? That was her first instinct, as she knew that many men sought relief, as they called it, elsewhere when their wives were with child. But Charles never had. They had always managed. And in any case, he had always been so busy with his businesses, first the lumber business, then the retail stores and more lately the canals and railroads, that he had never had time to stray. So, what could it be?

"What is it, Charles?" she asked again. "Whatever it is, tell me, and we shall get through it together," she assured him in a calm tone.

He sighed again, kissed her hand again, and then let it go, moving to stand with one hand on the fireplace mantel. He bent his forehead briefly to it, then stood and turned to face her.

"I have lost it. My investment—our investment—in the North Branch Canal."

Charles had recently bought the North Branch Canal in a final attempt to circumvent what he saw as the state's blockage of its development.

"Governor Bigler—?" she began, but fell silent as her husband nodded heavily.

"He does not wish to do anything which might benefit our neighbor, New York," Charlie began. "Which, of course, the North Branch and the Junction Canals would do. But it would also benefit Pennsylvania. But he does not see that." He sighed. "And further, he believes our Commonwealth can best weather any financial storm, such as those that have struck in England and elsewhere, by selling off any interests in railroads and canals," Charles informed her, his tone bitter. "I think that is foolishness: the railroads and canals will allow the east to supply the west, allow progress, allow goods and materials to make even greater expansion across the land, and that will ensure our future," he explained, sounding for a moment much like his usual confident self.

Elizabeth frowned. "That seems unusual for the Governor," she offered quietly, thinking. "He encouraged Sam Morse, didn't he? He had the foresight to see that the telegraph would be a vital way to link our huge country and perhaps someday the world," she murmured, and her husband nodded.

"Indeed he did," Charles agreed. "And where better to run telegraph lines than along the railroads and canals?" he asked rhetorically. "The land is already cleared, it would not be difficult to set the poles and lay the cable..." He sighed again. "I cannot understand his reasoning, but it matters little. The North Branch Canal is closed."

Elizabeth waited a beat, then took a breath. "Are we ruined, Charles?"

Her husband first looked down at the carpet, a Turkish one in now-faded shades of red and gold that had belonged to her father, and then back at her.

"Near enough, my dear. Near enough."

Chapter Two

Marseille, France October, 1792

The interior of Le Bac was as densely smoky as it normally was of an evening, and the fog outside, which entered as patrons did, only added to the murky atmosphere. The small tavern smelled, not unpleasantly, of wood and pipe smoke, sawdust, and ale.

Marquis Antoine Omer Talon sat hunched in his usual shadowed corner, the wide brim of his dark leather hat pulled low to hide his features.

His fine straight nose, rather full lips and large oval brown eyes were not often seen, even at night, and in any case would likely not be known to the other patrons of Le Bac: they were to a man rough sailors from the port, just a block away, and only concerned with enjoying what little leisure time they had on dry land.

But the agents of Robespierre were everywhere. Who was to say they might not have followed Talon here, he worried, and even now be searching for him?

Talon shifted uneasily in the wooden chair, and took a sip of his drink. It was the tavern's basic red wine, a cheap, sharp-edged Rhône and not at all to Talon's more refined tastes. Still, he couldn't abide the more popular ales, disliked the fortified wines so prevalent in the area, and got heartburn if he drank whiskey. So...the inferior Rhône it was.

The fireplace of Le Bac was some distance from Talon's spot, the better that he might go unnoticed in the semi-darkness. France's former Avocat Général shivered slightly beneath the thick woolen cape that draped his shoulders.

" 'Soir," murmured a wiry, slender man of middling height, dressed in brown wool leggings and breeches, with a black wool coat and hat. The man sat down, setting his own thick glass filled with wine on the small table that was now between them. He tugged at a knobbly, knitted scarf around his neck and opened a couple of buttons on his coat, revealing a glimpse of the bright yellow silk waistcoat beneath.

He sighed, then rubbed his long-fingered hands together and looked expectantly at his neighbor. "Ça va?" he asked in a low voice. Nonetheless, he was smiling slightly, and his tone suggested that he really cared about Talon's answer.

Talon shrugged. "I'm well enough," he answered shortly. "You?"

The new arrival, whose name was Bartholomew LaPorte, broke into an amiable grin and took off his hat, showing wavy brown hair that fell rather lustrously nearly to his shoulders. He had a long nose paired with merry eyes in a face whose complexion recalled sun-filled summers past.

"I'm fine, fine...better than fine, my friend, for I bring good news!" LaPorte shared in an excited whisper, his black eyes snapping with excitement. LaPorte sipped at his drink, then made a face, said, 'pah!' in distaste, and wiped his mouth on his coat sleeve. "They call this ruby port?" he asked rhetorically of his companion. But his voice was low: no sense offending the proprietor, who left them to themselves and never bothered them when they met at his establishment, often for hours at a time.

Talon shrugged. He had been waiting for LaPorte. He expected that they would meet, because they did so several evenings a week, to just visit, sometimes, but sometimes also to plan. Unlike himself, who kept to his little room in North Saint Catherine Street, and to the shadows when he had to go out, LaPorte was free to roam the city. He heard what was going on: a useful thing if one were on the run, as was Talon.

LaPorte himself was a refugee, but not from the revolutionaries or pseudo-government in power in France. Rather, he'd been forced out of Spain, and all his assets seized a couple years before, when France and Spain went to war. It had been one of the seemingly endless wars in the series that together comprised the French Revolution, with one nation allied along side others against an opposing conglomerate of nations.

The result had been that LaPorte had fetched up in Marseille almost penniless. But the cleverly optimistic man who had made a fortune as a wine merchant in Cadiz was not about to be bested. Oh, no: he had his sights set on the new land, the place of opportunity: the United States.

Since that country was neutral in the French hostilities, it was a desirable refuge, and also boasted a large French population in some of its coastal cities.

LaPorte had been working on earning enough money to secure his passage for the past several months. Having much experience as a wine merchant and also having a reasonably good nose and palate, he had been able to find ready and abundant work among the merchants of Marseille. Although what he earned was nothing like the fortune he had amassed in Cadiz, where he'd traded chiefly in fortified wines like port and sherry, he was able to rent decent rooms and put some money by.

He was also able to befriend, in the course of his work, the merchant ships' captains and crews when they were in port, and thus be assured of knowing when passage might be available at a price he could afford.

Thus it was that he brought his 'good news' to Talon this rainy autumn night.

"The *Amaryllis* sets sail for Deal tomorrow, with the evening tide," LaPorte whispered now, leaning in towards Talon to speak.

That man also inclined his head to listen, enough so that the brim of his hat nearly touched his friend's forehead.

And friend he was, Talon thought. He and LaPorte had met by chance, if one believed in such things, at the Night Market several months before. Talon generally went abroad only at night and was careful where he traveled, so he would not become known. In the city of Marseille, which truly lived up to its reputation as a place for smugglers, pirates and other persons who operated in the shadows, people could usually live quietly with no questions asked if they so desired.

And Talon desired exactly that. At least until he could book passage out of France. But trying to get a berth on an outbound ship was exactly the kind of activity that could draw attention to himself, particularly if the ship's captain, or any of her crew, were chummy with the local gendarmes. Police here were almost as shadowy in ethics as many of Marseille's inhabitants: money frequently changed hands on the quay, ensuring that the police looked the other way whenever a below board portion of the 'import export' trade needed to proceed unmolested. So Talon feared that, should he try to secure passage, the police would inevitably be tipped off, and he would be captured and brought back to Paris—and the guillotine.

When Talon had encountered LaPorte in the Market, he had immediately realized the former wine merchant was exactly the sort of ally he needed if he was ever to escape France alive. LaPorte, whose broad langue d'Oc dialect fit right in and did not prompt second looks, as Talon's northern syllables did, seemed to know everyone. And everyone seemed to know—and like—him. The more circumspect Talon was not only drawn to this, he knew it was a trait that would allow LaPorte to easily achieve Talon's objective: a ship out of France.

They had struck up their peculiar friendship, the former wine merchant and the former Avocat Général to Louis XVI: an association that, in the French society that existed prior to the Revolution, would never have been possible. But now, well, Talon had not only initiated the meeting, he had encouraged further engagements with LaPorte, and that cheerful man had been sympathetic to Talon's plight and indeed, happy to try to help.

Both of them had, for different reasons, fixed on the new United States as their haven, Talon because politically the U.S. was safe for him, and LaPorte because he thought the new nation was a land of great opportunity. Both knew of the large French population in Philadelphia, and LaPorte had been glad that the city was also a thriving port.

'I can make a lot of money there,' he had said assuredly. 'I know all the best wineries and producers in Spain, and in Portugal, and in the south of France. I can be king of the wine trade in Philadelphia!' he had declared with enviable self-confidence. 'But, I suppose I shall have to learn English,' he had murmured then to Talon, sounding displeased.

'What is wrong with English?' Talon had asked curiously.

LaPorte had made a face, wrinkling his long nose and twisting his wide, expressive mouth. 'It is an ugly language I think,' he had offered in judgement. 'But—I shall learn it!' He sounded determined.

Talon had smiled. Perhaps, to his friend's ear, accustomed as it was to the softer, more elided phonetics of Occitan and Spanish, the more Germanic sounds of English did sound harsh. To him, however, a native of Paris and married to a noblewoman from Belgium, English was more familiar, and held neither attraction nor distaste: it had been a language he had needed to know for diplomacy, and so he had learned it. And, to clinch the deal with LaPorte, he had promised to teach him English on the voyage to the U.S.

Now, Talon moved his eyes to meet his friend's. "The *Amaryllis*?" he asked, and frowned. "But surely, that is not a passenger ship," he objected, low.

Most of the trade in and out of the harbor was, indeed, goods, not people, and Talon knew that ships whose primary purpose was moving passengers were few and far between.

"*Òc, plan segur*!" LaPorte returned, "yes, to be sure. But I have a plan," he told Talon, and laid one nimble finger aside his long nose, and gave a wink.

Chapter Three

The route would take the *Amaryllis*, a ship with English registry, south west through the Strait of Gibraltar, then north to Lisbon, Portugal. There it would stop to take on fresh supplies, offload some cargo and take on new. Then it would continue on, almost directly North across the Bay of Biscay to Brest, France's westernmost point on the continent.

This, LaPorte had cautioned, would be the most dangerous moment for Talon, because although the ship was technically part of English soil since it was registered there, calling at a French port would naturally be hazardous for a French royalist on the run from the new order in that country.

The clever man's solution to this and indeed the entire issue of getting Talon out of France without documentation was simple, but not easy, at least for Talon. It was essential that Talon board the *Amaryllis* without identifying himself or leaving any record that could be traced. There would be no mention of him as a passenger on that or any other ship, so he would be presumed to still be in Marseille, or at least in France somewhere, if Robespierre's men were hunting for him. Once LaPorte and Talon arrived safely in England, the latter could reveal his identity, confident of being sheltered there.

So the question was how to get Talon aboard, out of France, and onto English soil without notice, and without documentation.

Using a barrel from a friend who was a waterfront cooper and who owed him a favor, LaPorte had invited Talon to crawl inside the large wooden cask, which was then put with the rest of LaPorte's shipment of wine bound for London. LaPorte's brother, a seaman his entire life, had assisted with this project and had even signed on to the *Amaryllis* for her journey to England, to be at hand should his brother and Talon need help during the trip.

The barrels, including Talon's, were loaded into the *Amaryllis'* cargo hold by means of many hands and a rickety ramp that swayed with every step. Because the contents were supposed to be wine, the barrels were not jostled too much, but Talon was queasy nonetheless at the handling, and was oddly grateful when at last his barrel came to rest in the dark hold. However, the presence of some agents of the Republic as well as Robespierre's forces, who were patrolling the docks, had made LaPorte's scheme a necessary one.

Once the ship was underway, LaPorte's brother explained to the Captain that his brother Bartholomew had especially tasked him with the duty of checking the wine shipment each day for leaks. The Captain thought this was a bit over cautious, but he certainly did not mind: he and his crew even joked that, should a barrel of wine leak so severely that the leak could not be mended, they must be allowed to enjoy the escaping beverage. Grinning, LaPorte had agreed.

Whenever LaPorte's brother gained the hold—and it was fortunate he was a fairly short man like his brother, for the hold was low-ceilinged—he popped the lid on Talon's barrel, allowing him a few minutes of relatively fresh air, and to stretch his legs. Because Talon was taller than the LaPortes, however, this consisted largely of him bending over and from side to side, and walking a few stooped steps in a circle while trying not to bump his head on the wooden rafters above him. LaPorte's brother also brought Talon bits of food and drink, though the stowaway was not inclined to eat very much because of his sea sickness.

The journey to Deal took a week, and they were blessed with good seas and a favoring wind. No storms blew up to delay them, though in Brest, soldiers of the new army boarded the ship and examined the goods being transported.

This caused some consternation because the numbers of the barrels of wine and crates of other goods listed on the manifest were lower than the numbers actually in the ship's hold. The 'extras' would provide a nice little *'pour boire'* for the captain and the crew, since their sales would be pure profit. Bartholomew LaPorte was completely aware of the scheme since it had been part of the deal he had struck with the Captain to provide him passage at a cheaper rate.

He had paid for himself through to Deal, and used up much of his savings. He planned to try and borrow enough from somewhere in England to make his passage to the U.S. He could even work for his passage, if it came to that: he was only thirty-four, after all, still fit and vigorous. He wasn't even married yet! Though he intended to remedy that once he gained the U.S. and decided on where to settle.

In Brest, therefore, the crew and Captain of the *Amaryllis* were grateful when the French soldiers did not count their stock. The soldiers did, however, pry open a crate or two at random to verify the contents. And although they did not open any wine barrels, they did move a few, again at random, to be certain they could hear the liquid sloshing inside.

LaPorte urged them to be careful so as not to disturb the sediment in the barrels, and the soldiers—perhaps because as Frenchmen they very much understood and valued wine—heeded his plea.

LaPorte held his breath as they approached the barrel he knew contained Talon. Full barrels of wine weighed about 600 pounds and needed two soldiers to tip them gently so the liquid could make an audible noise as it moved inside. Although he had weighted Talon's barrel with a few rocks, he knew it was lighter than the others, for Talon weighed at most 200 lbs.

"I've had a leak in that one," he called from his vantage point at one side of the hold. He pointed to Talon's barrel. "Maybe it would be better to leave it alone?" he suggested. "But of course, you know best," he added deferentially.

Two of the soldiers carrying out the inspection frowned first at him, and then at the barrel, but moved on. Had their inspection caused a leak or a rupture, the resulting loss of income could have been claimed by LaPorte, and would eventually have come out of their wages. So they passed the 'leaky' barrel by.

Inside, Talon breathed a circumspect sigh of relief, careful not to be heard by any but himself. The tiny vertical air holes slotted near the top of the barrel were so cleverly done as to be nearly invisible; they allowed a little air inside, but could also make any noise from within the barrel audible outside it.

The rest of the inspection, and then the last leg of the journey to Deal, passed uneventfully. On a bright morning in late October LaPorte's brother popped the lid of Talon's barrel for the last time, and the former Avocat Général of France set foot on English soil.

The first thing he did was stretch up to his full height and take a deep breath of the clean, sea-scrubbed air. They were in a corner of the large warehouse type building on the wharf at Deal, near London, but although men were scurrying around moving barrels and large packets, crates and bundles of goods either coming or going, no one noticed them. In part, this was due to the fact that LaPorte's brother had positioned a large crate in such a way that he, his brother and Talon were partially screened from the others in the building. Additionally, all the workers were focused on getting the goods on the right ship or at the right doorway for pickup, and doing it as quickly as possible. Then they would have a few precious hours of leisure to spend as they chose in the small port.

Talon was safe, now that he was in England. There was, of course, no record of his arrival, but that should not matter if he kept a low profile until they could find a ship bound for the United States. It was possible, of course, that Robespierre's agents were in England, or even in contact with some few English sympathetic to the French Revolutionaries and the new government. These could be carrying on the hunt for Talon and other Royalists in England, and particularly at port cities. So keeping a low profile was the best plan.

LaPorte had discovered in his chats with the crew of the *Amaryllis* that ships bound for the U.S. that took on passengers left either from the Port of London, or from one of the other ports associated with the Royal Navy, like Portsmouth or Plymouth. However, London was the capital, and other ports connected with the Royal Navy could spell trouble for Talon should he be recognized. Talon had his identification papers, and although England was a safe enough country for him, there was no guarantee that someone, for some reason, upon discovering that he was a wanted man in France, might not just send him back across the Channel.

So LaPorte had decided on the small town of Southampton, a thriving port since Roman times. With the rise of the Port of London, however, it had lost favor in recent decades, becoming known more for its spa and health activities than for being a port. But trade there was once more on the rise now, although Southampton was still off the radar of the Royal Navy and much of the government. Ships from Spain, Portugal, Ireland, the North of England and Scotland and even the Baltics called regularly, and ships flying the starred and barred U.S. Flag had also begun to call. All of that made

Southampton, in LaPorte's opinion, ideal for his and Talon's purposes.

The LaPorte brothers said goodbye to each other at Deal, with Bartholomew's brother planning to sign on board another ship, bound for some exotic port. They promised to write, and Bartholomew told his brother that when he had settled in the U.S., he would invite him over for a visit. His brother seemed pleased.

To get to Southampton from the eastern shores of Kent, LaPorte and Talon would have to take a coach along the gravelly road that hugged the shoreline of the English Channel and then the Solent, with the Isle of Wight in the distance. This they did, and LaPorte was pleased if slightly surprised when his companion complained hardly at all about the relative discomfort of the journey.

The trip by coach to Southampton took the better part of two days, with an overnight stop near Brighton where they shared a quite buggy straw mattress with their other traveling companions. LaPorte had very little money left from his savings by the time he had paid for his seat on the coach, although he had earned a little on the wharfs at Deal during their brief time there. It seemed people everywhere were happy to pay for good Spanish wine, and pay handsomely.

When LaPorte and Talon saw the Isle of Wight through the grimy window of their coach on the second day of the journey, they smiled at each other: the Isle of Wight lay directly opposite Southampton, and in large part was responsible for the sheltered aspect of the port. Sighting it meant they were nearly there.

They secured lodgings at a little wharf-side rooming house. It did not afford much in the way of luxury, but it was clean, and the first thing they both did was to visit the public bath at the end of the street. There they washed, rinsed, and washed again, de-lousing, deflea-ing and otherwise de-infesting themselves so that they were once more as presentable as possible.

A plain but filling meal in a smoky pub on the opposite corner, where Talon and LaPorte practically inhaled the meat stew and crusty wholemeal bread, was their next stop. Talon pronounced the blackberry sponge and custard they ate for dessert 'delicious' and both he and LaPorte were pleased to find a very palatable vintage of sherry on offer at the small place.

Then it was back to their room, and the narrow rickety bed with a single sheet and a moth eaten blanket that Talon collapsed into almost as soon as he was in the door. It was the first real bed he had slept in for more than a week. His sleep was one of near unconsciousness, and he did not wake the next morning until LaPorte had dressed and left the rooming house to see if he could earn a few quick English pounds, and to size up their chances down by the water of booking passage to the United States.

Chapter Four

The two decker *Stout,* out of Rotterdam, carried 64 guns, some freight, and a few passengers, all bound for the port of Philadelphia via Southampton, England. It was the next ship leaving that port headed for the U.S. for several weeks, and since it would dock at LaPorte's and Talon's intended city of disembarkation, it would be ideal.

However, passage to the U.S. was not cheap and, because the French duo were the last passengers to book, all that remained were two higher priced berths in an upstairs cabin that had been converted with bunk beds to hold six people.

"It will be better than a barrel in the hold, even if the cost is dear," commented Talon with a reassuring smile at his friend. LaPorte had told him of the Dutch ship's departure for the U.S. in two days, and now they were having their evening meal in the same smoky little pub in which they'd had their first a day before.

But LaPorte's mein was not happy. This was unusual for him, Talon had learned, and seemed particularly so with the solution to their situation and the last leg of their journey in sight. Or so he would have thought.

LaPorte forced a smile and took a sip of his sherry. "Ah but my friend, I am afraid I cannot go," he murmured finally, eyes downcast.

"*Pourquoi toujours pas!?*" Talon blurted out, surprised.

LaPorte then explained that his savings were gone after the journey from Marseille to Deal, the lodgings, the coach trip, and other expenses of the journey. "I have earned a little extra, here and there," LaPorte said circumspectly, "odd jobs at the wharves, you see. But it has just been enough to enable me to eat," he explained, adding that he only had a few small coins left in his pocket. "And I will not be paid for the wine I shipped over until next month some time," he added. "Then I should have enough for passage, if any ships are traversing the Atlantic then," he finished quietly. As winter progressed, fewer ships took the risk of a crossing, so it was not guaranteed by any means that LaPorte would be able to book passage before spring.

Talon nodded solemnly.

"And by then, if I am at sea, I may never see a *sou* of what I'm owed," LaPorte continued in a morose voice. "I do not wish to arrive in my new country—'*avec rien mais charpie dans mes poches*'—with nothing but lint in my pockets," LaPorte finished, adding that his plan was to stay in Southampton and work the docks until he could secure passage and have a little money left for when he arrived in Philadelphia. "I hope I may seek you out when I land in the United States?" he asked his friend.

Talon shook his head in the negative, and LaPorte was confused: what could his friend mean? Talon also looked very merry about something, which confused LaPorte even further.

"There will be no need for that, my friend, for you shall come with me in two days hence, on the *Stout,*" Talon insisted. As he spoke, he reached over to his battered leather hat, which lay on the bench beside him.

"But..." LaPorte protested.

But Talon overrode him. "I owe you for all you have done for me," he continued, his tone more serious. "Were it not for you and your clever plan, I should still be in Marseille. Possibly dead, if Robespierre's men had found me." He paused. "And then, there was your quick thinking in Brest: if the soldiers had discovered me there..." Talon let the implication fall.

LaPorte shrugged. "I have been happy to help," he said simply. "And we have become friends," he added, smiling slightly. "And the company has been welcome. But while you still have savings, I do not," he concluded matter of factly. Things did not always go as one planned, he had learned, and the best thing was not to moan about it, but to make a new plan and get on towards ones goal.

LaPorte knew Talon's wife was from a wealthy family, and suspected that, although she had moved back to Belgium, Talon's cash was due to her. In truth, he had wondered from time to time during their journey where Talon secreted his stash of money: the man always seemed to have a ready supply of coins, yet LaPorte never saw any sack of money about his person or with his few possessions. But he had been quite occupied making arrangements, and in any case had not wished to offend his friend and traveling companion by asking.

Talon nodded agreement, but still smiled, and patted his leather hat that perched on the wooden bench beside him. Here in England, he was less cautious about showing his face and though the hat was never far from him, it did not remain constantly on his head as it seemed it had in France.

Now, he laid the hat in his lap and flipped it upside down, fingering the leather sweat band inside, where the crown met the wide brim. Sturdy lacings all the way around the crown held the band in place and also were decorative, as they were visible on the exterior of the hat.

"What are you doing?" LaPorte asked curiously. He cocked his head and stared at his friend. It looked to him as though his companion was pulling the sweat band away from the hat itself, although carefully.

Talon merely gave another sly smile, and then, having loosened about an inch-long section of the band, he plucked something out that had been tucked inside. This proved to be a piece of cotton, such as might be used to make a handkerchief, rolled up several times into a sort of tube.

As LaPorte watched, all thoughts of the chicken and gammon pie they had been eating for dinner gone from his head, Talon handed the length of material to him.

"What is this?" he asked Talon, frowning at the tube of cotton in his hand. On close inspection, it looked a bit lumpy, and it seemed to weigh more than it should.

"Unroll it and see," Talon instructed. Another rare smile quirked up one side of his mouth, and he took sip of his sherry with an almost jaunty flourish. "But be discreet," Talon advised.

Frowning in puzzlement, LaPorte obeyed, placing the cotton in his lap and then unrolling it with one hand while shielding it from the rest of the pub with the other. Inside were dozens of mostly round, clear stones ranging in size from that of a lentil to that of a *pois chiche* or garbanzo bean. LaPorte's frown deepened, and he looked across the table to Talon. "These look like..." he began, but stopped and hastily covered the stones as some entering patrons came near their booth on their way to their own.

LaPorte rolled the stones up in the cloth again, being careful to fold in the ends to make the packet secure. Then he looked expectantly at his friend.

Talon nodded. "They are. From the Royal Treasury, as it was," Talon said mildly, with a wry lift of one eyebrow.

"You took them?" LaPorte asked, trying not to sound scandalized, even though he was. He might deal in some off-book importing and exporting, might occasionally look the other way in favor of a good deal, but he didn't consider himself an outright thief, just a shrewd businessman. But this...

Talon nodded again. "I did."

He sounded completely without compunction.

"Well, my agents did," Talon amended. "And they were well paid, too." He sighed. "I knew the Monarchy would be overthrown. I also knew that the rabble among the Revolutionaries would not balk at emptying the coffers at Versailles and elsewhere," he added sourly. "Indeed, they plundered graves of our historic French nobility, took the jewels and gold buried with our ancestors and scattered their bones to the wind," he reminded LaPorte.

LaPorte knew this last was true: a desecration, and unjust, as well as a tragedy.

"So I intended to have my share before that happened," Talon finished. "I never did get paid for the services I performed for the King and Queen last year, as things were—tumultuous. And if the Royal Treasury was intended to be a type of insurance for the well being of the French people, is this not a valid use of some of its contents?" he asked in a bemused tone. "And I say 'some' because there was much, much more still there, all taken I am sure, by now, for the cause, or for distribution among the people." He sighed shortly and gave LaPorte a wry look. "At least, I hope that is what it has been used for," he cautioned. "But I do not know, and as I was no longer welcome in France, I could not wait around to find out. I consider these my, well, my retirement wages," he added with another wry expression. "I cannot have my wife's family thinking I am without means, after all," he concluded.

"Well, then, I cannot take them," LaPorte rejoined, pushing the cotton cylinder back across the table towards Talon.

His friend smiled and almost chuckled. "No, no, LaPorte, you misunderstand me," he reassured him and pushed the diamonds back towards him. "I have more. Many more. Enough to live very well for the rest of my life, regardless of where I choose to dwell," Talon revealed astonishingly.

In fact, the entire sweat band on his old brown leather hat was stuffed with scores of similar cylindrical cotton packets, each with various stones secreted inside. Some, like most of the ones he'd just given LaPorte, were un-faceted. Others had been cut and would probably fetch a higher price. Still others were not diamonds, but rubies of the highest quality whose price rivaled that of the diamonds.

At LaPorte's evident shock, Talon did finally chuckle companionably and go on with his meal. He urged LaPorte to put the packet of stones in a pocket and finish his pie before it got cold.

"It is far too generous," LaPorte protested later as they walked the short distance back to their rooming house.

"It is not," Talon insisted. "I have more than I really need. But it is better to overestimate than underestimate future needs, and the stones are easily transported and easily sold. As I said, my friend, were it not for you, I should be dead and have no need of the treasure. So how is it wrong to share with you, the *sine qua non* of my escape?" he asked rhetorically.

At LaPorte's look, Talon continued. "There's enough there for your passage on the *Stout*, and plenty more to set yourself up somewhere in the United States," he told his friend. "I hope, close by me, for we make a very good team, I believe," he added with another smile.

And so it was that LaPorte and Talon booked the last two berths on the *Stout* and left Southampton two days later on the evening tide, bound for Philadelphia. The majority of the other passengers were German or Dutch. There were no French aboard, for which Talon was very grateful, for although he was safe, one could never be sure of what tales others might carry back to those who wished him harm.

LaPorte had sold one of the smallest stones from his packet to a back-street jeweler in Southampton, who paid him in English gold guineas. The money was enough to pay his passage and buy his share of their supplies for the crossing, with some left over for when they landed. And there were still the rest of the stones in the rolled up cotton that was now his!

At some point, of course, LaPorte would have to find another discreet jeweler in the U.S. and sell more of the diamonds. But for the moment he tucked the heavy, lumpy cotton cylinder inside a seam of his chemise and put the guineas in his small leather coin purse. This he tied securely to his belt.

The journey across the North Atlantic would take about a month. With 'fair winds and following seas' they should land in Philadelphia in early December, and both LaPorte and Talon eagerly anticipated their arrival. Talon had written ahead to a few contacts in that city and was sure they would have a roof over their heads—quite possibly a very grand one—once they touched dry land.

Chapter Five

"You're clever with cards," remarked Talon. It was a bright, brisk morning somewhere in the middle of the North Atlantic and he and LaPorte were taking the air on the deck of the *Stout*. Talon had found that his seasickness passed quickly once the ship was in open water, and he enjoyed the bracing sea air, which seemed to keep any new attacks of queasiness at bay.

LaPorte, who—like his brother—loved the sea and had no trouble on board, nodded slyly at his friend. "I have spent much time on the docks," he answered obliquely, "waiting for shipments to arrive. 'Tis a good way to pass the time," he finished calmly.

"Well, yes, except for those who bet against you," Talon observed wryly.

For the past few nights, LaPorte had disappeared after their evening meal, returning to their upper berth in the wee hours of the morning. However, he had seemed in an ever increasingly cheerful mood and Talon had finally asked him where he had been going each night.

'Have you found a woman?' the former exile had asked in a low, slightly envious tone, one evening as his friend had made ready to depart. Talon hadn't seen women on board but had heard that there were a couple, special favorites of the Captain and crew, who traveled with the ship on her extended voyages to 'see to the needs' of the men, as Talon gracefully put it.

He, of course, was married, and remained faithful to his Belgian wife, difficult though that might be at times. But LaPorte, a single man with a *joie de vivre* that was attractive to everyone, and especially women, could take his pleasure where he wished.

At Talon's query, Bartholomew LaPorte had thrown back his shaggy brown head and laughed loudly. 'A woman? No, no my friend,' he had answered, still chuckling. 'Although I will confess I do, erm, miss female companionship,' he had admitted frankly. 'But I prefer girls who have not shared their favors with a score of others, or at least, not so obviously,' he had added.

Talon had nodded.

Then LaPorte had told him that he had been taking part in various games of chance on board, almost ever since they had watched the Isle of Wight disappear over the horizon after their departure.

'It took a few days for me to find a game, and fellow players, whom I like, and who are congenial,' LaPorte explained, adding that usually on board ship the various games of cards had changed makeup until everyone settled in with 'their' preferred group. 'I've found a few who play *hombre*,' LaPorte had continued. He'd paused.

Talon had looked at him expectantly.

'But not so well as I,' LaPorte had finished triumphantly. He'd confided to his friend what his winnings thus far had been and Talon had been genuinely surprised.

'You do not, erm, cheat?' Talon had inquired, low.

LaPorte had laughed again and shaken his head. His dark eyes had twinkled. 'I have no need to my friend,' he had said, but it was fact, not boast. He had explained that he had been taught his numbers by his grandmother, using a deck of cards. So, he had commented, counting cards was a skill that was second nature to him.

Now, Talon gazed at his traveling companion with shrewd assessment. LaPorte's cheery and somewhat simple demeanor hid a very quick mind and a high intelligence. LaPorte was, certainly, friendly and of a sanguine disposition. But he was also very clever. His familiarity with cards helped, surely, but it was his brain —if Talon had known the term 'eidetic' he would have used it—that meant that his friend could engage in games of chance and nearly always win—and win big. It was also a major reason for LaPorte's fast absorption of the English lessons Talon had been giving him as they sailed westward. By now, LaPorte's English, while still heavily accented, was nearly as good as his instructor's.

LaPorte nodded happily at Talon. "You are correct, those who bet against me do not come away overjoyed," he admitted, still smiling.

"But—don't they suspect you're cheating?" Talon asked.

"But I am not!" LaPorte rejoined. "They inspect the deck and weigh the dice each evening before we begin," he explained. "And I lose here and there,"

"On purpose," Talon interjected knowingly.

LaPorte nodded. "Òc! Yes, when the pot is not so very big," he finished. "And I do let the others win something, from time to time," he continued. "But I come away with the lion's share." He took a deep breath of salt air and his face grew more serious though not sad. "It is for when I settle in our new land," he reminded Talon. "I want to do as much with your gift as possible," he explained, adding that he had increased the money from the sale of the first stone many times over by playing cards at sea.

Talon nodded, poked his friend good humoredly in the ribs and chuckled. "Well done," he commented, and gazed at the ocean that stretched out ahead and all around them. It was a blue grey color with a few small whitecaps but nothing alarming. A light breeze billowed the *Stout*'s sails as she headed west.

"We should be turning south soon," LaPorte informed him: more knowledge gleaned over the gaming table.

In the evenings, Talon had generally retired to his bunk to read one of the many books from the *Stout*'s library until he was tired enough to sleep. Still careful about those with whom he spoke, he preferred to keep to himself. With a German copy of Walpole's Castle of *Otranto*—who knew German sailors enjoyed Gothic tales? —he was even teaching himself a smattering of German, although he suspected he might have little use for much of the phraseology in the fictional book. The story and its setting were familiar because of a similarity to Shakespeare's Hamlet, which he had read.

So while Talon was learning German and staying out of the way of his fellow passengers, LaPorte was learning English, increasing his stash of money, and learning about transatlantic voyages. Despite the fact that he'd sent and received numerous shipments of wine across the Atlantic, this was the first time he himself was making that trip, and it fascinated him. He was curious about the maps the Navigator used, and about the sextant and other tools and observations the Captain and crew employed to make the journey.

"We'll want to avoid the iceberg field," he told Talon now, adding that to the north, pack ice often formed from drifting icebergs that had calved or broken off huge glaciers at the North Pole and made their way south on the Labrador Current to the Atlantic. "Our captain is a bold one, for most ships sail south along the west coast of Europe until they reach the Canary Current off the coast of Africa," LaPorte explained admiringly.

Talon gazed out at the ocean to the middle distance, imagining the route in his mind's eye. He nodded, and waited.

"This they follow then, westward across the Atlantic, until they find the Gulf Stream. That takes them northward to the east coast of the United States." LaPorte paused. "But by that route, the journey takes far longer," he continued informatively. "Going directly west, straight across the northern Atlantic, can cut the time in half, but one must be cautious not to go too far north," he finished.

Most of the icebergs, LaPorte told Talon as they walked, turning into the brisk breeze on deck, came from the glaciers of western Greenland. By the time an iceberg reached the Grand Banks off Newfoundland, it was only about a fifth of its original size, LaPorte said, adding that this was the region where smaller icebergs, called 'growlers' could often be found, although many larger ones were still intact: and a threat to ships.

"Once the icebergs reach the waters of the Gulf Stream, they melt rapidly, of course, but we want to turn south before we encounter any," LaPorte finished.

Talon looked intrigued, and he turned his large well-shaped eyes to the north, the direction easy to gauge on this sunny morning, and let out a low hum. "Well, I should not be sad to see an iceberg," Talon murmured, a bit longingly. "A small one," he reassured LaPorte.

LaPorte looked at his friend. "We are about at 45° latitude and 45° longitude, turning south at 47° longitude and making for 39° latitude and 60° longitude," he murmured. So you may see some as we move south west along that tack." He added that from that position, Philadelphia would be almost directly west, for it lay at 75° longitude.

Talon shook his head in admiration. He was smart, and he was good with figures, but LaPorte was truly a savant, at least as far as he was concerned.

As his friend continued to talk about navigating the open sea and how using a sextant enabled ships to know where they were even though there was no land mass to use as a point of reference, Talon's eyes glazed over.

He patted LaPorte on the sleeve of his coat. "Better you than me, my friend," he said good humoredly. "I am glad you know all of this. But as for me, I shall merely be happy to land at last on U.S. soil."

LaPorte blushed a little at his friend's obvious admiration, then shook his head. "Well, we shall do that, and not long now, for I make it more than half the journey lies behind us," he announced confidently.

Chapter Six

LaPorte was right, in that once the *Stout* turned south, the Gulf Stream swept her along quite quickly. However, winds from the north also meant choppier seas and fewer pleasant times spent on deck. Talon, while he wasn't badly sea sick, for he had gained—as LaPorte said—his '*amariner*,' or 'sea legs,' felt unwell enough to carry on his pursuit of the German language during most days, taking just enough food in to keep his energy level up.

LaPorte, meanwhile, seemed unaffected by the *Stout*'s suddenly rolling decks and swamped portholes, and went about his business as cheerfully as before.

It was not as though the food on board was especially appealing, at any rate. As was customary, he and LaPorte had brought a small pile of provisions on board for themselves, consisting of a few live chickens who could be fed on table scraps, packets of cured and salted meat, dried fish, dried fruits including apples and plums, and a sack of small, underripe oranges which LaPorte had bargained for on the wharf at Southampton. A type of hard, baked flat bread was available on board, as were raw grains which they could cook into a sort of porridge. Some others in their cabin had brought cheese, and LaPorte engaged in a brisk trade with them so everyone had some meat or fish and cheese with their meals.

Because the passengers in each cabin cooked and ate their own food, the system worked reasonably well. At this point with more than half their journey gone, though, only the least appetizing stores remained. The chickens had been eaten and a soup made from the bones. The soup was gone. The oranges were gone. Beer—the drink of choice on board—was rationed more carefully to be sure it would last until they put into port. The porridge remained, and a little of the flat bread, but it too was being rationed more than at the start of the trip, and some bits were moldy or had been nibbled by the mice and rats that also shared the ship, and their provisions.

So meals were usually gruel with something added to it, either dried fruit or bits of salted meat or fish, and sometimes a small chunk of cheese. Filling enough, and nutritious enough, but not very appetizing—at least to Talon's refined palate. Although he'd become used to eating several notches down from the level to which he'd been accustomed in France, the limited ship board menu coupled with his Général malaise meant he didn't eat much as the ship headed for port.

Talon had seen an iceberg—several, in fact—as they had made their turn southward. They had been far enough west to be able to spot the pack ice in the distance, for they were far enough north that the icebergs had not melted away completely. Talon borrowed a spyglass and marveled at the sight.

But then, the *Stout* had made quick and steady progress southward and although the waves remained frisky, as LaPorte put it, there were no more icebergs.

Great joy spread throughout the ship on the day that sea birds were spotted overhead. That meant that land was within a day or two's journey, and that, barring a last minute misfortune, their trip was nearly at an end. The following evening, a distant beam marked a lighthouse, and quick measurements taken with LaPorte's beloved sextant by the ship's Navigator showed that the ship was approaching Lewes Point in the new state of Delaware, south of the Delaware Bay and the entrance to the Port of Philadelphia.

The ship's crew deftly turned, aimed their vessel north west and within a few miles, another smaller light shone out ahead.

This was, LaPorte explained excitedly—for nearly all the passengers including the two Frenchmen were on deck—the lighthouse at Cape Mey Island in the new state of New Jersey. These two lights marked the entrance to the Delaware Bay and guided sailors in towards the port. As they drew near, the bells from both lighthouses could be heard.

Because navigating the Bay could be tricky, especially at night, the Captain pulled into a small inlet of the Maurice River on the North shore of the Bay, and dropped anchor for the night. They would make their way through the rest of the Bay and into the mouth of the Delaware River the following morning; he expected they would dock around noon in Philadelphia.

"So we have our first sight of the United States," Talon said to LaPorte as they gained their cabin that evening: it would be their last aboard ship, and Talon was amazed that the worst thing they'd encountered had been a bit of rough sea.

"Well, Antoine, it was dark, so although I may have gazed upon it, I did not actually see it," LaPorte replied with a wink and a chuckle. "But tomorrow, with the rising sun, I shall."

The Captain's plan went off without a hitch, for they set sail again the following morning, moving slowly and carefully through the Bay with the Captain and his Navigator consulting charts they had of the bay's topography, and then they moved into the channel of the Delaware River. In daylight it was an easier manoeuvre, and the Captain had done it several times before.

As they pulled up alongside the wharf at Philadelphia, for here the river was deep enough that they did not need to disembark into smaller boats to make the final leg of the journey, Talon could hear bells in the city begin to ring.

"It is mid day," he told LaPorte with a smile. Eagerly, he scanned the bustling wharves, to catch his first glimpse of the people meeting the ship and bustling to and fro along the quayside.

"We have a good Captain," LaPorte replied, sounding satisfied. He, too, stared out at the teeming dock as the ship slipped into her berth and the anchor dropped for the final time on this journey. "Welcome to the United States, my friend," he said, turning to Talon.

They shook hands, and then embraced. Then it was time to gather up their belongings, say goodbye to their ship mates and the Captain and crew, and make their way down the long gangplank to set foot, finally, on U.S. soil.

Chapter Seven

A tall man in rather grand livery of blue and grey approached Talon and LaPorte as they made their way among the throngs on the dock.

"You are Messieurs Talon and LaPorte?" the man in livery asked expectantly. He had been told to watch for two men, traveling together, and disembarking from the *Stout,* and had been given a cursory description of Talon's features.

Talon nodded. LaPorte looked intrigued.

The man in livery nodded. "I am Visser, Butler to Mr. Theophilus Cazenove," he informed them, looking proud. Cazenove, a well-heeled and popular merchant from the Netherlands who had settled in Philadelphia and was engaged in much trade and land purchases, was one of the people to whom Talon had written when they left Europe. He was not surprised, somehow, that it was Cazenove among the three or four contacts he had notified of his journey, who had responded first. Talon was sure the others would make themselves known to him eventually.

Visser led the two men to a handsome coach and four, loaded their luggage, ushered them inside the plush conveyance, and took his own spot inside on the bench seat opposite them, near the door. Although the turnout included the coachman, a footman and a postilion—the latter for show, for the four horses knew the city streets well—Visser would be the one to assist Talon and LaPorte into and out of the carriage, once the footman had opened the door.

As the little party moved from the wharves and docks onto Spruce Street and then along the curving Dock Street, they passed Bell's Print Shop, several churches of varying denominations, and some grand townhouses. At

Walnut they turned left, or west, for a block, then north again on Fourth Street until they came to High Street—what would after 1800 become known as 'Market Street.'

Even now, early in 1793, the reason for the eventual switch in names was evident: a covered open air market spanned High Street between Fourth and Front Streets, where all manner of goods—many from the ships docking just steps away—were offered for sale.

Talon and LaPorte gazed in fascination at the arched roof that capped the wide boulevard as the coach turned left, then drew to a halt before a gracious townhouse on the corner of Fifth and High Street. Granite walls surrounded narrow gardens on either side of the townhouse and rose up from the pavement where a few beautifully dressed people promenaded.

The men wore top hats or tricorns and wigs, their embroidered velvet coat sleeves peeping from heavy woolen capes in forest green or rich blue, and tall leather boots keeping the slush on the pathway from their cream colored breeches. The ladies, for there were a couple arm in arm with gentlemen, boasted soft woolen hooded capes in shades of gold and plum, their brocade gowns in jewel tones showing slightly as they walked. LaPorte noticed that the ladies all wore pattens with their shoes, the better to keep their feet and dress hems from the wet on the pavement. Although they had hoods, and the day was very chilly, it was clear and dry after wet snow overnight, and the ladies showed off prettily dressed hair with feathered hats perched on top. LaPorte thought to himself that the hats were decorative, but did little to keep the wearer warm.

The footman opened the coach door and Visser leapt out, then assisted Talon and LaPorte to the pavement. Out of the muffling confines of the coach, the two émigrés' senses were assaulted by the sounds and smells of the bustling city. The clatter of horse shoes on cobblestoned streets from the several carriages and wagons traveling up and down High Street was the loudest. Shouted advertisements from the nearby market added to the din, and snippets of conversation from passersby floated like a descant atop it all. Although the air was clean and fresh, a lingering odor of manure wafted from the streets and the river, just a few blocks away, lent its distinctive tang as well.

Then the tall black double house doors atop a short flight of marble stairs opened—yet another footman—and the two men were whisked inside to the warmth and hospitality of Cazenove's house. The doors clunked shut and Talon and LaPorte were once more enveloped in quiet. The foyer was floored in alternating squares of black and white veined marble. Wall sconce lamps burned brightly in glass chimneys. A huge mahogany table with a gilt mirror atop it stood to one side, ready to receive calling cards. A small burgundy upholstered and gilt love seat occupied the facing wall. Landscapes in oil couched in gilt frames hung on the pale green walls and a beautiful staircase led to the upper floors. As one's eyes were drawn upward by the staircase, the shimmering chandelier in the middle of the foyer ceiling was brought into view, as were the stenciled vines and leaves all around the edge of that same ceiling.

Visser took their cloaks and hats—Talon, as always, kept his hat in one hand—and led them into the first reception room. Here they were invited to sit, and the same footman who had opened the doors brought in a small silver tray with a sparkling crystal decanter and three slender glasses. Inside the decanter, port glowed a beautiful, deep ruby red.

Both Talon and LaPorte accepted a glass even though it was not yet noon, and were told by the ever vigilant Visser that the master of the house, Theophilus Cazenove, would be with them shortly.

"This is a beautiful house," LaPorte said, low, but the admiration in his voice was evident.

Talon nodded. "Indeed. I believe Cazenove had some trouble before coming to the United States," he went on informatively, sipping at his port and gazing around the well-appointed room. "Business investments that went poorly," he added. Then he shrugged. "He seems to have recovered."

The first parlor was quite an impressive room. Its ceiling, like that of the foyer, was stenciled around its border in a similar vine and leaf pattern, the greens and golds mirroring the colors in the Oriental rug that centered on the wide, polished wooden planks. Bird's eye maple moulding ran along the bottom and top of the room's walls and the doors were made of the same. Several upholstered and gilt chairs and settees were scattered around the room in conversational groupings. More oils—these were mostly of people—adorned the walls and an ornate liquor cabinet of carved, dark wood with elaborate blue and white porcelain embellishments occupied an entire corner.

LaPorte was just about to venture the opinion that if they could do half as well here in the United States as their Dutch host appeared to have done, they would be lucky men, when heavy steps were heard on the stairway and then across the foyer, and then the door to the parlor opened.

"Welcome, welcome, *mes amis*, to the United States, and to Philadelphia!" Theophilus Cazenove declared, entering the room and immediately using up most of the space in it, it seemed, for he was a very large man. He was also a very effusive man, who shook hands vigorously with both Talon and LaPorte and then commanded that his guests sit once again.

Happily, he moved to the little silver tray, poured himself a glass of port, waving away the attentive footman who had followed his master's entrance with silent steps, and sat himself down in the middle of a bottle green brocaded love seat. Silver buttons twinkled from their host's oyster colored embroidered court coat. Striped ribboned garters adorned his calves just below the hem of his bright blue breeches, and a cream and scarlet brocaded waistcoat spanned a not inconsiderable belly.

Cazenove wore a powdered wig which dusted his shoulders, and his complexion was florid, his smile wide. Both Talon and LaPorte had noticed the slight limp in their host's heavy gait and in lieu of the ubiquitous buckled shoes, Cazenove sported a pair of soft leather slippers. Talon suspected gout, no doubt from the rich food he had heard that Cazenove loved. But since it didn't seem to bother his host much, he thought it wouldn't bother him much, either.

Chapter Eight

Mary House ran, appropriately for her surname, a boarding house just a half a block from the Cazenove mansion. It was here that Talon and LaPorte secured rooms. LaPorte had got the name of a discreet jeweler from Visser—it was always best to ask those in service, he had found, rather than gentlemen, for this type of recommendation—and had sold another of the smaller rough stones, thus replenishing his store of ready cash.

The House Boarding House was quite upscale: though a boarding house, it boasted well appointed rooms and an attentive (and well-paid) staff. It also cost much more than regular boarding houses, and attracted a well-heeled and quite genteel clientele. James Madison had booked in there, as had George Washington, until his friend Robert Morris had offered him accommodation in his own home.

That home of Morris' had by the early spring of 1793 become the United States President's Home, and President George Washington resided there, not two blocks from Cazenove's mansion. Morris was building another residence at a little distance from the city center, but was still a frequent guest at social gatherings at what was beginning to become known as 'Society Hill,' and at Cazenove's mansion.

Theophilus Cazenove had a reputation for living well. A place at his dinner table was a sought after invitation and his highly valued and equally talented chef turned out meals that were, literally, the talk of the town. All of the city's 'best people' frequented Cazenove's home and table and in this way, Talon and LaPorte quickly met the movers and shakers of the early United States in their first couple of months in the new country.

They also met a bevy of young French women, plucked from aristocratic adolescences in France and transplanted to the still slightly wild United States. Although Talon was a married man, the girls flirted with him nonetheless and he became, had the term been known at the time, LaPorte's 'wing man.' Aware that his friend sought to find a wife, marry, and settle in the U.S., Talon kept a ready eye out for suitable partners.

At several of Cazenove's dinners but more frequently at evening dances and 'suppers' given at the Society Hill homes of the French aristocrats, LaPorte was introduced to the daughters of the nobility and gentry. Although he was courteous to them, and seemed quite pleased with one or two, none of them appeared to suit him so well that he wanted to make her his wife.

"You've got the *crème de la crème* here, Bart," Talon declared expansively late one evening as he and LaPorte wended their way back to the boarding house after a particularly lively evening at the Liancourt mansion. The streets were mostly empty, dark and glistening with dew in the waxing gibbous moon's light. A street or two over, they could hear the measured footsteps of the Night Watchman echoing. A moment later, the bells from Old Saint Mary's Church to the southeast tolled solemnly, twice. Other churches followed in succession, chiming near and far to the east, the north and finally to the south, where the African Methodist Church was located at Sixth and Lombard.

"Two o'clock, and all's well," came the satisfied call from the Watchman, whose steps now turned and moved away, becoming more and more faint.

Both Talon and LaPorte had drunk quite a bit, and Talon in particular was waxing philosophical. "'Tis a fine country we've come to," he noted with contentment, nodding to LaPorte as they continued their journey homeward. "With some of the prettiest and noblest daughters of France here, for your choosing. You couldn't do any better for a wife," he added with a nudge to his friend's ribs.

LaPorte nodded. "I know. You do speak the truth." He paused. "But I should like to find a place and settle down, first, I think, and then find a partner. Perhaps someone from this land, too—not an émigré like me, I mean," he added, thinking aloud.

"You mean a Redskin? A Native woman?" Talon joked and LaPorte laughed aloud.

"No, no—although that surely would be interesting," he teased back, mischievous. "No. I mean I don't necessarily have to marry a French girl," he clarified.

Talon allowed that of course, LaPorte could marry whom he wished, but added that in his opinion, French women far surpassed any others both in beauty and in wit. "One must have wit, for when beauty fades..." he added in mock lament.

"Indeed, so," LaPorte rejoined thoughtfully. "But good common sense and a kind heart—those are qualities I think are more important than beauty. And of course, she must have a good mind: I shouldn't want to marry a dullard," he added with a chuckle.

The question of marriage was ever present but clearly secondary to the question of where to settle. Talon was considering Philadelphia, because he hoped, in a year or two at least, to be able to return to Europe and be with his wife in Belgium if he could go there safely. Therefore, a port city seemed the most logical to him, and the society of Philadelphia intrigued and attracted him. It was different from that which he'd known in Paris to be interesting, but similar enough to be comforting.

LaPorte, however, was open to settling outside the city; ideally, he said, he would like to have a large farm where some food crops, dairy cows, sheep and cattle could be raised, and which would be near good transportation so that he could engage in the thing he was best at: trade.

"You won't find any vineyards here, at least not any whose product is worth exporting," Talon cautioned sourly one mid day as they were heading to Cazenove's for dinner.

LaPorte shrugged and smiled, his open countenance cheery and hopeful. "'Tis no matter: I shall find something else to sell and buy and make money from," he told his friend. "I still have connections in shipping, you remember. I would imagine that people living beyond the coastal cities in the U.S. would pay a pretty *sou* for commodities like salt, sugar, silks, and yes, even wine," he explained. "While people in Europe, or elsewhere along the U.S. coast, perhaps, might be happy to pay a premium for timber, perhaps slate as well, and other treasures the interior of this great land can provide," he finished.

In the salons and at the dinners, suppers and dances, both men had heard talk of various logging, quarrying and mining endeavors just a couple hundred miles away from the coast and Philadelphia. It was clear that LaPorte, in particular, was intrigued.

Now, Talon nodded: the growth in the cities had to be fueled by the building of houses to shelter the influx of residents. Building products like stone and timber could not generally be found very close to the cities and so were either imported from Europe—Italian marble was quite the rage at the moment—or located, harvested or mined, and brought in from the more rural sections of the country.

What LaPorte said made a great deal of sense, and the two friends entered Cazenove's dining room a few minutes later ripe for the conversation that they would encounter that day.

Cazenove was part of a consortium of Dutch bankers that would become the Holland Land Company in a few more years. He acted as the purchasing agent, initially buying federal bonds. Currently, they had expanded and were embroiled in the speculation for 'wild lands' in rural parts of the United States. Cazenove was in the process of buying up millions of acres of land in Western New York State and also in Northern Pennsylvania, with an eye to building canals along the native rivers which would give the interior of the country excellent access to trade.

In northern Pennsylvania in particular, he had made a point of purchasing both the Connecticut titles to the acreage, given by King George III of England, and the Pennsylvania titles, given by William Penn. Therefore, the consortium's ownership of the thousands of acres could not be questioned. However, it also meant that it had cost more, and so would sell for a higher price. That day around Cazenove's table Senator Robert Morris waxed eloquent about the region's natural beauty and resources.

LaPorte and Talon had met Morris before, of course. He had been instrumental in their introduction to the President, George Washington. Two of the other guests that day were also known to them: the Marquis de Lafayette and his brother-in-law, Louis deNoailles. One man, John Nicholson, was a stranger, although he was friends with Morris and had come as his guest. Nicholson was perhaps Pennsylvania's pre-eminent post-Revolutionary land speculator and entrepreneur and was deeply involved with the project that would establish a permanent Federal City for the new United States.

Philadelphia was now serving as the Capital, as New York and other locales also had. But no place had been truly suitable to be the Nation's Capital: to Nicholson and others working to create it, the Capital should not only be the center of the Federal Government, it should belong to all the people and be created specifically as that.

Another stranger at the table to LaPorte and Talon was John Keating. Although Irish by birth, he had been brought up in Poitiers, France, and was fluent in the language and customs. A former soldier, he was descended from a man whom King Louis XV had ennobled, and friends in the U.S. with President Washington and others in that elite circle.

It was a smaller than usual gathering, but the reason shortly became clear, for Morris and deNoailles were engaged in business negotiations concerning specific lands along the North Branch of Pennsylvania's Susquehanna River, near the New York State border. Because the consortium that Cazenove represented owned that acreage, he was also involved: he and Morris were coming close to an agreement on a price as well as on the exact size of the tract.

But there was more to the scheme, LaPorte and Talon discovered that day over their smoked gammon with asparagus, turkey pie, and apple cobbler: Lafayette and his brother-in-law wanted to establish a large, regional settlement of French nobility in the interior of the country and thought the land Cazenove owned along the river might just be ideal.

Chapter Nine

Both Lafayette and deNoailles had fought in the American Revolution on the side of the Colonists and so were familiar with the 'back country' of the new nation. Although they still had money, their fortunes had suffered greatly, not only because of the Revolution in France but also because of the subsequent crash of the European financial markets. Thus, they were not flush enough to engage in land purchase schemes on the scale that Cazenove's consortium could. Yet they knew that in order to establish a large French settlement somewhere in the Eastern U.S. they would need ready cash, and a great deal of it.

To this end, they decided to seek other investors who could join with them to purchase the acreage, and who would own part of the land and also the settlement. They would share in any profits from eventual timbering or farming or quarrying or other merchandise produced by the settlement as well.

"Our principal desire is to provide a refuge for those fleeing the new regime in France," deNoailles explained quietly as they ate Cazenove's delicious meal. His French cook had outdone himself, enrobing new asparagus spears, bright green and firm, in a perfect *sauce à la hollandaise*. "Philadelphia cannot house them all."

"What about the settlement on Lake Otsego in New York State?" queried Morris. "And the other one on the Chemung River?" he added, referencing small encampments of French refugees.

Cazenove was just about to reply that these were very far out in the wilderness, even more so than the tract they were proposing to settle, but Lafayette spoke first.

"There is, of course, the large French Mission in the Illinois Country," he said thoughtfully.

"You mean, Cahokia?" Morris rejoined. "Yes, of course," he agreed. But his tone was slightly dismissive. "There is Louisiana, and Charleston, too," he added, still sounding as though any of those choices would be inferior to the scheme he was promoting.

"Upper New York, Illinois, South Carolina and Louisiana for that matter, are all quite far away," deNoailles offered.

"Louisiana at least has a port: New Orleans," his brother-in-law put in. "And South Carolina is on the coast. But Upper New York and Cahokia are inland, and while they are along rivers, 'tis far from the Atlantic," he concluded.

LaPorte listened eagerly as the men continued to outline why they thought a French colony in the interior of Pennsylvania would be a good idea. The place they had in mind, part of the lands Cazenove's consortium had acquired, was on the mighty Susquehanna River. This would make it accessible to trade and travel. Admittedly, it was not a fast or easy journey to travel between the considered locale and port cities, especially as one had to use the river in some stretches and fight its current, or travel very primitive roadways.

But byways and turnpikes were improving all the time, and even now, it was faster and easier to travel from northern Pennsylvania to the coast than it was from either Illinois or Louisiana. And, should Cazenove's idea of canals running alongside the river come to fruition, ease and speed of travel would be multiplied and the area become even more desirable.

Excitedly, the men around the table named various families they thought would be happy to settle in an exclusively French colony set in one of the large valleys of the Susquehanna.

"And of course, if Her Majesty and the children manage to escape Paris and imprisonment..." Talon put in. The men around the table nodded, and tried to look hopeful. King Louis XVI and Queen Marie Antoinette had been forced out of Versailles a few years earlier and had fled to Paris, where they had been imprisoned in the Tuileries. They had escaped, however, and headed for the Austrian border where, it was rumored, Antoinette's brother was waiting with troops to march on France and restore the monarchy.

That had never happened, but it made the Queen less popular, since some thought the plan traitorous. At the end of the previous summer, in 1792, the King and Queen and their children had been captured and imprisoned again, and revolutionaries had begun a large scale massacre of royalists.

The men around Cazenove's dining table that day in the spring of 1793 had only lately heard that King Louis XVI had been guillotined on January 21. Marie Antoinette, however, and the children, were still behind bars in the Tuileries. The older son had died shortly after the start of the Revolution but the younger son, Louis-Charles, was alive, and referred to by Royalists as 'Louis XVII.'

It was the hope of many, not just Cazenove's guests, that the Queen and her son the King, along with his two sisters the 'Princesses of France,' could escape somehow. Talon's proposed refuge in the rural woods and fields of northeastern Pennsylvania was perhaps the first to offer an actual destination for the royal escapees.

"That would be a brilliant accomplishment," Morris replied to Talon with a smile. "But we would have to build a very great town, if it were to house the Queen."

"Perhaps only for a few years, while she is in exile," Talon continued, sipping at his glass of chilled hock.

"Until the rabble is suppressed and the monarchy restored, you mean," Cazenove weighed in. Then he shook his head. "I am not confident of that, my friend: not since the execution of the King. I think the revolutionaries mean it to be permanent and the Queen is on borrowed time. If she manages to escape, and if she makes her way here, I expect she would live out her days here."

"Even more reason for ample acreage, farms and room for livestock as well as a great town where all the refugees may dwell in style and comfort and peace..." began Morris again.

"And a very *grand maison* for *la Reine*," LaPorte put in, excited at the thought.

Everyone looked cautiously optimistic, and nodded.

"We would need many people to settle there," Morris cautioned. "And we must devise a way that they might afford to purchase the land," he continued, very thoughtful. "So many have had their fortunes seized, or lost, because of the wars and the Revolution," he finished, nodding sympathetically at Lafayette and deNoailles, and also at LaPorte who had shared the story of losing his Spanish fortune in the political struggles between that country and France.

"The unrest in Saint Domingue, too, may also attract refugees from those islands," put in Lafayette thoughtfully. Both LaPorte and Talon had heard of the slaves' revolt in the French occupied islands, and some refugees with loyal slaves had already begun arriving in Philadelphia. They all expressed their agreement.

It seemed, LaPorte thought to himself as he tasted the turkey pie—the rich brown gravy was delicious—that everyone had been inspired by the American Colonists' uprising against the British: the French citizens followed suit a decade later, and now the slaves in Saint Domingue were demanding rights and freedoms, too.

And it also seemed, he thought, as he rolled the exquisite hollandaise sauce on his tongue, that everyone felt the United States was the place to establish new settlements: asylums, refuges, places where those fleeing violence of any sort could re-establish themselves and forge a new life. It was the spirit of the times.

It suited those fleeing oppression or violence that financiers whose place in Europe's political and banking worlds had become precarious felt that investing and speculating in land development in the United States could help them recoup their losses, and re-establish themselves on firmer footing. Talon had told LaPorte of a Frenchman who had been great friends with the American Ben Franklin. This man, along with Jacques Necker, the French Minister of the Exchequer, had bought up thousands of acres along the north-eastern tier of Pennsylvania, hoping to lure immigrants. And the Priestly family's community to the west, in Northumberland, was well known, too. There had even been a small French colony begun by the Fouriers in LeRaysville—named for Franklin's friend, Jacques Donatien LeRay de Chaumont. Established on the community living pattern of Brook Farm in Massachusetts, Fourier's settlement had failed, as its ideal had. But even in failure, these enterprises pointed to the enthusiasm people felt for establishing themselves in a new place and beginning afresh.

Morris and Nicholson along with Keating had tentatively agreed to back the venture deNoailles had outlined a couple of weeks before. That day at Cazenove's table, the particulars were hammered out after the plates containing the apple cobbler, which was rich with butter and cinnamon and topped with a hot creamy vanilla bourbon sauce, had been licked clean. Over port, and with their long clay pipes smoking genially, the men decided on an initial settlement of nearly 20,000 acres, spanning both sides of the Susquehanna River's North Branch. After a brief discussion it was decided that prices would vary between $2 and $3 per acre, and plots of 200 acres would constitute a 'share' in the company.

"Most people will not have the means to pay $600 all at once," Keating noted with a slight frown.

LaPorte gave a covert look to his friend Talon, who sat opposite him at the table. Talon, he knew, had enough gemstones secreted in the brim of his hat to buy many, many shares in the new venture, or possibly all 20,000 acres! He himself, because of Talon's payment to him for 'services rendered' as Talon phrased it, had enough to buy quite a few. But might such an outlay of cash not arouse suspicion?

Talon met LaPorte's eyes intensely for a long second, and then returned his attention to his pipe. LaPorte nodded almost unnoticeably, and let out a long breath. Talon was right: sit tight, and wait.

Chapter Ten

Keating snapped his fingers a second later, and his brow cleared. "We could defer the payment, say, for two years? Until they have established themselves and begun to turn a profit," he suggested happily.

"Make it three years," Nicholson advised, joining with enthusiasm. "The winters in that area can be very harsh. Crops could fail," he cautioned.

Everyone nodded.

"There will, of course, be dividends issued yearly, once the initial payments are made," Keating assured them, and all looked pleased. "Dividing the profits from the settlement's income in trade."

Morris spread out a pen and ink map of the region, and pointed with one stubby finger. The main settlement, he explained, would be a town or village on the south bank of the river where, according to deNoailles, the land was a fertile alluvial plain already in agricultural use by early settlers from whom the land had been purchased by Cazenove's bankers.

These early settlers would be relocated, and Morris along with his partners agreed to buy the land from Cazenove on behalf of the new settlement.

"It will be an *azilum*," commented Talon, "a true refuge for the Queen, and our French aristocrats and nobles who must flee...or face the guillotine," he noted with excitement.

"I know the Prevosts, the Homets and others who will gladly come to our new community," deNoailles said again.

"We could send people to meet ships docking here in Philadelphia," suggested LaPorte. "If any French families are on board, they can tell them about our French Town, and they can buy a plot of land and settle down here in the new country!" he explained enthusiastically. "That way, we will earn back the money to repay your investment," he added to Morris and Nicholson.

Keating proclaimed that a capital idea, noting to LaPorte that he 'was always thinking up a profitable angle,' to which LaPorte nodded and smiled. Then, the group decided to offer half acre plots with two story log or 'timbered' houses on them, and additional holdings in the agricultural segment of the settlement. Morris made a sketch showing a central boulevard 100 feet wide, leading to a large structure where Queen Marie Antoinette could reside. Branching off of this central thoroughfare were smaller streets about 60 feet wide, where the houses and properties of the residents would be located. Each house, Morris indicated, would be set on a lot of about a half an acre. Centered in the residential area, Morris indicated spaces for a sizable town square of about two acres, around which he indicated a church, a few shops and even a theatre. A large orchard with apple and pear trees, and cultivated gardens would flank the main settlements. Pastures for grazing and tilled fields for large scale crops would be placed beyond those. At the bottom of the central north south roadway, at the river's edge was a quay, or wharf for river boats. Morris optimistically drew in several roads besides the one that currently existed, leading over the mountains that stood guard over the new settlement, although it would take years for all of those decent roadways to be carved out of the steep, rocky terrain.

Nicholson did some quick figures on a slip of foolscap and when the scratching of his quill ceased he informed his companions that the selling price for each half acre plot and two story house would mean an immediate return of some 400 percent over the purchase price.

"That's even before we clear land and sell timber and whatever else we may find," put in Talon, looking quite cheerful. "There is sure to be slate and bluestone to be quarried."

"To our friends coming from France, and used to French land prices, 'twill seem a bargain," added Lafayette. "Especially with the generous terms," he shot an appreciative look at Keating and Nicholson.

"There is some mining for coal south and east of this land," said Keating quietly. "A way to ship it up to New York State without having to fight the river current would mean a boon for any settlement along the way." He sighed. He had long thought to use the Susquehanna as a transport route for goods, but the river's tricky navigation in spots meant that his beloved vision of steamboats plying the water bringing goods from ports to inland settlements was likely never to be realized.

However, Keating was experienced in the import and export line, and if nothing else was delighted to have made the acquaintance of LaPorte, whom he thought would make an excellent lieutenant: someone he could have on site to oversee what he hoped would be a brisk trading business.

"You mean, my idea of a canal!" Cazenove rejoined quickly now, and explained that linking the fledgeling Erie Canal system in New York State with the Delaware Canal system near Philadelphia could mean 'riches' for the people involved as well as for the towns and villages along the canal route. Including, perhaps, French Town. "I have often thought of such a scheme," he continued enthusiastically. "There is a group working on the Schuylkill and Susquehanna Canal," he informed his colleagues. "But they are just beginning the first section, a portage canal at Great Falls on the lower Susquehanna." He paused, clearly thinking great thoughts. "Perhaps, with your French Town along the North Branch of the river, other trading depots such as Tioga Point and Wilkes Barre would be interested in financing such a venture!"

Cazenove's canal idea was shunted to one side, however, as the group made their plans for the more immediate concern: the establishment of the French Town colony.

Of the group, only Lafayette and deNoailles had actually seen the region Morris and Nicholson spoke about. However, they described the acreage they were purchasing in such glowing terms that both LaPorte and Talon found themselves anxious to relocate there, LaPorte permanently and Talon at least temporarily. It was decided that the '*Grande Maison*' should be built first and then the houses for new residents. This way, people who were not planning to settle permanently could still visit the colony and stay at the Grande Maison—at least until the Queen arrived.

Another impetus for people, including LaPorte and Talon, to leave congenial Philadelphia that spring was the looming summer. The warmer months were known all up and down the East Coast as the 'sickly season,' when fevers of various types were widespread. It had become commonplace for those who could to leave coastal cities for the summer, and Philadelphia was no different: the government recessed and President Washington left, to return in the autumn.

Most cities' open drains and sewers as well as undeveloped marshlands near the ports provided a lush breeding ground for insects, which carried diseases. Additionally, the influx of arrivals from ships docking at these ports meant new strains of germs, including Yellow Fever. Although no one understood germ theory in 1793 or knew the connection between insects and illness, they did know that summer in Philadelphia could be deadly.

Thus, they headed for points inland such as Northampton Town and Bethlehem—which had its own water supply, an innovation that kept it relatively disease free— or further north, to towns such as Wilkes Barre. Although the numbers escaping the illnesses varied from year to year, as many as a third of the 50,000 people dwelling in Philadelphia in 1793 would seek cooler climes where the disease bearing insects did not thrive.

In the late spring of 1793, therefore, LaPorte and Talon decided that, since Cazenove and Morris were moving inland for the summer and the others were either resuming or starting different journeys, the time seemed opportune for them to make the trip north and west towards the land Morris and Nicholson had purchased on behalf of themselves and other refugees. They would stay there until the weather turned, then return to Philadelphia for the winter. That way, they could become familiar with the area and its people, and LaPorte intended to choose his plot of land and negotiate some acreage to farm as well. When they told Morris, Nicholson and the rest of their wish to travel north and west to see with their own eyes the site they would call home, and to which they would be inviting other French refugees, Morris in particular seemed overjoyed.

It turned out that the investors—they had yet to decide on a name for themselves—had decided to send two scouts to make sure the land was as they thought it would be. Major Adam Hoops and Charles Felix Bué Boulogne. The latter had been involved with a couple of other immigrant settlements and although these had failed, the investors thought that this would make Boulogne particularly cautious before he gave his approval for this new French colony on the Susquehanna. As for Hoops, he had travelled with Général Sullivan in 1779 when he went up the Susquehanna through northeastern Pennsylvania and into New York in an attempt to push back the Native Americans. Therefore, Hoops knew the area well. He'd also spent time in France, and so knew the language, and the people. He had assured Morris and the other investors that he would make sure that the acreage where they were planning to establish French Town would meet the expectations of the noble families they would solicit to settle there.

Thus it was settled that LaPorte and Talon would accompany Hoops and Boulogne on their journey.

Talon thought he might travel to Belgium once they returned to Philadelphia, if it were safe then, to visit with his wife and family, and to enchant them with the idea of re-settling at French Town. He could bring them over with him when he returned, or go back with LaPorte to the new colony the following summer, and send for his wife and family once some houses had been built and land had been cleared.

Talon also planned to take out citizenship papers in Pennsylvania upon his return, and swear his fealty to the Commonwealth. That way, he thought, no one could say a foreigner was purchasing the land at French Town: he would be a citizen. Although the disputes over the Royal land titles from George III and the titles for the same land from William Penn had been mostly resolved, Talon did not wish to risk any disruption in his plan to settle in the United States. It was expected that about that time, several of the other families deNoailles had mentioned, and perhaps even the Queen, would also be settling there in their new home.

The acreage was now called French Town, but would shortly become known as 'Asylum,' or in the French manner, 'Azilum,' because so many in the initial group of investors and planners referred to it as such. Additionally, they decided to call the company holding title to the lands, 'Asylum Company.'

Chapter Eleven

As predicted, the trip out of Philadelphia and north, then west to the land that would become Azilum, was neither fast nor comfortable. Both Talon and LaPorte were used to hardships in travel, however, and had prepared well for their journey, packing their belongings in leather valises and acquiring sturdy coats, hats and shoes. Although in theory they would be riding in coaches or on horseback for much of the trip, one never knew what might happen, and it was best to be prepared.

Hoops and Boulogne were already in the Wilkes Barre area on other business, and had sent word that they would wait there for Talon and LaPorte, and then lead them onward to the land that would become Azilum.

A weekly coach service between Philadelphia and Bethlehem had been thriving for thirty years, travelling along the King's Road. This highway had been established in the 1760s along the path of the Minsi Trail, which had been a Native American byway. The coach service had been started by George Klein: his sons now ran the business and handled the coaches, which left every Thursday from the King of Prussia Inn, arriving at the Sun Inn in Bethlehem on Friday.

Several settlements had sprung up along the King's Road following the establishment of the town of Bethlehem by the Moravians in 1741. By the time the coach had reached the small settlement of Sellers Tavern, about 20 miles along and thus nearly precisely half way to Bethlehem, so many passengers had availed themselves of the coach that Talon and LaPorte were squeezed together along the narrow bench seat inside the conveyance.

The large inn that gave the settlement its name was a boon, however, since it provided decent rooms and excellent food. The two Frenchmen spent a pleasant enough night there and were happy to find their coach less crowded the following morning, when their driver informed them that it should be a quick trip to Bethlehem, for the weather was still fair and the road dry.

"Ye'll be at t'Sun Inn by dinner time, have nae fear," he said congenially, his Germanic accent distinctive.

LaPorte and Talon were cheered to realize their guide had been correct, for although their coach made several stops along the way to pick up or drop off passengers, they pulled into the Sun Inn's cobbled courtyard just after 1 p.m.

"'Tis a beautiful country," Talon sighed as he and LaPorte went for a walk along Bethlehem's main roadway following their dinner at the Sun Inn. Although the cuisine had not been what either Frenchman had been used to—gone were the delicate sauces and complex interplay of spices so familiar in French dishes—it had been tasty and filling: roast pork with stewed cabbage and dumplings, sweet noodles with poppy seeds, and preserved fruit pies. Now, both men wanted to stretch their legs.

They ambled slowly down the broad, cobbled street, admiring the stone buildings on either side. Although it was still light out since it was just 4 p.m. on a spring afternoon, all of the windows in the residences had small candles shining brightly, framed in many cases by brilliantly white net curtains drawn back to either side. Talon and LaPorte had noticed the same thing at the Sun Inn, and took it to be a custom brought with the Moravians from their homeland in Germany.

Residents walked up and down the street, patronizing shops or businesses, or visiting friends, many in traditional Moravian garb. Men wore wide brimmed hats not unlike Talon's, but with long vests and coats.

LaPorte admired the style and vowed to find and purchase a similar accessory before they departed.

The women's dresses were mostly black or other dark colors, topped by white half aprons, cloaks in greys or greens, and somewhat elaborate white head gear that completely hid their hair. This was quite a change for the Frenchmen, who had been chiefly associating with French women who wore bright colors in silks and satins, or floral muslin frocks, and dressed their hair elaborately, even in Philadelphia.

"I suspect it is part of their beliefs," Talon murmured in French to his companion as they turned left from the main street onto Church Street.

LaPorte nodded, and then smiled as the bells began to chime the hour from the Old Chapel, on the next street. "Hecke-wel-der Place?" LaPorte read the name of the small street from the etched stone plaque on the side of the Chapel.

"German," Talon supplied with a smile. "An interesting language, but not one I know very well," he commented, thinking of his perusal of the German book on the transatlantic voyage.

The two friends walked on, turning as they did, so that they made a large square around the center of town, and returned to the Sun Inn refreshed and ready to plan the next leg of their journey.

Over a supper of halušky, pickled gherkins and the wafer thin, sugary cookies the Moravians would become known for, Talon and LaPorte sipped the slivovitz, or apricot brandy, and plotted their next steps.

"We will likely stay west of the mountains," LaPorte advised, tracing the route he supposed Hoops and Boulogne would use. "Even though it is spring time, at elevation there will still be snow, and ice."

Talon nodded mildly, and took another sip of his brandy. This slivovitz was strong stuff! But the taste was redolent of apricots, and delicious. He wondered if eventually the little settlement of Azilum could produce something like this, perhaps from the fruit trees they were planning to grow.

"Antoine!" came LaPorte's voice sharply, but he was smiling. "Are you listening?" he asked, slightly exasperated.

"Ah, yes, yes, my friend, I am listening," Talon insisted.

"I think you've had too much brandy," LaPorte returned sarcastically.

Talon shrugged, then shook his head. "No, no: I was just dreaming…of a day when Azilum perhaps could produce its own version of this," he confided, lifting the small glass of amber liquid, and then downing the remaining brandy in a single gulp.

LaPorte grinned, then sighed and pointed to a map he carried with him of the commonwealth of Pennsylvania. "We are here," he said, pointing one determined finger to a spot on the map. "We are going here," he continued, pointing to another spot. "But tomorrow we set out for here, Wilkes Barre, to meet our scouts."

Talon squinted at the map in the candlelight. "It says, 'Lehigh and Lackawanna Path?'" he queried.

LaPorte nodded. He explained that this road was again built on a path originally traversed by Native Americans. This one ran from the Forks of the Delaware through Fort Allen to the Nanticoke Creek, where Wilkes Barre now was. The 70 mile trip would be made on horseback this time, and again split up over two days. They would stop at an inn LaPorte had heard of, in Little Gap, roughly half way along their route.

The same driver who had so ably brought them from Philadelphia had agreed to source two good horses for them, and LaPorte and Talon had paid a very reasonable price for the beasts. They would be brought to the Sun Inn the following morning, Saturday, and the two Frenchmen would set off on their journey north.

Some re-configuring of their satchels was needed since they would have to carry everything with them on horseback, but both managed, and by 9 a.m. on Saturday, LaPorte and Talon had clip-clopped out of Bethlehem atop their two brown and white horses, and by 10 a.m. they were making good time at a fast trot traveling through the green hills and aiming for the mountainous ridge they could see in the distance before them.

Chapter Twelve

"They call it Little Gap because it is in an area where the mountains do not quite form a ridge, and passage across is possible nearly all year 'round," LaPorte informed Talon. The two were pausing briefly in the small settlement whose name they were discussing, to rest and water their horses and purchase sustenance for themselves before attempting the somewhat arduous trail through the mountains and into Wilkes Barre.

Although they were, as LaPorte had noted, west of the much higher north to south Pocono Mountain Ridge, the lower mountains that ran east to west were unavoidable. Switchback roads were the order of the day except for areas, like Little Gap, where passage could be had without going over the ridge.

Talon nodded, and returned to the cold dried beef and hard cheese he was eating. Along with a roll that was just slightly stale, this would be his main meal this day, and he hoped they would find more substantial fare at the end of their journey, in Wilkes Barre. Hoops and Boulogne were staying at the River Inn in Forty Fort, just north of Wilkes Barre along the Lehigh and Lackawanna Path, which was the main road they were traveling.

The scenery was breathtaking as LaPorte and Talon spent the day riding along, and rather different from what either had been used to seeing. The places they had lived in Europe had not been mountainous, and so the drudgery of climbing over the peaks before them was somewhat alleviated by the unique experience as well as the beauty of their surroundings. Also, despite the fact that it was nearly summer time, the air was cool and clean, a refreshing change from steamy and often smelly Philadelphia, the wood smoke of Paris or the sea air of Cadiz or Marseille.

Hillsides, newly green, burst with flowering shrubbery: *kalmia latifolia* the mountain laurel, as well as various types of azaleas and rhododendron colored the landscape, and birds sang, it seemed, everywhere. Several times as the two French men trotted along the well worn dirt roadway they spied herds of white tailed deer as well as other wildlife, like foxes.

They had been told about the native American 'mountain lion,' a large carnivorous feline that roamed freely in the wilds of northeastern Pennsylvania. There was no such animal in Europe, and at first LaPorte had thought the sailors who were telling him about the puma were joking. However, he'd verified the tale with so many people he felt sure the creature truly existed; secretly, he wouldn't mind seeing one, even though it might spell danger. But with all the deer available for easy meals, LaPorte thought that the big cats probably wouldn't bother them, as long as they stuck to the road and traveled by day.

Getting to Wilkes Barre, or actually Forty Fort, by sunset meant a day of nearly continual riding because they could not go at a very fast speed due to the uneven and often mountainous terrain. Even their stop at Little Gap had been very quick, and LaPorte kept urging his companion on if Talon seemed to be lagging behind.

"Nearly there—see—the town is below," LaPorte pointed out the settlement of Wilkes Barre and to its north, the Forty Fort area, as he and Talon achieved the summit of the final mountain before the long descent into what was called the Wyoming Valley. The Susquehanna River bisected the valley, and then led north and west: they could see it gleaming grey in the late afternoon light as their mounts began to trot down the switchback road that led to civilization. A couple of lights began to wink on as they descended, and evening drew near.

Forty Fort had been named for the fort that stood at the center of the small community. It in turn had been named for the forty settlers from Connecticut who had founded the town. During the Yankee Pennamite Wars and the Revolution, the fort had been a necessary feature, and it was still in use.

An early settler, Nathan Dennison, had built quite a grand home nearby, followed by more settlers who had built their own dwellings. The town had developed a central market area as well as residential streets branching outward and along the river. Settlers were raising families and building homes, farming nearby land, engaging in trade in the small town center, or joining in with the burgeoning mining business nearby. Inns like the River Inn where Hoops and Boulogne stayed were popping up as well.

Since there were only a few main roadways that led into Wilkes Barre and then out towards Forty Fort and Pittston, which was a mining center, it was not difficult to figure out which way to go. Most roads had signposts to point the way, and once LaPorte paused to ask a passerby, to be certain they were headed in the right direction.

They availed themselves of a ferry near Nanticoke, so they would be on the same bank of the Susquehanna as the River Inn, and by dark they were riding up to its front steps.

Lanterns illuminated the three story inn. Talon and LaPorte dismounted; Talon in particular was delighted when two stable hands appeared quickly to assist them. The boys led their horses to the stables where they would receive a well deserved brushing down, water, and food, as well as cozy stalls for the night.

The River Inn was a curious mix of rustic and refined, Talon thought as he looked around him. Outside, it looked like a very large private home, finished in dark brown paneling, with a sturdy front door of wide planks flanked by lanterns that illuminated thick slabbed stone steps. There were many windows, and through several of these light of varying intensity shone out into the dark night. The windows were outlined in whitewash and sported black shutters; the Inn was capped with a dark grey slate roof. A discreet sign in front of the establishment enlightened passersby that this was, 'The River Inn, prop. Jas. Brown.'

"We are expected, I believe, by Monsieur Boulogne and Monsieur Hoops?" Talon told the Innkeeper, who had welcomed them almost as soon as they had knocked on the front door, and led them to a reception area. Here, the Innkeeper entered their names in a Register with an enviably flourished script, and handed over a key to the room they would be sharing.

"Indeed, indeed, gentlemen: your party awaits you in the front parlor," Mr. Brown told them genially, and led them to the sitting room where Hoops and Boulogne were, indeed, waiting, each with a glass of whiskey.

Talon continued his survey of the inn, finding the same mixture of simplicity and elegance inside as he had outside. Huge, hand hewn beams joined by pegs supported the ceilings, but the walls were nicely painted in either a soft creamy yellow or that peculiar blend of aqua and green so loved by Colonial interior decorators. The floor of the foyer was bare wood, but the planks were polished to a high sheen, and where the heaviest foot traffic was expected—from the front door to Mr. Brown's desk—an Oriental carpet in dark hues that wouldn't show dirt easily had been laid.

On one wall of the foyer, someone of an artistic bent had painted a representation of the river and the surrounding area, and two tall backed wooden benches stood ready to receive waiting visitors. Wrought iron wall sconces held candles, and a still life painting of fruit and freshly caught pheasants held pride of place opposite Mr.

Brown's desk. A wrought iron chandelier with beeswax candles burning brightly hung in the center of the ceiling, illuminating everything.

The parlor to which they were led boasted a smaller cousin of the chandelier in the foyer, and was warmed by a 'Franklin stove' although it was actually the improved version tweaked by David Rittenhouse in the mid 18th century. This was kept burning steadily, providing a good warmth to the room at all times. Even though it was summer, Talon noted, the evenings and nights were cool, especially near the river. A couple of covered candle lamps stood on small tables in the parlor as well, and these provided extra light.

A brightly colored Oriental rug centered the room over more polished wood, and small upholstered settees along with chairs and tables were scattered throughout to create intimate groupings where guests of the Inn could hold reasonably private conversations. The windows were traditional: Colonial nine over nine single hung. In the parlor they were ornamented with dun colored draperies in a rather coarse linen type fabric, now pulled shut against the gathering gloom.

Talon's musings were cut short by the two men who, upon his and LaPorte's entry to the parlor, sprang up from their seats around a small table near the stove, and bowed formally.

"Monsieur Talon! Monsieur LaPorte!" they exclaimed happily, and then everyone shook hands, following the less formal custom of the United States. The two men were Hoops and Boulogne, who had been waiting at the Inn for the arrival of LaPorte and Talon, whom they thought of as their 'charges.'

Hoops and Boulogne were the scouts, the ones with backwoods and wilderness experience. Talon and LaPorte were principals involved in the Asylum Company who would shortly be taking ownership of the land along the

North Branch of the Susquehanna. It was, therefore, the scouts' considered opinion that they were the ones to look out for the welfare of the two businessmen on their journey.

"How fortunate you are able to join us," Charles Boulogne began, motioning to one of the Inn's staff to bring two more glasses and the bottle of whiskey.

"I do hope we will not be a bother, or a hindrance," LaPorte replied with a smile. "We are not professional outdoorsmen, such as yourselves," he added, encompassing Hoops in his smile. LaPorte and Talon had discussed the scouts and what they might be like, and had decided to let the backwoodsmen take charge.

Adam Hoops shook his head, but he was pleased at the man's comment. "Not to worry," he reassured them. "Much of the trip to the site of your French Town is by boat, now, up the river, and some by road," he informed them, adding that the next morning, if Talon and LaPorte were ready, they could begin the journey north to the small town of Tunkhannock. One never knew with businessmen just how adaptable they would be to the rigors of travel.

But to his continued surprise and pleasure, both LaPorte and Talon assured the scouts that they would be ready to travel on the following morning.

"We can break our travel in Tunkhannock, at Wall's Tavern," Boulogne put in as the whiskey arrived. He poured each of the newcomers a hefty shot. "*Salut et bienvenue!*" he said, raising his own glass and downing what remained of its contents.

Hoops did likewise, as did LaPorte and Talon, and then Mr. Brown sent over supper, which the scouts had ordered earlier. Talon and LaPorte were cheered to find a thick fish stew before them, along with a loaf of fragrant, crusty fresh bread and a crock of sweet butter.

"This is very good," Talon murmured, unable to hide his tone of surprise.

"The fish is from the river," Boulogne told them. "Very fresh, and everything else is local as well." He paused. "They have a decent cook here: not what you were used to in France, or even Philadelphia, but quite good nonetheless."

LaPorte nodded and ate happily. "We have become used to simpler dishes and less seasoning," he commented, slathering a round of bread with the creamy butter. "But that does not make them any less," he added with a grin.

As they all ate supper, Hoops continued to outline the trip they would start the next day. To Tunkhannock by road, then they would continue upriver by Durham boat towards the site. "We cannot make the trip from Tunkhannock to the site in one day: we will need to spend a night or two somewhere, and much of the question of where depends on how the river is," Hoops continued. "I try, if it is feasible, to stop at my old Army companion's house: it's right on the river, and the family who lives there now welcome visitors," he finished expansively. "From there, we can decide whether to continue by road or by boat, and where to stop, and how to most swiftly reach the site."

"Oh, we shall be ready!" LaPorte assured the two men with a smile for Talon, who nodded his agreement. "We are very anxious to see the place with our own eyes," he added.

Chapter Thirteen

The ride to Tunkhannock was similar to the ride up from Philadelphia, except that the terrain was more hilly. They followed the river as it wound through rocky outcroppings and deep, forested fields, passing a few small settlements where the ground was arable. They arrived in Tunkhannock in time for dinner, settled themselves at Wall's Tavern and Inn, and enjoyed another abundant if plain meal: roast chicken, peas with onions, mashed winter squash and potatoes, cheese and a good selection of alcoholic beverages. The four men sat together at a table and shared the platters of food 'family style.' This was the way most taverns and inns served food to their patrons; it was luck that allowed Talon, LaPorte, Boulogne and Hoops to have their own table.

To LaPorte's surprise, the tavern had a decent port, which he enjoyed. "I did not think, so far, erm, inland, that they would have much besides whiskey," he commented to Talon later as they got ready to retire for the night. Although the tavern had dormitory style accommodation for the budget conscious travelers who were in the majority, they had a few private rooms used by upper class people, military officers and the occasional brave woman traveler. Hoops and Boulogne shared one of these, and LaPorte and Talon another.

"Yes, I am surprised at the level of, well, of— civilization," Talon said, his tone hopeful. "Perhaps our site will not be as isolated as we feared," he added, smiling.

LaPorte shrugged. "Whatever it is, we will make it wonderful," he said confidently.

"How do you stay so cheerful?" Talon asked as they blew out the candle and settled into their narrow beds in the darkness. Around them they could hear creaks and murmurs as other patrons also went about their nightly rituals. Below, sounds of conversation and occasional bursts of laughter echoed faintly from the tavern, where several patrons still lingered.

"Why should I not be cheerful?" LaPorte countered with a chuckle.

Talon shook his head, moving against the rough weave of the pillowcase. "It just seems that you always see the positive, that you're always looking forward," Talon replied. "It is an enviable set of mind, Bart," he added, low. "I wish I were more like you."

At this LaPorte laughed aloud, then shushed himself into a chuckle. "Oh, my friend, do not wish that," he counselled, smiling in the darkness. "We each are as we are, and 'tis nothing to be gained by wishing we were otherwise. Rather, I try to be the best of myself, to give the best of myself, no matter what I am engaged in," he finished quietly.

Talon sighed. "Well, you have done so: 'tis true that without you I probably would never have left Philadelphia," he commented. Of the two of them, Talon had been less eager to leave the comfort of the city, and had been less entranced by the prospect of French Town. But LaPorte's enthusiasm for the new venture had been contagious, and Talon had been impressed by the investors' talk and plans, and so he had agreed. "Indeed, as I've said before, I probably never would have got out of France, much less made this remarkable journey," he mused.

LaPorte shrugged, then replied sleepily, "Omer, I think you have more mettle than you give yourself credit." LaPorte was happy to accept Talon's gratitude, and the former French Avocat Général had paid him well, almost too well, for what he thought of as his small part in Talon's deliverance. Now, LaPorte yawned. "Good night, *ami.*"

"Good night, *ami*," Talon replied happily.

They boarded the Durham boat headed upriver the following morning after a breakfast of ale, bread and cheese. Neither LaPorte nor Talon had ever seen a boat like the Durham before, though Hoops and Boulogne were familiar with them.

"'Tis much larger than I had expected!" Talon exclaimed, sounding relieved. The boat, pointed at both ends to aid navigation and about sixty feet long and eight feet wide, was drawn up to a dock on the south west side of Tunkhannock. It bobbed lightly in the water, as it was empty. But once the passengers and freight were loaded, it would settle down smoothly.

"What, did you think we were going to put you in a canoe?" Boulogne joked with a grin as they boarded.

Talon had the good grace to look chastised, and grinned back, shaking his head.

To his and LaPorte's pleasure, their good horses would also be making the trip up the river on the boat, along with mounts belonging to their guides. LaPorte had expressed surprise at this, but the scouts had explained that the Durham boat could carry about fifteen tons while only displacing twenty inches of water in the river. This meant that it didn't run aground often, especially now in the summer time when spring rains had swelled the river to a good height.

Hoops in particular took great delight in showing his 'charges' the details of the boat, from its flat bottom "the better to navigate on rivers," he explained, to its sawn planked deck. There were small decks on both ends of the boat and a walking board along each side, with cleats in the tread for security. The boat's navigator operated a long 'sweep' or steering oar, and a couple of other crewmen used long poles to help push the boat along, walking the cleated passages along the side of the boat. A single mast amidships was fitted with two square sails.

These, Hoops explained, helped propel the boat upriver when the wind was right, for upriver was traveling against the current. Although the Susquehanna was wide and slow in some places, in others it narrowed and the current could be quite fast. That was when the navigator's skill and the sails came into play, as long as the wind was blowing in the right direction.

Once everyone had been loaded along with their goods, horses, and any cargo the boat was carrying, it was untied from the dock and the crew pushed away from the pebbled shore into the middle of the river where the channel was most navigable. A light wind from the south meant that the sails could assist in places with the movement north and west, and the crew ably guided the boat along, upstream, towards its first port of call in a small town called Mehoopany.

Here, a few people alighted, for Talon and his friends were not the only passengers on the boat that day. No others boarded, but some cargo was offloaded and soon the boat continued on its way.

"Our next stop is Meshoppen," Hoops said. They were congregated on the forward deck, sitting on the sun warmed planks, for the Durham boat didn't carry niceties like deck chairs. LaPorte had produced a small bag of peanuts from one voluminous pocket and shared them out as they chatted and admired the scenery.

"All the towns have peculiar names," Talon said as they watched fertile fields backed by dark green forests and rocky hillsides slide past them.

Hoops nodded. "The Native peoples who lived here, and despite Général Sullivan's efforts, some still do," he added in a low tone. "They are called Lenni Lenape, as is their language. Their names for these places along the river have been adapted by the settlers," he explained.

"They're not exactly as the Natives pronounce them, but they are better suited this way to the English tongue," he chuckled.

"Look!" Boulogne suddenly exclaimed, pointing towards a high outcropping of rock they were just passing.

Hoops, LaPorte and Talon looked.

"Bald eagles," Boulogne said excitedly.

"That is the symbol of this country," Talon said, marveling at the two large birds that flew above them. They seemed to be protecting a spot high up on the rocks.

When he suggested this, Hoops nodded. "They have a nest up there," he said, adding that when he'd made this trip previously he had noted that the eagles were often sighted in this area and that nests belonging to them could sometimes also be spotted.

To prove his point he directed his party's attention towards a particular place high up on the rock face where just visible they could see some branches and other bits of detritus.

"That is the nest. Their hatchlings are doubtless in there, waiting to be fed, and the adults are guarding them as we pass," Hoops explained in an almost reverent voice. "They will be fledging soon," he added, sounding excited.

"Beautiful!" exclaimed LaPorte.

They were nearing Meshoppen now, where they would again offload some cargo. Here, a few people boarded the boat as well, but before much time had passed, the boat was once again headed upstream.

As the sun rose, it was obscured by some high clouds that presaged rain within a day or so. This kept the temperature on the deck of the boat cooler than usual and so the journey upriver was pleasant. In addition to the eagles, other wildlife was seen as the boat passed almost silently along. The passengers spoke among themselves, but quietly, and many enjoyed the passing panorama as LaPorte and Talon and the scouts did.

LaPorte's peanuts were the only food they ate all day, however, and as the afternoon waned, Talon's stomach growled.

"We will stop at my friend's house for supper and the night," Hoops told them happily, adding that their luggage and horses could continue by boat and be waiting for them when they caught the next day's boat to Wyalusing. "Well, he built it, or had it built. They've sold it now, but the family there is very kind, and used to welcoming river travelers," he amended.

"From Wyalusing we go by road?" Talon asked, curious.

Hoops and Boulogne looked at each other. "'Tis more by trail or track than road," he admitted. "Although once your settlement is accomplished, roadways will no doubt be built," he assured them.

Chapter Fourteen

They had a choice, Hoops and Boulogne explained to LaPorte and Talon as the Durham boat was propelled upstream towards Braintrim, of routes to take to get from Wyalusing to the site of their settlement. They had alluded to this before, and indeed had told the two Frenchmen frankly that the route they were taking was not the most popular one to gain that area of Pennsylvania.

'Most travel the river west and then come north,' Hoops had said dismissively.

'Is that easier, or faster?' Talon had asked.

' 'Tis not faster,' Hoops had said definitively.

Of course, the fact that he and Boulogne had been in Wilkes Barre had been the deciding factor in the route Talon and LaPorte took to meet them for their journey, but it was interesting to hear about other options.

Now, to get from Wyalusing further west, Hoops explained that the easier way was to ride along the north bank of the river on the old Native American Path that was fast becoming a highway, albeit a dirt one. "It is travelled heavily," Hoops noted, "and the surface is a good one."

"Well that sounds like the way to go then," LaPorte agreed.

"Yes, but although your Asylum Company owns land on both sides of the river, it is my understanding that the settlement is destined to be on the south side, where there is much arable land," Boulogne put in.

Talon and LaPorte nodded.

"Crossing the river there, where there are few settlements and fewer good roads, can be tricky," Hoops continued. "We want to take the best advantage of both." He paused. "If we were to ride along the Native American

Highway from Wyalusing, there is no ferry until we reach Towanda, and that is a few miles past the place where your settlement is to be," he outlined, sketching in the air to allow everyone to understand better.

"What is the other way?" LaPorte asked, still cheery.

"We cross at Wyalusing, on their ferry," Hoops answered. "And then take the trails along the south side of the river until we reach your site," he finished.

"How long will that take?" Talon inquired with a slight frown. He knew that there would be no real accommodation once they gained the land that the Company owned but he was anxious nonetheless to reach it. Even a tent on land that was theirs, he felt, would be better than a bed in an inn.

"'Tis but a dozen miles," Hoops answered. "But it is not fast going, and will take the better part of a day."

"If we take the next boat upriver to Wyalusing, then take that trail, we will not be at your site by nightfall," Boulogne cautioned.

"Could we not disembark completely at your friend's son's house in Braintrim, and ride to Wyalusing early the next day rather than wait for the boat?" LaPorte queried. "Would riding not also be faster?"

"It would," Hoops concurred. "And yes, we could do that. I think my friend—well, it's his son, James Smith, who lives there—would do his best to accommodate us," he replied. Four horses would be a tight squeeze in the barn, he thought, if he remembered right, but he knew the family well and was sure they would do what they could.

"That was the best meal I've had in a while," LaPorte told Talon quietly. It was evening, and the two of them had gone for a walk together after the feast that had been provided for them by the Smiths.

James was the son of Hoops' friend, Dr. William Hooker Smith, who now lived in Pittston and was involved in the mining business. Dr. Smith and Hoops had both served under Général John Sullivan, traveling with him on 'Sullivan's March.' That was how Hoops had come to know the area so well, and become friends with Smith. When Smith had acquired several hundred acres of land and built a house, Hoops had been a frequent guest when passing through, even though Dr. Smith had never lived there, having built the house primarily for his son and family.

The Durham boat had called at the small wharf in the late afternoon, and as had been decided, all of their bags and the four horses had been offloaded. The Smiths were happy to see them if a bit overwhelmed by all the extra mouths both human and equine. But as Hoops had hoped, room was made and the travelers were welcomed inside.

Hearing that they had not eaten since the morning, directions were given and before long a number of cold and hot dishes were laid out on the rough wooden table in the house's Keeping Room, and Talon, LaPorte, Hoops and Boulogne were invited to eat. James Smith sat with them, not eating, but sipping at a tankard of small beer and talking with the travelers. His wife, having said her greetings, disappeared with the children, and the household staff, having provided the meal, continued with their usual chores.

Talon had once again absorbed the details of the furnishings in the house, for it was the first private home in the U.S., outside of the rather grand ones in Philadelphia, that he had visited. It was more rustic than the River Inn had been, but like that establishment, some elements of refinement could be seen: painted walls, another wrought iron chandelier in an upstairs room, and a couple of upholstered chairs in the parlor.

Downstairs in the Keeping Room, however, which faced the river and which led to the house's *de facto* main doorway, the walls were merely whitewashed and the space dominated by the huge stone chimney and double fireplace, some eight feet square, and finished with a solid beam of black walnut. More hand hewn, pegged, black walnut beams striped the low ceiling of the room, and herbs hung from one of them near the chimney's warmth. Small windows caught the sun as it sank towards the western river's edge and flashed a golden light through the room.

The hand-made table had benches, but Smith pulled up a couple of chairs for his visitors, and Talon took advantage of the kindness. A small fire in the first fireplace warded off any evening chill and the travelers spent a congenial few hours eating, drinking and talking with their host.

Now, Talon nodded his agreement at LaPorte's opinion of the Smiths' table and the two continued their walk along the river bank. Beyond the Smith house, they could see a couple of dim lights in the west. James Smith had told them that several families had begun to settle in a small village about a half mile upriver, and LaPorte and Talon knew it was the lights from these dwellings they were seeing.

"I am not sure we should continue all the way to Azilum by horseback," LaPorte ventured hesitantly.

Talon gave him a look. "Why not?"

LaPorte sighed. "Hoops and Boulogne told us the trail on the south side of the river would be 'rough going,'" he reminded Talon. "I fear it will be very rough." He paused. Far be it from him to say that he thought his refined friend, the former Avocat Général of France, might not be prepared for such a rigorous outdoor trek. He hoped Talon would come to that conclusion on his own.

But Talon was silent.

"Once we reach the site, we will need to secure lodgings," LaPorte continued. "Nearby. Close enough that we can ride overland to the site as we wish to."

Talon nodded. "Hoops mentioned an inn of sorts not far—'over the mountain' was the way he described its location," he added, sounding doubtful.

LaPorte nodded. "The site is surrounded on one side by a ring of low mountains," he explained. "South of those heights we come into lower land, with villages. And inns. I am not sure if there is a very good road between the site and those settlements," he continued. "But there is a decent path, Hoops maintains."

Talon, who had been looking down as they walked and talked, for the ground was not very level and he didn't wish to twist an ankle if he stepped wrong, now looked up. He gazed at the Smith house in the foreground, lights showing from several rooms' windows and the big front door open to the cooling evening river breezes. He lifted his eyes to the roadway beyond the house: a well worn dirt track that would lead them to Wyalusing.

"Perhaps..." Talon began, "we can see how the ride tomorrow morning goes, to Wyalusing," he suggested. "If this 'roadway' proves less easily traveled than we might wish, we could perhaps conclude that the "track" on the south side of the river to Azilum would be beyond at least my capabilities," he offered self-deprecatingly.

LaPorte smiled to himself and let out a long breath. "We could do that, surely. And perhaps in Wyalusing we could find another Durham boat, or ride, as Hoops said, to Towanda, and ferry across the river there."

Talon allowed as how the 'Native American Highway' to Towanda didn't fill him with confidence of an easy ride, either, but it would probably be preferable to—

and faster than—the 'track' on the south side of the Susquehanna.

Chapter Fifteen

The ride to Wyalusing the following morning was not too bad. The road was hard packed earth and obviously a major thoroughfare for the region. Although the river was still the best way to move if one were headed downstream, going upstream by water was challenging, as their trip from Tunkhannock had shown. Both LaPorte and Talon understood why the roadway that ran between Braintrim and Wyalusing was preferred for travelers heading west.

The weather held: it was warm, but dry, and they were able to keep a steady, quick pace that brought them to Wyalusing. On the way, Hoops explained that the Moravian missionaries who had come to the area more than two decades before had shortened the Native American 'machiwilusing' and given the village its slightly shorter but still unusual name.

They passed by a cluster of a few houses snuggled right up to the roadway, called 'Friedenshutten,' and Hoops said this was where the Moravians had originally settled, for down towards the river the land was good for farming.

On the road there were others on horseback, a few carriages and wagons, and even a couple of people walking, some with bundles and others without, but all looking as though they were on a mission.

Wyalusing in 1793 was a bustling small town, its future as a shipping port for logging and other enterprises easy to envision. LaPorte, Talon, Hoops and Boulogne called in at a tavern the two scouts knew well from previous visits, and over tankards of small beer they broke their fast with fresh-baked bread and creamy butter. They had left the Smith house at daybreak and had worked up quite an appetite on the road. LaPorte had carried a few apples from the Smiths' stores, stuffed in his pockets, and had shared them as they rode but hunger still overtook them.

Hoops had a quick conversation with the tavern's proprietor and returned to the small table, where his three companions sat, to outline their route choices for the rest of the journey.

As LaPorte and Talon had discussed the evening before, there were three ways to get to the site from Wyalusing. First, they could continue on upriver on another Durham boat. However, the tavern owner had told Hoops that no boat was scheduled until the following day. This route would be easy, but it would take time.

The second way was the 'path' that Hoops and Boulogne had traversed before, along the south side of the river. Given the fact that it was an uneven trail of varying elevations, the scouts thought the party of four might make it to French Town by nightfall if they left at dawn the following morning. However, that would leave them without overnight accommodations.

"Could we not pitch a tent?" LaPorte asked, curious.

Hoops and Boulogne frowned at each other, and then at LaPorte. "We could set up camp, yes, but we would have to set a watch, for American panthers roam the hills near there, and could make an easy meal of us," Boulogne told them.

LaPorte closed his mouth and nodded. "Maybe not a tent, then," he conceded.

The third way was to continue to ride along the 'Native American Highway' they had traveled on that morning, all the way to Towanda. There, they could take a ferry and back track a relatively short distance along the southern bank of the river to the site.

"We could stay tonight in Towanda," Boulogne added. "The ferry tomorrow and the short ride would bring us to the site by mid day. Then, we could travel on to a nearby inn where we would remain while we visit the site and the surrounding acreage," he continued.

"I am sure that the innkeeper in Towanda would be able to recommend lodgings to us near our site," Hoops put in confidently.

Everyone considered the three options quietly. They all seemed to have merit, but also drawbacks.

"There is one more thing," Hoops put in, and everyone looked at him, curious. "There are some clouds in the sky that tell me rain is on the way, probably tomorrow, possibly by this evening," he said.

Everyone nodded.

"I'm starting to think that putting up a tent on the site would definitely not be a good idea," LaPorte admitted in a humorous tone. "Between the American panthers and the rain."

Talon chuckled. "I think we should stay on the roadway, all the way to Towanda, and seek lodging and advice there," he said.

Hoops and Boulogne seemed to agree, noting that this route was probably the easiest and safest, for it was well travelled, and Towanda was a larger town even than Wyalusing, with several inns and taverns and people who could help with advice.

Having fed and watered their horses, the four men set out late that morning for Towanda. The fifteen mile ride should take just about two hours if they kept a good pace, which they intended to do. That would put them in Towanda in time for dinner in mid afternoon and before any threat of rain might get them and their belongings soaked.

Although the sky in the west began to be occluded with greyish nimbostratus clouds, the freshening breeze that heralded rain on the way was a welcome boon to the riders, for it was still warm and now the humidity was higher from the approaching rain.

As they had on the journey that morning, they saw several others on the 'Native American Highway' both on horseback and in carriages and wagons. They passed many slower-moving flat bedded wagons piled high with freshly hewn logs from the forests north and east of Wyalusing, evidence of settlements being built all along the roadway.

They passed through Wysox, where a few houses marked the village with farms spreading out in all directions and a small mill on the creek.

"'Tis not far now," Hoops said, pointing ahead of them. "The ferry is just there," he added and LaPorte, Talon and Boulogne could see the landing where the ferry plied its way across the Susquehanna from its north side to its south bank. The big town of Towanda was just beyond ferry route, which made it very convenient for travelers and no doubt contributed to the town's fast growth.

"Just look at all this green," LaPorte murmured to Talon as, a short while later, they and their companions and horses stood on the flat deck of the ferry and crossed the greyish green river. "So many colors of green, I could not count them all," he breathed, gazing at the forested hills in the distance, the river bank with its cattails, and the broad expanse of fertile farmland in between.

Talon gave his friend a crooked smile and shrugged. "You're a poet," he said, not for the first time, and LaPorte grinned back at him.

"There's a very good boarding house run by Widow Ellis and her three daughters," said Josiah Bennett, the proprietor of the Towanda Tavern where the small travelling party decided to stay that night. The four of them had been shown to two rooms, washed the travel grime off their faces and hands, and had arrived at the establishment's dining room for the mid afternoon dinner. Their horses were being similarly attended to in the capacious stables behind the tavern and would, they were assured, be ready for them the next morning.

"Is it near the place we are heading?" Hoops asked Bennett, a trusted acquaintance from previous journeys in the area.

"No more than two miles if that, from Half Moon River Terrace," Bennett replied easily.

At Hoops' frown, Bennett told him that the settlers who had been farming the land there called the land inside the horseshoe shaped bend in the river by that name.

Hoops passed this on to Boulogne, Talon and LaPorte, but only LaPorte's eyes lit at the Romantic fancy of the title. Boulogne merely nodded, and Talon shrugged, concentrating on his meal.

The travellers had before them a significant repast of a meat pie, a good chunk of cured ham, pickled vegetables, and a selection of fresh and dried fruit. It was high summer and the first harvests were nearly in, which meant that fresh food was abundant.

A 'sallat' of greens in a large shallow bowl sat in the middle of the table, and LaPorte in particular took heaping helpings of the vibrant leaves, which he ate with gusto alongside his heavier meal choices.

For dessert, or 'pudding' as Bennett called it in the English fashion, there was a pound cake, fresh strawberries and cream, nuts and soft, fresh cheeses.

"I can send word now of your arrival tomorrow, so they will be ready," Bennett offered, referring to the Widow Ellis' boarding house.

Hoops nodded and thanked the man and they all continued their meal.

Afterwards, they relaxed and lit their long clay pipes and sat back to digest the dinner and speak about the next day's journey. They would again leave quite early, although they would breakfast at the tavern. The riverside trail they would take was fairly flat, but somewhat winding. Still, it should only take them the morning to reach their site.

"We can see it, and then find Mrs. Ellis' place and settle in," Talon noted, sounding relieved at finally being able to be in one place for more than a night.

"Indeed. And then we can travel as you wish, to the site and the surrounding areas, for as long as you wish," Boulogne said. "The journey back will not be so difficult, as we may choose to go nearly the entire way by boat, for on our return, we will be going with the current," he explained. They would still have to ride from Wilkes Barre south to Bethlehem and then further south to Philadelphia, but the entire journey, having been made in one direction, would not be so problematical going in the other direction.

"Well, what do you think?" LaPorte asked Talon in a low voice that night once they had gained their bed chamber. Both men were lying down on the narrow beds, listening to the thunder and rain from the storm. Occasional flashes of lightning illuminated the small room, which only held, besides the beds, a table, chair and a pitcher and bowl with a clean if limp face cloth draped at one side.

"I think America is an amazing place," Talon replied quietly. "So much room! So much opportunity. The land is rich in resources as well as being beautiful in a way that France is not—or has not been for centuries."

"It is unspoiled, that is certain," agreed LaPorte. "And there is a lot of money to be made." He paused. "But do you not think it, well, a hard sort of place?" he queried, turning on his side to face his traveling companion.

Talon frowned as another flash of lighting dazzled their eyes, and then almost immediately a great crack of thunder shook the building. "Hard?"

LaPorte chuckled. "I mean to say, for example, there are very few roads and what there are are not very grand. The towns are bustling, 'tis true, but they seem—not gracious. Not elegant—they are all busy working towards the goal of being self sustaining," he explained. "Which is a worthy aim, and one I myself espouse," LaPorte noted.

Talon nodded. "Ah, I take your meaning now, Bart." He paused. "Yes, you're right: there seems to be very little time set aside for entertainment, leisure, the arts, for example."

"Exactly. And so I wonder how the noble families we know, our friends who must flee the guillotine, I wonder how they will manage here, for it is very very different from what they are used to."

Talon yawned and shrugged. "They shall have to manage if they wish to live," he offered dourly.

"And perhaps we can make our —I think of it as 'Azilum' to be honest, more than 'French Town,'—" he confided, "a little bit more—refined—a little bit more like home," LaPorte murmured as he, too, felt sleep overtake him.

Talon yawned again, and rolled onto his side. "Why not wait until we've seen the place?" he suggested mildly, and in the next breath, he was snoring.

Chapter Sixteen

The rain had mostly gone by the time the four men breakfasted, and before they were long out of Towanda, the sun was breaking through any remaining clouds and drying them up.

"It should be a good day," Boulogne offered with a smile.

The trail was narrow but not too hilly; still, the four of them rode single file in many places. Although LaPorte and Talon were anxious to see the land that would become their settlement, they had to exercise patience, for they could not consistently ride at a fast pace.

All around them were the native flora of northeastern Pennsylvania: refreshed now after a rain, the leaves of oak, walnut and maple and the needles of pine and hemlock glistened and gleamed in the sunlight.

Wildflowers clumped at intervals along the path attracted bees and perfumed the air: the pink, flat, furry heads of Joe Pye Weed and the bright yellow coreopsis were everywhere. Tall stalks of wild indigo in deep purpley-blue made a nice contrast and the orange Turk's Cap Lilies were just starting to make their elegant appearance.

In his mind, LaPorte was already planning for gardens and orchards at their new 'Azilum': not only would they grow vegetables and fruit, though, they would have herbs and flowers—even some of these wild flowers would be pretty in a garden. He recalled the plans Morris had shown them back in Philadelphia: how that seemed to be another life, now, as much another part of his existence as his time in Spain!

They rode all morning with the river on their left. Several boats passed by, most going downstream although a couple were earnestly struggling upriver towards Towanda. On the river they saw several water birds, including more bald eagles, nesting in cliffs at the river's edge. And alongside their narrow path, although they did not see any American panthers, they did see many white tailed deer, squirrels, chipmunks, rabbits and even a bobcat in the distance at one point.

"Don't shoot it!" exclaimed Talon to Hoops, who had readied his rifle in case the bobcat would attack.

"He won't come after us, anyway, but best to be prepared," Hoops replied, and lowered his gun.

It was just about noon, for the sun was blazing directly overhead, when the four of them came to a stop at Hoops' signal.

"We have been on the land that the Azilum Company owns for some time," the scout told his companions. "But ahead lie the fields that we think will be the site of the settlement," he explained. "It has been farmed for quite a while, by the earliest pioneers, and because it is right along the river, it benefits from spring flooding. Higher land a little to the south would be best for the building of houses and roads, and the town itself," he concluded.

They rode on, and in a few moments had broken through the lattice of the wooded trail and found themselves at the edge of a wide, green expanse.

LaPorte took a deep breath, then smiled happily. "Ah…it is so very green!" he exclaimed again. "Let us go forward!"

The four of them rode across the flattish plain and Boulogne and Hoops gestured to where they thought the farmland of the new community should be, and then where they thought the town itself might best be constructed.

"I can see building a hunting lodge, up there," Talon pointed to the hills that protected the site from southerly winds and invaders, for the hills were about

2000 feet high and heavily forested. Yes, there would be a road, or roads, through the hills and southward in due time, but now there was nothing to mar the arboreal expanse except outcroppings of rock.

"Like Louis XIII's?" LaPorte asked with a grin. That king's hunting lodge outside Paris had become, over time and with many additions, Versailles.

Talon bit his lip, and waggled his head. "Mmmm... not quite so grand, I shouldn't think," he confided to his friend. "But you have to admit, 'tis a perfect spot for a hunting lodge," he insisted, gazing again at the hills.

After a long morning of riding, measuring, surveying, discussing and evaluating, Hoops led them a little further east, towards a house he explained belonged to a gentleman who had struck a deal with Cazenove when the land all around him was purchased. The deal, Hoops outlined, sold the land to Cazenove but allowed King to remain on the property in perpetuity or until he or his heirs chose to vacate it. When Morris and the other investors of the Azilum Company bought Cazenove's consortium's tracts of land here, they had honored the agreement.

"So, our 'Azilum' has already a settler?" Talon asked warily as they drew up before a two story house in dark brown, with what Talon thought of as 'daub' showing in between the exterior plank siding. The house was quite close to the river, but on a little rise which protected it from flooding. There was a very small barn and a couple more outbuildings, but it was clear that the resident was not a farmer, at least not on a large scale. A few chickens scurried from under their horses' hooves as the four men rode up towards the house's entrance, and Talon suspected that the barn contained a cow, perhaps, or two, for milk, and a pair of horses both for riding and to pull the small carriage he spied at the side of the barn.

He noted a good sized vegetable garden at one side of the house and a small stand of fruit trees beyond that.

"His name is John King, and he is a most genial man," Hoops assured Talon. "He is an Englishman," he added. "Made quite a bit of money in England before he came over to the United States, and engages in philanthropy, mostly, now."

"Philanthropy?" Talon queried, doubtful. What was there around here to be philanthropic about, he wondered. Trees? Rocks? Grass?

"I think it is a very good beginning!" LaPorte the optimist declared, and dismounted. He was ready to meet Mr. King, not knowing that the acquaintance would change his life.

Chapter Seventeen

John King welcomed the four travelers happily, for Morris had written ahead and explained that the Azilum Company's scouts, along with two investors/settlers from France, would be surveying the area. Therefore, Boulogne, Hoops, LaPorte and Talon were expected. King insisted that they stay with him for at least that night, and then said he would gladly send word of their delay to the Ellis Inn, and then give them directions to it, where they could go the following day and stay for the rest of their trip.

"How long do you expect to be here?" he asked as they all trooped into his dining room and chose seats around a large table. It was, conveniently, dinner time, and King's cook had laid out quite a spread: hot roast chicken, cold roast beef, green beans, summer squash, a fresh loaf of bread with just-churned butter and honey, and something new to Talon and LaPorte: sweet corn. King explained that the vegetable was just coming into season and was best when it had been cooked and eaten the same day it was picked. "This was picked this morning," he added, helping himself to a portion.

"Several days," Hoops replied to King's query. "As you no doubt know, the Azilum Company's holdings contain several thousand acres. While we cannot hope to survey all of it, we do intend to at least visit the areas surrounding the new settlement as thoroughly as we can," he finished.

King nodded as he tucked into his dinner. He'd poured a chilled white wine to accompany the meal. "You might want to extend that, if you can, until the leaves begin to change: 'tis a most beautiful sight," he advised, his broad face alight with anticipation.

"We do not wish to tarry so long so that the journey back to Philadelphia is hampered by winter weather," Boulogne offered cautiously. He thought the area that Morris had suggested, and that he and Hoops had now just seen to confirm, would be very good for the proposed settlement. He could see it becoming a gracious and successful town along the river in time. But right now, there was nothing there but open space and wild animals, and he had no wish to be marooned here by an early blizzard.

King chuckled. "Ah, 'tis true, we can have snow as early as October," he admitted.

King was a slightly paunchy man of middling height with assessing blue eyes and greying hair beneath a short white wig. LaPorte guessed the man's age to be somewhere in his early 50s, but he was still quite spry and moved like a younger man. He himself had no family: his wife had died and they had not been blessed, as he said, with children. However, he had a large extended family including nieces, nephews and cousins, most still in England, but some of whom had emigrated to the United States.

"Whereabouts in England are you from?" LaPorte asked, curious. He was also curious about how King had made his money, but felt asking such a question so soon after being introduced to the man would be gauche.

"Essex County—do you know it?" King asked hopefully, looking around the table at his guests.

They all shook their heads.

"Ah. Pity. 'Tis a wonderful part of England," King sighed. He explained that the town he was from dated back to prehistoric times. "Before the Romans, even," he said proudly. Called 'Leigh' or more properly, 'Leigh on Sea,' it had been for centuries right on the main shipping route to London. However, a generation back, the deep water access Leigh had prized became so silted that large ships could no longer call, and so the port declined. "I took the decision, as that began to occur, to leave and come here," King explained.

"And what business did you have there, back in Leigh?" Talon asked mildly.

LaPorte grinned to himself. Hoops had told them that King had been 'in trade' but had not said what kind. 'In trade' was a phrase that could mean anything from shopkeeper, to skilled craftsman, to..."

"Shipping," King replied happily. "Most goods coming up the River Thames were headed for London, 'tis true, but some were bound for points north, and so were offloaded at Leigh," he explained. "That was my business, and a thriving business it was, and had been for my father and grandfather as well," he continued, smiling. "We would warehouse and then send all manner of goods on, over land, to Colchester, and even as far as Norwich some times," he noted, naming a town in the north and east of England, that faced the North Sea. " 'Twas faster, and cheaper, than sending goods to London and then up from there by road," he added.

"Shipping!" LaPorte exclaimed, delighted, and quickly told their host of his own work in Spain, and then in Marseilles. "I hope to develop something similar here, once our little colony is established," LaPorte told King confidently.

King nodded. "There are trading posts in Wyalusing and Towanda and Tioga Point," he noted.

LaPorte nodded: they had been told that.

"But having a stop in between Wyalusing and Towanda would be fine, and there is no lack of natural resources such as timber and shale, which could be sold," King replied, nodding.

Talon reminded LaPorte of the apricot brandy they had tasted in Bethlehem.

"Why, you could perhaps make something like that, if you could grow the apricots," King agreed as they all finished their main courses and started in on the dessert course that had been set out by King's butler-cum-footman. A sweet cake loaded with dried fruit was one offering, along with custard tarts, a selection of cheeses, and nuts. "I myself have a few apple trees and pear trees," he added.

"There is of course the apple brandy grown in Normandy," Boulogne put in, helping himself to a custard tart.

"Calvados!" LaPorte rejoined happily.

"I should imagine any fruit could lend itself to brandy making," Talon murmured. "But I doubt that there would be enough to make that our largest commodity," he added.

"No, no, that will be, as Mr. King says, timber and shale, and bluestone?" Hoops agreed, but finished on a question. He had heard of bluestone being quarried fairly easily as the stone was close to the surface and could be liberated by hand.

King nodded. "Indeed, bluestone: not only very attractive, but durable and much in demand for walkways and such. With increasing settlements along the river, bluestone could become a brisk trade," he advised.

Chapter Eighteen

They stayed the night with King, whose large house offered a level of comfort that LaPorte and Talon, especially, relished. A feather stuffed mattress and smooth linen sheets as well as relatively abundant hot water with which to wash were luxuries they had not known since leaving France, really, although their boarding house in Philadelphia had been very good. Still, it seemed that King had created for himself a little spot of comfort out here in the Pennsylvania wilderness, having brought over furnishings of every description from his home in England. Although his home along the Susquehanna was rustic by European standards, it offered both tranquility and indulgence, and King seemed extremely content there.

Late in the evening before they retired, as they were all having their last sips of the excellent port King had offered, the conversation turned to family. Talon expressed his hopes of returning to Belgium to see his wife and children, and perhaps luring them to return with him, to Azilum. He, like LaPorte, had begun to call the settlement that, rather than French Town, and the name seemed to resonate, for Hoops and Boulogne and now even King, had begun using it as well.

King told them about a cousin who had recently landed in Philadelphia and was in a bit of, as he put it, 'a pickle.'

"He came over with his family, their passage paid by John Lambert, the Legislator. He has a large plantation in New Jersey and my cousin and his family were to work on it until the cost of their passage had been paid."

LaPorte nodded: he was all too familiar with such schemes, having thought to avail himself of one similar in order to make his way across the Atlantic. At least until Talon had paid him with the cache of diamonds he still had hidden, sewn inside his chemise.

"However, my cousin felt he could make more money working in Philadelphia, and more quickly pay Mr. Lambert back," King continued. He shook his head and gestured to a letter half opened on his desk: they were gathered in what King referred to as his 'study' to have their port and smoke their pipes.

"It did not work out the way he had hoped?" Hoops questioned.

"No. Mr. Lambert is not a trusting soul," King replied sourly, and explained that the legislator from New Jersey had claimed the cousin had 'run away' and sent him to debtor's prison. "Of all people, my cousin would never defraud anyone, least of all a benefactor, and least of all someone who holds the fate of his wife and children in his hands!" King insisted.

"That does not seem right," Talon opined. "This Lambert should have at least given your cousin a chance to see if Philadelphia would be a more profitable place to earn money to pay his debt," he agreed. "But why did your cousin not wish to work on the plantation?" he asked.

King shook his head again, then scratched at his scalp beneath the wig. "I believe it was as he said: he thought he could make more money and make it faster in the town, rather than on the plantation," and he gestured here to the letter once again. "He adds that he explained this to Mr. Lambert. He is no stranger to hard work, from what I know of him," he offered. "He is my Aunt's grandson, so, my first cousin once removed, and he worked as a Forester in Hatfield before deciding to emigrate." King shook his head.

"What was his reason for leaving England?" LaPorte queried.

King shrugged. "Not unlike mine: things changed. The towns and villages in Essex grew larger, and the forests grew smaller, so less need for foresters," he explained.

"'Tis the same throughout Europe," Boulogne offered grimly.

"But here," King made an encompassing gesture with one arm, "here there are forests aplenty where my cousin might use his skills."

"Including skills useful in the logging industry, I imagine?" LaPorte asked eagerly, and King nodded.

"Indeed. In Philadelphia he had begun work in the shipyard, securing timbers for the building of new frigates. But Mr. Lambert felt the lure of the sea might tempt him to run off before his debt had been paid," he told them sourly.

"How ridiculous," Talon offered.

"And surely your cousin cannot earn any money while in prison," LaPorte chimed in.

"No. But after so many days, they will call the debt paid, even though it is not," King replied.

"That just sounds mean spirited to me," LaPorte grumbled.

King nodded agreement. "Yes. Which is why I am making arrangements to have money from one of my Philadelphia banks transferred to Mr. Lambert, to pay off my cousin's debt," he revealed.

"Why—how wonderful!" LaPorte exclaimed.

"And then," King continued, "I shall bring the whole family here, to your 'Azilum.' They can stay with me until their debt to me is paid, and then decide what they wish to do," he added in satisfaction.

"I shall look forward to meeting them," LaPorte told King sincerely.

The next few days were spent mostly on horseback. Talon and LaPorte, who were not used to it, complained quietly and mostly to each other about being 'saddle sore.' Hoops and Boulogne, who rode horses every day, had become inured to the discomforts such a lifestyle could bring. The four men saw forests with trees of all types, and more of the wildlife they had noted before. They did not see an American Panther, however, much to Talon's dismay, for along with the iceberg, a mountain lion would have been an amazing memory to bring back and share with his family in Belgium.

They did find the small boarding house King had recommended. It was at some distance south of the area of the proposed settlement and so gave them a good home base from which to visit the outlying regions. It was clean, and the food was good and plentiful, if basic. But there was not the level of comfort that had been so welcoming at John King's house by the river. Still, it was only for a few days and what they saw on their daily rides was so unendingly fascinating, at least to LaPorte, that he did not mind the rough sheets and the rather hard beds. Talon found the region less interesting, for, as he kept saying, there was nothing there.

"Yet—my friend," LaPorte would reply. "Some day, there will be many towns and villages, and roads traversing this whole part of the land," he declared confidently on one of their last nights before setting out on their return to Philadelphia.

"I will be happy just to see our Azilum settled and thriving," Talon returned, somewhat dour.

As Hoops and Boulogne had predicted, the trip back to Philadelphia down the Susquehanna River to Wilkes Barre was much faster and easier than the trip up it had been. From there, the road to Bethlehem seemed somehow shorter as well, perhaps because they had already traveled it.

The four parted ways there, at the Sun Inn, since Hoops and Boulogne had another commission to survey land around what would become Lancaster, and so were headed west. But LaPorte and Talon took the stagecoach that traveled to the King of Prussia Inn in Philadelphia and so were back at Mary House's Boarding House at the end of September.

Talon in particular was quite delighted to be back in Philadelphia, not only because they could dine almost daily at their friend Cazenove's table and stay in their comfortable boarding house, but because it was still early enough in the year that some ships were scheduled to sail out of the port for Europe. He was hoping, of course, to make his way to Belgium.

However, things were still chaotic enough in France, they learned over several dinners at Cazenove's, to make Talon's journey unadvisable.

Disappointed as he was, Talon joined in with LaPorte, nonetheless in describing the site for the settlement, which they decided to name Azilum, as well as their adventures getting to and from the spot. Morris, Keating, Nicholson and the rest were fascinated to hear everything, and a bit relieved at the Frenchmen's report that the site appeared perfect for a settlement.

"It will require much hard work, to clear all the land and establish the town," cautioned LaPorte. "But with enough people, it will be easily enough accomplished," he concluded.

"Monsieur Boulogne has sent word," interrupted Morris. "He has already purchased a plot and intends to return there as soon as his current surveying assignment is completed," Morris informed everyone. "He will be the first settler at 'Azilum,' and says in his letter that he will secure local workers and aid us in setting up the new colony."

"He was much taken with the place," agreed LaPorte.

"And it is beautiful—even if we did not see a mountain lion," Talon put in.

"But we need people—our own people—on site, to supervise the laborers, to direct and delegate, so that everything is built correctly and that the town is laid out according to plan," Morris continued and Nicholson, Lafayette, deNoailles and the others nodded in agreement.

They all turned their faces to Talon and LaPorte.

"Antoine," began Lafayette with a smile. "Would you be willing to supervise the town's construction? And Bartholomew, would you consider being your friend's lieutenant, as it were?" he asked.

Talon sat back in his chair with a surprised 'whump.'

"We know how disappointed you are not to be able to return to your family," Lafayette added in low, sympathetic tones. "Perhaps having this—project—would help to pass the time. And you—" here he included LaPorte in his glance—"could choose your own acreages yourselves, there, on site, pick out exactly the spot where you want to settle down," he added as an incentive.

Talon looked around the table at each of the men in turn: they looked hopeful, encouraging even, and he felt a happiness inside at being thought worthy of such a task. To build the town to house the Queen! And the Dauphin, and the rest of the royals, not to mention nobles and other fellow Frenchmen.

"It would be an honor," answered LaPorte gravely. "As for me, yes, it would be an honor." He turned to his friend. "Antoine?"

Talon nodded slowly. "Yes, I agree." He paused and smiled slightly. "It would be an honor."

Plans for Azilum, then, would go forward. Talon and LaPorte decided to return there as soon as possible to join with Boulogne and ready the site. Meanwhile, they would work and plan for that return.

LaPorte made contacts at the docks and learned what commodities from the interior of the country would be most desired for shipment elsewhere. He also carried out his idea to meet ships as they docked in Philadelphia, to make any French émigrés aware of the new settlement.

Word was sent ahead to Boulogne, advising him of Talon and LaPorte's imminent arrival, and asking him to secure a cadre of laborers who could begin work on the settlement itself as soon as possible. They would need carpenters, foresters, blacksmiths, and stonemasons as well as less skilled laborers to dig and level and perform similar tasks to help create Azilum. Additionally, negotiations were made with a prominent man in the region, Matthias Hollenback, for monetary credit and for the shipment of other necessary goods to the site. These would come up the river on Durham boats, arriving at Azilum's newly constructed dock. The dock would be Boulogne's first task.

Fortunately for Azilum, the winter of 1793-1794 was quite mild, and so LaPorte and Talon decided to take advantage of it and leave Philadelphia at the end of November, and head northwest.

Chapter Nineteen

Several families of French émigrés had been happy to hear about Azilum when they disembarked in Philadelphia, and had agreed to purchase land and settle at Azilum. The majority would arrive at the site early in the summer of 1794, once the site was more habitable. However, a few were eager to settle, and would make the journey the same month that Talon and LaPorte returned.

Additionally, residents of a small French settlement in upstate New York had heard about Azilum, and decided to move there in the late spring of 1794. Notable among these were the D'Autremont family, the Prevosts and the LeFevres.

Talon, eager to help out and anxious for a good population at Azilum, sent a boat up to carry these French people down to Azilum. Talon and LaPorte arrived in early December and through most of the month continued to work with Boulogne and the laborers who had been hired. The first thing to be built was the small church, which looked lonely and vulnerable all by itself along the large town square. However, soon other buildings joined it, although the priority was, of course, homes for the settlers who had arrived and then the Grand Maison for the Queen.

The town was laid out very much according to the plan that Morris had sketched one evening at Cazenove's house. Five streets, each about 50 feet wide, marched north to south. The central boulevard, however, was 100 feet wide, and quite grand. Nine other streets going east to west crossed these, and in the center was a large town square.

"'Tis land that is plentiful in rocks and stones," noted LaPorte one day as he and Boulogne watched the progress of the laborers who were removing the turf and smoothing one of the 14 roadways of the town. It seemed that in every foot of sod uncovered, a rock or stone the size of a man's fist—or head in some cases—popped up. Larger boulders had also been dug out from the deep earth when foundations for the houses had been being prepared.

The workers were piling the manageable stones at the sides of the roadways and would edge them with the stones when the road was completed. Boulders that could be dragged had been harnessed in leather straps and chains, and pulled by oxen to a growing pile. If the boulders had been too large to unearth completely or move, they had simply been incorporated into the foundation of whatever house was being built. LaPorte was not sure what Boulogne or Talon planned for the boulders, most the size of a man's chest and twice as thick. However, at least they were all tidily collected at one edge of the town.

"The main Boulevard will be cobbled," Boulogne told LaPorte now. "We certainly have enough raw material!" He added that the other roads would receive a layer of river gravel that would help them remain passable.

LaPorte chuckled and agreed. "It might be nice to plant trees along that Boulevard," he suggested.

"Lombardy poplars!" Boulogne exclaimed, recalling the way those tall, graceful trees lined the boulevards of his native Paris.

"I can get some for us," LaPorte said quickly, recalling that Morris had made use of the trees extensively in his new home on the outskirts of Philadelphia. LaPorte was sure he could write to Morris and find out where he'd sourced those trees, and acquire some for Azilum.

Once the roads had been laid out, the construction of the more than 200 house lots that were planned began in earnest. Each lot was a half acre in size and would contain a two story main house with a separate cookhouse and in most cases a second small, separate structure to be used as a dining room. These would be connected to the main house by a covered walkway, which some residents would extend into a porch that ran along part of the house itself. The design was intended to keep the odors of foods out of the main house.

The local workers, whose houses were not constructed this way, and whose households did much of their cooking at the main hearth, found this to be quite an interesting concept. Some laughed over it: not, of course, when Boulogne or anyone else from the settlement was around.

Although foundations for the houses and cookhouses were dug, these were only a few feet deep; however, the foundations for the dining rooms were several feet deep. The reason for this was that the undercroft of the dining room was to be used as a root cellar and a wine cellar by the families. Here, the stones and rocks that had been unearthed as the cellar had been excavated were re-laid to form firm walls, and both exterior and interior methods of access were built.

LaPorte and Talon had selected their plots. Not surprisingly, LaPorte's was directly adjacent to Talon's. Both their plots were next to a third, where construction had already begun on the Grand Maison. They would live in the Grand Maison until their homes were completed, for they did not expect the Queen to arrive until spring, at the earliest.

"We have the best views," Talon said happily as the two friends regarded the vast empty fields before them. Indeed, they could see clear down to the river, and the dock was just east of the border of Talon's property. "We shall build a very grand house for *la Reine*," the former Avocat Général continued, looking over one shoulder at the nearly completed mansion. "One that the Queen will feel at home in," he added with a wistful smile. "And when my family comes, I shall have already built another home for them here—not quite so grand, perhaps," he finished with a chuckle.

Talon had written to his wife to explain the delay in his return to Belgium, and had suggested that she prepare herself for a trans Atlantic journey when the 'incivilities' in France ended. He'd spoken glowingly of the new Azilum and had hopes of receiving a positive reply from her soon. Mail, of course, took a long while to travel between Europe and the U.S., so it would likely be a few months before he had her reply.

The Grand Maison was, indeed, very grand. The army of workers contracted by Boulogne had begun construction as soon as Talon had arrived and chosen the plot and by mid December the Grand Maison was habitable. Talon and LaPorte took up residence, knowing that until the Queen and her children came over, there would just be the two of them, the occasional visitor, and perhaps some remaining settlers who would stay there while their homes were being built.

However, the majority of those who would come that autumn—nearly thirty families—had arrived and were installed in their houses: it was surprising how quickly they went up with all the good local labor. More homes were constantly under construction, too, so they would be ready for the influx of settlers expected the following spring.

Every day, and sometimes twice a day, river boats docked at Azilum to offload furniture, livestock, raw materials and other supplies that had been forwarded by future residents or ordered by current ones. LaPorte and Boulogne's Lombardy poplars arrived and were hastily planted in hope that they would settle into the ground before the worst of the winter.

About thirty homes were erected that autumn, although the construction of chimneys for the new homes would have to wait until spring. Franklin stoves that had been shipped up kept those who were living at Azilum that first winter comfortable enough, and even once the fireplaces were functional, the stoves would serve as good sources of extra warmth.

Each house was two stories high; glass for the windows had come upriver from Philadelphia, and the houses had plenty of good, bright windows overlooking the site. Shutters protected the valuable glass during stormy weather. Although the houses were built of logs, they were squared off on the edges, and the pine shingle roofs kept the structures dry.

"I think that makes them look more finished," Talon noted to Boulogne as the two of them looked over a completed home. "And the shingle pattern on the roof is very pretty," he added with a nod to the roofer who had done the installation. He had taken care to overlap the shingles so they were textured in appearance rather than flat, and the roof itself had been made sturdy by the application of pine pitch to repel moisture. Never one to waste a resource, LaPorte had overseen the extraction of this pitch from the wood, and it was used liberally throughout the construction of the site.

Inside, the houses had smooth plank floors and most of the plank walls were papered with interior decorating items that had also come upriver. Each floor had two large rooms: on the main floor, these were generally parlors or studies, while upstairs were the bed chambers. Some residents had brought items of furniture from France, but local cabinet makers and furniture turners were kept very busy making tables, chairs, beds and other accoutrements that were needed.

Talon had designed the Grand Maison to be built of logs and pine shingles, like the other houses, but it was more than twice as large: about 80 feet long and 60 feet wide. Its two stories were capped by a large attic and before winter set in eight fireplaces on each floor were connected to four chimney stacks.

If the other residents, who had to make do with Franklin stoves, resented this they did not say. In any case, Talon was such a genial host that the small group of émigrés who were already at Azilum often gathered at the Grand Maison for dinner and sometimes in the evening, for entertainment.

Both floors of the Grand Maison contained large salons or rooms, as well as bed chambers on the upper floors, and long halls with wide staircases to connect everything. This house was filled with light from numerous windows and even some 'French doors' which were really just long windows that functioned as doors. The interior walls were of hand planed wooden planks; some wallpaper decorated certain rooms but much of the wood was merely smoothed to a satin finish and left as it was. Black walnut wood was used to make the stair rails and newell posts, providing a nice visual contrast with its dark color to the lighter oak and pine used elsewhere.

Just before Christmas, harsher weather settled in, so work at the site was suspended until early spring. The river also became impassible because of ice floes and so the shipment of goods was halted until spring as well.

The animals: cows, sheep, pigs, chickens, horses and a few goats as well as the oxen, were snuggled into their respective barns, located on the 'town lots' at the edge of the town proper's western border. In the spring, most of the animals would be turned out to pasture once fences were erected, a task that had not yet been begun. Also at that time, fruit orchards and vegetable gardens would be planted in the town lots; of these there were seventeen five acre parcels and fifteen ten acre parcels.

Chapter Twenty

Christmas Day dawned bright and cold, with some scattered snowflakes in the air and the sun a brilliant disk in a pale sky. Talon and LaPorte had borrowed a Moravian custom and erected a Christmas Tree out of some scrap pine boards and branches and placed the creation in the center of one of the large reception rooms in the Grand Maison.

Talon had hosted the traditional French Christmas Eve *Reveillon* dinner the night before, and was giving an all day open house type of reception following the morning church service on Christmas Day. He had invited not only the current residents of Azilum but also their neighbor John King, who had been so kind to them when they had first come to the site, and who had continued to be a great friend, fascinated to watch the new village take shape. The laborers, all home now with their families, had also been invited, and it was hoped that some would brave the chilly, snowy ride to the site.

The Christmas Tree consisted of four open, tapering triangles made of planks about three inches wide and an inch or so thick. On these, Talon and LaPorte had wound branches of the pine and hemlock trees that had been felled for lumber, securing them with nails as needed until the entire creation seemed to be of fragrant needles.

The Moravians traditionally decorated their Christmas Trees with candles and Bible verses copied onto scraps of paper. The former were supplied by Talon, and he affixed a number of candles in small holders to the tree. The latter had become a project for the six children who currently resided at Azilum. Varying in age from three to nine years, the two boys and four girls were tasked with choosing a favorite verse from their Bibles and copying them carefully onto small pieces of paper.

When LaPorte had explained the idea to Madame Heraud, she had been delighted to welcome the children to her house and oversee the project. A former school teacher in France, Mme. Heraud was not only perfect for this job, but she hoped, once all the settlers had arrived, to start a school at Azilum for the children. Surely, there would in time be more than six!

On Christmas Eve day, LaPorte had collected the paper verses, delighted to see that Mme Heraud and her pupils had taken the initiative to cut the scraps of paper into pretty shapes: stars, circles and small open books. These had been hung using the scraps of yarn that had been attached to them by the children, and had made the tree in Talon's reception room look quite festive.

A small church had been built just off the large town square. The same dimensions as one of the houses, it was one large open space. Carpenters had hewn benches for worshippers to sit, and a Franklin stove kept the place warm. On Christmas Eve, the families who lived at Azilum gathered to hear the Gospel of Matthew and sing 'Un Flambeau, Jeanette, Isabella,' and then 'Il Est Né, le Divin Infant.' Then they had returned together to Talon's house for the *Reveillon*, at which time the Tree was revealed and exclaimed over by everyone. The children proudly showed their parents and relatives which verses they had copied out, and all enjoyed the repast laid out by Talon.

Traditionally, the centerpieces of the *Reveillon* supper are the thirteen desserts, one for each Apostle, and one for Christ, as well as the *'tourtière'* or meat dish. In France, many fine and intricate pastries and sweets were served, and at Azilum for the Christmas of 1793, it was very much the same, for right after the church had been built, a large bake house had been erected. *Petits* fours, *éclairs*, *baba au rhum*, *madeleines*, tarts, *palmiers*, chocolate mousse, spice cake, *pot de crème, pralines, profiteroles, tarte tatin,* and of course the yule log or 'Bûche de Noël' were enjoyed by the small group of settlers who remarked that this Christmas was one of more hope and joy than any they could recall in recent years.

In France, the meat dish was usually the finest cut of beef, enrobed in pastry and baked. However, with supplies being somewhat sketchy until the settlement was completely functional, the settlers had borrowed from the Quebecois and had used ground meat mixed with potatoes. Spiced with nutmeg, garlic and more—for the French had brought their spices with them and planned to grow or trade to keep their stock supplied—the fragrant *tourtières* were laid out on a long table and accompanied by pickled vegetables and a variety of breads. To wash it all down, Talon had uncorked a case of his best champagne which had been carefully brought up from Philadelphia.

Now it was Christmas Day, and given the late evening the night before, Talon and LaPorte didn't expect any visitors until mid day. This feast was different than the *Reveillon*: no less plentiful, but less formal.

By noon, the few first residents of Azilum had begun arriving in a small but steady trickle, and Talon welcomed them all magnanimously. Then, some riders on horseback or in small carriages began to trek down the primitive road that led into the settlement: the laborers had come with their families, proudly showing off what they had been busy building these past several weeks.

Last, a fine carriage made its way along the well travelled road between the main town and Talon's Grand Maison and John King's home on the eastern edge of the clearing, and that man alighted.

"Welcome, John, welcome!" declared Talon, pumping his friend's hand and ushering him inside.

"Thank you, Antoine," King replied happily. "I've seen this house go up, timber by timber, but you have done a grand job of making it a home," he complimented Talon. "'Tis a fine place!"

Talon had the good grace to look modest, even though he, too, thought the house was quite fine.

"John, how wonderful to see you again, *Joyeux Noël*!" LaPorte said as he hastened towards the foyer to greet their friend. He shook King's hand as one of Talon's servants took that man's cloak.

"You are very welcome, do come in and see the house, and have something to eat, and drink!" Talon urged merrily.

Chapter Twenty-One

Talon's Christmas Day Party was a great success. All the visitors who had not been at the *Reveillon* exclaimed over the beauty and gracious proportions of the Grand Maison, and were both impressed and delighted by the food Talon's cook had prepared.

Greatly expanded from the repast of the evening before, the Christmas Day feast included several roasted turkeys stuffed with chestnuts, stewed cranberries, eels fresh from the river in a rich cream sauce spiced with dried herbs and precious saffron, various potted meats, cheeses, nuts, and an even wider selection of cakes and tarts to tempt everyone's palate. Talon's chef had emigrated from France and been snatched up as soon as he'd set foot off the ship by LaPorte. There were also pumpkin tarts, tarts made of dried fruits and berries, hot mulled cider, beer, and of course, wine. Apple tart, or 'tarte Tatin' was a favorite, but the little 'petits fours' made their appearance, enrobed in thick ganache and decorated with more chocolate. More champagne had been uncorked and Talon also offered port, hock, and cider for those who didn't imbibe.

People loved the furnishings, especially the Christmas Tree: for many, it was the first one they had ever seen, and they were intrigued with the idea.

"Could we not just chop down a suitably sized tree?" queried one man to another as their wives exclaimed over the little Bible verse decorations.

"'Twould be less trouble than fastening all those branches to a frame," agreed his friend.

Other visitors to the Grand Maison deemed it suitable for the Queen, to be sure, for it had parlors and bed chambers enough to house quite a retinue as well as the Queen and her children.

The large windows gave onto the frost covered land and the ice-jammed river reflected the dozens of beeswax candles that illuminated the interior of the home. Talon had made the reception rooms as welcoming as possible, bringing down some settees and love seats from upstairs bed chambers so that everyone might have a spot to sit and talk, or admire the room, or the view out of the windows.

Most seats were at least partially occupied although many visitors were so busy greeting friends and milling around the long table that held the food and drink that they appeared quite happy to do their socializing standing up. Roaring fires in the great fireplaces threw warmth into the large, high ceilinged rooms, keeping everyone comfortable, and a weak winter sun did its best as it shone in through the windows.

"I shall not ask you what these windows cost," commented Monsieur Beaulieu to Talon, sounding only a bit envious.

"Ah, but, 'tis for the Queen," Talon reminded him. "And all the houses have ample windows," he added.

"Oh, yes, you are right, of course," agreed the man with a sigh. "Still, my wife complains that all she can see from our beautiful glass windows is mud and bare trees and ice, and now snow."

Talon knew, of course, that many of the newcomers to Azilum were not used to rural landscapes outside their windows, and also not used to the weather in northeastern Pennsylvania. Near Paris, where most were from, although winter was cold, it was not quite as snowy as it was at Azilum, and adapting to being virtual shut-ins when roads were impassible due to snow would take some time. He hoped that the colony's other advantages would outweigh what some of its new residents appeared to consider its drawbacks.

"You have not been here long enough to see what it is like in summer, and in the autumn when it looks as though all the hillsides are on fire," Talon continued to Beaulieu, who had arrived in November. "Just wait. Spring is coming."

"I hear that there are two other great houses being built, however, at a little distance from here," noted Beaulieu. He himself, having organized his own household rapidly, had purchased another parcel and would in the spring construct a larger dwelling that he intended to operate as an inn. "They planned one for the King and one for the Queen, but now have revised it so one house will be for the children and one for the Queen," he told Talon.

"Yes, I know of that, and I suppose the Queen could have her choice of homes, in that case," Talon replied. "She could certainly live here until those houses are ready —I understand they are nowhere near finished!" he declared with a wry smile.

Beaulieu chuckled. "You pinched all the good laborers," he told Talon. "But come spring, I expect they will make progress."

In January of the new year, word came that Queen Marie Antoinette had been guillotined the previous October. Despondent, the little group of Azilum settlers held a memorial service at their chapel, and found themselves ever more grateful to have escaped France, since at this point it appeared they would never be able to return. The two houses a few miles away from Azilum that had been begun as homes for the King and Queen were never finished, the project abandoned.

Talon, too, was downhearted, and in his weekly letters to his wife in Belgium, he begged her even more urgently to consider joining him in the new Azilum. He told her that the Grand Maison, which he had been living in and using as his own home, for all intents and purposes, would now be his in fact as well as practice, and he regaled his wife with details about how lovely and grand the place was.

However, her replies, when they came, were not favorable to such a move and Talon felt that she had perhaps become more fond of the happy, secure life she led with their children and her parents in Belgium than she might be of a new life in the wilds of Pennsylvania, with him.

LaPorte tried to cheer his friend, suggesting that once the colony was thriving with all of its houses occupied, gardens producing and livestock flourishing, Mme. Talon might be more amenable to making the journey.

"I wish I could go and see her," Talon repeated. But he had been tasked with overseeing the initial build and settlement, and until the weather broke and construction was complete, and the majority of the settlers arrived, he could not in good conscience leave.

All LaPorte could do was reassure him that yes, he would be able to go to Belgium, although not right away.

Meanwhile, in March with warmer weather, construction began again and in addition to installing chimneys and building more houses—the goal was to have fifty completed for the initial influx of residents—the laborers got busy on the roadways that led to and from the settlement. Existing roads were widened, and leveled where possible. A couple of new roads were built, too, leading from Azilum to other villages in the area.

"We need a ferry," LaPorte remarked one unusually warm May afternoon. He had just returned from a trip to Wyalusing which, on the improved road, was easier going than before but still a dozen miles, the round trip taking the better part of a day.

"Where do you think would be a good spot for one?" queried one of that spring's new arrivals, one Charles Homet. He had been a steward in the King's household and had fled France early on, when the royal family first tried to escape. His wife, Maria, had been one of the Queen's Ladies in Waiting. A native Austrian, she had met Homet when they had both been on the same ship bound for Philadelphia. The two had married shortly after they had arrived on U.S. soil and been part of the French social scene. However, when they had heard about Azilum, they had immediately made plans to move from Society Hill to the new settlement. Maria, in particular, had long cherished the hope that her Queen would also escape and take up residence at Azilum, in which case she would be there, ready and waiting, to take up her duties as Lady in Waiting.

However, that was not to be, but the Homets remained since they liked the settlement and knew many of the other refugees. Their home was at a little distance from the main village, but they were considered residents, nonetheless.

Maria, by dint of her former position, became something of a leading light in Azilum society and was often to be found with her coterie of ladies enjoying a promenade in the fresh air on a fine day, or leading a sewing circle at her home if the weather was poor.

Now, LaPorte turned to Homet and answered him. He'd left early for his errand in Wyalusing, which involved banking and communications with Hollenback and other financial backers, and had returned to Azilum in time for dinner at three o'clock. He, Homet, Talon and a few others were seated in what was now Talon's grand dining room, beginning that repast.

"There is a narrowed area of the river a bit farther downstream," LaPorte answered. "Near the grist mill."

Homet's eyes lit up. "Ah! That is very near, only a couple of miles," he said enthusiastically. Then he frowned. "Do you really think we would have enough traffic to warrant a ferry?" he asked LaPorte, then looked to the rest of the men at the table, silently seeking their opinions.

Most of them who had been listening to the conversation nodded.

"It would certainly make trips to Wyalusing faster, and more and more people are building homes and farming the land all around there," one man, whose name was Aristide Aubert duPetit-Thouars, said genially. A retired soldier who had fought gallantly in the French Army and Navy, duPetit-Thouars, or 'the Admiral' as most people called him, had come to Azilum from Philadelphia where he'd fled to once the Revolution began.

Homet looked thoughtful, and finished his dinner in silence.

"How did you manage in Wyalusing?" Talon queried. The business had been part of the ongoing issue trying to settle the Pennsylvania and Connecticut land titles. Although Cazenove had thought that by buying out both titles the problem had been solved, it continued to impact Azilum, as did Morris' money troubles.

That April, the formal Plan for Azilum had been finalized, with Morris named president. DeNoailles, Keating and Nicholson were named managers. But in an effort to settle the ongoing title dispute, Morris was using up much of his credit. He would eventually transfer his shares in the Azilum Company to Nicholson. Meanwhile, Morris' money woes impacted the credit—and the cash flow—of Azilum from such financiers as Hollenback, and

LaPorte had gone to Wyalusing to handle correspondence related to this.

"I believe once the letters I posted today are received, we will all be back in order," LaPorte replied with a smile. "And soon, we will be able to trade more than just lumber," he added, looking at one of the other men at Talon's table. This man, Monsieur Maurice, had recently begun to oversee a small quarry near the settlement where good Pennsylvania bluestone was abundant.

Maurice nodded. "Yes, the laborers are making progress," he confirmed, adding that by the end of that week, two ox drawn carts of bluestone slabs should be arriving at Azilum's wharf, for shipment downriver to Wilkes Barre. "Someone is building a grand house, and ordered several tons," Maurice noted in satisfaction.

"If word gets around, that could be another profitable export," Talon said happily. The lumber from the seemingly endless forests on the land owned by the Company was the settlement's stock in trade, but Talon and LaPorte knew it was always smart to diversify. Flax had been planted as a cash crop, as had some vineyards from which the colonists hoped to make wine. When the weather had broken earlier in the spring and the maple sap had started running, they had tapped and collected gallons upon gallons of syrup which they had boiled down into the liquid sweetener and also dried and made into 'maple sugar.' These items had also gone down and up the river in trade.

Always with an eye to what was needed and what might turn a profit, LaPorte had gone in with another refugee named George Heier and opened a mercantile shop. Two residents, Blecons and Colin, had opened a haberdashery, but a mercantile shop with a wide assortment of goods including material that the haberdashers could purchase for their trade, was a real need.

Hollenback had a trading post and store upriver in Tioga Point, and of course there were several such concerns in Wilkes Barre, and a couple in Tunkhannock. But LaPorte had realized within a month or two at the site that Azilum needed its own such outlet, and set about establishing it as soon as the weather broke.

Heier managed the store, but LaPorte contracted with local artisans for the goods they carried and by letter with importers out of Philadelphia who could supply items not locally made like silk and some spices. The shop was very new and well patronized, and so far had held its own. But LaPorte sunk most of the profit back into it so that he and Heier could expand the range of items they carried.

The Admiral, du Petit-Thouars, that spring began to take over LaPorte's functions as overseer, as LaPorte himself had not only become busy with the mercantile shop, but he had become increasingly involved in the business end of Azilum rather than the practical, material end of the colony. It was an arrangement that suited both and LaPorte was always very busy.

As Talon had predicted, several single young women had arrived with their families to settle at Azilum, and LaPorte took pains to meet each one and get to know them. One in particular, Therese Dandelot, had caught his eye and they had gone for a couple of walks together. Her father, a former officer in the French Army, had invited LaPorte for dinner as well, usually a sign that the parents favored what they thought might be a match.

But LaPorte had not decided. He liked Therese, but he did not find his heart moved by her, and still hoped to find a woman he could both respect and cherish.

Chapter Twenty-Two

Although the settlers may have been dismayed when they arrived in the fledgeling Azilum, so far from the cities and towns they knew and fraught with so many unusual dangers, they did not show it. With typical French resolve, they set out to make their new home what they wished it to be. Once the good weather came, they planted gardens, built fences to surround their properties, constructed stone walls for grander or more definitive properties, and got to work on bringing their houses up to the standards they had known in France—or at least, as close as they could get.

Tapestries, silver plate, furniture and ornaments from France, all brought upriver by Durham boat, made the interiors of their rustic houses relatively fancy. Outside, they planted flowers from seeds and cuttings they had brought from France or Philadelphia. A few even built little gazebos and other 'follies' on their properties, and took great pride in creating a kind of oasis in the wilderness.

There were a number of nobles among the settlers, as well as those who, like Homet, had served at the King's Court. But there were merchants and tradesmen as well, making for a well rounded and microcosmic settlement. Although some members of the upper class turned to trade in their new settlement and started up small businesses, most were unused enough to working that they hired out or employed servants and carried on much as they had before.

In particular, the ladies would amuse themselves as they had in France, or in Philadelphia: they visited, they sewed, they went for walks and picnics, they rode their horses around the settlement and beyond in fine weather, they played games and in the evening after elaborate mid day dinners they would enjoy a light supper, play music, and dance. Pianofortes and similar instruments made the journey upriver to Azilum to provide the settlers with harmonious sounds.

The men rode, too, often to look over the plots of agricultural land they owned which others worked for them. They met with others of the same social stratum to discuss business, banking, and even the hardiness and health of livestock and crops. They dined, and joined in with the ladies in some amusements like dancing, games and music.

Soldiers, shopkeepers, farmers, bakers and other tradespeople also came to Azilum and soon not only established their homes but set up new concerns to ply their trades. A blacksmith, a tin smith and silver smith, a baker, the haberdashery and LaPorte and Heier's mercantile depot, Le Marchand, were among the first. A mill that could make 'bolted' or white flour was also built, as well as the grist mill further downriver and two sawmills to handle the lumber the settlement produced. The grist mill and the sawmills were at a little distance from the site because they were water powered and needed to be situated to take advantage of that. The flour mill, however, was designed to be drawn by horses and so it could be located near the square—and the baker.

Although the settlers had of course brought clothing with them to Azilum, new clothes were always needed, often in the elaborate styles they had known while in France although some of the ladies sported the '*bergère*' hats that Marie Antoinette had favored while at her 'Hameau,' the rustic village she had built at Versailles. Some of Azilum's ladies even said among themselves that, the Queen would have felt very much at home at Azilum. 'We even have sheep!' one young woman had declared fervently.

The men—those who were not merchants or laborers of course—sported pale breeches and cutaway court coats in shades of blue and gold and even salmon color. The ladies wanted embroidered cotton or silk for the warmer weather and brocades for the winter, and universally wore '*la Robe Francaise*,' or the 'sack back gown,' which had full length pleats across the shoulders in the back, falling to the hem. Both genders employed yards and yards of lace around their cuffs and collars and soon a mother and daughter lace making team was also a going concern in the town.

Beekeepers whose hives graced the far perimeter of one of the 'town agricultural plots' supplied honey and beeswax for candles.

Weeping willow trees were planted near the river, and more Lombardy Poplars than the ones along the boulevard—which had survived the winter—graced other portions of the village, in particular, the border between the residential area and the more agricultural zone. Thousands of apple and pear trees were planted in one area on the fertile plain and many residents had several trees in their gardens as well. Some were espaliered, but in the gardens particularly, people preferred to cluster the trees so as to create small groves.

Three taverns were next to open, operated by Monsieur LeFevre, Monsieur Heraud and Monsieurs Regnier and Becdelliere. The little chapel which was the domain of Monseigneur Carles, who had been a Canon of Guernsey, was soon joined by a theatre.

In addition to the chapel and the theatre, a school for the children of Azilum was erected around the town square, and a great bell, shipped upriver from Philadelphia, called the students to class each morning and dismissed them in the afternoon. Along with the church clock, which was rung at six a.m., noon, and six p.m., this gave residents a way to mark the hours of every day. Some had pocket watches, of course, and the richer homes had case clocks that had made the journey up the Susquehanna, and many gardens sported sundials. But the bells were another and very pleasant way to mark each day's progress, tolling out and echoing faintly from the hills that rose up on the opposite side of the river.

Talon had an outdoor pavilion constructed as well, near the square, where in the warmer months people could dance to an orchestra made up of slaves from Santo Domingo who had come with their families to Azilum. The uprising there around the same time as the Revolution in France had meant that many French families from that island fled to Philadelphia, bringing their slaves with them. Some chose to make the journey to Azilum, and again, the slaves came too. A dedicated community of smaller and less grand cabins was set up for them on the northern edge of the settlement, quite close to the river.

By the time the Pennsylvania forests turned from green to gold and red, and then brown, the French settlement of Azilum was well on its way.

In April of 1795 word came that the Duc de Rochefoucauld Liancort was making a tour of Canada and the northern United States and was planning a visit to Azilum. His estimated time of arrival was in late May, 1795. Having survived two winters, now, Azilum was becoming truly established, even doing a relatively brisk trade in some items not carried at other trading posts and shops in the area.

LaPorte, who had sold a few more of his rough diamonds for cash while in Philadelphia and during the early years of Azilum's and his own establishment, had not had need to dip into his stash for a while, because his business concerns were quite successful. Although his house could not rival the Grand Maison, it was neat and clean with a large porch and pergola attached, a cook house and a dining room nearby, and an expanse of lush green grass just waiting to be turned into a garden. Indeed, like LaPorte himself, his property seemed to be waiting—for the right person to arrive, and make it a real home.

With the news of the Duke's imminent visit, Talon readied six of the best bed chambers in his Grand Maison, for Rochefoucauld was said to be traveling with five friends. Not only was Rochefoucauld a Duke, and thus a peer of France, his father had been the Master of the Royal Wardrobe, an intimate of Louis XVI and his grandfather before him.

Everyone followed Talon's example, excited by the impending visit. To them, it seemed as though the Duke's arrival would signal a re-establishment of ties to their beloved France. Even though it was currently ruled as a Republic, not a Monarchy, the visit gave the refugees hope that this would not be permanent. The younger son of Louis XVI and Marie Antoinette was still alive as far as anyone knew in the spring of 1795. Although he was reported to be sickly and was at any rate only ten years old, should the Monarchy be re-established, he could take the throne, they thought. (Word that the Dauphin had indeed died in prison in June of 1795 would reach the colony later that summer.)

Additionally, Louis XVI's two brothers could either rule with the boy as Regents, or, if the child should not survive, rule in their own rights. '*La Monarchie n'est pas morte!*' was a comment heard often, at least at Azilum. 'The Monarchy is not dead!'

Gardens were weeded and tidied, roads received new layerings of gravel, and quarried bluestone was delivered by the cartload for installation as pavements, porches, walkways and more. Home improvement projects that had been approached casually and leisurely were now attacked with vigor.

Talon planned another open house type of reception for the visitors a couple of days after their arrival, to showcase everything Azilum had to offer.

'What if the Duc decides to settle here?' Talon had asked LaPorte one evening after supper as the two friends had sat on LaPorte's veranda and smoked their long clay pipes, and watched the early spring night settle down among the hills and the river. Talon's voice had been calm, but LaPorte had sensed his friend's anticipation.

'Well, he could not find a better spot,' LaPorte had agreed genially.

The frenzied preparations had also meant an extremely busy spring for LaPorte and Heier's mercantile store: draperies that had been delayed in their creation by more pressing tasks were now 'desperately' needed before the arrival of the Duke, and so bolts of silk and brocade came upriver and into the Mercantile and then went out again to be sewn into window treatments. Satins, dress and gown silk fabrics, muslin, embroidered cottons and lawns and even gingham in bright colors and patterns were requested, acquired and purchased without so much as the turn of a hair, because even the servants and the laborers in the farms and fields wanted to have new clothes to show off when the Duke arrived.

Equally in demand was, of course, lumber and other construction materials like nails, to finish off half finished outbuildings, barns, stables, and garden ornaments. The two weavers in the village were kept constantly busy with requests for rugs, linens and other items they excelled at creating. Azilum's sheep could supply some of the wool needed for certain things, as could its flax crop. However, cotton and silk in particular still had to be shipped up by the bolt, and cotton and silk thread for custom work arrived, too, in vast quantities. More than once, both weavers' shops were literally burning the midnight oil.

One early evening—for the shops closed for two hours in mid afternoon for the dinner break, then re-opened and stayed open until about seven o'clock—after a particularly hectic day, LaPorte was in le Marchand, having sent Heier home for the day. He had inventory and ordering to finish before he, too, locked up and headed for home and was hoping for a quiet evening where he could get much accomplished.

LaPorte had just pulled out a long inventory list of sewing supplies that desperately needed updating, and had begun counting tiny items like buttons, hooks, ribbons, spools of thread, embroidery floss, and needles. It was a painstaking task and not one LaPorte relished. However, a good chunk of the mercantile's trade came from sewing and lace making endeavors—which had just expanded with three new trainees—and so he did not want to run out of anything. He also took pride in stocking the newest in style and fashion, things that even people from outside the settlement sought out his shop for.

He was taking a moment to admire some new hand painted buttons with scenes of ladies and gentlemen in pretty gardens when the small bell that Azilum's silversmith had designed let out its cheery tinkling to signal the arrival of a customer.

"Good evening! *Bonsoir*!" called LaPorte from behind a counter. He rose and turned, saying, "how may I be of service? *comment puis-j'être utile?*" Then he shut his mouth with an audible click and just stared.

The most beautiful young woman he had ever seen stood on the other side of the counter. She wore a simple navy and pink floral print *robe Anglaise* trimmed in white lace, with a pink underskirt and a navy wool shawl around her shoulders. Matching navy mitts covered all but her fingertips and she grasped a small beige leather reticule. Brown hair waved gently around her face and was swept up behind in a cascade of tight ringlets. No jewelry sparkled from her ears or neck but LaPorte thought the girl's shining hazel eyes were adornment enough. Thickly lashed, those eyes gazed at him expectantly from beneath fine straight brows. A Roman nose gave character to the visage and the girl's naturally rosy lips were at the moment turned up in a little smile.

"Good evening, sir," the girl replied in an English accented voice. "I require some boot black and some embroidery floss—red if you have it," she told him. The smile bloomed to show even, white teeth and a dimple on one cheek.

LaPorte, for one of the first times in his life of nearly 40 years, found himself at a loss for words. Moreover, his mouth had gone suddenly completely dry.

Thinking that perhaps the man's English was not good—although why this should be so, for both English and French were spoken equally at Azilum—the young woman tried again, this time making her request in French: "*Bonsoir, M'sieur. J'ai besoin d'une botte noire et d'un fil de broderie rouge, s'il vous plaît?*"

"Ah, *oui, oui,* yes, that is…" LaPorte shook himself out of his stupor and replied, stammering. "I understood you the first time," he admitted sheepishly. "Forgive me for, for—not replying swiftly," he finished, feeling foolish.

Quickly, he set about getting the items that she had requested and set them on the counter between them for her inspection.

"Oh, yes, this is exactly right. What do I owe you?" the young woman asked.

LaPorte told her, and watched as she counted out some coins, and then tucked the embroidery thread in her reticule, grasping the boot black jar in one mitted hand.

"I—I do not recognize you," LaPorte ventured bashfully. He could feel his heart beating so hard he was sure this young goddess could hear it as well. He was surprised it was not making the front of his silver and black satin waistcoat pulsate, it was dancing so violently within his chest.

But she merely gave him another dazzling smile and said, "we have just lately settled here, at Azilum, that is, my family and I," she amended.

For a moment, LaPorte was dismayed: she spoke of her family: she was married?

"Your family?" he echoed, feeling his mouth go dry again.

"Yes, my father, John Franklin, my mother, and my sisters," the young woman elaborated, still smiling.

"Ah..." It was more a sigh than a reply and LaPorte realized that of course, the young woman wore no cap, as a married woman certainly would have. "*Enchanté*, Miss Franklin," LaPorte finally said with a slight smile. He inclined his head.

Miss Franklin just smiled again, then turned and left le Marchand.

"Franklin!?" Talon exclaimed the next day when LaPorte told him of the encounter. "Then John King's friend Mr. Franklin, and his family, must have arrived!" he deduced with a grin. "I wondered why he hadn't visited last week. Now I know why: too busy getting the Franklins settled in, I shouldn't wonder. They're staying with him, I think," he added.

Talon and LaPorte were riding out to check on the condition of the roadway from Charles Homet's ferry landing to Azilum. Even this had to be made as perfect as possible for the Duke's arrival.

LaPorte digested this information as they rode along at a leisurely walk, which enabled them to adequately survey the condition of the road. Talon continued, explaining that once Mr. Franklin's debt to their friend King had been paid off, he planned to purchase a plot of land at Azilum and settle down.

"How much of his debt is still owed?" LaPorte asked with a frown.

Talon shrugged. "I do not know."

Thoughts of Miss Franklin were never far from LaPorte's mind for the next several days, but he, like the rest of the residents of Azilum, was busy readying everything for the Duke's arrival. However, he did find himself riding past the King homestead, even though it was completely out of his way, at least once every day, hoping to catch a glimpse of Miss Franklin. He was rewarded for his determination twice, but only once did Miss Franklin notice him, and return his wave.

Chapter Twenty-Three

When the Duke arrived with his companions—it turned out there was only one, plus a servant man who did for both, along with three horses and the Duke's dog, Cartouche,—Talon's six bedchambers were turned into two suites, a dressing room and a bed chamber for the servant. The Duke was clearly delighted to find such gentility amidst what he had perceived until then as the quite wild interior of the country. They came across the river on Charles Homet's good ferry, with no mishaps like those which had plagued them before on other ferry crossings, about which the Duke would regale his hosts repeatedly. Then they traveled the newly improved roadway the short distance to the town of Azilum, where they were greeted with much fanfare.

The sight of Talon's Grand Maison was one that made the Duke and his companion, Monsieur Guillemard, smile broadly; when they were brought upstairs to their bed chambers they became almost giddy.

Each bed chamber was prepared with feather mattresses, cotton sheets, down comforters, scores of candles in holders and sconces, dressing tables with large mirrors, desks, comfortable upholstered chairs and settees, and armoires for all the luggage. Talon had put his entire household staff—and he employed several—at his guests' disposal so that all of their attire might be cleaned and laundered, boots shined, shoes repaired, whatever was needed.

Additionally, once the Duke and Guillemard had taken a drink of hock and had a quick meal of fresh bread and cheese, large bathtubs were brought up to their bed chambers, and filled with steaming water by a parade of servants both young and old, male and female. The tubs were then draped in soft linen, and supplied with soap, brushes and washing cloths. Fires were kindled in the bed chambers' fireplaces even though it was a warm day at the end of May, just one month before the summer solstice. Then, the Duke and Guillemard were invited to bathe.

All manner of pomades, oils, dentifrices, lotions and creams were also made available on the dressing tables and the two honored guests were left to wash and relax in their respective rooms. Their servant, Joseph, overwhelmed at being given his own bed chamber, also had his clothing attended to. He told Talon's housekeeper that he would be happy to wash himself once his employer, M. Guillemard, was finished.

Dinner was a bit later than usual that afternoon at Talon's, and it was an intimate affair, with just Talon, LaPorte and their honored guests. They ate at one end of a long dining table, set with china and glassware, silver and gilt, and Talon's cook supplied *Lapin à la Moutarde*, roast chicken, new peas, asparagus, potatoes Lyonnaise, and a tart of dried fruits with brandy with whipped cream for dessert.

"This was an amazing repast!" the Duke exclaimed as they all pushed back from the table and lit their pipes. Guillemard nodded enthusiastically.

"Yes, the provisions on the road were, well, unreliable," he told Talon and LaPorte, making a face.

"Salt beef. Salt fish. Stale bread. Moldy cheese of indeterminate type," the Duke put in. "Eggs. Many eggs. I am as fond of eggs as anyone, but there does come a time..."

LaPorte and Talon listened avidly as the men described their journey thus far in more detail.

"And the bugs, *mon Dieu*, and the sleeping arrangements!" the Duke said, with a small shiver of distaste.

"Not what we are used to," Guillemard noted quietly.

"Soap is cheap and it costs little to be clean, for the river is right there, for water, and firewood abounds," LaPorte pronounced flatly.

"And if for whatever reason you do not wish to heat the water, well, as my friend says, the river is right there," Talon added with a smile.

Guillemard nodded. He was a fair complexioned man who looked to be in his thirties, with light brown hair caught back in a queue and sky blue eyes. His face bore the marks of his mixed French and English heritage, for, having come over with William the Conquerer, his ancestors had settled in the agriculturally rich county of Kent and intermarried with the local English of Anglo Saxon roots. Freshly washed and with laundered clothing, he presented a genial and attractive appearance.

The Duke, who was nearing fifty years of age, was a slight man with his freshly washed and pomaded greying hair drawn back in a queue as well. A broad forehead and expressive brows dominated his face. Serious of mein, he had during dinner smiled and laughed more than he had since he'd begun his journey in early May, and appeared very happy to have arrived among his compatriots as well as in a situation that provided him with the comfort to which he used to be accustomed.

"And the roads!" chimed in the Duke now. "*Mon Dieu*! In places there were holes that could swallow a man. Sometimes, these had been covered over with planks but many of these had rotted away. And in other places there were no roads at all, not even a pathway." He shook his head. "Art has hitherto but little meddled with the roads in Pennsylvania," he murmured. "You would do well to remedy that situation so that your colony can be accessed easily," he added with a nod at LaPorte and Talon.

Talon explained that they hoped to bring the longer roads that led towards Towanda and along the river to settlements to the east, like Wyalusing and Braintrim, up to the standards of the roads immediately around the town. But, he added, this would take time.

"*Bien sûr!*" agreed the Duke. "And I will say that from my brief glimpse riding in to your town, and from my experience here, at your house, Seigneur Talon, Azilum has attained an uncommon degree of perfection, especially considering its infant state," he finished.

Talon looked extremely pleased at this, and murmured for the Duke to please call him 'Antoine.' To Talon's delight, the Duke reached over and clasped his hand firmly.

"Then you must call me François-Alexandre," he replied heartily.

"He's quite the scholar," Talon told LaPorte the next day. The object of their discussion was, of course, the Duke, who was, along with Guillemard, out riding along with the Admiral, duPetit-Thouars. The Admiral was showing their guests around Azilum, pointing out the mills as well as the agricultural areas and the adjacent farms and dwellings along the Loyalsock Creek.

LaPorte raised an eyebrow. He and Talon were in le Marchand, and for the moment all was quiet. Everyone was busy outside, for it was a fine, sunny day, and they were hoping to catch a glimpse of the distinguished visitor.

The huge reception and ball, where most of the residents would be introduced to the Duke and Guillemard, was set for the following evening at the Grand Maison.

"D'you know, he's keeping a journal about his travels?" Talon went on. "He was telling me how delighted he was to find a desk and fresh quills, because he makes notes as he goes but while he's here, he will be able to organize them and put everything in order, writing it down properly!"

LaPorte looked impressed. "I should like to read that some day," he said. "If he ever publishes it?"

"Oh, I think it's meant for his friends, but we could always ask him to send us a copy—or bring one, and visit again."

"He does seem to quite like our Azilum," LaPorte said then with a nod. "And he has some very good ideas about ways to improve."

"I look forward to hearing what he has to say when they return from their tour today," Talon put in. "And Guillemard's people are farmers and they raise cattle back in England, did you know?"

LaPorte shook his head.

"He was telling me about it over breakfast," Talon continued. "His father and grandfather specifically breed bulls and cows to get particular traits—for example, thicker coats to withstand cold and harsh weather, or producing more milk or leaner beef," Talon explained.

LaPorte nodded eagerly. "I will have to speak to him about that, then," he said firmly. "We need to find a few good bulls to liven up our cattle and now is the time to do that, since so many were lost this past winter because of the cold," he told Talon.

The previous winter had been exceptionally harsh and snowy, and the livestock at Azilum had suffered. If Guillemard could give them some pointers as to how they could over winter their animals in more comfort, and also about ways to improve the strains of dairy and meat cattle they raised, it would be a huge boon to Azilum.

Chapter Twenty-Four

Everyone came to the reception and almost everyone stayed for the ball, which ran into the small hours of the next morning. Talon's chef had called in a few cooks from other households, notably the deSybert and Buzard cooks, to help him prepare a feast for the 200 people expected. The day was fine and warm, and the evening cooled pleasantly.

Talon ordered fires kindled in the fireplaces but he also had the tall windows in both reception rooms opened, to allow the breeze from the river to waft in. The rugs were rolled up and the pocket doors between the reception rooms were tucked away and chairs and settees were set about the parlors so people could have a seat while they ate, or chatted, or rested.

The dancing would be in the reception rooms; at one end of the second, a table the width of the space was set up, covered with fine linen and by the time the reception began at eight o'clock, covered with all sorts of food: de-boned stuffed duck, grilled rabbit, fresh eels in sauce, whole stuffed baked bass from the river, what looked like an entire side of beef roasted and sliced thinly, all manner of fresh vegetables, some rolled in a pastry crust to create little tarts, potatoes Anna, potatoes *Dauphinoise*, and more. Dishes were not only succulent, they were presented in an elaborate manner, with bunches of herbs accenting platters or designs cut into the crusts. Everything was sized appropriately as well, for this was a buffet, not a meal where diners sat at a table, so food was meant to be eaten with fingers, or simply a fork.

The wine and champagne flowed freely as well, and by about ten p.m. Talon, looking around his crowded home, felt happier than he had in a very long time.

LaPorte circulated among the guests, who numbered almost everyone in Azilum, as well as some friends from outside the colony. He had enjoyable chats with Azilum's old friend—and now major shareholder—John Keating, about the canal building efforts taking place. Both of them still thought, as Morris and others had a few years before, that a canal along the north branch of the Susquehanna would mean riches for Azilum as well as the other settlements in the area. LaPorte was excited to hear that some progress was being made further north, and further south, on canals, and had hope that such construction would soon come to Azilum's shores.

He also enjoyed talking to Monsieur Prevost. Originally from Paris, he had fled France with all of his fortune and was here, as he had there, engaged in much philanthropy. Along with his wife and the widow of his brother, he maintained a household on the Loyalsock Creek, a few miles from Azilum.

Madame Prevost introduced LaPorte to her sister in law, Madeline Prevost, heavy-handedly suggesting that as she was widowed and he was without a wife as yet the two might do well together. Although LaPorte found nothing to dislike about the woman, who was in her early thirties he estimated, and quite pleasant in appearance, he also found nothing to really attract him.

Still, he engaged her in cordial chatter for a few minutes, and then moved on. He expected John King to arrive, and of course, an invitation had been sent to the Franklins as well, who were still living with their friend. It was the Franklins, above all, whom LaPorte found himself watching for, glancing out the tall windows towards the drive that swept up to the house every few minutes.

Madame d'Autremont, another widow, whose husband had drowned during his escape from France, was holding court, as it were, along with Charles Homet's wife and the Duke. The two ladies considered themselves among the leaders of Azilum society and so had taken it upon themselves to be sure that the honored guest was well looked after, and never bored. LaPorte would not be surprised if one of them—probably Madame d'Autremont since she was not married—had already politely insisted that the Duke open the ball with her at his side.

LaPorte smiled to himself. The Duke could do worse. But he could do better. And clearly, he was not here looking for a wife. His wife and his three grown sons were all back on the Continent, waiting for the day when they could return to France and take up their lives.

As that thought crossed LaPorte's mind, he raised his eyes once again to the front door of the grande Maison and a gabble of happy voices met his ears.

"My dear friend, welcome!" Talon was greeting John King while a servant took that man's cloak and hat. King and Talon shook hands and King looked around with a satisfied air.

"You've done yourself proud, Antoine," King said in a low voice, but LaPorte heard him as he approached.

Talon nodded.

Behind King stood a tall slender man, a shorter, somewhat rounded woman and Miss Franklin.

"Antoine, may I introduce my friend and colleague, John Franklin, and his wife, and his daughter," King said a moment later. "This is Monsieur Antoine Omer Talon, one of the founders of Azilum and my great friend," he said to the people with him.

The man tipped his hat, and the two women curtsied.

"Aha! And here is another great friend and the man who is Monsieur Talon's right hand, as it were, Monsieur Bartholomew LaPorte!" King continued, catching sight of LaPorte as he drew up to the small party.

Everyone bowed and curtsied again.

"Monsieur LaPorte has a very profitable business trade here, and also a wonderful shop, where anything you wish for can be obtained, isn't that right, Bartholomew?"

LaPorte smiled, a bit embarrassed, and allowed that he did his best. He thought he saw Miss Franklin smile slightly at the mention of le Marchand, but could not be certain.

Servants took the trio's coats as Talon and King moved off to make their introductions to the Duke and Guillemard, and LaPorte made a motion with his hand to encourage the Franklins to follow suit.

"Once you've been introduced, do avail yourselves of the buffet," he said genially to Mr. Franklin. He wanted to directly address Miss Franklin, of course, but that would be rude. Although they had now been introduced, it was most proper that he speak to her father or possibly her mother when all three were with him. And above all, although he had not yet formed his exact intentions with regard to Miss Franklin, LaPorte wanted to be proper and make a good impression.

Mrs. Franklin wore a heavily beribboned lace cap atop her hair that had been styled in an up do. The hair's bouffant quality led LaPorte to surmise that much teasing of her own hair and possibly some embellishment with hair pieces helped to create the fashionable look. Her gown was of a dark royal blue silk brocade shot through with gold, and unlike most of the gowns of the ladies in attendance, it was a *robe Anglaise,* with no pleated train falling from the shoulders as with a *robe Française.* Several inches of creamy lace fell from the elbow length sleeves and also adorned the scooped neckline of her gown. The gown's skirt was not split in front to show a decorative underskirt, but all of one piece. She wore pearl bobs in her ears and pearls at her somewhat stout neck. White gloves hid her hands, but she carried a pretty fan with a scene of swans swimming under a starlit sky painted on it. She had clearly, thought LaPorte, put on her very finest clothing for the Reception and Ball.

Mr. Franklin was also in his best: brown hair pulled back with a green velvet tie into a neat queue, cream colored breeches, silk hose, polished black shoes whose buckles shone brightly, a satin vest in dark green brocade, snowy linen and an impeccable beige tailcoat that looked a couple of years out of fashion but was nonetheless immaculate. It also seemed a little tight on the man, and LaPorte guessed that he didn't wear it often.

But it was Miss Franklin, and her attire, that LaPorte gave the most attention to, and which in turn gave him the most pleasure. Like her mother, she wore a *robe Anglaise*, but her pink brocade gown was split in front to show a flowered silk petticoat beneath in tones of pink and lavender on a cream ground. Lace dripped from her sleeves, ruffled around the scooped neck of the gown, and edged the hem of the overskirt. As before, her hair was caught up in ringlets that cascaded to the nape of her neck with other wisps and curls framing her face. She did not wear a cap, but did have a lace band in her hair, and she—or her mother—had tucked little silk flowers made from scraps of the pink brocade in amongst her curls. Small pearl drops swung from her ears, and white gloves covered her hands. She had a small fan, too, decorated with a pastoral scene in colors that complemented her gown.

LaPorte stood to one side as the Franklins were introduced to the Duke and Guillemard once King had been presented. Then, as the three moved off, he ushered them towards the table of food and invited them to partake.

"Might I bring you some wine?" he asked Mr. Franklin, but he included his family in his gaze.

Mr. Franklin, unused to such attention, particularly from one whom he considered to be above him in rank, nodded 'yes' and before he had a chance to inquire what types of wine Talon was serving, LaPorte had disappeared.

He reappeared as the Franklins found a love seat and a chair in one of the parlors, and settled down to eat. LaPorte presented Mrs. Franklin with a flute of champagne, which she looked very pleased about. The ladies had removed their gloves to eat and Mrs. Franklin grasped her flute in chubby fingers that flashed with a gold ring, and a ruby one. Then LaPorte handed another flute to Mr. Franklin.

"Might I fetch champagne for Miss Franklin?" he asked Mr. Franklin deferentially. "Is she of an age to ..." he asked quietly.

"Oh, goodness, yes, she is sixteen!" Mrs. Franklin put in happily. LaPorte noted she had drunk half her champagne already.

"Half a glass, if you would be so kind," Mr. Franklin amended, and LaPorte hurried off.

When he returned, he handed the flute of champagne, half filled as her father had requested, to Miss Franklin, and for a moment as she grasped the stem while LaPorte still held onto it, their fingers touched. She raised her eyes to his.

Chapter Twenty-Five

LaPorte knew he couldn't remain dancing attendance on the Franklins, much as he might wish to, so he busied himself with the other guests, joining in conversations here and there as the mood took him. He was most intrigued to hear Guillemard as well as the Duke giving advice to Monsieur Dandelot regarding his cattle. A couple of others joined in and seemed quite intrigued with the pointers the two visitors gave them.

He also heard Dr. Buzard talking with the Duke about the benefits of vaccinations, a relatively new concept that had proven successful in England and was now becoming popular on the Continent and in the more forward-thinking areas of the U.S. Smallpox, in particular, was a scourge that killed or disfigured many every year, but the newly-formulated vaccine had proven an effective preventive and the Duke was much in favor of it.

Franklin joined the doctor and the Duke at one point, seemingly very interested to hear what they were saying, and LaPorte went and stood in the group as well.

"We had a dreadful time of it on the ship coming across," Franklin was explaining to the Duke. "Smallpox killed many in the crew and several of the passengers, and those who did not die are scarred," he added in a low voice. As he spoke, LaPorte looked more closely at the man: the gentle light from the candles was kind, but now that he knew what to look for, LaPorte could see the tell tale shallow, round depressions scattered across his face. It did not disfigure him so much as give him a rugged appearance, however, and LaPorte wondered if smallpox had also ravaged Miss Franklin, or if she had been spared. He had not noticed any evidence of the disease, but his encounters with the young woman had been brief, and had benefitted from the more forgiving interior lighting.

"Did your wife and daughter..." he began tentatively.

Franklin smiled slightly. "They suffered the disease, but less severe cases, although it still left its mark," he told LaPorte, sounding sorrowful.

The Duke then said that he could send word to his physician in Philadelphia to have enough vaccine sent to Azilum to make everyone safe from the disease, and Dr. Buzard looked both grateful and impressed.

"Who can say what other diseases we might be able, some day, to prevent," the Duke then said excitedly.

"Yellow Fever?" suggested LaPorte, recounting how he and Talon left the city for the interior of the country once summer arrived, to avoid the instances of Yellow Fever that routinely decimated the population. That particular year, 1793, had been a very bad one, too, with thousands succumbing to the illness.

The Duke nodded. "Yes, I myself always summered in the country for that very reason," he agreed. "'Twould be a boon if a prevention—or a cure—for that scourge could be found," he finished.

LaPorte moved away from the group then, ostensibly to re-fill his glass of champagne. However, he also wanted to find Miss Franklin and ascertain that she was enjoying herself.

He saw her talking with some other young women from Azilum, so he did not interrupt, happy that she had found companionship. As he circulated among the guests, though, he kept an eye on her and finally, just before he knew the dancing would commence, for the little quartet of musicians was setting up in a corner of the second reception room where the food had been, Miss Franklin's friends scattered and she was left on her own.

She watched the bustle of the food table being dismantled for a few moments, then smiled as the musicians began to tune their fiddles. Then, she walked over to one of the long windows that faced the river and gazed out.

"May I fetch anything for you, Miss Franklin?" LaPorte asked quietly at her elbow. "Some more champagne, perhaps?" he asked, noting that there was just a drop or two left in her glass.

She turned, surprised, and shook her head. "Monsieur LaPorte!" she said. "You are so kind. Thank you. But I require nothing at this moment," she replied with a smile. "I was watching the musicians," she added shyly.

"Ah yes, they are some of the, erm, slaves—" he could not think of a more politic word—"who come with a few of the families who settled here," he told her. "They play remarkably well," he added with a smile.

The little group of musicians also entertained the settlers of an evening, but tonight, in honor of the Duke and the gala reception, they had outdone themselves with newly-made clothing in brilliant colors and patterns.

For a couple of beats LaPorte and Miss Franklin just stood side by side, looking out of the window and towards the river that was only about a hundred yards away. The moon was a waning gibbous and had risen a short time before in the east. But LaPorte and Miss Franklin were looking north, so the mighty Susquehanna appeared as a thick black ribbon beyond the greyish swath of grass that led down to the river's edge. Above, the hills were moonlit, a lighter shade of textured grey that marked the forests. Above that shone the stars.

"I have never in my life seen stars such as I have seen here," breathed Miss Franklin.

"'Tis the pure, clean air," replied LaPorte genially. "Very little smoke or anything else to interfere with the view of them," he added. "Not like in cities. You lived in cities in England?" he asked her, curious.

Miss Franklin shook her head. "We lived in Essex when I was a child, a county outside of London. But then father began working in London, and so we moved there, and then we came to this country and lived in Philadelphia for a time," she elaborated, filling in the blanks in LaPorte's knowledge of her past.

They were silent again for several long seconds and LaPorte wondered what he could say next to keep the conversation going.

"You can tell the time by the stars, did you know?" he said next. It was true: you could. Each night, the constellations rose at certain times. As the days progressed, the rising times became later and later.

Miss Franklin shook her head. "No I did not know that. Tell me?" she asked boldly, but her eyes sparkled with interest.

LaPorte explained, and Miss Franklin gazed out at the stars as he spoke.

"Look to the right—that's east, you see," LaPorte told her, gesturing as Miss Franklin leaned her head over so far it nearly touched the window, and looked to her right. "In the morning, now, you'll see Venus rise, just before the sun," he said.

"But Venus is a planet, not a star, is it not?" Miss Franklin asked, frowning a bit and turning to look at him.

"Yes, yes it is." That was interesting: not many people, let alone women, knew the distinction between planets and stars. Unless they were scientists, anyway. "But it, too, moves across the sky relative to us here on Earth, because of its orbit around our sun," LaPorte explained.

Miss Franklin, satisfied with his answer, nodded.

"Right now, the late spring sky holds many interesting groups of stars, or constellations," he continued. "Look over there," he indicated. "That bright star is called Altair."

"Altair?" Miss Franklin repeated, curious.

"Ah, yes, many of the stars have names from Persia or the Orient," LaPorte explained. "They were the first astronomers, long before Galileo or Copernicus."

Miss Franklin smiled.

"Antares, Betelgeuse, Fomalhaut, Mira, Andromeda..."

"Andromeda? But surely that is from Greek Myth!" Miss Franklin put in, pleased that she could make a contribution. Monsieur LaPorte seemed to know a great deal about the stars, after all.

"Indeed it is!" LaPorte agreed, delighted. "The ancients named the stars as well after their own legends. The Silk Road opened their contact with the East, and astronomy became another gift they gave civilization," he commented.

"What other stars are named after the myths?" Miss Franklin asked, sounding eager. "I had a book of Greek and Roman Myths as a child, which I loved, and read constantly," she added shyly, looking down.

"Ah! Well...let's see...hmmm..." LaPorte scanned the sky visible through the window for a star that he knew with a Greek or Roman name. "Ah! See there, that sort of crooked W on its side, just up over the hills?" he pointed north again and Miss Franklin, following, nodded.

"Yes."

"That's not just one star, it's a group of them, known as Cassiopeia's Chair."

Miss Franklin repeated that to herself in a whisper. "It's a funny sort of chair: it looks as though one might fall right out of it!" she giggled.

LaPorte chuckled along with her. "Yes, it does, you are right!" he agreed.

They were silent for another long minute. Then:

"In the fall, when the nights start to get cold," LaPorte began, his voice low, "look in the east and you will see Orion rising after sunset. You can tell him by his belt: three stars, just so," and he showed her with his hand. "And behind him follows his dog, marked by Sirius, one of the brightest stars in the sky," LaPorte continued. "We call Orion the hunter, because when he becomes visible in the sky, hunting season is upon us," he added.

Miss Franklin looked rapt.

LaPorte wondered if she really were so interested, or just being polite.

"Oh, Monsieur LaPorte, I do hope I remember that," she said earnestly.

LaPorte smiled at her. "I am certain you shall, Miss Franklin."

She smiled back, hesitantly, and then said, "if I do not, Monsieur LaPorte, perhaps you will remind me?"

Chapter Twenty-Six

The rest of the evening at the Reception passed mostly in a blur for LaPorte, whose brief encounter with Miss Franklin had solidified the suspicion he had had from the moment he had seen her in his shop weeks before: he was in love. Probably, he thought, for the first time in his entire life.

He could not stop thinking about Miss Franklin: her clear hazel green eyes, her gently waving brown hair with golden highlights, her sweet smile, and her quick and agile mind. If he were to be honest with himself, it was the last characteristic that pleased him the most, although the fact that she was pretty to look at didn't hurt one bit.

The dancing began shortly after LaPorte and Miss Franklin had their astronomy lesson at one of the Grand Maison's tall windows, and LaPorte, who loved to dance, made it his mission to be sure that every lady got to dance at least once. If their escorts or husbands were too busy chatting away with the Duke and his entourage about medical advances or animal husbandry—not that those weren't interesting topics and possibly very beneficial for Azilum—then he stepped in and made sure to lead them onto the polished wooden floor for a gavotte, a minuet, or a sarabande.

The musicians played a great variety of tunes, some fast, some slow, and most of the dances were done in a 'longways set' of couples down the double reception room, men on one side and women on the other. Although LaPorte wanted, of course, to monopolize Miss Franklin he called upon his strength of will to dance with several other women before he approached her. But he kept an eye on her, and was pleased to see that she danced several times, including 'La Caroline et la Sabotier' with the Duke himself.

Miss Franklin was now standing with her mother and a couple of other ladies, a few feet from where Mme. d'Autremont and Mme. Homet were. LaPorte had already danced with each of those worthies, and as his feet moved towards Miss Franklin he wondered if he shouldn't ask her mother to dance first, rather than ask the daughter.

Mr. King saved him the decision, whisking away—if moving the somewhat chubby Mrs. Franklin could be described thus—the older lady and leaving Miss Franklin with the Mesdames Prevosts. LaPorte had already danced with them, too.

"Miss Franklin," LaPorte began as he drew up to the women. He ran a hand through his dark brown hair and smiled as he gave a little bow.

She looked directly at him and smiled back, glad he had finally come to ask her to dance, for she assumed that was his purpose. And truth be told, she had been waiting.

"Ah, Monsieur LaPorte, you honor me overmuch!" interrupted Madeline Prevost rather loudly, extending her hand towards him. She gave him a brilliant, if slightly champagne-infused, smile.

"Madame," LaPorte smiled in an automatic courtesy at the sister in law of Monsieur Prevost without realizing the meaning of her coquettish remark.

Then he did.

"Ah...erm..." he stuttered, but saw no way out of the situation that would not rudely rebuff Mme. Prevost.

"You made such a splendid couple the last time you danced," Miss Franklin spoke up quickly. "Do let us have the pleasure of watching you again!" she insisted, her smile more brilliant than her rival's.

LaPorte and Mme. Prevost moved out onto the dance floor for the next tune, and Monsieur Prevost's wife moved closer to Miss Franklin.

"That was nicely done," she murmured. "Thank you. I do fear Madeline would have been in quite a snit if Monsieur LaPorte had corrected her assumption in public," she continued.

On Miss Franklin's other side, Theresa Schillinger Homet and Marie Jeanne d'Autremont sidled closer and began to nod their heads in agreement, having heard and seen the entire exchange.

"Take comfort in the fact that Monsieur LaPorte was clearly about to ask <u>you</u> to accompany him to the dance floor," advised Mme d'Autremont, invoking the wisdom of her years, for she was a bit older than the other ladies in their little group of four.

Miss Franklin blushed. "Oh, I am not sure..." she began dismissively, but Mme. Homet reached over and put a hand on her arm.

"But I am," she said, raising one blonde brow. She turned slightly and regarded the dancers. "He is one of the leading men of this settlement and society," she murmured as she watched LaPorte, who was light on his feet and clearly enjoyed dancing, even with a partner not of his choice. "'Tis a pity he is so much older than you are."

Miss Franklin said nothing. To say that she didn't think about age would make her sound either stuck up or stupid. To say that she hadn't thought about LaPorte in that way would be a lie, for she had. To say that she didn't think he thought of her in that way would be disingenuous. So she said nothing.

"I have wondered why he has never married," Mme. Prevost put in thoughtfully.

All three of the other women in their little group said, 'hmmm...' and continued to gaze at the man under discussion.

"He certainly seems to enjoy the company of women," offered Mme. Homet with a smile.

Then, as the dance ended, they all shrugged and resumed their air of nonchalance as LaPorte and Madeline Prevost left the dance floor and moved back towards them.

The musicians began another tune and this time LaPorte turned directly to Miss Franklin and bowed, extending his hand.

"Miss Franklin, will you do me the honor of a dance?" he asked in a voice just a bit louder than necessary. The immediacy with which she had taken his gloved hand in her own kid-sheathed palm made him think her answer would be 'yes.'

It was a typical 'set' dance as most of the others had been, with little physical contact except for the touching of hands during turns and other figures. However, the leisurely pace encouraged conversation: dancing with someone was one of the cleverest ways to get to know them. Dancers not only could ask questions of their partner but also could see how the other person moved, and how the two of them moved together.

LaPorte and Miss Franklin moved well together, their steps seeming effortless. Miss Franklin was certain that she could feel a spark, like when a flint had been struck, each time her gloved hand met LaPorte's, and she wondered if he felt the same.

Another important element in set dances was eye contact between partners, and as the dance progressed, both LaPorte and Miss Franklin were grateful for this practice, since it gave them unbridled liberty to stare at each other.

"Have you brothers and sisters, Miss Franklin?" LaPorte asked at one point.

"Three younger sisters, Monsieur LaPorte," she answered. "They are, of course, at home, as they are but eleven and eight years of age, and the youngest but three months old." She paused. "Erm—have you any family here?" she asked, curious.

LaPorte shook his head and Miss Franklin found she quite liked the way his chestnut hair waved across his forehead. He wore it slightly longer than most, but it was handsome and thick and fleetingly she wondered how old LaPorte was. Her companions had not been specific, but they had seemed to think he would have been a more suitable companion for someone of Madeline d'Autremont's age, rather than hers.

"I have a brother, but he is a sailor, always out on the open seas," he told her. "I have invited him to visit, and perhaps he shall in a year or so," he added with a smile. "My father was a teacher, back in Paris. Both he and my mother are long dead," he added with a sadder shake of his head.

"You must miss being part of a family," Miss Franklin suggested compassionately.

LaPorte thought about how to answer this as he took both her hands in his and made a full turn in the dance. Then, as that part of the dance was finished, they were 'out' at the top of the set, which meant that for the next few moments they could just watch—or talk.

"I have been on my own for so long, and so busy with businesses, and then coming here and helping M. Talon, and now working hard to make Azilum truly as it should be, I think I have been too busy and tired at the end of each day to miss having a family," he answered truthfully.

Comprehension flickered in Miss Franklin's eyes.

"And, you, Miss Franklin: you enjoy being part of a family?" he asked obliquely. Well, he could hardly ask her if she wanted to have a family of her own some day soon, could he?

She nodded. "Indeed: my sisters and I are very close, and my parents have been both my teachers and my friends," she replied earnestly. "I think they have prepared me well," she added daringly.

That comment, of course, had several interpretations. But Miss Franklin hoped that LaPorte would know it was her subtle way of telling him she was interested. In him.

He sighed, but it was a happy sigh, and he smiled. "Well, now that most of the work here is finished and le Marchand is turning a good profit, and I have the leisure to take up other business opportunities as they arise, should I so wish, I may also have the—inclination—to pursue, well, other things as well," he said softly.

Miss Franklin just looked at him, her hazel green eyes shining in the glow of the many candles. The dancing had brought a pretty flush to her face and bosom, and she was breathing rather quickly—perhaps more so because of what LaPorte was saying than because of the dance. "Other things," she replied, her voice low, "such as astronomy?" she smiled.

LaPorte nodded and chuckled. "Yes, *certes*," he agreed.

The next part of the dance was half way over: there was not much more than a minute left for them to speak confidentially before they would be dancing again where conversation would not be as private.

"And more," he continued quickly, quietly. "Perhaps now my desire for a family, for a wife," he whispered that word, "will be—indulged." LaPorte looked meaningfully at Miss Franklin, who to her credit met his eyes with hers unflinchingly. There might be rules and manners to be followed, surely, but this was still the American Wilderness, and some times, she felt, one could bend the rules a little in pursuit of one's goal.

She thought she knew the subtext of LaPorte's comment, but it would not be seemly for her to assume or comment on any assumption. So she replied, obliquely,

178

"you might wish to follow the dictates of Socrates in this matter."

She was surprised when LaPorte thought a moment, then said, low: "sound advice, indeed, Miss Franklin, and advice I intend to take, if I may, with your cooperation."

Chapter Twenty-Seven

They had not said too much more to each other for the rest of the evening, but Miss Franklin could not help but repeat the exchange over and over in her mind as she and her parents returned with Mr. King to his house in the early hours of the following morning.

Socrates had many famous quotations: it was not a given that Monsieur LaPorte either knew many of them or knew the one that had been uppermost in her mind, Miss Franklin reminded herself.

'By all means, get married: if you find a good wife, you'll be happy,' was the bit of wisdom that she had been thinking of. Could LaPorte have thought of the same quote? His response could have been just formulaic: 'sound advice...I intend to take [it],' were it not for the last three words: 'with your cooperation.'

Why, if he had not been thinking of that quote, would he need her cooperation? It had been a baffling conversation but an enchanting one nonetheless and Miss Franklin was burning to know more about LaPorte.

"Papa, do you not think that was a wonderful reception?" she asked as they said their goodnights at the top of the stairs.

"I do, Elizabeth," he replied fondly, for his oldest child was a favorite of his. "And you seemed to have a wonderful time," he added indulgently.

"As did I, my dear," Mrs. Franklin called from the doorway of the bed chamber they were using. "Now come along!"

"I did, Papa. Good night, Papa, Mama," Elizabeth Franklin replied quickly, and scuttled off to the other bed chamber, which she shared with her two younger sisters.

The Duke stayed for two weeks, all tolled, along with Guillemard and of course, Cartouche, who greatly enjoyed loping through the settlement, the gardens and the fields. He was very respectful, however, and not at all destructive, and made friends with the other dogs that already lived at the settlement. Of the several cats he was less sure, and gave them a wide berth. But, as his master was fêted and regarded as a VIP, so Cartouche seemed to be held in the same high esteem by everyone at Azilum.

When the Duke left, the glow of his visit persisted for several weeks, and everyone at Azilum seemed to be in an especially good mood. That is, at least, until word came at the end of June that the younger son of Marie Antoinette and King Louis XVI had died in prison. The direct line of Bourbon Kings of France, since Henry IV in 1589, was now finished. Louis XVI's two brothers, of course, were still alive and had escaped the guillotine. But it was not quite the same, everyone felt, and as the sulky, sodden skies of July with its humidity and rain rolled in, Azilum's residents appeared quite glum.

"While Le Dauphin was alive, there was hope," noted Lucretius deBlacons to his wife, the former Mademoiselle deMaulde. Together with Monsieur Mancy Colin they ran the town's haberdashery and worked closely, therefore, with LaPorte. They relied on him for sourcing supplies they required for their shop. This day, the deBlacons and LaPorte were having dinner at the new Inn, just established at Azilum. It was run by Francis de la Route's wife, the former Mademoiselle de Bercy. De la Route himself partnered with Monsieur DeBecdelliere in trade also.

The Inn, which was along the road that led up the hill south of the town, was called Auberge de Confort, and stood to be a welcome sight to travelers coming to and from Azilum. It was about a half hour away by horse or carriage, so it was popular for dinner with residents as well. On fine days, groups of ladies would set out in wagons and carriages to walk among the nearby forests and fields, for they greatly enjoyed the outdoors. Sometimes they packed a picnic and made a day of it. Other times they would leave in the late morning and stop at the Inn for their dinners, before returning home in the late afternoon.

Since this particular day was rainy, no such parties occupied the sparkling and cheerful dining room of the Inn, and LaPorte and the deBlacons had the place to themselves. The food was very good, and they drank beer or wine and anticipated their dinners with relish.

"Yes, of course," LaPorte agreed now. "But while some family remains, I still have hope," he sighed.

Indeed, Louis XVI had had four brothers: Louis, Comte de Provence, who would later style himself as Louis XVIII of France; Charles, Comte d' Artois, who would later style himself Charles X of France; Xavier, the Duke of Aquitaine and Louis, the Duke of Burgundy. The last two, Xavier and Louis of Burgundy, had died young.

The deBlacons wagged their heads in a gesture of doubt, but LaPorte smiled. "We must always hope," he told them as the waitress brought their platters, heaped with fresh seasonal vegetables and the specialty of the day: Lapin A La Bourguignonne.

LaPorte himself was by nature a hopeful man, and an optimist. As he dined with the deBlacons that day he was thinking, not of the precarious state of the French monarchy—though he still had hope about that, as he had just asserted—but about the hope he had with regard to a much more personal matter: Miss Franklin.

He had been putting off a visit to her father to formally ask permission to court her since the night of the ball. Such behavior was unusual for him, because he generally attacked matters directly, and swiftly. But first he had told himself he should wait the few more days until the Duke had departed to approach Franklin. There was no good reason he should do so, but he told himself that he should. Then, he had found himself very busy at le Marchand since his partner had fallen ill for a week and a half with a summer cold. Following that, he had told himself he should avoid visiting the Franklins in case he had caught Heier's cold and could be contagious.

And so the weeks had passed.

Now, he had to admit to himself that his audience with Franklin was a daunting mission, for he was not in control of the outcome. What if Mr. Franklin refused? LaPorte had been telling himself since the evening of the ball that Franklin would have no good reason to do so: he, LaPorte, had money, owned several successful businesses, and had his own house, three horses, a carriage, and several agricultural plots of land worked for him by others at Azilum. Even without revealing his 'secret stash' of diamonds, he was, LaPorte thought, a good prospect for a husband.

What had stopped him from visiting the Franklins at John King's house—although he rode by several times a fortnight and once or twice in the past weeks he had been King's guest for coffee or a drink—was the vast difference in age between him and Miss Franklin. He was thirty-seven years old. She was sixteen.

There were other eligible bachelors at or near Azilum much closer to her in age, although nowhere near as well off as he was. And, since 'absence makes the heart grow fonder' was very true for LaPorte, he doubted anyone could love Miss Franklin more than he already did, and was prepared to do.

Chapter Twenty-Eight

It had been the brandy after dinner with the deBlacons, LaPorte thought, that had given him the nudge he needed to bid them farewell when they rode back down to the intersection at the base of the mountain. They continued on straight ahead, towards Azilum's town square. He turned right, mentioning that he wanted to stop in to see John King, whose house was next to the eastern edge of the small village of Azilum.

That was true enough, but when he arrived at the King home, he knocked, was admitted, and asked to see Mr. Franklin.

The tall man, fortunately, was home, having been reckoning the accounts for King's enterprises, which he handled. He met with LaPorte, therefore, in the small room he used as a study.

"Do please sit down, Monsieur LaPorte," Franklin began kindly, motioning to a heavy wooden armchair with a curved back.

LaPorte smiled and sat. Franklin resumed his seat behind his oak desk, steepled his fingers and looked inquiringly at his visitor.

"Ah, thank you for seeing me, Mr. Franklin," LaPorte began. "I trust you and your family are well?"

"Yes, quite well, thank you. And yourself?" Franklin replied genially.

"Oh, yes, well. My partner at le Marchand has been ill, however, so I have not had a chance until now to come to speak with you," LaPorte replied, sounding more mysterious than he intended to.

Franklin raised one brow. "I do hope he is recovered now?" he asked, concerned, for he was a kind man.

"He is recovered now, yes..." LaPorte agreed, nodding his head.

"And so?" Franklin urged. He had an inkling about why LaPorte had come to visit, and had asked to speak particularly to him: he'd seemed quite taken with Elizabeth at the ball for the Duke a few weeks before, and Franklin had noticed. He'd also seen LaPorte ride by the King house at least once a week, and knew LaPorte had dropped in to visit with the Franklins' benefactor more than once. Now, LaPorte's obvious nervousness at speaking to him amused Franklin a bit: LaPorte, along with Talon, were the leading men at Azilum. Both were quite fluent now in English as well as French, albeit with an accent on the latter. Franklin would have thought that LaPorte wouldn't be nervous about speaking to anyone.

"I should like to ask your—erm—you permission, sir, to walk out with your daughter, sir," LaPorte blurted out finally.

Franklin bit back a smile. He couldn't say he was surprised, and in some ways he was very pleased, although the difference in the age of his sixteen year old daughter and LaPorte was a concern. Still, he decided to have some fun with his visitor.

"My daughter? But she is but a babe, just three months old!" he teased.

LaPorte smiled nervously and shook his head. "No, sir, your other daughter," he explained.

Franklin smiled again. "Susanna is but a child, still, eight years old," he told LaPorte gently.

LaPorte looked stunned, and then relaxed a bit as he recalled Elizabeth having told him that she had three younger sisters.

"Ah, no, Mr. Franklin, the other daughter," he said, and was about to add, 'the oldest,' but Franklin cut him off.

"You mean, Rebecca?" Franklin affected surprise. "But she is only three years older!" he protested.

LaPorte frowned. "No, sir; it is not your young daughters of whom I speak, sir, 'tis the oldest: Elizabeth," he explained finally. "Miss Elizabeth Franklin."

"Aaaaah!" Franklin gave a wide smile and chuckled. "She is my favorite child, perhaps because she was my first," he added, his tone somber. He had known, even hoped, this day would come, that some fine young man would seek to pay court to his child. He couldn't ask for much finer man than LaPorte, Franklin thought. But— "She is but sixteen," he cautioned.

LaPorte nodded. "I know."

"And if I may ask, Monsieur LaPorte, you are—?" he left the question unsaid.

But LaPorte knew what he meant. "I turned thirty-seven this past April," LaPorte answered quickly.

Franklin hid his surprise: he had thought LaPorte was perhaps thirty, for considering everything he had done thus far in his life, he could hardly have been younger. But he was nearing forty! He himself was only 42.

"But I assure you, sir, I have the health and the mind of a much younger man," LaPorte went on. "And does it not give you, as a father, some measure of— confidence and consolation—to think of your daughter being under the guidance and tutelage of an older man? I am settled, I am experienced, I have several thriving businesses and most importantly, I find myself completely captivated by Miss Elizabeth Franklin." He paused.

Franklin was giving him a long, interested, yet assessing look.

"I pledge my life to her happiness, and I promise to make certain she will never want for anything," he told Franklin, thinking of his diamonds. "Even after I die, if I should die before she does, she will never want for anything," he repeated firmly.

Franklin took a deep breath. "I see that you are sincere, Monsieur LaPorte, and I have no doubt that you are very fond of my daughter," he began.

"Indeed, sir, though I do not know her very well, and wish to know her better, I do believe I love her, sir," LaPorte put in.

Franklin nodded agreement. Then he stood. "I must ask Mrs. Franklin," he told LaPorte.

LaPorte also stood. "And you will ask your daughter her feelings in the matter?" he asked, solicitous. "For if she does not wish it, I should not ever want..."

Franklin smiled: that concern showed him exactly how much LaPorte really did care for Elizabeth, he thought. The man was willing to put his own needs and wants aside in favor of hers.

"Yes. If Mrs. Franklin agrees, we shall speak to Elizabeth and send word," he told LaPorte with a kind smile.

Chapter Twenty-Nine

"Monsieur LaPorte wants to court our Elizabeth?" Susanna Brown Franklin parroted her husband's news in surprise.

"He does. I do believe he is very serious."

"But—how old is he?" Mrs. Franklin asked shortly. He told her on a sigh.

"He's nearer my own age than our daughter's!" she protested. She was 35 and had given birth the winter before to a fourth daughter. She and her husband were hoping that the next baby would be a son. The idea that her oldest daughter might soon marry and have children close in age to her own was not what gave Mrs. Franklin pause. It was the age of Elizabeth's proposed suitor.

"He is very well off, my dear, and very highly thought of, and quite refined," Franklin reminded his wife. "You yourself complimented him on his dancing, and remarked to me several times since we made Monsieur LaPorte's acquaintance on his acuity, wit and genial nature," he added. "And you cannot argue that he is a wealthy man."

"I know I did, I know," Mrs. Franklin replied testily. "But—thirty-seven?" she shook her head, and the lace on her cap fluttered. "It just does not seem right."

Her husband paused. "I think Elizabeth may not mind, though, Susanna," he said gently.

His wife looked up at her husband and brushed a self conscious hand across one cheek. The smallpox they had all endured on the voyage from England had scarred everyone, including herself. Although powder could help to disguise the marks at home she wore no 'maquillage' and knew that the small craters that dotted her skin in places could be seen.

"She is a wonderful girl and could find a man closer to her own age for a husband, I have no doubt," Mrs. Franklin said staunchly, defending her oldest child. "And the way she wears her hair, well, you cannot even see the scars," she added with a sniff.

It was true: Elizabeth's smallpox scars were mostly along her hair line, and since she wore her wavy brown locks with tendrils around her forehead and cheeks, which fortunately was the fashion, they were generally quite hidden. But Susanna feared that the imperfections might hamper her daughter's attractiveness, particularly to prospective suitors. Still, she didn't think she had to settle for someone more than twice her daughter's age.

"Should we let the man's age disqualify him from courting our daughter?" Franklin asked softly. "Aside from that—and to my mind, Susanna, it is a small consideration—he is an excellent prospect."

Mrs. Franklin bit her lip and took a breath. "Very well. If she wishes it, then, I give my permission. Not my blessing, you understand, for I think she would do better with someone closer to her own age. But I shall allow it, husband, since you seem to feel it would be a good idea. And woe be to you if they marry and our Elizabeth is made unhappy, or a young widow," she warned with a scowl.

Franklin sighed. He didn't think LaPorte would make Elizabeth unhappy. And if she were to become a young widow, well, at least she would be a rich young widow, he thought to himself.

Elizabeth's parents spoke to her that evening after supper, once the baby and the two younger girls had been put to bed.

"We have had a visit from a man who wishes to pay you court," her mother began stiffly.

Elizabeth looked up from her embroidery, surprised. She had hoped, it was true, that Bartholomew LaPorte would come to call after the ball for the Duke. She had hoped he would speak to her father and ask to court her. But the weeks that had gone by since the ball had quenched the fire of that hope, and she had become resigned to the fact that their conversation and dance at the ball had been just that: conversation. And nothing more. Since she had been out when LaPorte had visited earlier that day, she did not know that what she had dreamt of early on had finally occurred.

"Indeed, Papa? Mama?" She giggled a little bit. "I cannot imagine, who?" She asked, cocking her head to one side like a curious bird.

"Monsieur Bartholomew LaPorte," her father answered, sounding quite happy about it.

Elizabeth gasped. "Truly? Monsieur LaPorte?!" she exclaimed, and dropped her needlework in her lap, and clapped her hands over her mouth in surprise. "Monsieur LaPorte?" she asked again.

Her father chuckled. "The very same. Make no mistake, he is the very man," he reassured his daughter.

"He is very old," her mother put in sourly, stabbing a needle into the crewel work she was laboring over. It was meant to be a kneeling cushion for the little church and she was trying to make a pattern of gold leaves on a burgundy ground.

Elizabeth looked at her mother. "How old?" she asked curiously. "I know he is older than I am..."

"He is thirty-seven," her father replied, and Elizabeth giggled again, and looked over at her mother.

"Why, Mama, that is only two years older than you are!" she declared merrily. "So he cannot be 'very old,' for you are not 'very old,' indeed, you are still quite young! You've just had a babe!" she protested, still giggling.

Her mother bit her lip and looked chastised, but still not really amenable to the match.

"What say you," her father asked her kindly. "Do you like Monsieur LaPorte?" he asked Elizabeth.

"Yes, Papa, I do." Her answer was quick, and certain.

"Might you wish that he be allowed to pay you court?" he asked her, solicitousness making him very formal.

Elizabeth gave both her parents a wide smile. "Oh, yes, Papa, Mama, I do wish that, very much!" she answered with so much enthusiasm that the certainty of her wish was in no way doubtful.

Father and Mother exchanged a glance. Mrs. Franklin shrugged in surrender and Mr. Franklin said he would write to Monsieur LaPorte immediately and let him know their decision.

LaPorte had visited Mr. Franklin on that rainy Wednesday afternoon. He received Franklin's note informing him that he would be permitted to court Elizabeth on Thursday morning. Friday after dinner and before supper he arrived at the King house once again, and requested to speak with Miss Elizabeth.

LaPorte had taken special care with his appearance. Although he generally took a full bath once a week before attending church on Sunday, he'd made special ablutions on Thursday evening and on Friday he'd dressed in a new dark blue brocaded waistcoat, grey breeches and coat, all with silver buttons that winked in the sun. His neck stock was snowy white and freshly laundered as were the silk hose he wore. Even the silver buckles on his black shoes sparkled. On his head he wore the hat he'd obtained in Bethlehem, the one that was nearly a twin to Talon's venerable brown leather one, but upon admittance to the King house, LaPorte removed this.

He was ushered into the smaller parlor where, too nervous to sit, he circumlocuted the room until he heard the door open, and Elizabeth's light step.

"Miss Franklin!" he said, turning, and seeing her standing a few feet away. He bowed.

"Monsieur LaPorte," she replied with a small curtsey.

"It is a pleasure to see you again," LaPorte said fervently, and gestured to the small settee upholstered in gold brocade with pink flowers.

Miss Franklin sat, and arranged her skirts so that LaPorte really didn't have room to sit beside her. Her reticence did nothing to dampen LaPorte's enthusiasm.

He took a chair done in matching upholstery, and she noticed that he flicked the tails of his coat back quickly before he sat. Most of the nobility did not do this, for they had servants to iron out any wrinkles. She had no doubt LaPorte did as well, so she wondered why he was careful of his clothing. Later, when they knew each other better, she would ask him, and he would tell her that he saw no point in intentionally wrinkling the clothing he wore and making more work for his servants. 'They have enough to do without having to pick up after a slovenly master,' he would tell her, and Elizabeth would be pleased.

Now, she nodded and said that it was a pleasure to see him as well.

"Your father and mother have spoken to you?" LaPorte asked hesitantly.

"Yes, they have."

"And—you are agreeable?" he asked, wanting to be sure.

Elizabeth took a deep breath. "I have a question, first, Monsieur LaPorte," she told him.

He waited.

"The ball for the Duke was nearly two months ago. Why did it take you such a lengthy time to come and see my Papa and ask to court me?"

LaPorte was surprised: she was quite direct! Still, better direct than simpering allusions, he thought, and so he answered her with equal directness.

"I was fearful your father would say no," he admitted. "I am generally not fearful of much, you see, but in this case the result was completely out of my hands, out of my control," he explained. "And so I was afraid. I made excuses to wait: first, until the Duke departed. Then, we heard the devastating news of the Dauphin. Then, we became extremely busy at le Marchand and then my partner took ill with a heavy cold..."

"Ah, summer colds are the very worst!" Elizabeth put in quickly and compassionately. "Has he recovered?"

"Yes. But then I still delayed, telling myself that I might be contagious, if I had caught his illness," he admitted. "But then it appeared that I was quite well, and so on Wednesday I just—decided." He shrugged. "I had run out of excuses, and because I think of you almost every waking minute, putting off asking your father to court you had become torture."

"But surely, if he had said 'no' that would have been a kind of torture?" Elizabeth sparred mischievously, quite relieved and pleased by his answer.

"Oh, indeed, but of a different kind," LaPorte agreed quickly. "It would have been a definitive torture, and so, much easier to handle. It is not knowing that is the worst form of agony, I think," he finished.

Elizabeth smiled at him. "You may be correct, Monsieur LaPorte, for I found myself in similar straits until my parents spoke to me Wednesday evening." She paused. "I had initially thought that it was because of my —disfigurement," she said softly.

La Porte frowned in confusion. "Disfigurement?" he echoed, baffled. "I see no disfigurement."

Elizabeth gave him a long look and then lifted the curling ringlets on one side of her face, turning her cheek towards him so it would catch the lamp light. "There was smallpox on our ship coming over," she reminded him. "I —and my whole family—bear the scars," she said quietly.

LaPorte shook his head as he peered at her face, and then smiled. "But, my dear Miss Franklin, that is as nothing—no more than freckles, indeed! And rather than scars, I count them as evidence of your strength of constitution and survival of the scourge," he added stoutly.

"Then, you do not think me—..." Elizabeth began, re-arranging her hair in its customary style and gazing with hope at LaPorte.

"I think you are the most beautiful woman I have ever seen," LaPorte said firmly. "And I have seen many beautiful women," he added with a nod. "I thought so, the moment I saw you, that afternoon in my shop. You came for embroidery thread."

"And boot black. I remember," she joined in shyly.

There was a long pause when both were silent. Elizabeth looked down at her hands, folded in the lap of her flower sprigged blue *robe Anglaise* and LaPorte gazed fondly at the top of Elizabeth's head.

"I had almost given up my hope that you would come, as the weeks went by after the ball," she said then, raising her head but speaking so softly that LaPorte had to strain to hear her. "But not quite. And so, I suffered."

LaPorte looked stricken. "Oh, my dear Miss Franklin, I never thought about that, about how you might feel, waiting. I am sorry to have distressed you and only ask that you allow me to make it up to you."

Elizabeth gave him another smile. "You may, Monsieur LaPorte."

Chapter Thirty

Talon was very happy for his friend LaPorte and entirely approving of his choice of companion. Although both were still very occupied with the business of running Azilum, and LaPorte in particular was also busy making certain his shop was well stocked and turning a profit, and that his other interests were also doing a brisk trade, LaPorte found time a couple of evenings a week to call on Miss Franklin. Sometimes they would stand in the small garden of King's home and talk, or watch the stars. Miss Franklin learned all about various constellations and the phases of the moon from her suitor. He learned about her family, their home in England, and the circumstances that had brought them to Azilum.

Sunday afternoons often found them walking from the King house to the river and taking out a small rowboat that Mr. King kept pulled up onto the shore.

"I shall teach you to swim," LaPorte told Miss Franklin.

"Swim!" Miss Franklin exclaimed, sounding intrigued.

"Yes, indeed. I can swim, and my brother can as well, but of course he is a seaman so he ought to know how to survive if his ship should sink," he added with a laugh.

"Is it difficult to learn?" Miss Franklin asked, curious.

"Why, no, not so very hard," LaPorte replied, rowing lazily along the shore and keeping them in the shade where it was cool and where Miss Franklin's skin would not become brown. "First you learn how to kick your feet and legs. Then you learn what to do with your arms. Then you put the two together. That requires coordination, but I have seen you dance, Miss Franklin, and you should have no trouble at all," he had replied gallantly.

Whenever they were together, they talked almost without pause, discussing any news that had come via the mail carrier who made the arduous trip from Philadelphia once a fortnight. They also talked about the wildlife around them, and the trees and flowers, and LaPorte was pleased to learn that Miss Franklin knew quite a bit about gardening.

Once the weather turned cooler, LaPorte would call for Miss Franklin in his carriage and they would go to the Grand Maison where they could always be certain of having chaperones around somewhere to maintain Miss Franklin's reputation. Chaperones notwithstanding, the couple had managed a few rather chaste kisses but as the months went by these became more fervent, and Miss Franklin often had to be sure she had composed herself and caught her breath afterwards.

But it was the conversation that flowed so easily between them that most pleased the couple. Miss Franklin learned all about LaPorte's many businesses, including le Marchand, which she admitted fascinated her.

'I should not mind helping you there, if you ever were to need my assistance,' she had suggested at one point. LaPorte had told her that he would be delighted if that were to be the case one day. However, when he thought about the future, and Miss Franklin, he did not picture her working in his shop.

LaPorte learned about the intricacies of the deal that King had struck with John Lambert, the New Jersey plantation owner, in assuming the Franklins' debt. 'Papa worries that it will be several more years before he will have worked off the debt to Mr. King,' Miss Franklin had explained one day while they were helping festoon the

Maison with greenery, for Christmas was only a week away now.

LaPorte had asked how much her father still owed, and Miss Franklin had named the sum. It was large: several times the man's yearly wage, for the debt was for passage for the entire family. And Lambert had tacked on a penalty fee for King because of his settlement of the Franklins' debt. He claimed King's action would deprive him of valuable workers for several months until he acquired more, so the figure was quite high. 'I am not meant to know, but I overhear Papa sometimes talking to Mr. King.'

'Is not Mr. King a most kind landlord?' LaPorte had queried. "He allows your father to work anywhere in the area where he may acquire employment, in addition to handling his affairs, is that not so?" he asked.

'He is indeed very kind, and yes, that is true,' Miss Franklin had confirmed. 'But our room and board here, with Mr. King, comes out of Papa's wages, and so there is not that much that is left to pay down the debt.' She had sighed. 'Papa is very much his own man. I know he wants to be free of the debt, and independent.'

'And would you leave Azilum once the debt is paid off?' LaPorte had asked, trying and failing to keep the fear at such a prospect from his voice.

'No, Papa says there is much here to attract him and allow him to earn a good living,' Miss Franklin had replied, and LaPorte had let out a long breath he hadn't realized he had been holding. 'And that is another reason he wishes to be free of the debt, so he may pursue those interests,' Miss Franklin had finished.

Once the winter arrived and all the crops had been harvested and the business of timbering and quarrying slowed, LaPorte would sometimes join the Franklins and Mr. King for Sunday dinner. Often he would reciprocate by inviting them all to the Grand Maison for dinner in return, especially if there was to be an 'evening' following the meal.

Mrs. Franklin greatly enjoyed these entertainments, although her view of her daughter's suitor was still somewhat sour. She was not entirely sure exactly why she felt this way, for she liked Bartholomew LaPorte well enough. She just didn't wish to have him as a son in law. She was certain it was the age difference, and her husband tended to agree with his wife.

However, they had given their permission for the courtship because LaPorte had been so insistent. Clearly, Elizabeth had been happy about the development and since she had begun seeing LaPorte she had been the happiest they had ever seen her. But both parents privately wished that with time, her keenness for her older suitor would wane, perhaps if she met other men, more her own age.

There were such young men at the evenings held at the Maison, and without appearing to be doing it, Mrs. Franklin always took pains that Elizabeth should be introduced to all of them. Elizabeth was always polite to these young men, of course, but even Mrs. Franklin could see that her daughter only had eyes for LaPorte.

The two of them always conducted themselves properly, but anyone bothering to look could not miss the gazes of adoration that passed between them.

LaPorte had always insisted that there never be secrets between him and Miss Franklin. 'I remember that you thought I was not sincere in my interest, when I initially delayed in asking your father if I might court you," he had told Miss Franklin solemnly one late winter afternoon. "I never want you to doubt me, or my intentions, or to have question of what I am doing.' They had been sitting in one of the parlors at the Maison. The door was open, and people wandered or bustled by frequently, but if they kept their voices low, they had a modicum of privacy.

'And what are your intentions, Monsieur LaPorte?' Miss Franklin had asked lightly. She thought she knew, and when changing for her 'walk' with Monsieur LaPorte earlier that afternoon, she had taken special care. Surely, the big moment would come soon, and she wanted to be ready. She'd chosen a new *robe Anglaise* in a deep moss green silk. It was trimmed in ivory lace at the neck and sleeves but was otherwise unadorned. Elizabeth had thought that it would do very well for what she hoped would be a special afternoon. As their meetings had become more ardent, she had become more eager for the matter to be decided, and had found herself almost breathless once she had asked that all important question —though her tone had been casual.

Now, LaPorte had smiled at her and engulfed one of her small hands in both of his. 'I wish, Miss Franklin, to ask you to do me the honor of becoming my wife,' he had said quietly. 'And if you are agreeable, I shall ask your parents for their blessing.'

Miss Franklin had gazed a moment at LaPorte's large, strong hands. They were warm and firm and held her hand as though it were the most precious thing in the world. Then she had looked up at him, meeting his dark brown eyes with her own clear hazel ones.

'I am most agreeable, Monsieur LaPorte,' she had answered quietly. 'And I think you may call me Elizabeth,' she had added.

This time, LaPorte wasted no time in arranging another meeting with both Mr. and Mrs. Franklin, and he presented his case.

"I am, as you know, well off, with several businesses and a thriving mercantile," he told the couple frankly, but with as much modesty as he could muster.

The three of them sat together the next evening after supper in Mr. Franklin's small study. Tiny glasses of brandy were before them, but LaPorte had only taken the merest sip.

"Most importantly, however, I am deeply in love with your daughter Elizabeth," he continued. "And I wish to spend the rest of my life making her happy, building a life and a family with her, and protecting her from all harm and distress," he concluded.

"You wish to marry Elizabeth?" Mr. Franklin asked. He had thought this was LaPorte's ultimate wish when the man had asked to court Elizabeth. But now that he was faced with the fact of LaPorte asking permission to marry his daughter, Mr. Franklin found himself unwilling to let her go. At least, not immediately.

"I do indeed, sir," LaPorte confirmed, nodding his head. "In the spring, or perhaps June, which is always a good month for weddings," he suggested. It would be difficult to wait until June, he thought, for it was just February. But if Elizabeth would like a June wedding, he would wait.

"And have you spoken to Elizabeth?" Mrs. Franklin asked archly.

"I have, madame, to ascertain if she were amenable to the suggestion. And she is," LaPorte assured her.

"But she is still so very young," objected Mr. Franklin.

"Yes, she is," his wife chimed in, seizing on the fact like a drowning woman clutching at a life preserver. "And with the vast difference in age between you both, it might be best to wait a little while and see if you are still of this mind when she has, erm, grown up a bit," she added doubtfully.

"I will do whatever you wish, only say you do not oppose the marriage," LaPorte told them fervently.

"It is not that we oppose it, exactly," began Mr. Franklin.

LaPorte interrupted him. "I sincerely hope not, sir, for you gave your permission for me to court Elizabeth, and surely you knew that I, as an honorable man, intended marriage eventually, should things work out," LaPorte put in, his voice even but stern. He gave Franklin a very long look.

"Of course, of course..." Mr. Franklin replied, attempting to smooth the Frenchman's ruffled feathers.

"I would not trifle with any woman's feelings," continued LaPorte earnestly. "Especially not Elizabeth's, for I love her so dearly," he finished, and his voice softened at the last.

Mr. Franklin exchanged a look with his wife, who frowned, then gave a small shrug and cast her eyes down towards the brown figured carpet on the floor.

"Well, then, you have our blessing," began Mr. Franklin slowly. "But we ask that you wait."

"How long?" LaPorte asked bluntly. "I agree, Elizabeth is young, but she is not a child," he put in frankly.

"Until she is eighteen," Mrs. Franklin answered quickly.

"Eighteen?" LaPorte echoed, disbelieving. Elizabeth would not turn eighteen for more than a year. It seemed an eternity.

"Eighteen," confirmed Mr. Franklin.

LaPorte took a deep breath. "But we may consider ourselves engaged?" he asked, but it wasn't a question. The Franklins may have conditions, but so did he. "I intend to give her a ring, very soon," he added.

Grudgingly, the Franklins agreed.

Chapter Thirty-One

"I shall be eighteen next April," Elizabeth told Bartholomew when he had, the next day, informed her of her parents' demands. It had turned unusually warm for February, and the sun was strong. It reflected off the snow pack and made the day even more temperate, and Bartholomew and Elizabeth had decided to go for a walk on the still frozen roads of the settlement. They walked with her arm in his, and he held her close. "We could be married the following day," she finished with a grin for him.

LaPorte laughed aloud: Elizabeth had a wonderful way of lightening even the darkest subject. "Would that not be somewhat precipitous?" he asked gaily.

She shook her head, and beneath her rather old fashioned calash bonnet, her brown curls fluttered prettily around her face that was just beginning to flush with cold. "They said we must wait until I am eighteen," she reminded him. "I do not want to wait a moment longer."

"I do not want to wait at all," LaPorte confessed, giving her waist a squeeze through all of her skirts and petticoats and her thick cape. "But I shall, as long as you promise not to tire of me."

She stopped, and faced him, and took both his gloved hands in her own, which were covered in wool mitts. "I shall not tire of you, Bartholomew," she promised sincerely. "You are the most fascinating man I have ever met."

The colony of Azilum thrived and with the arrival of another spring came another growing season. Before then, however, just two weeks after the discussion with the Franklins, Bartholomew made a journey to the jeweler in Towanda he had struck up an acquaintance with when he'd first arrived at Azilum. He had sold some of his diamonds here, but that day in early March, his mission was a different one.

"Choose the stone which will make the finest ring when faceted," he told the jeweler, and he spilled out a few of his largest rough diamonds into the other man's hand. He himself had chosen them and they were, to his eye, the finest of the bigger ones that remained. The diamonds—large and small, mostly rough but some faceted—were with him at all times. He had even asked one of the Maison's servants to sew a sturdy little pouch in which he secreted his stash. He wore the pouch on a piece of rawhide around his neck and was never without it.

The jeweler gasped, for although the stones were rough, they were quite large, as large as marbles. Then he pointed to one in particular. "This has the best color," he said. Then, with his loupe, he examined it. "And it is quite clear," he added with a nod.

They negotiated the cost for cutting the stone in the popular round 'rose cut' and then setting it in a ring of fine gold, and LaPorte paid him and promised to return in two more weeks to collect the ring.

For Elizabeth's birthday that year, Bartholomew gave her the ring, and she proudly slid it onto the third finger of her left hand. "It is truly magnificent," she breathed, holding her hand aloft so the diamond could catch the light. They were seated in Mr. King's front parlor, where LaPorte had asked Elizabeth to join him. He had been invited to dinner, a special one, for Elizabeth's birthday, complete with cake and presents. But this last present was, she thought, the best.

"Only a year now," he replied with a smile, and kissed her thoroughly.

The colony amused itself throughout the year with several 'evenings' at the Maison. Usually these began an hour or so after mid day dinner, and they would go on until about ten in the evening, or later sometimes. A supper was always served, but beforehand the various amusements included games of cards or backgammon or chess, sometimes dancing, or music, for there were a couple of very fine pianofortes at the Maison. They were not so fancy as a ball, but they filled in the evenings when the residents of Azilum were without any outside visitors.

Elizabeth, who played the pianoforte well, was always delighted to entertain those assembled and when another of the company played, LaPorte discovered to his happiness that his fiancée had a charming if untutored voice.

They also played charades and performed various tableaux from history and literature with the audience trying to guess what was being portrayed.

One evening in May at one such activity, the tableau that was chosen was, 'The Abduction of Persephone,' with Elizabeth playing Persephone and Bartholomew playing Hades, the God of the Underworld who snatches the young maid while she and two friends are gathering flowers.

Behind the closed doors that divided the double reception room into audience and makeshift stage, and that hid the players as they prepared for each scene, Elizabeth and two of her contemporaries from the settlement huddled together to discuss how they would portray the three young girls. Bartholomew, who knew exactly what he needed, slipped out the back door and made his way down to the Maison's servants' quarters.

Upon his return, he was festooned with a large red blanket of woven wool that was clasped across his chest with a big silver buckle. Beneath that, he had removed his coat, vest and shirt, much to the consternation but secret delight of the young ladies. Mme. d'Autremont, who was acting as backstage assistant cum chaperone also found herself admiring the muscles on LaPorte's naked chest—what she could see of it beneath the blanket—and had to employ her fan rather more than the temperature in the room warranted.

LaPorte had also brought with him a large wheeled cart—the best he could do on short notice, he muttered to Mme. d'Autremont, who merely nodded. It was to symbolize the chariot Hades rides in.

For their part, the young ladies were no less titillating: it was, after all, Classical Myth and as such had to be portrayed authentically. Elizabeth and the two other girls, Mademoiselle Clarice Boulogne—the scout's younger sister who kept house with him—and Mademoiselle Mathilde deVilaine, whose parents ran the maple sugaring operation at the colony, were all dressed in colorful gowns and several petticoats. Although they sported 'round gowns' which were the style now that the panniered split skirt had fallen out of fashion, the colonies had not yet caught up to the English and European 'Empire' gown that mimicked the dress of Classical Greece and Rome. Called 'Regency' in England and even 'Directoire' in France in the early part of the next decade, it featured lighter materials and high waistlines. But Elizabeth, Clarice and Mathilde all wore the natural waisted heavier gowns in patterned silk with petticoats beneath to make the skirt stand out from the body.

"These will never do," tut-tutted Mme. d'Autremont, regarding the trio. "You are meant to be Classical Goddesses!" She quickly sent a servant to fetch items she specified to her, and the servant rushed off. She returned after several minutes along with Mme. d'Autremont's own lady's maid, bearing three chemises of white linen, each adorned with various types of lace. Mme. d'Autremont hustled the three young ladies out of the reception room and into an unused parlor across the wide central hall. There, she quickly ordered them to help each other off with their gowns and petticoats, much to the surprise of the girls.

After a good deal of giggling, the girls stood only in their own chemises and stays, and Mme. d'Autremont and her lady's maid popped one of the d'Autremont chemises over each girl's head. The articles of clothing were quite voluminous, for Mme. d'Autremont was not a small woman. However, the same servant who'd run to fetch the chemises had also returned with several lengths of bright ribbon, and in a moment each girl had a ribbon tied under her bust, gathering the chemise behind her. The effect was quite charming and reasonably accurate although the long sleeves of the chemises were problematical.

"Can we not use the ribbons again?" asked Elizabeth, demonstrating what she meant on Clarice: she wound a length of ribbon around one of the girl's wrists and then crisscrossed it up her arm to her shoulder, where she secured it carefully in a small knot. Her engagement ring winked and flashed as she worked and Clarice murmured—not for the first time—what a beautiful piece of jewelry the ring was. Elizabeth smiled. "If you don't move too much, it should be fine," she cautioned of the ribbon work.

Everyone grabbed for ribbons and followed Elizabeth's lead.

"Now, we only need flowers," said Mathilde, but the clever servant had thought of that too, for she now reappeared in the parlor with three small pots of african violets.

"These are from the kitchen," she said shyly, offering one to each young lady. "They like warmth and moisture, but a short trip upstairs will do them no harm," she smiled.

Thus equipped, the young ladies returned to the reception room where LaPorte waited. They positioned themselves accordingly, with Mademoiselles Boulogne and deVilaine holding their flowers and looking horrified while Miss Franklin appeared to struggle as LaPorte took hold of one of her beribboned arms and pretended to drag her off. She flung her other arm, tightly grasping the violet pot, out in desperation towards the two other ladies.

"You are so beautiful," whispered LaPorte to Miss Franklin, caressing her arm rather more than necessary.

Indeed, the figure-revealing chemise allowed him to see as much of his fiancée as he ever had: even more than when he had taught her to swim the previous summer, for then she had been bogged down by petticoats and accompanied by her next younger sister as chaperone.

"Sssssshhhhhh, now I am meant to be terrified," giggled Miss Franklin. The two other young ladies sighed in delight: Monsieur LaPorte was so romantic!

Mme. d'Autremont flung open the dividing doors and the assembled audience gasped in delight.

"Orpheus and Eurydice!" called out one person, guessing incorrectly.

"*Non!*" declared Mme. d'Autremont, who quite enjoyed her job.

"Europa being taken by Zeus!" called out another.
"*Non!*"

"Theseus and Helen?" queried another.
"*Non!*"

Surely they could guess it, now, Elizabeth thought. She couldn't keep herself from gazing at Bartholomew's chest. It occurred to her that she had never seen a man's naked chest before, although she had of course seen drawings and paintings and statues. But Bartholomew's was—so close! So real, so alive. And very attractive.

"The abduction of Persephone?" called out someone else, and everyone broke character and clapped as Mme. d'Autremont called out, "*OUI!* Yes! *Vraiment, truly so!*"

Chapter Thirty-Two

That evening after the light supper and liqueurs that followed the tableaux, LaPorte asked Franklin if he might escort Miss Franklin home, alone, while her parents went on ahead. Franklin gave his permission.

It was a chilly evening for May, and although Miss Franklin had returned to her gown and petticoats after the portrayal in Mme. d'Autremont's chemise was finished, she was very glad of the light wool blanket Bartholomew wrapped around her as she stepped up beside him on the front seat of his elegant horse trap.

"Thank you, Bartholomew," she said quietly.

"I want you to stay warm and well, my dearest," he replied honestly. Then he flicked the reins and the horse moved ahead. Bartholomew kept him to a slow walk, however, wishing to prolong his time alone with his fiancée. Such minutes were precious and hard to come by, and especially after the excitement of their shared tableau, both felt the need to prolong their interaction.

They were silent for several minutes, and then Bartholomew said, "I have had a thought," and proceeded to tell Elizabeth of his idea.

"Do you think it will make your father and mother allow us to marry sooner than next year?" he asked when he had concluded.

Elizabeth's eyes were shining in the light of the moon. "I do not know, but it is worth asking him," she replied. "It is most—aggravating—to wait," she agreed, and she cupped Bartholomew's face in her hand briefly.

He kissed her palm, then sighed deeply. "It is indeed. When I am busy all day with the shop, or making deals for trade, or surveying the colony to make certain everything is as it should be, I find it easier to bear, for I can pretend, then, that when the day's work is ended, I shall return home, to you," he whispered. "'Tis only once the evening falls and work ceases that I return to an empty house, or to the Maison, where my companion M. Talon, although a good friend, is not you," he confessed. "And then...I long for you."

Elizabeth sighed, and laid her head on Bartholomew's shoulder. "And you can truly afford to do this?" she asked quietly of the idea he had shared. The King home was visible now, in the distance, and she knew they had only a few more minutes together. Her mother and father were probably even now looking out of the parlor window, waiting for LaPorte's trap to arrive.

LaPorte laughed lightly again. "I can indeed, my dearest one," he replied. "When we are married, I shall explain to you all of my accounts and holdings, for I wish you to know everything."

Elizabeth smiled. "But is it not usually the other way around?" she asked. "I mean, shouldn't my father be paying you something, my dowry?" she explained. "I can bring nothing to this union," she added softly.

Bartholomew shook his head. "If he would only give me you, that would be enough," he muttered. "You need bring nothing beyond yourself, for you are all the riches any man could ever wish for."

The idea LaPorte had had was one he'd been considering for months, ever since he had begun courting Elizabeth and he had learned the details of the Franklins' debt to King. When her parents demanded that they wait to get married, he had nearly offered his deal then, thinking to force their hand and allow them to get married more quickly. But he had waited, perhaps hoping that once the Franklins saw how happy their daughter was wearing his ring and being officially his fiancée, they might relent.

But they had not. And so, he had told Elizabeth his idea: if her father would allow them to marry now, he would pay off the Franklins' debt to King, and give Mr. Franklin a management position in the timbering and forestry business he owned. "That way, your father will earn more money and can either buy one of the houses available here at Azilum, or build his own as he wishes," Bartholomew said now as the horse's steps drew them ever nearer to the King house. "And he will be free of his debt, for this would be a gift to him, and to your family."

"I think it is a wonderful idea, and one that perhaps will convince Papa to change his mind," Elizabeth replied happily. "I know how it wears at him to be a bonded man."

In June of 1796 came word that Charles Maurice deTalleyrand was to pay a visit to Azilum, and as it had ahead of the Duc de Rochfoucauld's arrival, the colony swung into frenzied preparations.

A diplomat and crafty businessman, Talleyrand was temporarily in exile in the United States, like so many of his countrymen. However, word would come later in 1796 that he was no longer on the list of undesirables and so he would return to France.

However, Talleyrand did not know of his pardon as yet. Having made the acquaintance of Cazenove in Philadelphia and wishing, like others, to escape the coastal cities in the warmer months, and having heard of Azilum, he had decided to pay a visit to his fellow émigrés. He stayed for a month, fêted and honored much as the Duke had been. Talon enjoyed having the diplomat to stay at the Maison and LaPorte enjoyed exchanging views on commerce and trade with him.

Although Azilum had a prime location right along the river, Mr. Hollenbeck's trading outlets downstream and Tioga Point upstream were fierce rivals. Azilum's trade with outsiders and American settlers was good, but not as thriving as the colony had hoped, or forecast to its investors. Additionally, some prejudice on the part of the residents of Azilum towards the English speaking settlers nearby became known. While the American settlers felt no such prejudice and indeed thought the French people quite refined and elegant, hearing that those whom they admired thought them ruffians was a hard pill to swallow, and some bad feeling developed. So any tips or ideas from Talleyrand as to how Azilum might build its trade and handle its competition, or counter any negativity, would be welcome.

Talleyrand's arrival brought some of the curious from surrounding towns and even as far as Towanda to visit Azilum, and towards the end of the diplomat's stay, another grand ball was held, to which not only residents of Azilum and their friends were invited, but also any of the local residents who wished to come.

Elizabeth and her mother had made new gowns for the occasion, for recent mail deliveries had brought issues of Ackermann's Repository and revealed to them the startling and significant changes in European and English fashions. LaPorte had gifted them the beautiful China silk they had ordered for the gowns, and although Mrs. Franklin allowed her daughter to accept the gift, she had stubbornly insisted on paying for her own bolt of pale blue material.

Likewise, LaPorte's idea of paying off the Franklins' debt to King in exchange for permission to marry sooner had been met with a quiet but firm refusal on Mr. Franklin's part.

'For then I should be in debt to you,' Franklin had objected. 'I will not trade one indenture for another.'

'No, it will be gift,' LaPorte had insisted.

The two men were walking together one afternoon after Sunday dinner at the King home, and had chosen the path by the river for their discussion.

'I cannot allow you to do that,' Franklin had replied. 'Mr. King is a fair and kind employer,' he had added on a sigh. ''Tis the length of time it will take before I am once again my own man that wearies and troubles me,' he admitted solemnly, the lines in his face looking deeper than ever.

'Then, what about taking a position at my timbering and forestry business?' LaPorte had asked. 'You earn wages here, handling King's business, and doing whatever other jobs you can fit in around that, but I could double that salary,' LaPorte had told him, tempting the man. 'Additionally, I have a young man in my employ who would be better suited to doing the work here, as overseer for King's estate. I'll even pay his wages myself, until your debt is cleared, as part of the deal. You would vastly reduce the time until you could pay Mr. King back in full," he explained with hope.

'I do not take charity,' Franklin had said firmly. 'And I will not allow Elizabeth to wed before she is eighteen,' he had added.

''Tis not charity!' LaPorte had exclaimed, becoming quite agitated. Yes, he wanted this to work out, for he desperately wished to marry his beloved Elizabeth. But it seemed to him that Franklin was being intentionally difficult. 'Monsieur Pernaud died last month in that landslide near Liberty Corners and I need a new supervisor.' LaPorte paused. 'King tells me himself your talents are wasted here: you have bookkeeping skills, management skills and a good eye for what other people enjoy doing and do best. You have forestry and timbering experience. You would make a fine supervisor,' he had declared. 'And, the job would carry no commitment from you to allow us to wed before Elizabeth's eighteenth birthday,' he had said reluctantly. But it was meant as an incentive. Once Franklin were working for him, LaPorte thought, they might become better acquainted and

Franklin might object less to the marriage and be willing to allow it to happen before April of 1797.

Franklin had deliberated, and walked a few paces, then gazed for a full minute out at the river, which that day had been green and sparkling in the summer sun. Then he had sighed and his shoulders, which had been very rigid, had slumped. But his face had cleared and he'd looked relieved.

'Your offer of the position of supervisor is a welcome one, and I believe you are correct: I shall make more money and be able to pay Mr. King what I owe him more quickly,' the other man had finally admitted.

LaPorte had been pleased that Franklin had at least taken the job he'd offered. While he understood Franklin's point of view about the debt, he still hoped the man would change his mind, and had told him that he could take all the time he wished to consider his offer, that it would always be available.

Elizabeth and her mother sewed their own gowns for the ball, for frugality had always been their manner even when pennies counted because of the family's debt. They found that the new Regency styles were not only to their liking, they were simpler to make and required much less material. Additionally, Mrs. Franklin was pregnant again, this time with, they hoped, the much anticipated son, and the higher waist would hide the developing bulge nicely.

Elizabeth on the other hand was as slender as ever. Gazing at her daughter one day as they were preparing to do a final fitting for the gowns, Mrs. Franklin sighed: Elizabeth's hips were as narrow as a boy's, she thought, and her bust was only a little more developed. The new Regency style accentuated the latter the best it could, but her oldest daughter had still not developed what Mrs. Franklin thought of as the rounded contours of womanhood. Still, Elizabeth was surely an adult, with monthly reminders of her readiness to be a wife and mother.

"Elizabeth, are you sure?" Mrs. Franklin asked that warm June day. LaPorte's visit to Franklin had been the day before, and both women knew that LaPorte's offer had been rejected although the position in his business had been accepted. The situation, and the offer, had been the topic of much conversation as well as meditation for both parents and daughter.

The two women had brought their sewing out onto King's back veranda where the cool river breezes brought some relief. Elizabeth had arranged chairs in the shade, and they had sat down.

"About what, Mama?" Elizabeth asked, smiling as she adjusted a little cap sleeve on her yellow silk gown. It was woven with yellow silk on the warp and white silk on the weft, so that when Elizabeth moved, it shimmered, and the color changed back and forth, like a marigold in the sun. Just looking at it made her happy, although at the moment she was sadder than usual because of her father's refusal. Every passing day found her longing for Bartholomew increasing, though she took comfort in the fact that if her father's dictum that they wait to wed had been meant to make her lose interest, it was not working.

"About wedding Monsieur LaPorte," her mother said, with a glance at Elizabeth's diamond ring.

It flashed in the light as Elizabeth took a stitch.

"As sure as I've ever been of anything," she replied firmly. "I do wish Papa would let us get married sooner," she added regretfully. "And I wish he had allowed Bartholomew to pay off our debt to Mr. King."

Her mother laid a hand on her belly. "As do I, Elizabeth. But your father..." She sighed. "With the baby coming this winter, it would not be the best time,

Elizabeth, for you to be away: I shall need you here, at home," she added.

Elizabeth nodded: she was aware of that. But she could still wish that things were different.

Her mother sighed again. "Your poor Papa. He works so hard, and wishes so much to clear the debt we owe to Mr. King," she murmured, taking up her stitching again. She was feeling more unwell with this pregnancy than with any of her others and while she tried to tell herself that was a sure sign it was a boy she was carrying, she was most often too tired and ill to really care. As long as the birth was a quick one and the child healthy, she didn't mind if it was another girl they would add to their family, though she knew her husband would be disappointed.

"I know. But his new position in Bartholomew's business will bring in much more money, so Papa should be able to repay the debt quite a bit sooner," Elizabeth replied encouragingly.

Her mother nodded. "'Tis true. But your father feels, well, he is anxious for it to be finished." She paused. "And another child, even a son, was not in the plan," she finished quietly. Another mouth to feed, even if it were a boy, was more expense to keep the Franklins and that meant less money available to pay back on the debt.

Elizabeth was silent a moment, then had her own inspiration. "If Papa would allow me to marry sooner, however, the cost of feeding and clothing me would no longer be his, and the arrival of my baby brother," and here she smiled at her mother, "would not be such an onerous burden," she suggested. Goodness, she thought, what a scheme: Bartholomew's cleverness must be rubbing off on her! "And I would still come and help you with the baby, of course! I would, after all, be living just up the road."

Her mother gave her a solemn look, and Elizabeth was startled to see how old her mother appeared in that moment. Maybe it was the unforgiving daylight, or maybe it was just because she was so tired and felt so unwell. Mrs. Franklin sighed heavily. "Your father—finds it difficult—to let you go," she began slowly. She put down her sewing as though doing that as well as explaining were too much for her. "'Tis that which is, in the main, keeping him from allowing you to marry now, I know it." She paused, and shifted uncomfortably in her chair: really, where were those cooling river breezes? "You have always been his favorite, because you were our first child," she told her daughter, and her voice was soft and sweet. "Parting from you will be a challenge for him."

Indeed, when Franklin had shared Bartholomew's offer, and his refusal, with his wife, Mrs. Franklin had been quite cross with her husband.

'You would wish to be indentured until we are both old?' she had asked him in a scathing whisper. 'You prefer that to being debt free and able to enjoy our lives while we are still young enough to enjoy them?' she had asked. Then she'd placed her husband's hand on her belly, where he'd felt the baby move. 'You want to work yourself into an early grave rather than see your son grow to manhood?' she had finished, knowing that that argument was the finest in her arsenal.

Franklin had bowed his head, and then drawn his wife into an embrace. Against her lace-capped hair, he had whispered, 'Susanna, let us wait until she is eighteen,' he had said. "'Tis only a few more months.' And she had known that he would insist on that, even though the age of consent at that time was much younger.

Now, Elizabeth bowed her head and a hot tear escaped one eye. She quickly brushed it away, not wanting it to mar the silk she worked on. "I think Papa wishes me to be an old maid," Elizabeth said, low, but her words carried an edge. "I think he would prefer it if I never married."

Her mother shook her head, and took up her sewing again. "No, Elizabeth, that is not so. Your Papa just needs time to become used to the idea, but he does, indeed, want to see you happy," she reassured her daughter. "He will do almost anything to be free of the bond," she continued, thinking of the extra odd jobs her husband always took on that meant he was home very little and always tired. "But letting you marry now, well, that he is not willing to do." She sighed again. Then her lips settled in a firm, thin line. "He even asked if I would be willing to sell my ring," Mrs. Franklin muttered, low. "Lord knows this ring is all I have left of my own family," she continued, her eyes flashing with anger as she regarded the fine ruby on her right hand.

"That was great-great grand mama's ring!" Elizabeth said, sounding shocked that her father would have even thought about selling it, let alone actually suggesting it.

The family knew the tale well: Susanna Brown Franklin's mother had inherited the ring from her mother who had inherited the ring from her mother. That lady, Elizabeth's great-great grandmother had been Chief Lady in Waiting to Queen Anne, who had, as James II's younger daughter, ruled England from 1702 until her death in 1714. According to family legend, the Queen had gifted her Lady in Waiting with the large ruby set in gold upon her death, and the ring had been passed down ever since within the family.

Now, Elizabeth's mother nodded, and polished the ring against the cloth of her skirt. "Yes. I will not part with it, until I give it to you," she told her daughter with a determined smile.

Chapter Thirty-Three

July brought its usual heat, the departure of Talleyrand, and news from Belgium that Talon's wife was gravely ill.

"I must return, even if I die in the attempt," Talon told LaPorte solemnly. Travel to Europe for those on the traitors' list was still chancy. Talon was packing a small valise and planning to leave the next morning, saying he would send for the rest of his personal items once he'd reached Brussels safely.

"Ah, my friend, I understand completely, but I wish —I shall miss you," LaPorte finished quietly, and handed Talon a pile of neck stocks which had been hastily laundered, dried and folded neatly. "You will not be here for my wedding," he said sadly. "I would have wished you to stand up with me," he added, an unusually rueful smile on his lips.

Talon gave his good friend an arch look. "By rights, you should already be married, my friend, and I would have been proud to stand up with you." He sighed. "I do not understand Franklin's delay," he muttered, jamming a couple of shirts into the valise with little regard for creasing. "You are an excellent match—older than Miss Franklin, to be sure, but hardly so old that you would not make a fine husband. And you adore that girl," he added firmly, this time stowing a couple of balled-up pairs of hose in a corner of his valise. "What more could a father wish for?" he finished rhetorically.

"I think Franklin just is finding it hard to part with Elizabeth," LaPorte replied sadly. "And that does not surprise me, for he has known her her entire life, and she is such a joy to be with, I can only imagine the delight living with her must bring. I have only known her for a year and yet I feel a pang here," he touched his chest, "each time we must say *adieu*," he told Talon. "So I think I understand what her father must feel." He sighed. "Still, I wish he would change his mind."

Talon, whom LaPorte had told of his idea to offer to pay off Franklin's debt in exchange for the lifting of the embargo on an immediate marriage with Elizabeth, nodded solemnly. "I wish that too, Bart," he told his friend. "You are a very kind, and compassionate man," he added frankly. "I would have liked to have seen you settled and happy before I leave."

"Ah, well, that can't be helped: you must go to your wife, now, and I will be all right: 'tis only a few more months now, until Elizabeth is eighteen," LaPorte finished, sounding determinedly cheery.

Talon gave him a look, and continued packing.

"I'm sorry you never did get a chance to build your hunting lodge," LaPorte continued. He had been folding and re-folding a waistcoat as they talked and now handed it to Talon.

He took it with a smile and fitted it into the top of the valise. "I know, my friend. But family comes first." He sighed. "I had hoped my wife and children could someday follow me here and love it as I do. But..." he trailed off, then set his mouth in a thin, determined line, and clicked his valise shut.

He planned to ride hard the entire way to Philadelphia, feeling that if he rode night and day, changing horses as needed at various inns, he could make better time than even the Durham boat. Additionally, the road over the hills that surrounded Azilum had been much improved and many people were now using it to travel, in addition to the mail coming twice a month.

The letter containing the news of Mme. Talon's illness had only been six weeks old. Talon had no way of knowing if his wife still lived, but he vowed he would waste no time in arriving at her side.

He decided that since LaPorte had been his 'right hand' while he had been the colony's Director, he should become Director in his stead. He had already sent word of his decision to Keating and the others who were still invested in Azilum, noting that he felt under LaPorte's leadership the small French settlement would continue to thrive. There had been no objection to the appointment from the other investors.

"You'll be moving in here, now," Talon told LaPorte as he hefted his valise.

"Ah, no, Antoine, for you will return some day, surely?" LaPorte objected.

But Talon shook his head. "No, my friend. I doubt if I shall return. If I make it safely to Brussels I shall remain there. Azilum, now, is yours. I have every confidence that you will make it as great as ever."

And so, next morning, Talon departed and LaPorte moved most of his belongings from his house—which he'd never really lived in, having spent most of his time at the Maison, with Talon—to the larger edifice. If his four bed chambered house with the garden and the view of the river had seemed empty without Elizabeth, the Maison was nearly unbearably so. Except for the fact that the servants kept bustling about night and day, and for the fact that Mme. d'Autremont, the Homets and other good friends stopped by frequently, LaPorte would have sunk into a depression.

But such was not his nature. And so he made the best of things. And Elizabeth, too, visited as much as she could. LaPorte continued the tradition of dances and 'evenings' and various amusements and summer waned, and autumn arrived.

Elizabeth had, by then, begun to plan her small spring wedding with her close girlfriends Clarice and Mathilde. She'd also made a good start sewing her trousseau and with their help had amassed quite an array of pretty gowns in the new high waisted style, a new cloak, petticoats, and several new chemises in silk and linen.

Both girls would be bridesmaids, as would Rebecca, the oldest of her three younger sisters. Elizabeth was still determined to marry Bartholomew in April, immediately after her birthday, which was just a week after Bartholomew's. The weather, she thought, would be fine if perhaps a bit chilly, and she had begun work on a new pale pink brocaded silk gown that was to be her wedding gown. The lace makers in the settlement had already woven the fine net that would veil her head and were working on the intricate lace that would border it all the way around to where it fanned out in a small train over her gown. LaPorte had given the brocaded silk to his fiancée, and had charged her bridesmaids only what the material for their new dresses had cost him.

A letter from Talon had come in October: he had arrived safely in Brussels. His wife was recovering, he wrote, though still poorly, but his children were well, as was he. LaPorte was much cheered by this, and wrote back immediately, filling Talon in on all the doings of Azilum. He missed his friend a great deal, but found consolation in carrying on the good work they had begun. Franklin was proving, as LaPorte had thought, a very good supervisor, which left LaPorte free to check on his other interests and throw himself into his new position as Director of Azilum.

On one of the darkest, coldest days of early January, 1797, Mrs. Franklin's labor pains began. The midwife was sent for, as well as the settlement's doctor, and although it was not a first baby, the labor was long and very hard.

"Another sign that it is a boy," gasped Mrs. Franklin as she struggled with another contraction.

Elizabeth wiped her mother's forehead with a cool cloth. "We all hope so, Mama," she reassured her.

"Boys' heads are bigger than girls' and often cause problems," the doctor murmured. Mrs. Franklin may have successfully birthed four girls, but in his estimation, her hips were on the narrow side even if the chubbiness of approaching middle age disguised that.

The midwife, who had been examining Mrs. Franklin yet again, stood now, and stretched her back out. "That's true, Monsieur le Docteur, but this child is breech, and that is a bigger problem," she declared, explaining that the baby was trying to be born feet first.

"We must turn him," the doctor said immediately, and the midwife agreed, although it was a very chancy procedure. However, if mother and child were to survive, it was the only one.

The child, when it was finally born, was a boy, but tragically, he had suffocated when the umbilical cord had wrapped around his neck. It was possible that the manoeuvre that the doctor and midwife had applied to turn him into the correct head first birth position had tightened the cord, too, and ultimately caused his death moments before he was born.

Mrs. Franklin nearly died herself from loss of blood and exhaustion, after nearly two days of hard labor and significant birth trauma.

Elizabeth, her sisters and her father as well as the doctor and midwife, took turns standing vigil at Mrs. Franklin's bedside. A week passed, and then two, and the doctor and midwife finally declared that Mrs. Franklin would live, perhaps, if she rested in bed for the foreseeable future.

"She is extremely weak, and has lost a great deal of blood," the doctor explained to Mr. Franklin and Elizabeth. "She needs 'round the clock care if she is to live."

LaPorte had visited every day during the crisis and had done what he could to help out around the house since nearly everyone was in attendance at the sick bed. He had even helped Mr. Franklin dig the small, unmarked grave for his son and bury him at the edge of the settlement's small graveyard. And, knowing that Elizabeth's mother needed nutritious and easily palatable sustenance, he had ordered the cooks at the Maison to make a large pot of broth from the bones of beef cattle, pigs, sheep and chickens as they were slaughtered, and to extract the precious bone marrow and mash it into the broth. Every day, he had sent a servant from the Maison over to the King house with a pottery tureen of this broth for Mrs. Franklin. Both doctor and midwife said the special broth had made all the difference in their patient's recovery.

Now, it was late February, and Elizabeth sat with Bartholomew in Mr. King's small parlor. She explained that although her mother would probably live, she would be recovering for several months. "Were it not for your excellent soup, she may have died," she told her beau with tears of gratitude in her eyes. "But as it is, I am needed here until—until she is well again, or as well as she can be," she finished.

Yes, her younger sisters, especially Rebecca, who was now 14, could pitch in and help run the household and do the chores that had been her mother's portion of the family's indebtedness to Mr. King. But Elizabeth felt she could not leave until she knew her mother and sisters and father would truly be able to manage without her.

"I understand, my Elizabeth, your Mama needs you, as does your Papa," LaPorte replied gently.

"But—Bart—you need me too, and I need you, and I am torn," Elizabeth anguished. "I do so long to be your wife," she whispered, clasping his hands tightly.

"And I your husband. You do not know how much," LaPorte replied solemnly. "But if you did not feel so for your poor family, you would not be the tender hearted, kind, loving woman I adore," he concluded simply. "And so, we will wait until your mother is recovered and you can come to the marriage bed with joy, and not sadness, in your heart."

Chapter Thirty-Four

Spring came, and then summer, and Mrs. Franklin improved, but very slowly. Sometimes, Elizabeth wondered if her mother were intentionally wallowing in her invalid status to keep her from marrying LaPorte. But since her mother had never expressed any reluctance to see her marry, except for her reservations regarding LaPorte's age, Elizabeth dismissed that thought as unworthy of both her and her mother.

Azilum did well under its new Director, for LaPorte was a forward-looking man. Now, in addition to making sure his own business interests were thriving, he brought his attention to detail and his talent for trade to Azilum's ventures and soon the colony was turning a profit, albeit a small one.

The political situation in France had not changed. A few more exiles arrived at Azilum's gates: they bought homes or had them built, and were soon part of the settlement. They farmed or engaged in skilled workmanship, for Azilum now had three carpenters, two blacksmiths, a silversmith who also did pewter work, three mills, extensive crop farming, sheep and cattle along with goats, pigs and chickens, two weavers who made wool rugs and cloth as well as linen material, a seamstress, the milliners and shops that had been original to the settlement, as well as le Marchand. Maple sugaring had proven to be a good cash export for the colony, since a fine stand of sugar maples on the property yielded gallons of the sweet liquid and the settlers soon learned how to boil it down and filter it into syrup. The honeybees still only provided enough honey for Azilum itself, but the apiary was doing well, at least. Timbering and quarrying were always in demand, and the potash, pitch and other byproducts some clever residents of

Azilum had figured out how to make were also in demand all along the river.

LaPorte suspected that it would only be a matter of time before other trading posts secured their own supply of these unique commodities, but while Azilum was still the only purveyor of them, he intended to make the most of it.

As Talon had, LaPorte made sure to arrange plenty of entertainment for the residents of his village. Some, like him, had been there several years by now, and were tiring of the area's natural beauty and relative security. LaPorte knew that most of Azilum's residents were not, as he was, truly invested in their new country and settlement. They were merely biding time until they could return to France. If that time ever came. They refused to give up hope, which was, he supposed, to be commended. But this meant that they were largely unhappy with their situation, and easily overtaken by ennui.

The entertainments combatted that, to some degree. LaPorte arranged outdoor dances in fine weather at the pavilion Talon had ordered built just off the town square. Concerts were another feature of some of the 'evenings' held at the Maison, just as Talon had done. During the day, inhabitants of Azilum who did not work went riding, or boating or picnicking in good weather. When the skies poured or it was cold they gathered at the Maison or at one of the inns that had become established now, and shared a meal, whiling away the afternoons playing cards. Ladies had sewing circles and also began to gather in groups on dry days to visit the shops at Azilum and then enjoy the mid day meal together.

LaPorte took Elizabeth out riding a couple of times a week, for she loved horses and was becoming a competent rider under his tutelage. The fresh air and getting away from the sickroom and her chores at the King house were also a boon to her. Just being together, while it was still a kind of torment, was sweet for both of them, and every Sunday after church, the Franklins would have Sunday Dinner at the Maison with LaPorte and whoever else happened to be staying at the mansion.

Mrs. Franklin, who was no longer bedridden by the end of the summer, still did not travel out of the house, and so her daughters took turns staying with her while the family went to church and dinner, and LaPorte always sent back a large hamper full of delicious food for both Mrs. Franklin and the family member who had stayed behind to look after her.

In November, when the Americans celebrated Thanksgiving, the residents of Azilum followed suit and at the King home much cause for thanks was to be had, for Mrs. Franklin was now walking unassisted and able to spend nearly an entire, normal day at the house without taking to her bed. She did not engage in any strenuous labor as she had before: that was done by the girls, including Elizabeth. None of them had ever been a stranger to hard work. But Mrs. Franklin was able to do mending and sewing and to help look after her youngest child, now two years old.

She had also, for the first time since her confinement before her son's birth, attended the brief church service that had been held that morning, for the weather was fine and she had been well wrapped by her solicitous family.

King and LaPorte joined the Franklins at the King home that mid day. Wonderful smells were emanating from the cook house and wafting into the clear cold air. The King cook as well as the older Franklin daughters were busy preparing roast wild turkey, vegetables, and special desserts. That evening there was to be a 'Harvest Home' celebration at the Maison, including music and dancing: not a formal ball, just a dance, but everyone was excited about it and planning to show off their new winter clothes.

Mrs. Franklin, who had not been allowed to so much as stir a pot in preparation for the dinner, had met LaPorte in the front parlor along with King, and then asked to speak with LaPorte privately. She had brought him into her husband's study, where Franklin sat behind his desk.

As LaPorte entered the room, Franklin rose, came around, and offered his hand.

"You have been a most patient man, Monsieur LaPorte," Franklin said.

Mrs. Franklin sat carefully on a small chair and looked at the two men, who then also took their seats.

LaPorte smiled, but said nothing.

"All these long months, you and Elizabeth have waited," Mrs. Franklin said.

"I know Elizabeth was most concerned that she be here to help all of you while you recovered," LaPorte returned. "And I agreed with her that here was her first duty," he finished with a slight smile.

"Your generosity in naming me to the position of Supervisor of your timbering and forestry business has enabled us to not only get through this time when Susanna was unwell," Franklin continued with a smile for his wife, "but enabled us to pay more towards the debt we owe Mr. King. You were correct: I should be able to be a free man once again sooner than I would have without your assistance. I am grateful," Franklin said.

"I am grateful to you, because your ability in running my business has allowed me the time to focus on being Azilum's Director, a position I had not anticipated I would need to assume. But with Talon's departure..." LaPorte replied genuinely. "So you see, it worked out well!" he declared with his typical joviality.

He still wondered why the Franklins had sought him out specifically: this day was a celebration, and he had hoped to spend most of it with Elizabeth, and he had yet to even say hello to her.

"My wife's illness, and the loss of our son," Franklin began, and his voice broke, "has made me realize a few things." He paused. "I should have realized this before, but I was blinded by my tender feelings for Elizabeth. And by my own selfishness," he admitted.

LaPorte was silent.

Mrs. Franklin gave her husband's hand an encouraging squeeze.

"It is clear to everyone who looks upon Elizabeth, and you, how happy you are together and how happy you make each other. If you both still wish it—" Franklin began.

"And I cannot imagine it would be otherwise—" interjected Mrs. Franklin, who gave LaPorte an unusually sweet smile that reminded him of Elizabeth's—

"Then you have our blessing to marry as soon as you both wish it," Franklin finished.

LaPorte was stunned. He had known that, with Mrs. Franklin's recovery the days until he could marry Elizabeth had to be numbered. But he hadn't expected such support from her parents, or for them to agree to the marriage so soon.

"I—I thank you, both," he stammered.

"'Tis we who thank you, for everything you have done," Mrs. Franklin said gently. "You have been a real friend to us, through thick and thin, and our daughter could find no finer man to wed, I am sure of it," she concluded.

"I—I shall—have you told Elizabeth?" LaPorte asked.

Franklin shook his head, and smiled as well. "We thought to leave that happy task to you," he told LaPorte.

"I shall ask her, then, if I may, before dinner, when she wishes the wedding to be," LaPorte replied, his voice joyous and his smile wide. "Perhaps spring time!"

LaPorte drew Elizabeth out of the cook house and her duties preparing that day's meal, and brought her along the covered walkway and into the main house, then into King's small parlor which was unoccupied. He told her what her parents had discussed with him, and her cry of joy was audible throughout the house.

"Oh, but Bart, that is wonderful!" she exclaimed, taking both his hands in her. Happy tears shimmered in her eyes.

"'Tis, indeed, my dearest one. Now you must name the date," LaPorte demanded indulgently. "Do you wish a spring wedding? The apple and pear trees in blossom would be lovely..." he said, referencing the colony's extensive orchards.

"Spring?" Elizabeth echoed. "You wish to wait until spring?" Her voice was faint.

"No! I wish to marry you this very day," LaPorte reassured her immediately with a chuckle. "But I believe the curate is otherwise engaged," he told her and Elizabeth let out a sigh.

"I thought, perhaps, after all this time, you..." she began in a shaky voice, and wiped a tear from her cheek.

"Time has altered nothing, except it has increased my anticipation," LaPorte said, and proved what he said with a kiss that left them both aching and breathless.

"Then—let us speak with Father Carles tomorrow, and ask him when he might be able to hold our wedding!" declared Elizabeth insistently.

Chapter Thirty-Five

December 11, 1797, was a clear, crisp Monday, and that morning was the morning of Bartholomew LaPorte's wedding to Elizabeth Franklin. Elizabeth and her bridesmaids wore their fine dresses that they had made nearly a year before, and Mrs. Franklin, leaning heavily on her husband's arm, walked slowly to her seat in the front pew of Azilum's chapel. Nearly everyone from the thriving community attended the wedding: it had been so long in coming, and both Elizabeth and Bartholomew were such favorites of the settlers that to miss it would have been almost unthinkable.

Following the service, a large wedding breakfast was held at the Maison, which of course was now Elizabeth's home as well as Bartholomew's. It was decorated with greens in anticipation of Christmas, which was just two weeks away. Beeswax candles stood tall in crystal holders and candelabra, and mirrored sconces reflected their gentle light into the large well appointed rooms.

The newly-wedded couple were fêted with champagne, and the cooks at the Maison had outdone themselves with an array of delicious foods. Dancing followed, and the party continued well into the afternoon, until the cool blue of a December evening drew in, and the last guests departed.

The servants had prepared Bartholomew's bed chamber in advance of the wedding night: Elizabeth's clothing and personal belongings had been brought to the Maison and installed in a room connected to the master bed chamber on one side by a small door. This was to be her dressing room. Bartholomew had an identical space on the other side of the bed chamber.

The bed chamber had been cleaned thoroughly, bed curtains laundered and re-hung, and linens changed. New pillows were brought in, roundly stuffed with goose feathers, and a new mattress piled high with the same adorned the rope bed, which was pulled very tight. Chamber maids had hung bunches of dried lavender here and there in the bed chamber and more new beeswax candles had been placed in all the sconces and holders. A fire, freshly kindled, blazed and crackled comfortably from the marble fireplace and warmed the room nicely.

Elizabeth had chosen one of the chamber maids at the Maison to function as her lady's maid, for now she had no sisters to help lace her stays. However, on this evening when she and her new husband retired to their bed chamber after a supper of leftovers from the party and more champagne, she did not engage the services of her new attendant: Bartholomew had whispered to her earlier that day that he wished to undress her himself.

The intimacies of marriage, and of the marriage bed, were surprising to Elizabeth, but also extremely pleasurable. From the moment that she felt Bartholomew's fingers deftly undoing her stays, to its removal and the feel of his nakedness against her silk chemise, to that article's disappearance and the sparking warmth she felt when they touched skin to skin all along the length of their bodies, to what followed, it was all most thrilling, she found, and most satisfying.

She had not been prepared by her mother for what were often referred to as the 'rigors of the marriage bed.' She had, of course, seen farm animals mating, but it had only been the whispered discussions and speculations—many of them wildly incorrect—that she had had with Clarice and Mathilde, which had given Elizabeth any inkling of the pleasure which could be garnered.

Both of her French friends had been brought up by mothers who had been reared at the French Court. Thus, they knew all about flirtation and courtship, something which had stood Elizabeth in good stead during the long dreary months that she'd had to wait to wed. Clarice and Mathilde had also known something of lovemaking although Mathilde, especially, had been given to somewhat incomprehensible stories and flights of fancy.

'I heard that the man sprouts horns and rides his bride like a stallion rides a mare,' she had told Elizabeth breathlessly once, when their conversation had turned to the latter's upcoming wedding and wedding night.

'No,' Clarice had corrected Mathilde. 'I heard from Maman and you know she and Grandmère were friends of la Pompadour,' she had said, speaking of Louis XV's official mistress, 'that first the woman must—...' and here she had whispered something that had sent all three girls into fits of embarrassed giggling.

In fact, on her wedding night, Elizabeth discovered that only some of what her friends had told her was true. And she also discovered that all of it was wonderful: exciting, perhaps a bit scary at first, but wonderful. And the way she felt afterwards! More relaxed and yet more alive than she had ever felt in her life.

In the early hours of the next morning while it was still dark grey outside, Elizabeth and Bartholomew found each other for a third time. When they had finished, Bartholomew leaned over and lit a candle, placing it on a small table near the head of the bed.

"I want to show you something," he whispered.

Elizabeth, lying back on her downy pillow, replete and relaxed, giggled. What more could he have to show her, she wondered?

Catching her eye and reading her mind, Bartholomew chuckled. "No, my dearest one, this is something else," he murmured, and reached around his neck, and removed the piece of leather cord on which the small pouch was fastened. He was never without that pouch. Even making love to his new bride, it had hung suspended around his neck.

But now it was time to share with her his great and wonderful secret.

At her husband's action, Elizabeth sat up in bed, pulling the soft linen sheets to her chest and watching him in the candle light. Her hair spilled over her shoulders and down her back and she split her attention between the small pouch her husband held and its mysterious contents, and his own nakedness. He seemed completely unselfconscious and she reveled in being able to examine every inch of his nicely muscled, fit physique.

Bartholomew opened the little pouch, then reached for her hand. He turned it palm up, then kissed her palm.

A shiver of desire ran through her and she looked at him beseechingly in the candle light.

"In a bit, ma petite," he assured her with a cocky smile. For him, the marriage bed was turning out to be everything he'd hoped, and more, and he was eager to continue.

But now, he grew serious. Carefully, he upended the little pouch against Elizabeth's upturned hand and poured its contents out. Or, most of its contents: there were still so many diamonds that Elizabeth's single small hand could not hold them all.

She gasped. "But—what??"

Bartholomew grinned. "'Tis my inheritance, I suppose you'd call it," he told her, and related the story of his and Talon's escape from France. She had heard most of that before, except for the detail about Talon's own fortune, smuggled out of France and shared with LaPorte.

"Oh, my darling Bart, how wonderful!" Elizabeth had exclaimed, finally understanding how her husband could have always been so assured about money. Yes, his businesses were doing well, but there had always been another layer of security, it had seemed, an assuredness. And now she understood why.

"And there's a bit more," Bartholomew said, carefully pouring the diamonds back into the pouch and hanging it around his neck.

"More?" Elizabeth echoed faintly. She eased back into the pillows.

"I met with Mr. King just before our ceremony, and paid off your family's debt to him. Your father is now a free man. Call it my wedding gift to you," Bartholomew said, low.

Elizabeth said nothing, but tears sprang to her eyes, and began to roll down her cheeks.

"And I told your father—you may have noticed, we disappeared together during the party? No? No matter," Bartholomew continued. "I told him what I'd done and then I gave him the deed to my house, for I no longer need it, and this way he and your mother and your sisters can move right in, for I've had it cleaned and freshened. It is sparsely furnished so they can add whatever they'd like, and this way," he said again, hurrying on as though he wanted to get everything said quickly, before his bride could object, "your family will be just a short walk away, instead of a carriage ride to Mr. King's or wherever your father might have built a house."

Elizabeth just stared at him. "You —gave—my family your house?"

Bartholomew nodded. "Are you not pleased, *ma petite*?" he asked, concerned.

"Oh, Bart, I am overjoyed!" she replied feelingly. "Such generosity, such kindness!" she exclaimed. "I am overwhelmed," she added, throwing her arms around him and peppering his face with kisses.

He chuckled. "If you are pleased, I am pleased," he told her happily. "Now, dry your tears, and let me see that smile…"

Chapter Thirty-Six

During the summer of 1798, the settlers at Azilum, like most of the residents of the United States, were preoccupied with the news from abroad, for Napoleon had occupied Cairo and waged the Battle of the Pyramids, defeating the Ottomans. In late August, they heard about the Battle of the Nile in which Lord Admiral Nelson was wounded, but led the British forces to victory over the French nonetheless.

Such unrest, coupled with Napoleon's apparent megalomaniac wish to rule all of Europe and the Middle East succeeded in dashing even the faintest of hopes of a return to France that some few settlers at Azilum may yet have fostered.

Faced with this, LaPorte outdid himself in keeping the little colony running as smoothly as he could, and keeping the shops and traders supplied and happy. However, even with Elizabeth's help, it was an uphill battle. Many of the residents had finally lost heart, and murmured more and more often about packing it all in and moving, if not back to France, then to Philadelphia, or to other French-dominated settlements that were less rural and longer-established than Azilum. Elizabeth was a natural diplomat, and usually able to persuade others to be more sanguine about their and the colony's prospects.

She had assembled around herself a coterie of some of the leading young women, both single and married, at Azilum and nearby. They met at least twice a week for sewing circles and shopping excursions that did accomplish needlework or the acquisition of goods, but accomplished more with lively discussion, exchange of ideas, and news about practically everyone at Azilum.

Elizabeth greatly enjoyed this society. As the oldest child, she had been her mother's right hand and while she had had friends, certainly, as a girl, her duties at home had been the priority. Now, she had several servants to assist her with her daily work, which left her free time to socialize with her friends, visit her family—but on her terms—and enjoy riding, picnicking, dancing and social events at her leisure. She took up watercolors and spent much time trying to capture the beauty of Azilum's surroundings.

Her position now as the *de facto* First Lady of Azilum also made her the leader, especially among Azilum's women, in most things. She was the one to share news of the Egyptian Campaign, for she and Bartholomew read every newspaper almost the moment it was delivered. They discussed the events they read about, too, so when Elizabeth disseminated the news to her friends at their gatherings, she presented a balanced and informed view. Many of the other ladies had, of course, also read about Napoleon, Nelson and the rest, but they found exchanging ideas with the others in their group to be most enlightening.

Bartholomew had read about, and shared with Elizabeth, the development of coal gas as a fuel for lamps: a man in Cornwall had lit his house with such lamps. The small article in the Wyalusing Courier, a local newspaper that arrived at the colony the same day it was printed, that Bartholomew read suggested that the 'thermolamp' might have larger applications.

"Can you imagine, *ma petite*, having all the homes and streets lit with such lamps?" he asked Elizabeth the morning that they read about the invention. "We could turn night into day, and make work more productive, and make it safer for people to walk abroad in the evening. And it would be so beautiful!" he sighed.

Elizabeth had smiled at him, and agreed that it would be very useful and no doubt attractive. "I wonder if it has an odor, like our oil lamps do?" she queried with a slight frown.

At her next sewing circle, held on the Maison's front terrace, which was shady and caught any breeze at all, and so more comfortable on warm summer days, the ladies debated the relative merits of the new gas lamp versus the familiar oil lamp. Most thought that if the gas were easier to obtain, cheaper than oil, and had no smell, or less of a smell, it would be a good thing.

"I still prefer beeswax candles, they smell so lovely," noted Clarice Boulogne, who was now Clarice duMaurier, having wed that spring. Elizabeth had been one of Clarice's bridesmaids and had been happy to stand up for her friend, who had been walking out with Monsieur duMaurier for several months. He was a skilled patisserieur, and ran a specialty shop next door to Azilum's bakery. Given the settlers' taste for fancy pastry, he was always busy. Word had spread beyond Azilum of his delicious confections, too, such that twice a week he sent orders to upscale shops in Towanda, Wyalusing and Tunkhannock.

"I agree. I love the smell of beeswax," Elizabeth confirmed with a smile.

"I should imagine that, erm, at the present time, you are particularly sensitive to odors and tastes, is that not so, Madame?" asked Maria Homet with a sly look at their hostess. Gathered together that day were Elizabeth, Clarice, Maria, Elizabeth's sister Rebecca, Mathilde, Marie d'Ohet LeFevre, and Julieanne Scheufeldt, the daughter of one of the original settlers of the land that was now owned by Azilum.

Elizabeth looked over at Maria and bit her lip. She and Bartholomew had told no one, not even her family, yet, that she was pregnant. It came as no surprise to either of the newlyweds, given how attracted they were to each other and how frequently, now that they were married, they indulged that attraction.

She fingered the string of gold beads at her neck, a gift from Bartholomew when she had told him of her condition, and smiled.

"We were waiting, to be sure everything was as it should be," she said softly. "And the styles now are so forgiving," she added with a smile. In her lap, not only her Empire style dress but also the embroidery she held hid the firm and not inconsiderable swell of her belly. By her reckoning she was five months along, and due in early November.

Her friends exclaimed with delight, then, and asked if they might share the good news. A little embarrassed by all the fuss, for she still conducted herself as she always had, Elizabeth said that yes, they might share the news, but asked that Rebecca go right away to tell their mother and father. "I wouldn't want them to hear it from someone else," she told her sister, who, happy to leave sewing for any reason, sped away, smiling happily.

Elizabeth had, indeed, changed very little about her daily routine once she was certain that she carried a child. She had ordered the new 'short stays' from le Marchand: a revolutionary style, this corset stopped below the bosom at approximately the place that the Empire style gown's waist sat. The short stays effectively produced the correct silhouette in the new style gowns, but left the lower part of the torso unconstricted except for the wearer's chemise. Although many women just enlarged their regular, longer stays during pregnancy by inserting sections of material, Elizabeth felt that with the current styles, the longer stays were not needed in general, and particularly if one were pregnant.

Her chemises had fit well enough until just recently. She had been considering enlarging them, too, by inserting strips of cloth around the middle, but

Bartholomew had surprised her with a gift of several silk and cotton chemises in a looser, larger size.

'What extravagance!' Elizabeth had exclaimed, scolding him but pleased nonetheless. 'I could have altered a few of my own,' she had added.

'*Certes*, but then you would need new ones any way once the babe is born,' Bartholomew had told her with a nod. 'Now, you have special ones to use now, and it is to be hoped, many times in the future,' he had whispered lovingly. They both wished for several children, and Elizabeth, thus far at least, was enjoying being *enceinte.*

It had been late evening when they had been preparing for bed, and Bartholomew had followed his gift and his rationalization of the expense by helping Elizabeth to shed her tight chemise and then lovingly dropping one of the new silk ones over her head. It flowed beautifully and comfortably over her expanding belly and both she and Bartholomew had been delighted.

She still planned to make a pair of 'jumps' or 'jupes' which were essentially padded material that laced as tightly or loosely as the wearer wished, but which were generally unrestrictive, for the last month or so of her pregnancy. For that, now that she had Bart's gift, she could use the oldest of her old silk chemises, stuffed with carded wool from one of Azilum's sheep. She wasn't quite certain of the pattern for the jumps, but she knew her mother could help her make them.

She still walked several miles every day, visiting people in the village, stopping at shops and seeing friends. She still rode, too, and told Bart that she had ridden before she'd realized she was pregnant, so clearly it did her and the child no harm. She still went on picnics and she still danced, for she loved dancing, and she wanted to do all the things she enjoyed while she still could. She suspected that some activities would become uncomfortable as the birth drew close.

Chapter Thirty-Seven

Bartholomew had written to his friend Talon to share the good news of the start of his family, but on the evening of November 3, 1798 he wished more than ever that his good friend were with him at the Maison. Elizabeth was in labor, her mother, the doctor and midwife in attendance, and Bartholomew, who had barely spent an hour away from his bride since their wedding, was agonizing in his dressing room, just one door away.

The doctor had suggested that Bartholomew at least go downstairs to one of the reception rooms, or to his study, or a parlor, or better still, to the Franklins' home or another friend's. He had promised to send word, but Bartholomew had been adamant.

'She is my life, my breath, my soul. I can no more leave her than I would leave myself,' he had said, and stubbornly taken up his vigil in the little antechamber.

All he had heard since the early evening when Elizabeth, who had said she'd felt too unwell to have mid day dinner as usual, had taken to her bed, had been running feet as servants fetched and carried, and the occasional whimper from the bed chamber next door, along with snatches of low conversations.

Even though Elizabeth had lain down in their comfy bed originally, her discomfort had resolved over the space of a couple of hours into concentrated pains. Once that happened, she found that walking around the bedchamber, holding on to her lady's maid for support, was the best thing to do, and shortly after she began that, her water broke and her mother, the midwife and doctor were sent for.

Bartholomew heard the tall case clock downstairs in the foyer strike midnight. Then one in the morning. There were still murmurings and steps from the bed chamber and in the hallway and finally, he went to the connecting door between his dressing room and the bed chamber he shared with Elizabeth, and opened the door silently.

Elizabeth was sitting in a wooden birthing chair which he supposed had been brought in at some point: part of the fetching and carrying, he was certain. He had no idea where it was from, but would later learn that it belonged to the Franklin family.

Surrounding his wife were her mother, her lady's maid, the doctor, the midwife, and two other female servants of the Maison. Quantities of freshly laundered and folded linens stood at the ready. Elizabeth was grasping her lady's maid's hand with such force, Bartholomew wondered if the girl's bones wouldn't break. Her mother stood behind her, rubbing her shoulders and whispering encouragement.

His Elizabeth had a determined look on her face: her long hair swept back and fastened to fall out of the way, down her back. Her chemise and her face were both wet with perspiration, and the fire was roaring in the fireplace, making the room almost uncomfortably warm. Still, Elizabeth was the most important, and she wore only her silk chemise. She sighed as the labor pain passed, and then she looked up and saw him.

"Bart!" she called, and held out one hand to him. She sounded glad, and frightened all at once.

"Oh, non, Monsieur, you..." began the doctor, stepping quickly away and trying to keep Bartholomew from advancing towards his wife.

But Bartholomew firmly, yet gently, set him aside and went to Elizabeth. He grasped her other hand and stood flanking the birthing chair as Elizabeth felt the next pain begin and screwed up her face with the effort.

"Push, Madame," encouraged the midwife, who had emerged from beneath Elizabeth's chemise. "Monsieur, it is not usual for the husband to attend," she commented curtly to Bartholomew.

He merely shrugged. "I was with my wife at the beginning of this, and like her, I shall see it to the conclusion," he said softly, but his tone brooked no countermanding.

The midwife gave a grudging smile and returned to her task, thinking to herself that in a way, she wished all husbands loved and respected their wives as much as Monsieur LaPorte did.

"There's my good girl, Elizabeth, you can do this," whispered her mother. The lace lappets on the woman's cap fluttered as she bent to her daughter's ear.

Elizabeth took a deep breath, and gave another push.

"I can see the head, Madame," the midwife said a few moments later. "One more push, maybe two," she told Elizabeth.

The doctor peered at Elizabeth and nodded his concurrence.

Elizabeth nodded. She pushed again. Then, for the first time, she cried out.

"*Ma petite!*" Bartholomew exclaimed anxiously. He felt helpless. He had promised to always keep Elizabeth safe and unharmed yet here she was in agony because of something he—well, they—had done. How could he bear it? How could she?

"One more—the shoulders—..." murmured the doctor, who was again peering under Elizabeth's chemise, his head next to the midwife's.

Elizabeth took another breath and gave another push even though she cried out again, and then sobbed. But seconds after the pain when she felt her skin tear to allow her baby to emerge, she heard a lusty cry.

The midwife caught the child and quickly poked a finger around his mouth and up his nostrils to clear them, then she gave him a little smack on his flank. Reflexively, the child cried, and the satisfied midwife busied herself tying off the umbilical cord and wrapping the infant in one of the clean, soft lengths of material.

"You have a boy, a son," she told Bartholomew and Elizabeth. "A fine, big boy," she added. The baby was, indeed, very big: surprising, because Elizabeth had not gained a great deal of weight or even looked full term. She had been, as the midwife murmured to the doctor, '*tout bébé.*'

Wordlessly, Elizabeth stretched out one hand and the midwife deposited the bundle in the crook of one arm, for she still held Bartholomew's hand fast in her other hand.

"We have a son, Bart," Elizabeth sighed.

Tears glimmered in both their eyes.

Chapter Thirty-Eight

It had been a difficult birth in the sense that Elizabeth's hips were, as her mother had always said, very narrow, and the baby, a healthy big boy they called 'John' had weighed nearly four kilos, quite large, even for a boy. But Elizabeth recovered after a time, although she did not heal completely until the following spring.

She took great delight in nursing little John, eschewing the ready services of the wet nurse who had been called in. Some of the grander (and older) ladies had taken advantage of this option, provided by some of the younger women in the settlement, when they had birthed their children. The belief was that without nursing, new mothers could fit back into their corseted clothes more quickly, and the children seemed to be done no harm by having another woman nurse them for the first several months or so. However, Elizabeth chose not to do this, and decided to wear padded stays rather than boned corsets until such time as John was weaned to make it all easier.

It was a quiet, but joyful Christmas for the LaPortes, and nearly everyone in Azilum and the surrounding area came to visit and congratulate the young couple on the start of their family. John was baptized in Azilum's little chapel by Monseigneur Carles and afterwards the LaPortes gave a big party at the Maison where everyone ate, drank and danced until the early hours of the late December morning. The baby, and Elizabeth, who was certainly not yet recovered enough to dance, retired early for the night, but Bartholomew remained, although he did not dance. He was the consummate host, and made certain that every one of his guests was well taken care of and happy.

John was a bright, active and lively baby who began to walk just before his first birthday and began to talk around the same time. His first word was, not surprisingly, 'Mama' which was followed quickly by 'no,' 'Papa,' *'oui,'* and *'ferme,'* which meant 'farm' in French, although he pronounced it 'fem.' There was, however, no doubt as to his meaning, for he clarified the syllable by pointing his chubby fist and finger out towards the fields of harvested grain.

He appeared to be exceptionally healthy, throwing off most illnesses quickly and with no apparent harm. Additionally, he was exposed to both French and English since his parents were from different countries and spoke different languages as their native tongues. Thus, he grew up fluent in both.

Azilum continued, but the winters of 1797-98 and 1798-99 were very cold and harsh, with winds and snow buffeting the little settlement. Drifts closed the roads and pathways to all but the most determined, who had to trudge through knee high snowbanks in most places.

By spring of the new century, several residents at Azilum were packing up and moving on to other, less remote and more established colonies of French émigrés, including Philadelphia, Illinois and New Orléans. These moves had been brewing for years, almost since the colony had been established. While it sorrowed those who stayed, it did not surprise them.

Bartholomew went about his business as Azilum's Director, making sure that the remaining inhabitants' farm lands were prosperous, that their animals were healthy, their houses were kept in good repair, and that the timbering, quarrying and other businesses that had begun continued to produce.

The maple sugaring and potash trade fell off when, as Bartholomew had forecast, neighboring trading posts identified and secured their own sources for those products and began offering them. Those other establishments, which were admittedly larger than Azilum, could sell more of the items and therefore undercut the price Azilum had to charge in order to make a profit. It finally it put an end to those lines of commerce at the French community.

With the rest of the United States, the residents of Azilum grieved at the news of the death of former President George Washington in December of 1799. Like the rest of the country, they also discussed the Presidential election, scheduled for the autumn of 1800, and the two candidates: Thomas Jefferson and John Adams.

Early in 1800, Elizabeth was pregnant again, but sadly within four months had lost the child. She and Bartholomew grieved quietly together but were buoyed by the knowledge that miscarriages were not uncommon. They had great hope, still, of giving John several younger brothers or sisters.

Elizabeth's 'sewing circle' of friends had shrunk a bit because of the families who left the settlement. However, she and the Homet and LeFevre ladies, along with her own mother and sister Rebecca, one or two other women of Azilum, and occasionally the Prevost ladies, still met at least twice a week at the Maison. Following Elizabeth's lead, they often brought their children with them, and everyone gathered to talk and sew while the children played under their watchful gazes.

Rebecca, who was now seventeen and who still disliked sewing, often read while the rest of the ladies sewed and the children either napped or played. She enjoyed Shakespeare, Wordsworth and the poetry of Goethe, which Maria Schillinger Homet was teaching her to read in that lady's native German.

The women's afternoons were conducted in a mixture of languages. Although Elizabeth spoke French fluently, and the French residents of Azilum spoke quite good English, French was the usual language at the settlement. However, in informal settings like Elizabeth's 'sewing circle' the mixture of women from both linguistic backgrounds—as well as Maria Homet's Austrian-German background—meant that many words and phrases slipped gracefully from one tongue to another.

In June of 1800, much excitement greeted the bulletin, brought in the twice weekly mail run, that the U.S. Capital had finally moved from Philadelphia to the newly constructed Capital City, which was named Washington.

"A fitting tribute to a great man," commented Bartholomew to Elizabeth as they read the news together one morning.

She nodded, then sighed.

"What is it, *ma petite*?" Bartholomew asked solicitously.

Elizabeth revealed that just the afternoon before, two of her friends whom she had been close to since she had moved to the settlement had told her they and their families were planning to leave.

"They are moving to Philadelphia: they knew its days as the Capital were drawing to a close and realized that many grand houses will be vacant since the government and its leaders will be in Washington," Elizabeth explained. "They prefer the city, with its advantages," she added wryly. "Even if they do have to flee the fever every summer," she finished, sounding irritated.

Bartholomew nodded slowly, sadly. "Yes. Many have found the past several years here—a challenge," he finished quietly. "I can understand if they wish to return to a more—refined—life, perhaps," he added, sounding as though his understanding made him even more regretful. It would be difficult to keep Azilum prosperous and thriving if there were not enough people at the settlement.

"Do you think others will come to live here?" Elizabeth asked worriedly: of the original sixty families, only about half remained. Some of the empty houses had been taken down already by residents of nearby towns, the wood used to build new homes away from Azilum, for several villages had popped up in the region and new settlers were arriving constantly. Although the departing families had given their permission for the homes to be demolished, since they had sold the timber to the nearby residents who wanted the cut and finished wood, the several vacant lots that now pockmarked Azilum gave it a half-abandoned air. And although Bartholomew had very much wanted to object to the decision to remove and re-use the timber, it belonged to the departing families, and he could not deny them getting some money back on their investment in Azilum.

"I do not know, *ma petite*. But we can hope," Bartholomew replied encouragingly. But his tone was not as sanguine as his words.

Bartholomew and Elizabeth continued to hope for Azilum, as well as for another child. Although Elizabeth became pregnant readily enough, she seemed unable to carry the child beyond a few months, even if she stayed in bed—something she tried in desperation, finally, in the summer of 1802. John was now three and a half, and she very much wanted to expand their family.

However, even though Elizabeth and Bartholomew had convinced themselves that bed rest would allow her to bring the baby to full term, it was not to be.

"I do not understand it, Bart!" cried Elizabeth when the worst had happened. She was in their bed, and Bart had crawled in beside her and held her close. "I gave you a wonderful healthy son, right away! No problems at all!

Why can't I give you more children?" she agonized, and then wept inconsolably.

Bartholomew held her, and rubbed her back and tried to be strong. But every time one of their babies died, vanished in a rush of blood and a flash of pain, he felt it as deeply as Elizabeth did. Now, his own tears fell on her long brown hair and he gave a deep sigh.

"It is not your fault, *ma petite*," he reassured her.

"Oh, Bart, it clearly is my fault!" she contradicted him, and sobbed afresh, her cheek pressed to his nightshirt.

"The doctor and the midwife both said there had been damage, when John was born," Bart murmured softly. "You remember?"

Elizabeth nodded, then hiccuped. She was so grateful for her husband's understanding, but each time she lost a baby her sorrow and sense of loss grew until it had become almost untenable.

"So perhaps there was more damage—inside?— more than we know. Perhaps you just cannot have any more children, Elizabeth," Bart said gently.

"But—I want more children. And so do you. And I know our John would love a brother or sister..." Elizabeth replied faintly. She looked up at her husband, who kissed her and wiped her wet cheeks. "Can we keep on trying, Bart? Please? We cannot just give up!" she insisted.

"Oh, ma petite, of course we will keep trying, for there is nothing in the world I love more than you, and being with you. And if God sees fit to bless us with another child, it would be wonderful," Bartholomew replied. "But you have already given me the greatest gift, and more than I could ever want," he murmured, and kissed her again.

Elizabeth sniffled. "You mean, John?" she queried.

"Well, yes, but I meant, really, just yourself, and your love," Bart replied, and drew her close.

Chapter Thirty-Nine

On the heels of their bitter personal disappointment, the news arrived that summer at Azilum of Napoleon's pardon. He had granted amnesty to all those who had fled France during the Revolution. Should they now declare loyalty to him and his new government, they would be permitted to return to France. Although most of their familial lands and houses had been turned over to the State, Napoleon indicated that various provisions would be made to allow the nobles who had fled to re-take at least a portion of their properties.

It was an offer nearly everyone felt unable to refuse. Azilum once more swung into chaotic preparation, but this time it was not for the visit of a noble Frenchman or dignitary.

It was to pack up and return to France.

The Louisiana Purchase by the United States in 1803 solidified New Orléans' place in the new country, and many French émigrés from all over the United States flocked there, including several from Azilum.

By 1804, only the LaPortes at the Grande Maison, the Homets at their estate nearby, the Prevosts on their lands near the Loyalsock Creek, and the LeFevres remained of the original French Azilum residents. More of the timbers from the French houses were sold and within a decade nothing but foundations remained over most of the land.

Bartholomew struck a deal with the rest of the shareholders of Azilum to take over the remaining acreage of the settlement. Although his compatriots had fled, he was determined to remain, and keep his own businesses and properties going as well as he could. Timbering and quarrying began to fall off because the trading posts at Tioga Point and elsewhere were getting their material for trade from other, larger operations who could charge less money. Like the maple sugaring and potash ventures, these two also petered out. Also, because fewer and fewer residents were at Azilum, the pool of workers evaporated, and reluctantly, Bartholomew closed both the quarry and the timbering businesses, and concentrated on farming.

Elizabeth's father, now in his fifties, decided to join with his son in law Bartholomew and farm the vast acreage the latter now possessed. Bartholomew had sold off some of the outlying parcels to new area residents, and made a tidy profit, which he plowed back into his remaining fields. He focused on maintaining a decent trade in feed corn, and the rest of the acreage was devoted to crops that would provide the few families remaining with food all year round.

The shops, including le Marchand, closed, their timbers too gone to build other people's homes, and the families left at Azilum traveled the much improved roads to Wyalusing or Towanda for their goods, or took delivery from one of the river boats that still plied the Susquehanna, although less frequently now that roadways were better.

Livestock had remained a steadier business, however, because most of the families who had left Azilum had not taken their cows and pigs and goats and sheep along with them, but sold them at very low prices to the families staying at the settlement. So Bartholomew was able to keep these animals for meat and for wool, and would sell them as opportunity arose: those same new residents in outlying villages that were now dotting the rural landscape, though they had in some ways contributed to the demise of Azilum, in other ways were a ready market for the extra livestock and other commodities the little settlement had available.

Bartholomew also proved quite talented at animal husbandry, and began to make a little money by siring out some of his best bulls. So the LaPorte family was better off than most, and Bartholomew and Elizabeth freely shared what they had with the other residents remaining with them at the colony.

However, during these years when Azilum was diminishing and less secure than it had been, Bartholomew visited the jeweler he'd come to know in Towanda a couple of times, and sold a few of the diamonds he still carried with him in the little pouch around his neck.

Thus, although Azilum was fading into memory and its buildings were disappearing around them, the Maison still stood in good repair. Elizabeth, her parents and sisters, the Homets, the LeFevres and the Prevosts got together often to share a meal or have a party like the ones Talon and then Bartholomew used to host. Frequently they invited residents from the surrounding villages: the Terrys of Terrytown, the Dodges, the Seamans, the Gilberts, the Welleses, the Gaylords, the Spaldings, the Kinneys and several more. Dr. Jabez Chamberlain, who had served as Azilum's physician for a few years before moving back to his native New York State, returned to Azilum along with his wife Irene and their family, too, during this time, and took up residence in a recently vacated home not far from where the Franklins lived in Bartholomew's former house, and the Grand Maison.

The French refugees who remained had experienced, now, several years in the Pennsylvania wilderness, dealing with its weather, its wild animals, its challenging terrain, and other features of rural life. They had come to understand their neighbors, whom the original settlers of Azilum had perhaps considered rather coarse and unrefined. And so, they reached out, and created friendships and networked business relationships and in time some familial relationships were built as well.

In 1810, a large part of the county, including lands owned by Azilum and its principal settlement, broke away from Luzerne County, and was named Ontario County. Several of the leading families who were friends and associates of the LaPortes became leaders of the new county, and by March of 1811 the name of the new county had been changed to Bradford.

A year later, the War of 1812 saw blockades by the British and an uptick in the production of goods, especially cotton, in the United States. This was forced in many ways by the blockade, which meant that the United States could no longer import its textiles and other goods from overseas. Thus, they turned to their vast interior and learned how to make the things they needed themselves.

John, who was growing up during this interesting period, had been a happy and healthy boy, as he had been a happy and healthy infant. He raced through the tall stalks of corn in the seemingly endless golden fields that now were Azilum, he swam in the river, and rowed along the shore and to the several uninhabited islands in the river in search of adventure, for he had been much taken with Byron's 'The Corsair.'

John also showed a great interest in the inner workings of government and commerce from an early age. He followed the development of Ontario and then Bradford County with fascination and would constantly wish to discuss the changes around them in great detail with his father, usually after the mid day meal.

Bartholomew indulged his son, proud of the boy's mental acuity and grasp of the concepts of Federalism that were beyond his years. He also enjoyed sharing his own aptitude for trade and his understanding and exploration of the way various social changes impacted commerce with young John, who seemed as fascinated by this, and as eager to figure out a way to bring the most benefit to Azilum and the family from it, as was his father.

Although John attended a local school, most of the better part of his education came from his two literate and intelligent parents who doted on their only child and ensured he lacked for nothing and was exposed to literature, geography, science, art, music, mathematics, as well as trade, commerce and agriculture.

Although Bartholomew and Elizabeth continued to hope to add to their family, for Elizabeth was still quite young, by the time the second decade of the 1800s had dawned, they had stopped hoping, especially Elizabeth.

In 1807, Elizabeth's younger sister Sally married Nathaniel Terry and shortly began to have children: the first, a girl, was born that same year, with another girl following in 1810, a son the year after and then four more girls. Elizabeth, although she loved her sister and her nieces and nephew, was devastated when she herself continued to be unable to give Bartholomew another child, or John a sibling.

In 1810 Elizabeth's sister Rebecca married Edmund Dodge and a couple of years later began presenting him with what would become nine children. Again, despite her natural affection for her nieces and nephews and of course her sister, Elizabeth couldn't help feeling that Rebecca's fecundity threw her own barrenness, as she now called it, into sharp and damning relief.

Her depression deepened, and although she and Bartholomew never lost their great affection and love for each other, Elizabeth's overwhelming sense of disappointment, and of having been a failure, greatly saddened the once lively and happy woman.

Bartholomew, although he retained his naturally optimistic disposition, had his own share of grief during this period. Certainly, he was as saddened by the loss of their babies as Elizabeth, and he was also downcast because of the dénouement of Azilum. Although the community was still self sufficient, and he had plenty of money in the bank and the diamonds around his neck, it grieved Bartholomew to look out on what had once been a busy, thriving village and see empty lots and smoke coming from only a handful of cook houses.

In 1811, Bartholomew received word that his long-time friend Antoine Omer Talon had died at his estate in Gretz, in the north of France. The news had greatly troubled him, and he said to Elizabeth that he had lost his oldest friend. Talon's death, too, seemed to Bartholomew to be a harbinger of his own, and although he was only in his early fifties, he realized, for the first time that he could recall, that he would not live forever.

Although he found himself unusually glum in the days following the receipt of the news of Talon's death, Bartholomew took comfort by remembering the risky, exciting times he and Talon had shared in Marseilles and on the trip to the United States. He recalled with pride their venture to build the new colony of Azilum. And his one regret was that after Talon had left to return to his wife in Bavaria, they had never made the effort to meet up again.

He spent several evenings re-reading the letters from Talon he'd received in exchange to his own over the years they had been apart. Then he finally made his peace with the loss and returned to his former cheery demeanor.

In 1818, Elizabeth's mother Susanna, who had never been completely healthy since the traumatic birth of her last child, died, and her father, who still worked with Bartholomew on the vast farm that Azilum had become, moved into the Maison. Elizabeth grieved, but it seemed to her a smaller grief than it should have been. She and her mother had never been especially close and since Elizabeth had married, Susanna Franklin had not been a large part of her daughter's life. Still, it was another blow, and the guilt Elizabeth felt that she should somehow feel more saddened by her mother's death only made her more depressed and anxious.

Bartholomew tried to keep Elizabeth's spirits up, but he found himself busier than ever, even though Azilum was shrinking. There were fewer people to assist him and to whom he could delegate, although John Franklin was a worthy lieutenant. But he tried, and knew deep down that Elizabeth would have to find her own way out of her dark mood: he could but shine a light for her to follow, and wait.

Chapter Forty

Matilda Chamberlain was the daughter of the settlement's doctor, Jabez Chamberlain, M.D., who had come to Azilum from the Wyoming Valley in 1795. Although he had returned to his native Duchess County, NY, for a brief period, shortly after 1800 he returned to Azilum, and remained along with his children: Matilda, Adah, Gilbert, Jane, Maria, Oliver, John and Joseph.

Dr. Chamberlain rode several miles every day attending to patients in the surrounding towns and villages, and his wife Irene and the children settled in a house not far from the Grand Maison. John LaPorte had known Matilda, as well as her siblings, since the family had arrived.

The two were only 18 months or so apart, with Matilda being the elder. But they had been in the same classes at the local school, because Matilda's schooling had been interrupted when her family relocated to Pennsylvania from New York State. Since the two families lived almost next door to each other, John and Matilda had become fast friends despite their different genders.

Matilda was something of a tomboy, and delighted in accompanying John when he boated on the river, or hiked the nearby mountains. Like him, she read voraciously, and together they discussed not only what they studied in school, or read for leisure, but also what was going on in the wider world.

When the War of 1812 came, John was 14 and Matilda nearly 16, and both supported the United States' stance that Britain and Napoleon's France had been wrong to try to restrict U.S. trade. They found particularly heinous the attempts by the Royal Navy to snatch American sailors from U.S. merchant ships and force them to serve for Great Britain.

John in particular followed avidly the quick changes in Congress concerning trade agreements with Britain and France. Jefferson's Embargo Act had been repealed, but its replacement, which barred trade with both Britain and France, had been short lived. By the time the war began in 1812, a third bill that offered to restrict trade with one country if the other would drop its own sanctions against commerce with the U.S. had brought the disagreement to a head.

And meanwhile, the British were attempting to cause friction between the Native Americans and the U.S. over the fledgeling country's westward expansion.

John and Matilda often debated the merits of expansionism and whether or not the U.S. had a right to settle lands that were already settled by native peoples.

"But we've done that here," John pointed out one snowy winter afternoon after Sunday dinner at the Grand Maison where the Chamberlains had joined the LaPortes. It was a good thing the Chamberlains could walk home, as the snow, which had begun while they were all at church that morning, was already six inches high and showed no signs of stopping.

Matilda, who was lounging on the hearth rug in front of one of the massive fireplaces in a drawing room, rolled over and looked at her friend.

"Yes. I know all about General Sullivan's March to drive the native people out of this area," she returned solemnly. "That things like that are successful, though, does that automatically make them right?" she questioned.

John frowned at her and sighed. "Don't you think we have a — a mission, if you will— to build this nation into a shining example of what a country and a people ought to be?" he asked fervently.

"Well, yes, of course I do," Matilda answered calmly. "And I won't argue with you that Europe and

Britain have become quite…" she wrinkled her nose, "decadent. The things they think are important, and the ways they go about achieving those things, well, they're often quite corrupt." She paused. "But does creating, as you say, a 'shining example' mean we have to conquer and eradicate everyone else?" she asked rhetorically, "in some cases, people who have lived in this country for centuries?"

John didn't have an easy answer for that, though he felt that ideally, the native people should be able to live in harmony with the new America. But perhaps, he thought next, that harmony would be best achieved not by aggression but by cooperation. Perhaps Matilda was correct: a great nation would not diminish or dismiss smaller ones or different ones, it would learn from them and incorporate them into its vision of paradise on earth.

When he said as much to her, Matilda rolled back over to face the fire once more. "You read too much political theory," she grumped at him, but she chuckled: John's grasp of the various arguments for and against colonization and expansion was enviable.

Fortunately, the War of 1812 was a brief one, ending in December of 1814 with the Treaty of Ghent, and it left Azilum largely untouched though in Europe its impact was much greater. However, the LaPortes, the Chamberlains, John Franklin, and the few other families who remained joined with the rest of the U.S. in celebrating the war's end with a newfound spirit of nationalism.

Matilda, whose father set off early on his rounds and whose mother was busy tending to the younger children first thing, would begin her mornings on the days when newspapers arrived by commandeering a copy and haring off to the cook house or in fine weather the garden. There she would absorb all the current news of the day, much as John was doing at his own home down the road. When Matilda's mother, also an avid reader, finally got a chance to sit with the newspaper later in the morning, it was often smeared with grass stains or grease, depending on where her daughter had gone to digest it.

While John freely admitted his greatest interest was business and politics, Matilda confided to him that what intrigued her most in the news were the scientific discoveries of the day. Such an interest was not usual for a girl.

"I think it's remarkable the way everything just works, you know, John? Together," she explained one summer day when they were both in their mid teens, and were resting on the grassy bank after a swim in the river. "Even down to the smallest things. Look around us: everything works in harmony. The cattails growing over there, and the milkweed, they help clean the water for the fish and frogs and other aquatic creatures. Butterflies and bees pollinate the flowers when they feed on them. Birds eat the seeds and propagate the plants, ensuring an endless supply." She paused. "I suspect that this kind of inter-relation and harmony exists at the, erm, smaller level too, the microscopic level."

"What d'you mean, 'microscopic?'" John queried. He knew the word, of course, and had learned all about Van Leeuwenhoek's developments to increase the magnifying power of lenses and his subsequent discoveries. But he wanted to know what Matilda meant, specifically.

"Well, you know about the Dutch scientists' discoveries of tiny little beings in water, for example, things we cannot see with our own eyes?" Matilda answered.

John nodded.

"They've discovered similar tiny structures in plants and in our own circulation system, the way blood moves in our bodies," she continued, enthused. "I've read my father's copy of Hooke's <u>Micrographia</u> and the pictures are amazing! Only I wonder, if…well, if we can see all that now, much more than the ancients did with their magnifiers, because of the improvements we've made in ours, what else might we see if we continue to perfect our lenses and increase their magnification powers? Mightn't there be further, erm, levels, or layers of tiny constructs within those small things we see now?" she wondered aloud, explaining, she hoped, her fascination and her theory.

John nodded slowly. "You mean, say, within those 'cells' that Hooke found on cork, there may be other, smaller structures that make up the cells?" he queried. The idea astonished him, but it made sense. It was logical, so why not? So many things that a century before had never been dreamt of were now being discovered and proven.

"Exactly, John!" Matilda beamed.

John gave his best friend a long, appraising look. "How did you get to be so smart?" he asked admiringly.

Matilda smiled and shrugged.

Chapter Forty-One

It was an era when feelings and emotions were not openly discussed except with intimates, but John and Matilda talked over everything, and the better they came to know each other as the years passed, the more they shared.

Matilda, who greatly admired her father, had desperately desired to go to one of the newly established Medical Colleges and follow in his footsteps. When she had finished at the local school and told her family of her wishes, she had been heartbroken to learn that 'girls' could not become physicians, for no Medical College would accept them for the course of study. Matilda had run to John, to whom she had confided her dearest wish, and sought solace on his sturdy shoulder.

"I told you I knew of no Medical College that had ever had a female student," John said quietly as Matilda dried her tears and took a deep breath. He had tried to tell her in the hope that she wouldn't be disappointed. "Indeed, Medical Colleges themselves are quite new," he reminded her. This was true: most physicians merely apprenticed with established doctors and when they felt ready, hung out their own shingles, as it were. Matilda's father had done exactly that when he'd started out.

"Yes, I know you did, John," she replied, sniffling. "But I had hoped, you see, to be the first." Her face was passionate in its zeal, and it shone through her abject disappointment.

John paused. They were sitting in one of the 'follies' on the grounds of the Grand Maison: a small gazebo. It was spring time, and morning glory vines were snaking up the lattice work, tingeing the world inside the little structure a light green.

"I should have missed you, if you'd gone," John said, low. "To Medical College, I mean," he added hastily. He slid a glance over at Matilda, his hazel eyes gentle.

Matilda nodded quietly, then turned to look at him. "I should have missed you, as well, John," she confessed. "But oh, the opportunity! Had it been possible, I would have done it," she added, determined.

"Perhaps you can accompany your father, when he goes on calls?" John suggested. "It would mean you could assist him, perhaps, in small ways, and though you would not be a doctor..."

"It would be something. And it might be the best I could hope for, you are right," Matilda finished for him.

They often finished each other's sentences.

John smiled at her. She might be a visionary, but she was also practical.

"And, you would still be here," he added happily. "Not off at some Medical College miles and miles away."

He, too, had finished the local school, and was now considering what he might do next. Politics and business, of course, were his main interests, but initially he thought he would help his father and grandfather on the farm: both of them were getting up in years, and his assistance would be welcome. And he did like farming, though he felt destined for something more...eventually.

"But do you feel farming is enough for you, John?" Matilda asked now, solicitous. She knew the young man had interests as widely varied as her own, and somehow could not imagine him a farmer the rest of his life. It was a noble profession, to be sure, but she sensed that John would do many things, not just one, in his days on this earth.

John smiled, and stretched his hands above his head. His knuckles scraped the ceiling of the little gazebo for he was already, at 18, six feet tall. "'Twill do for a while," he told Matilda, still smiling. Then his face

274

clouded. "I do not wish to leave Mother..." he murmured, and sat beside Matilda on the bench.

They had often discussed his mother's solemnity and sadness, and the reasons for it, all buried in sorrowful little graves in the family graveyard. Matilda, though she understood John's wish to not give his mother further reason to grieve by leaving home, also felt that John needed to strike out on his own and be all the things she felt he could be.

"My father is a farmer, now, and yet he did many things before turning to agriculture," John continued. "That I farm for a while, now, does not mean I will not ever do anything else, Maddie," he told her, sounding just a bit defensive.

"I do understand, John," Matilda began, thinking to reiterate the arguments she had given her friend before, in favor of him finding work in a business or trade rather than staying on the family farm.

But he interrupted her. They were close enough that she took no offense.

"No, Maddie, I do not think you truly do," John said firmly.

In the past, he'd just listened to her opinion, not contradicted her or explained his feelings.

Matilda sat up and gave him her full attention. "Tell me."

He sighed. "I won't mind farming," he repeated. "And as I said, I do not have to do that for always. But whatever I do, I do want to stay—close. My mother has only my father, and me, and her father, of course, but he is quite old. And my father is not much younger, really, for he is much older than Mama." He sighed. "I feel—I feel that because I am my parents' only child," he continued, his voice low, "I feel that I must somehow be, oh, I don't know, everything to them."

"Everything?" Matilda echoed, frowning. That seemed like an awful burden to impose on oneself.

John nodded. "Yes. I must be a good son, and a dutiful one, and be a help to my father and a companion to my mother, and be a success at whatever I do, whether it's farming or something else. I must be a success, you see, because I am their only child: I cannot fail."

"But John, what about you?" Matilda broke in. "It's all very well to say you're all your parents have so you must succeed, and always please them and be near them, but what do you want to do, to be? After all, you must look at it also from your parents' perspective."

John cocked his head at her curiously.

"They love you more than anything in this world, and their greatest wish is for you to be happy," Matilda told him firmly. "Even if that should mean that you eventually leave Azilum, or make some mistakes along the way." She paused. "My parents love me too, that way, and I think their sadness was almost as great as mine when I learned I could not go to Medical College."

John nodded slowly. "But I want to make them proud," he said solemnly.

Matilda smiled. "You do, John, every day. And I see no reason for that to change, regardless of what you decide to do," she reassured him. "You know _my_ dream," she continued, her voice changing from inspiring to sad in a flash. "A dream that is not to be, because of the way our society regards my gender. But you: you're a man. You can do anything. Be anything." She couldn't help a tinge of envy in her tone. "So... if you could be anything in the world, what would you be?" she asked boldly.

No one, not even his father, with whom he had had many discussions about commerce and industry and the political workings of the nation as well as his possible future, had ever put that question to John quite so directly. He stared at her, and then took a deep breath.

"Really?" he asked. "Anything? 'Tis just a wish, right, Maddie?"

She nodded. "Yes."

"And you won't—laugh at me?" he murmured, holding her gaze with his own.

Solemnly, Matilda shook her head. "No more than you laughed at me when I said I wanted to go to Medical College," she agreed. Her voice still held sadness at that shattered dream.

"Well—I..." John hesitated. "I'd like to be President," he whispered.

Matilda sat back on the little wooden bench in surprise. "Of the United States?" she whispered back.

John nodded. "Oh, Maddie, I could do so much for our country, and for Pennsylvania of course, as well!" he enthused, and began to outline his dreams for political and social reform, business expansion, innovations in technology, and had he known it, sounding much like his father had decades before.

Maddie caught her lower lip in delight: she'd never seen John so excited, heard in detail about his plans. He was eloquent and passionate as he enumerated them. And he had some very good plans, she thought.

Well, if she couldn't go to Medical College, if her great dream couldn't be brought to fruition, perhaps she could help John achieve his, Matilda thought. And for her part, she would take John's advice and see if she could accompany her father on his rounds. That way, she'd at least be doing something worthwhile, and learning about medicine, albeit not in an official capacity.

Chapter Forty-Two

This encounter, a pivotal one among so many important ones in John and Matilda's life together, would guide and sustain both of them in the years ahead. Matilda began going on calls with her father, and continued to read whatever she could find about advances in science and medicine. John worked with his father and grandfather on the family farm, gleaning every bit of business acumen and clever strategizing from his father that he could—and there was a lot to learn.

As the years passed, John and Matilda became closer than ever to each other and finally the friendship turned to something more. By 1820, they were officially courting, and engaged a short time after that.

Elizabeth had become a quiet and solemn figure in the household by the time John began courting Matilda. Rather than be jealous of another person demanding her only son's affection and time, Elizabeth found herself in favor of the courtship and anticipating the union she felt was sure to come. In a very real way, her son's happiness increased her own, a testament to Elizabeth's natural kindness.

Elizabeth and Bartholomew had always liked the Chamberlains a great deal and grew to love Matilda almost as a daughter. Added to Elizabeth's contentment was a new friendship with Matilda's mother, Irene Gilbert Chamberlain. Although they had known each other for a few years, they were not very close in age. But Irene was a very intelligent and compassionate woman who, once her daughter's relationship with John blossomed, saw Elizabeth's unhappiness clearly since the Chamberlains were much more frequently in the company of the LaPortes than they had been before.

Irene found ways in which she might help her new friend feel less desolate. Although Elizabeth still held the 'sewing circles' once a week now at the Maison, she and Irene also met nearly every day, usually in the afternoons, and the two women would talk, not only about world events as their children did, and about things they read, but about how they felt. Elizabeth found herself able to unburden herself to the non-judgmental and sympathetic Irene, and found great solace in the friendship. She found release by confessing her guilt and fear to someone other than her dear Bartholomew, whom she didn't like to constantly bother with her concerns, since they had never seemed to change, only remain.

But Irene listened and comforted, much as Bart had always done, and gently drew Elizabeth out of her self-imposed prison with walks where they picked wildflowers and brought them back to sketch or press on the terrace at the Maison, or drives to one of the nearby towns to select fabric for new dresses, or word of a new dessert or dish that Elizabeth and Irene might want to encourage their cooks to try. For all that the river they lived next to had been named *Sisa'we'hak'hanna* by the native Lenape tribe, which means 'oyster river' referring to the large oyster beds at the river's mouth at Chesapeake Bay, oysters were not to be found at Azilum. But turtles were, and turtle soup was a delicacy that the two women urged their cooks to perfect—with much enjoyment for all.

On February 26, 1822, John and Matilda were married, and Elizabeth welcomed her new daughter with open arms. She was by no means the same effervescent, hopeful woman she had been when Bartholomew had fallen in love with her: grief and years had drawn lines on the smooth skin of her face and shadowed her clear hazel eyes. But Elizabeth's innate kind and sympathetic nature shone through, and she seemed happier, for which Bartholomew was glad.

John, too, was happy to see his mother become lighter of spirit, and he and Matilda took up residence in the Grand Maison, alongside his parents, Elizabeth's aging father, and just a short walk from the Chamberlain house. Matilda continued to go with her father to see patients until the autumn of 1822, when her first pregnancy became too noticeable and she contentedly remained at home in the Grand Maison, being looked after by her doting mother in law.

When Matilda gave birth to a son on January 25, 1823, Elizabeth had tears of joy in her eyes. The boy was named Bartholomew, in honor of his paternal grandfather.

John worked on the farm at Azilum for a few years, but soon opportunity came knocking and, with his mother restored to a general sense of equanimity and calm and his father as hale as ever despite advancing years, he accepted the appointment as Auditor General of the County in 1827. By then, he and Matilda had another child, a daughter: Elizabeth Charlotte, whom they called 'Lisette,' born November 25, 1825.

Following a successful time as Auditor, John was elected to the Pennsylvania House of Representatives in 1828, where he served until 1832. For two years he was even Speaker of the House, and spent much time in the state capital of Harrisburg. Matilda and the two children took a house in Towanda, but visited the LaPortes and the Chamberlains at Azilum frequently.

Matilda and John wrote every day to each other. Even though the letters weren't delivered for more than a week, they were still able, by this correspondence, to keep up with what was happening. John took great pride in hearing about his children's accomplishments and

Matilda delighted in the news John shared with her about bills before the House, and the changes coming to their home state of Pennsylvania.

Elizabeth's greatest joy, besides her darling Bartholomew, was now her grandchildren, and she looked forward to their visits to Azilum as much as she anticipated her son's return from Harrisburg. Often, although the young family would spend some time in Towanda, they would then make the journey down to Azilum and spend several quiet, blissful days there at the Grand Maison. John would hike and fish and swim and boat along the river, sometimes with Matilda by his side as they had done as youngsters. More often, little Bart was in tow, and afterwards Lisette once she became old enough.

Matilda suffered two miscarriages during this time, which saddened everyone, including Elizabeth. But somehow, helping her daughter in law through the sorrow that she herself knew only too well seemed therapeutic somehow for Elizabeth, and her emotional life continued to improve. For her part, Matilda recovered quickly both times, and reassured John that all was well with her.

In February of 1832, Matilda gave birth to a son, whom they named Samuel McKean. The birth, like all of them, had been easily accomplished at the family's townhouse in Towanda, with her father and a local midwife in attendance.

Elizabeth was overjoyed, now, with three grandchildren to spoil and coddle. Although John was still frequently away due to his work in government, her daughter in law Matilda and Matilda's mother Irene as well as the kind and comforting physician Jabez provided her with good company, and her dear husband Bartholomew was always nearby.

What remained of Elizabeth's sewing circle still met, but less frequently, although new ladies with their children and grandchildren now filled out its ranks.

Matilda and the children began to spend even more time with the LaPortes and the Chamberlains after Samuel was born, as in 1833 John was elected to the U.S. House of Representatives for the 17th District of Pennsylvania. He began to spend much of his time in Washington, the nation's capital.

When he had stood for the position, John had asked Matilda if she would come to Washington with him, if he were elected. Quietly, Matilda had told him that she would remain in Towanda, making frequent visits to Azilum to visit his parents and hers, and to make sure the children learned the history of the place and enjoyed its beauty and clean freshness.

'But I shall miss you too much, if you do not come with me,' John had protested, pulling his wife close to him. They had been in their bedroom at the Grand Maison, getting ready to retire for the night.

'I shall miss you, too, John,' Matilda had confessed. 'But if I stay here, you will have much reason to return, and return often, and thus truly remain in touch with your constituents,' she had reasoned. 'And that is, after all, why you are going to Washington.' She had paused. 'This is but one more step towards the fulfillment of your dream—our dream—and I want to do everything I can so that you are supremely successful at it,' she had explained.

John had smiled down at her, and told her once again how grateful he was for her constant support, and her belief in him. And then, he had agreed that she should remain in Pennsylvania with the family, and he had duly been elected, and gone to Washington. The two of them, as always, wrote constantly, and now that mail service had improved, news fairly flew between Azilum or Towanda and the nation's capital.

True to her word, Matilda spent some of her time at the family townhouse in Towanda, and the rest at Azilum. Spending time there not only provided her with adult company, it meant the children had many willing and eager babysitters, chief of whom was Elizabeth.

Although she loved all three of her grandchildren, Elizabeth felt herself particularly fond of her namesake, Lisette. The little girl was hazel eyed and brown haired, as was she, and seemed to have inherited much of her grandmother's original sunny personality. The two of them would spend a great deal of time together whenever Lisette was at Azilum, and Elizabeth taught the girl French, dancing, and water colors in addition to the subjects taught in school.

During Elizabeth's darkest days, she had put away the paintbrushes and easel she had so delighted in when she'd first married. However, once John was courting Matilda, Elizabeth had taken her watercolors out of storage and begun again to paint the hills and valleys, the river and the wildlife of her beloved home at Azilum. She passed her love of the region, and her love of capturing it on canvas, on to Lisette.

In 1833, John announced on one of his first visits back to Azilum from Washington, that he wanted to build a new house, right on the Azilum grounds.

"But you have a house, in Towanda, and your *pied à terre* in Washington, as well," Bartholomew put in, surprised. "And you always have the Grand Maison, you know," he finished. He was seventy five years old now, and although he was still strong, he could feel his health was faltering. Muscle strains seemed to pain him more, and took longer to heal, and colds and catarrhs troubled him a couple of times a year while when he was younger, they never had. "Why do you need another house?" he asked.

John smiled at his father. The two of them were in the little parlor on the main floor of the Maison. It was a summer evening, and they could hear Matilda and Elizabeth chatting on the terrace, and the more high pitched sounds of the children playing on the large swath of grass that fronted the Maison.

"Well, Papa, I was thinking of a more, erm, modern house, something in the new style," John replied. He didn't want to hurt his father's feelings, but after all, the Maison hadn't been his design: his friend Antoine Talon had designed it. But now the Maison was so dated! It was big and boxy, not comfortable despite all the fancy touches and gilt interior furnishings.

But to John, it was the hallmark of a bygone era. The architecture of the Maison actually reminded John of a fort more than a home. When he'd been a child, he had found this comforting, but now that he was grown he found he desired something more *au courant* and elegant, perhaps reflective of a more Classical design. He had seen some beautiful homes in Washington and the areas around it, not least of which had been Washington's estate at Mount Vernon. He wanted to create his own version of that, at Azilum.

"A summer house, in fact," he continued now, "somewhere that Matilda and the children could escape to when the weather is warm, and where I can seek respite as well, for you know the summers in Washington are hotter than anything."

Bartholomew nodded. "I suppose that might be nice," he conceded. He had already deeded over all of his acreage to John. Although Bartholomew didn't plan to die any time soon, he thought that as he was now in his seventies, it would be best if his son took ownership of the property.

Bartholomew and Elizabeth still lived at the Maison, along with Elizabeth's father, who was now quite feeble. Elizabeth spent much of her free time nursing her father alongside the maids at the Maison, who also took turns at the elder Franklin's bedside.

"Where might you wish to build?" Bartholomew asked John, reaching over to re-fill the long clay pipe he still smoked. Jabez Chamberlain told him it might make it more difficult for him to shake the bronchitis that now plagued him every winter, but Bartholomew had smoked since he'd been a boy, and was loathe to give it up.

John, who had grown into an impressively tall man of more than six feet, stretched out his long legs and folded his hands across what was becoming an expansive stomach. All those fancy Washington dinners and receptions, Bartholomew thought to himself, eyeing his son.

"Well, I was thinking, Papa: this house has the best prospect in the settlement," he began slowly. He knew every inch of Azilum: as a child, he'd run from one end to the other through the houses and boulevards, and later through the half buried foundations and overgrown streets. He'd learned to swim in the river. He'd fished that, as well as nearby streams, hiking the forests and hills and learning to ride a horse before he was seven years old.

"*Oui, oui, oui,* 'tis true! Antoine picked it for that very reason, and I built my little house just a couple of rods away," Bartholomew said, not for the first time, and gestured with one hand. By now, his wavy brown hair was almost completely silver, and rather sparse at the crown of his head, although there was still enough there to make it look full. His eyebrows had turned silver, too, and his snapping black eyes were a bit faded and surrounded by folds and wrinkles. Bartholomew's generous and ready smile had carved lines in the skin of his face and years of work outside meant his skin was almost constantly tanned, even in winter. He was still attractive though, and he had maintained his wiry and fit physique right into his seventh decade.

"So—where?" he asked John again, and John ventured the opinion that a spot just fifty or so yards south of the Maison, a bit further up the gentle rise towards the road and the hills, would be an ideal place for a summer home.

"It would catch the river breezes and give a wonderful prospect," John said again.

Bartholomew admitted that it would, and although he did not need to, he gave his son his blessing to build a 'summer home' at Azilum.

The House took three years to build, during which time Elizabeth's father, John Franklin, died. The Maison seemed emptier than ever now to Bartholomew, since it was just him and Elizabeth there. They kept most of the younger servants on, generously pensioning off the older ones, and when Matilda and the children were not visiting, the Maison seemed huge and sad.

"'Tis a relic of time gone by, John is right," Bartholomew said quietly to Elizabeth one chilly midwinter evening in late January of 1836. Matilda and the children were at her parents' home and the LaPortes were alone.

John's house was almost finished: just a few exterior niceties like shutters left to do now, and the interior decoration. He'd hired mostly local workers, but brought in some specialized craftsmen from Philadelphia and Washington. Compared to the new LaPorte House, the Grand Maison did, indeed, seem like something from a bygone and almost forgotten era.

Elizabeth looked up from the book she was reading as they sat in the small parlor, and smiled at Bartholomew. "'Tis our home, Bart, and I will always love it," she murmured. "Though I do think John's house will be very grand," she added with another smile.

Bartholomew coughed.

"That sounds worse than it did yesterday," Elizabeth said, concerned. A small furrow appeared between her brows. "Shall I make you a poultice?" she offered. A warm mustard poultice was good for chest colds, she knew, and Bartholomew had had this cold, or catarrh, for a week now. It had gone from his head to his throat to his chest, where it now appeared to have taken up permanent residence. She knew he was troubled with bronchitis and hoped this wouldn't turn into what had become her husband's yearly bout with the illness, yet again.

Bartholomew coughed once more, and spat into a handkerchief. He nodded. "A poultice would be good, I think, ma petite," he said gratefully to his wife. He looked over at her. In the firelight and the gentle glow from the oil lamp, the grey threads in her hair were invisible and the lines around her hazel eyes were softened. She was only in her early fifties, and to him, she still seemed very young. "When I go to bed." He added, then paused. "What are you reading?" he asked.

She told him.

"Will you read a little to me?" he asked. "My eyes can no longer see to read by fire and lamplight," he sighed. He coughed again.

Chapter Forty-Three

By the first week of February, it was apparent that Bartholomew's catarrh was not going to improve. Dr. Chamberlain, Matilda's father, attended, and confirmed that it was bronchitis, much as it had been in years before. Although he gave the nod for poultices and hot drinks to be continued, he drew Elizabeth aside and told her that he didn't think Bartholomew would conquer his bronchitis this time.

"It seems to have taken hold very firmly, this time," he began quietly. "He grows very weak," Chamberlain added.

"He has not eaten these last few days," Elizabeth replied, forcing her lower lip to stop trembling. "He takes but a bit of broth," she whispered. "In the past, his appetite has returned after a day or so, but this time…"

The doctor nodded, and, since they were in-laws after all, he gave Elizabeth a quick hug. "Be brave, Elizabeth," was all he said.

Elizabeth had sent word to John down in Washington to come home to Azilum as soon as possible, that his father was gravely ill. He arrived on February 10 and had a long talk with Bartholomew at his bedside.

Elizabeth, as was her custom, came late that night to the bed she had shared so long with her beloved husband, and tucked herself in next to him.

The doctor had been again, and left, not looking any more hopeful. John was asleep in the chamber he'd had as a child, down the long wide central hallway, and Matilda had come to be with him, though she had left the children with her parents, not wishing to disturb the house. The servants had banked the fires and retired to their beds, and the Maison was silent except for the crackling of the fire that was kept going night and day in Bartholomew's bed chamber.

The only other noise was the sound of the stertorous breaths her husband took. It seemed every breath was labored, an effort, much more than it had ever been before, and Elizabeth wished she knew what she could do to ease his struggle. She truly wished she knew what she could do to make him better, but she had begun to realize that that was not a possibility. She had prayed for a miracle, but now had begun to pray that Bartholomew would not suffer.

"*Ma petite*," murmured Bartholomew as he felt Elizabeth snuggle up next to him.

"Yes, Bart, I'm here," Elizabeth whispered, reaching up to stroke her husband's face. "Can I bring you anything?"

He shook his head fractionally on the plump down pillow. "No, my love, you have given me everything I want, always," he whispered, and a slight smile curved his lips.

"Oh, Bart, don't leave me, it is too soon!" Elizabeth protested in an anguished whisper. "Please!"

Bartholomew chuckled, and then coughed, but his cough was no longer productive and his skin was flushed, feverish. He opened his eyes, and they glittered in the firelight. "I cannot control my leaving, Elizabeth," he murmured. "I wish I could. For I shall miss you, and John, most of all..."

One hand fretted at the bedcovers and at his nightshirt.

"What is it, Bart?" Elizabeth asked, concerned.

With an effort, Bartholomew plucked at the rawhide that held the pouch of diamonds around his neck. "These—are yours," he whispered. "Take them."

Elizabeth drew back a couple of inches and shook her head. "No, Bart: they should go to John, surely?" she said quietly.

Again, Bartholomew shook his head a little bit against the pillow, but his meaning was clear. "No. John will make his own way just fine, and you can always help him. But these are yours. Forever. I promised. You will want for nothing. You will always have the best. These are yours," he repeated, gasping in between the words. He grasped the pouch, but he was too weak to pull it up over his head.

Elizabeth gently raised Bartholomew's head and slipped the pouch on its string out from around his neck.

He smiled. "*Ma petite, je ne cesserai jamais de t'aimer,*" he whispered.

Elizabeth bent down and kissed his lips, which were warm and dry. "Oh, Bart, I will never stop loving you, either," she murmured, fresh tears making her voice thick.

Bartholomew let out a long sigh, and closed his eyes.

Wordlessly, Elizabeth dropped the pouch around her own neck and tucked it inside her chemise where it lay, still imbued with Bartholomew's warmth, against her own soft skin.

With Bartholomew's death, the little LaPorte family cemetery at Azilum seemed to Elizabeth to be too full. She sunk back into her deep depression and gave away all her colored clothing, garbing herself only in black. But spring came, and then the yearly visit for the summer of Matilda and the three children: Bartholomew, who was thirteen, Lisette who was ten and a half, and baby Samuel, just four. And Elizabeth found herself, though still grieving her husband's death, able to smile a bit, and feel less hopeless than before.

John returned home at the end of session in Washington, in time for the family's removal to the just finished LaPorte House, their new summer home.

"Mama, you must come live with us," John entreated Elizabeth. "You are all alone now, in that old Maison, it is not right!" he insisted. "We have plenty of bed chambers, Mama, please. I worry about you down here all alone," he added.

Elizabeth regarded her son. Tall and handsome if a bit stout although he was not yet forty, he had his father's dark wavy hair and her own hazel eyes. In his determined chin she saw her own father's face, and in his warm smile she saw Bartholomew's.

Oh, how she missed that smile!

But she told him, quite firmly, that for the time being, at least, she was happy to remain at the Maison.

"But the roof leaks," John objected.

"Then I shall have it repaired," his mother replied with a tired smile. "Or, I can move to another part of the house where it does not leak. It is a very large house," she added, and chuckled.

Elizabeth got her wish and remained at the Maison, which was in any case just a few steps from John's new House. But Matilda and the children moved into the new French Colonial/Federalist dwelling that summer, which Elizabeth thought was quite grand indeed.

On her first official visit to the house once the family had arrived, her favorite, Lisette, came running down the bluestone steps of the front portico which faced the river and threw herself into her grandmother's arms.

"Oh, Grand-Mère, come and see, you must come and see, you have never seen anything like it!" Lisette chattered at her in French, pulling Elizabeth's hand towards the new house.

Elizabeth picked up her feet and moved in a more lively fashion along the pebbled path John had had built between the Maison and his own house, especially so that Elizabeth would be able to come and go easily between her house and his.

"Yes, *oui,* my pet, I am coming, Lisette," she said with a smile for the little girl, and followed.

Chapter Forty-Four

It was terribly exciting for Lisette to have a father so grand that he could build a magnificent summer house on the banks of the Susquehanna River, where they could all repair to once the warm months arrived. Their townhouse in Towanda was nice, and grand enough, she supposed. But the open fields and expansive beauty of Azilum had been familiar to her all her short life, and she loved it, far preferring it to what she thought of as 'city life.' Additionally, her beloved Grand-Mère for whom she was named lived at Azilum, just a few yards away in the Grand Maison which had all sorts of wonderful, if rather faded and old, settees and armoires and an ancient looking cook house and fireplaces so big she could stand up in them.

The death of Bartholomew, her adored Grand Papa, had saddened the little girl as well as her brothers, but Lisette seemed to find some of Bartholomew's own love of Azilum within herself, and soon carried on as happily as ever.

The new house made her even happier. Her father had taken time out to bring her to see it just before it was ready, before the family was due to move in and before anyone else had made any kind of official visit. Her brothers had been left behind: the older one, Bart, was busy helping their mother Matilda finish packing for the move, and the little boy, Sam, was still too young, her father had said.

So he had brought her, clothed in one of her better dresses and a new bonnet, her boots shined and buttoned up and little gloves on her hands. She had even carried a small, girl-sized parasol, to guard against the incipient freckles across her nose.

Truth be told, John adored all three of his children, but he had a special soft spot in his heart for his daughter. Perhaps all fathers did: he didn't know. But that day, seeing her in some of her best clothes and with a face looking both eager and enlightened, John had been a proud, and very pleased father.

It had been May, and quite warm, so John had driven them in his smart new phaeton, which was painted a glossy black with gold trim and the initials 'JL' emblazoned on its sides. Ten and a half year old Lisette had felt quite grown up sitting next to her distinguished Papa in the elegant phaeton behind the two matched greys whose silver manes and tails swished in the gentle breeze.

The road from Towanda to the Azilum settlement had been much improved—largely John's doing—although it had still curved prettily under ancient trees and along the river once it approached the Azilum lands. Before long, Lisette had spied the house in which the Chamberlains, her grandparents, lived, then a few more houses, and then the Grand Maison had come into view.

A few yards behind it she had seen a surprising, gleaming white structure. Although she had been at Azilum while the new LaPorte House was being constructed, it had been different, somehow, seeing it in its completed entirety.

"The exterior has been finished, Lisette," her father had explained as he'd guided the phaeton along the road, drawing nearer to the white building. "The painting was completed just last week, and the shutters installed as well," he'd added.

"That is why it looks so different?" Lisette had asked. "Before it was wood, and looked like all the rest," she'd put in.

"Exactly," her father had confirmed.

He had taken great pains with the new summer home, designing the layout himself with the help of an architect friend and with suggestions, of course, from Matilda. It was to be in the new fashion, with an attached open hearth kitchen, over which were some servants' quarters.

Two stories high, the house had a spacious attic as well as a full basement lined in bluestone and slate. As it sat on a small natural rise in the land, John thought the basement would remain quite dry. On the main floor there were reception rooms and parlors as well as a formal dining room. Four large bed chambers occupied the floor above.

Although the house was done in what was called the 'French Colonial' style because of the overhanging veranda at one side, its front elevation evoked the neo-classical lines of Federalist architecture. John had even incorporated the Italian Palladian style to a small degree, insisting on that type of three part window on the east and west sides of the house, just under the peak of the slate roof.

'But that is up in the attic!' Matilda had objected when he'd shown her the plans. 'And the windows, though pretty, are small. Would it not be better to have a larger one, over the portico?' she had queried. Most houses that had Palladian windows used that more traditional placement.

John had sighed. He had wanted to incorporate Palladian windows into his new home as a nod to Independence Hall in Philadelphia. After all, he had spent considerable time in that gracious brick building when he'd been in State government. But his architect friend had explained that since John insisted on broad, twelve over twelve windows in all the rooms of the house, there would be no place for a Palladian window, really, except at the landing of the stairway to the upper floor. And that prospect looked over the back entrance and the stables: not so grand.

Therefore, they had compromised by putting smaller Palladian windows up under the peaks of the roof, where the gracious detail could be seen from both western and eastern approaches.

The day he had brought Lisette to see the finished house, he had turned the phaeton and driven down a long, wide road, bordered on either side by large fields that had been turned and planted with corn already; the feed corn trade was still brisk, and John employed overseers to carry on the agricultural endeavors his father had begun.

Then a left turn had brought them alongside more fields, with the river to their right. To their left, as they continued, the LaPorte family burial ground had risen up on a small hill.

'Can we go visit Grand-Papa's grave today?' Lisette had asked in a small voice.

'Of course we can,' her father had agreed. He missed his father terribly, and had been pleased at his daughter's request, for he'd known that she still grieved for Bartholomew, her Grand-Père, as well.

Another turn had brought them onto a smaller road, which headed straight towards the Grand Maison and the heart of what was left of Azilum. Then, they had drawn alongside the big white mansion and her father had slowed, then stopped the horses at the front portico. He'd helped Lisette down onto the neatly clipped grass, and led her towards a bluestone walkway that extended to meet a pebbled path going north towards the river and the Grand Maison. In the other direction, it led up to the new house's columned front portico.

John LaPorte had handed the phaeton's reins to a young stable boy who had come running out when he'd heard the approaching carriage. The boy had deftly unharnessed the greys and led them to the carriage house at the back, where they would be fed and watered.

Then, her father had taken Lisette's hand and led her up the wide bluestone steps of the front portico and taken out a big gold key.

"Would you like to do the honors?" he'd asked her with a smile.

None of his family had seen the inside of the house yet, except of course, for Matilda, who had directed the placement of the new furniture they had bought, and had helped John with the planning and decoration. But even Matilda hadn't seen the house sporting its new, thick coating of gleaming white paint or its impressive black shutters.

"What's this?" Lisette had asked as she had taken the key from her father. She'd pointed to a funny sort of gold lever that projected from just below one of the sidelights of the front door.

John had reached over and given the lever a twirl, and inside a bell had chimed out prettily.

"It is a door bell!" Lisette had exclaimed delightedly. "Oh Papa, how clever!" she'd said. In Towanda, their four story brick townhouse had a knocker, which worked well of course, but didn't have the musicality of a door bell.

Then, Lisette had quickly inserted the key into the big lock, and turned it smoothly. Its tumblers had released, and the door had swung wide.

Chapter Forty-Five

"This is a magnificent house!" Elizabeth said a few days later to her son. The family had officially moved in for the summer just the day before, and as it was now Sunday, they had asked Elizabeth as well as Matilda's parents to come for Sunday Dinner, and see the new home.

Everyone had the same opinion as Elizabeth, and had been mightily impressed when John had welcomed them from the impressive portico with its bluestone base and noble columns, into the gracious foyer a short while before. An airy looking staircase wound upward to the second floor, its landing sporting a very large double window that brought a great amount of light in, particularly on this sunny May day.

In the foyer were marble topped tables with vases of fresh flowers and on one, a little tray on which people could leave their calling cards.

"We won't have a butler here," John explained. "At least not this year. But as it is a summer home, 'tis much less formal," he added.

Indeed, they would 'make do' with most of the staff they had at the Towanda house. The few they left behind were either daily workers or, in this case, the family butler who was taking the summer off to make a visit to his family in Ireland.

The staff roster included their Cook, two scullery maids, a footman, two upstairs maids—one of whom functioned as Matilda's lady's maid, John's valet, and the children's Nanny. Other local help, such as for the gardens and the horses and carriages would be called in as needed.

Now, visitors' eyes were drawn upward to the high plastered ceiling by a delicate fresco of classical vines and amphorae, painted in greens, golds and reds. The fresco bordered the ceiling, in the center of which was a grand chandelier of crystal.

So much for being less formal, Elizabeth thought with a private smile. John clearly had visited many grand homes in Washington as well as Philadelphia, in the course of his work in government, and had modeled this 'summer home' along the lines of those. He had also, she thought with great contentment, taken the lovelier aspects of the Grand Maison and recreated them.

A padded settee in a deep cherry red, with cherry wood carved in curvaceous lines, invited guests to rest once they entered, and the walls held a selection of paintings of Versailles, of Marie Antoinette, Omer Talon, and a couple of landscapes, as well as a watercolor Elizabeth had just done the week before of the new house.

"That's a wonderful painting, Elizabeth," noted Irene Gilbert Chamberlain, Matilda's mother.

Elizabeth smiled, and a blush tinged her cheeks. Normally, she didn't display her paintings, and indeed, had always only shown them to Bartholomew. But now that she and Lisette painted together, some of her work found its way to others' hands. When John had seen his mother's painting of the new house, he had immediately asked if he could have it. Unbeknownst to her, he'd had it framed, and hung it in the foyer of the new home.

"Isn't it a fine work?" John agreed happily, and everyone stood around to admire the watercolor, which showed the eastern aspect of the house with its deep, covered veranda.

"This painting of Monsieur Talon was Grand-Père's," commented Lisette, who had come dancing down the staircase to join her father in giving their guests the tour. She wore a yellow, green and white flowered frock that dropped in a bell shape to her mid calf and tied just above the natural waist with a wide yellow sash. Her hair was down and curled over her shoulders, although she'd clearly made an attempt to put part of it up in adult fashion, for a lop-sided pony-tail crowned her head. A yellow ribbon that matched her sash was tied onto this ponytail and fluttered behind her as she moved.

She pointed to the oil portrait of Talon which hung a bit farther down on the wall. "He is a kind looking man," she mused, gazing at the portrayal of one of the chief founders of Azilum. "Though not so handsome as Grand-Père."

"I wish we had a portrait of your father," Elizabeth said softly to her son.

"He never wanted to bother to have one done," John returned with a sad smile. "Or one of you," he added, sharpening his gaze.

Elizabeth smiled and shook her head. "Oh, no, John, no paintings of me, please," she answered. Her brown hair, now liberally streaked with silver, was worn in a timeless fashion atop her head, and her hazel eyes were almost as clear as ever. Although she still wore gentle curls of hair at either side of her face, her lace 'lappet' cap hid most of what she still thought of as her great disfigurement: the smallpox scars.

John, like his father, barely noticed the little indentations in his mother's skin along the hairline, and considered Elizabeth, now in her mid-fifties, a very handsome woman. He shrugged. "As you wish."

Then John opened a door on the left side of the foyer, and led his guests into what he called the 'first reception room.' He invited everyone to take a seat on one of the several upholstered chairs and settees. In one corner, a gilt showcase held a few precious items that had made the journey across the ocean with the original settlers and had formerly graced the Grand Maison, and before that some of the noblest estates and chateaux in France. Now that only Elizabeth lived in the Grand

Maison, she had begun divesting it of some of its furnishings, giving them to John, if he wanted them. Although John and Matilda had largely preferred new furniture, some of the china sets, glassware, vases and bibelots had found new homes in their new house.

A footman entered the room moments later, and offered a tray of small crystal glasses filled with a dark brownish liquid.

"And what's this, John?" Elizabeth inquired, taking a glass and sniffing its contents surreptitiously.

"Ah, I heard about this in Washington," her son replied, noting with satisfaction that everyone had decided to accept a glass. The footman withdrew, leaving the tray on a small table. "It's not a very new drink, but it's new to our shores, from Italy," John further explained. "Invented by a man called Carpano. It's *'punt e mes'* which means in Italian 'point and a half.' It's one note of sweet with a half note of bitter, and stimulates the appetite," he finished confidently.

Everyone nodded, especially Dr. Chamberlain, who noted that such 'tonics' were known to be good for the digestion.

"*Santé!*" toasted Chamberlain, lifting his glass somewhat.

Everyone echoed him by repeating '*Santé!*' or using the less formal, '*Tchin-chin!*' and took a sip. John downed his in one gulp: really, he would have to get larger glasses, he thought as he put his glass down on the tray. His chiseled face beamed with good will, even though his high collar was a bit annoying. But, it was the fashion now, and for this first official dinner party he and his entire family had dressed formally, and carefully. The striped silk waistcoat was new, even if his cream colored linen court coat was a year old, and he wore the new style long trousers rather than breeches, along with shiny black court shoes.

Everyone seemed to find the Italian drink palatable if not delicious, and since there was not very much of it, they managed to drink all or most of the liquid while admiring the reception room and chatting. Here, the ceiling was again bordered in a neo Classical fresco of vines and amphorae. No central light marred the smooth expanse of the plaster, though, but the room could be lit with several pretty oil lamps that were scattered on various tables throughout the room.

"As you see, these rooms face south east," John told his guests. "So there is always plenty of light and sun, and they stay quite warm."

The large windows were accented with floor-length brocaded silk draperies in a pale gold color. Since it was day time, the draperies were held aside by tie backs so that the spectacular view of rolling meadows, the river, and forested hills could delight visitors.

"No fireplace?" queried Irene, curious.

"Not in these rooms," John replied. "As you see, they are very comfortable in the day time and at night, well, we are likely to be in other rooms, or elsewhere..." he trailed off vaguely, and moved over towards a set of double doors at the end of the room.

Chamberlain smiled, and stood up, placing his empty glass on the small tray and moving towards John. "Yes, I notice you've been saying 'these rooms,' he told his friend with a smile. "Go on..."

With a minor flourish, John pushed aside one of the wooden doors, and then the other, sliding them neatly into embrasures, or pockets, on either side.

"Oh, how grand!" Elizabeth exclaimed as her granddaughter giggled and danced into the second reception room, now revealed beyond the double doors.

"It's a double reception room!" Lisette exclaimed, twirling a bit. "Papa says even though dances are still held at the Grand Maison, if we wish to have a dance here some time, we have only to roll the carpets up," she gestured to the cream, pastel and black bordered orientals in both rooms, "*et voilà!*"

"Hmmm...no need for a fireplace at a dance," commented Irene with a smile and a nod.

John chuckled as his guests moved through the double pocket doors, which formed a wide arch when opened, and admired the second reception room. In one corner stood a tall case clock, with wooden gears and a deep sonorous chime.

More upholstered chairs and settees were dotted around the room, and a beautiful new pianoforte was tucked into a corner, its dark wood contrasting nicely with the reception rooms' lighter moulding. The ceiling here, as in the first reception room and the foyer, had a fresco in a coordinating pattern.

"Papa says I may have music lessons on the pianoforte," Lisette said happily to her assembled grand-parents, who smiled and nodded indulgently.

"*Soyez certain que tu apprends aussi ton français, et bien sûr la littérature, les mathématiques et la science,*" noted Chamberlain as he ruffled his grand-daughter's chestnut curls. Music was all very well, as were the watercoloring sessions she had from Elizabeth, but Lisette needed to know more than just the arts, he felt.

Lisette grinned up at him. "*Positivement, grand-père: mon tuteur dit que j'ai une aptitude pour les numéros en particulier!*" she chattered back at him immediately. It was true: she was quite good at figures. Chamberlain smiled to himself. No doubt, Lisette had inherited some of her mother's aptitude for math and science.

"That is why she will do well with music," Irene told her husband gently. "And French," she added with a smile. Of English and Scottish extraction, she had struggled with the Romance language as a young woman, but she was comfortable enough with it now, although she preferred English.

"Is this—tiger maple?" Chamberlain asked a moment later as, frowning, he examined a part of the pocket doors' surface.

John bit his lip and smiled. "'Tis convincing, is it not?" he asked his father-in-law. "But no, 'tis pine, for pine is abundant here and makes a good interior finishing wood."

"But..." Chamberlain interrupted.

John chuckled and explained that an extremely talented woodworker whom he'd hired and brought up from Washington to work on the house had developed a way to score the surface of pine and then stain it differently so that it almost exactly resembled the far more costly tiger maple or birds' eye maple. "You'll see that in both rooms," he noted expansively.

Also in the second reception room was a dark wood gaming table.

"This was Grand-Père's," Lisette said, touching the wood almost reverently. "I'm glad you gave us a few of his things from the Grand Maison, Grand-Mère," she added, and skipped over to take her grandmother's hand. "It makes me feel like he's still with us."

Chapter Forty-Six

The tour continued, although they could smell tantalizing odors beginning to make their way past the door that separated the main section of the house from the new kitchen, and were eager for dinner time. Still, the new house was done so beautifully and John and Lisette, and now Matilda, who had joined them as they all trooped back into the foyer near the gracious staircase, were clearly extremely pleased by it.

"Ah, here are my sons!" John exclaimed as thirteen year old Bart and four year old Sam also arrived in the foyer. Bart held his younger brother by the hand. Sam was still wearing an oversized white shirt that looked like a short dress, along with a pair of short white trousers underneath, stockings, and little brown boots that reached to his ankles. His brother, however, had just begun wearing his 'adult' clothing, smaller versions of— and sometimes made over from—his father's waist coat and jacket. Today he sported a waistcoat of robin's egg blue and a jacket in a coffee colored linen and silk blend. With it, Bart wore a stiff collar and a white shirt and cravat, and long brown trousers, even though it was quite warm.

"And although we will show you the upstairs after dinner, right now, I wish to show you my sitting room!" declared Matilda with a sparkle in her eye. She looked lovely in a summer frock of ivory silk with embroidered flowers scattered throughout the fabric. The dress featured the stylish gigot sleeves that puffed out at the top of the arm and narrowed to tidy cuffs at the wrists. A lacy pelerine, so fine it provided mere decoration, floated across her shoulders and down the front of her dress to just above her bosom. The big, bell shaped skirt of the frock swept the floor, and three petticoats beneath created the required silhouette, and also provided a pleasing rustling as she moved.

Although at first her husband's desire for a 'summer home' had seemed unnecessary to her with the Grand Maison sitting just a few yards away and mostly empty, the beauty of the new house had entranced Matilda, and now she was almost as proud of it as he was.

With a smile, she opened the door off the foyer that faced the door to the first reception room, and led everyone in to the Ladies' Drawing Room: Matilda's exclusive domain. Irene and Elizabeth both gave a delighted, 'oooh!' and sighed.

A small parlor, the room was painted in pastels, with white woodwork. A pretty bureau, or writing desk—another gift from Elizabeth—stood in one corner of the room where it could look out over both the north and west prospects.

"To watch the children playing?" queried Irene of her daughter with a smile as she looked out the windows.

Matilda nodded.

Settees and chairs offered comfy places to perch, while another pianoforte, this one ordered up from Philadelphia, meant that the ladies could enjoy some music in a more private setting than that of the formal reception rooms.

"I see there's a fireplace here," Elizabeth said with an affirming nod.

"Well, the room faces north, north-west," her son explained.

"In the evenings, it can become quite cool, especially once the fire is banked," Matilda put in. "But look!" she said merrily, and moved to open a cabinet directly over the fireplace. "A blanket warmer!" she explained, showing the shallow cupboard with shelving whose back wall was right against the fireplace's flue. Warmth from the fire would heat the blankets placed on the shelves, which might then be used on particularly chilly evenings.

"How clever!" Irene exclaimed. "Was that your idea, John?" she asked.

He shook his big head, crowned with a fine head of dark brown hair that he wore short in the fashionable style. "No—my architect friend's," he admitted.

Although there were no frescoes on the ceiling in the Ladies' Drawing Room, several lovely pictures adorned the walls. Charming porcelain and glass statuettes and vases held pride of place on tables and mantel, and vases of fresh flowers gave a delicate perfume to the air. The space was proclaimed altogether delightful.

The footman opened a door on the far side of the room at this point, and announced that dinner was ready.

Matilda turned to her mother in law and indicated that she should go through the doorway into the next room. Irene followed with her husband, and Matilda and John brought up the rear of the short procession. Lisette and Bart tripped in after the adults, and their Nanny whisked little Sam away, up to the Nursery for his own dinner.

This room was the dining room. A bit more narrow than the others, it boasted another good sized fireplace. Although the day was warm, the single window here was shaded by a large apple tree which had been spared during the house's construction. Therefore, the dining room was quite cool, and a small fire crackled in the fireplace, to take the chill from the air.

A large mahogany table occupied the center of the room and took up most of the space. A huge walnut liquor cabinet, as tall as Bart was and inlaid with gold and hand painted porcelain, occupied one wall. It, too, had come over from France and had belonged to one of the first noble families to settle Azilum. A small chandelier hung suspended in the center of the room and was lit with beeswax candles. Silver candelabra were centered on the table along with a small, low arrangement of spring blossoms.

"Our first official dinner," said Matilda happily as she took her place at the foot of the table nearer the kitchen while John sat at its head. Bart and Lisette were given seats on either side of the large table, towards the middle, Lisette next to Irene and her husband, who sat near John, and Bart next to Elizabeth, who sat near Matilda.

"So formal!" breathed Lisette, her eyes shining in the candlelight.

"Normally, we would sit *en famille*," noted her mother with a quick smile for her daughter, who was, of course, learning all about etiquette, precedence and manners as part of her schooling. "And even though we are all family, we wanted to make certain our first dinner here was perfect."

"And it is, my dear, down to the last flower petal," her mother reassured her.

The food was perfect, too: savory lamb collops with local forest mushrooms, lemon and a delicious brown gravy; rich ramequins of cheese and rice; a sallat of fresh greens from the *potager;* fresh peas from the garden and boiled beets with herbs. A side offering of pickled vegetables including carrots, cauliflower, cucumber, and brussels sprouts rounded out the meal. A cool, creamy strawberry jellied ice followed, and then various cheeses, nuts and whole fruits, including the last of the apples and pears from the previous year's harvest. Azilum still had dozens of trees that faithfully produced bushels of fruit every year.

After dinner, the ladies retired to Matilda's Drawing Room, the children were released to go out and play, and the men remained in the Dining Room and shared port, perry made from Azilum's own trees, and cigars.

Before long, however, John and his father in law joined the ladies. Elizabeth and Matilda played a couple of duets on the pianoforte, and then Elizabeth played while Irene sang. The afternoon waned, and once the golden hour began, John and Matilda brought their guests up the beautiful curving stair to the bed chambers on the second floor.

"Normally, of course, visitors won't come up here," Matilda murmured as they gained the next level. A small landing here led off to each of the four bed chambers as well as up to the house's attic, where the children's Nanny and the most senior housemaid had their quarters. "Still..." Matilda smiled and gestured to a magnificent red lamp hanging suspended over the stairwell. A servant had already seen to the lamp and lit its small central wick, which descended into a little reservoir of oil. Although daylight still flooded in through the big window over the staircase's landing, the red lamp glowed, and Irene gasped.

"I have never seen red glass!" she exclaimed, staring at the fixture.

"John brought it back for us last autumn, after his trip to Italy," Matilda explained. John had gone abroad to discuss various trade agreements and had discovered a small glassblowing enterprise near Florence that was producing the ruby glass. The proprietor had explained that, although the Romans had made colored glass, including red glass, the methodology had been lost until it had recently been re-discovered by his grandfather, mostly by accident. 'Gold salts,' he had informed John, when added to the molten glass, resulted in the beautiful ruby color. John had been enthralled and had immediately commissioned this piece, destined for his new home.

On the far right of the small upstairs landing was a large room which served as the bed chamber for little Sam and for his elder brother Bart. Two narrow beds occupied opposite sides of the room, and a little desk stood next to one: clearly, Bart's part of the space. Sam's toys were lined up under one window, and the children's clothing was squirreled away in a closet.

Every bed chamber had a closet, unusual in most homes, but necessary because the LaPortes were wealthy enough to have a number of clothing choices, and so needed more storage space than just a peg behind the door.

Next to the boys' bedchamber was another large one: Matilda's room. Three big windows looked out over the river and the eastern aspect, and pretty porcelain bibelots decorated several of the surfaces. A large marble topped dresser was crowned by an adjustable mirror, allowing Matilda to accomplish her toilette in comfort and ease. A small dressing room connected to the bed chamber, and here Matilda could change her clothes throughout the day—although she generally just had two or three outfits per day, since here in the country things were much more relaxed than in the city.

The attic door was next in order on the upstairs landing, and although the LaPortes did not show their guests that level of the house, they explained that the area was warm and dry in the winter and cool enough in the summer thanks to the two Palladian windows on either end, which provided a cross breeze.

"Just like on the ground floor, you may have noticed the door behind the staircase," John pointed out to his family. "Not only does that lead out onto the veranda, for convenience, but if the day is very warm, both that door and the front door can be opened, and a truly cooling breeze comes right through the house, off the river," he explained.

The next room on the upper floor was bright and airy. Unlike the other rooms, it had a fireplace, and it was Lisette's. Dolls with porcelain and cloth heads and bodies, dressed in all manner and styles of clothing, sat around a little chest enjoying a tea party with a miniature china set. A few other toys were neatly placed in another corner, and the obligatory wash stand with pitcher and bowl was next to the large bed.

A couple of cradles, currently occupied by dolls, stood ready for future LaPorte children, something both John and Matilda wanted, and did all they could to bring about.

"On cold nights, Sam can bundle in here," Matilda said with a chuckle and a gesture to the big bed. "And the fireplace will keep everyone warm."

"Yes, I'm sure Bart would tough it out," commented John with a chuckle. His oldest child was stoic about many things, he was learning, a quality he admired.

John's room was the next, and last bed chamber. It had only one window, but a very large fireplace whose mantel extended around to a dressing alcove. Here, John had all the usual accoutrements he and his valet would require to dress: a shaving mirror, razor strops, cuff links, cuffs and collars, and a range of various hats for different occasions.

John had recently been named an Associate Judge of Bradford County. Since his term in the U.S. Legislature was up at the end of the following year, he had accepted the post, although he would only hear a few cases in 1837, until he was completely at liberty to sit on the bench. Because of this new appointment, a curly grey judge's wig also occupied a stand on one of the dressers.

By now, the golden hour had fled and the sun, having dropped below the horizon, had brought on the blue hour. Everyone returned to the main floor, where the servants had laid out a light supper. The children, who had been playing in the meadow next to the house, were called in. Little Sam said his good nights and was taken up to bed. Everyone else enjoyed the repast and, since the evening was drawing to a close, began to think about heading home.

Then the Chamberlains and Elizabeth took their leave, and the LaPortes began their first summer in their new house.

Chapter Forty-Seven

The LaPorte House was a wonderful respite for the LaPortes each summer: with the river so close, all manner of summer activities were, as always, handy, and the temperature was undeniably cooler than in Towanda, or Philadelphia. Matilda in particular found that the house and everyone's clothing stayed much cleaner, too, because at Azilum, no dust or dirt from highly traveled roadways, or soot from houses packed closely together, sullied anything.

Although John could afford to build the house, he had relied on credit: when the house was completed, he still owed rather a lot of money for the work and materials that had gone into it. Although he had contracts spelling out how the debts would be repaid, Elizabeth decided the time was right to make the acquaintance of the jeweler Bartholomew had done business with in Towanda. Early one morning in the early autumn of 1836 when the family had closed the House for that winter, Elizabeth took her pony trap and made the trip to the city. There, she introduced herself to the jeweler, who was delighted to make her acquaintance.

From the pouch of diamonds that Bartholomew had given her, and which Elizabeth had begun to wear, as her husband had, around her neck, she had withdrawn two stones. A fair deal was struck between her and the jeweler, and a couple of weeks afterwards when John stopped by the Grand Maison for a visit, she handed him the money.

"But, *Maman*, where did you—how—? What did you sell?" John asked, completely confused. He looked around the parlor where they sat, as though trying to find missing heirlooms: he thought Elizabeth must have sold some furniture or a gilt mirror or some precious memento of Old France.

Elizabeth shook her head and smiled at her son. "Your father left me some, erm, assets," she told him. "I am not without means, John. I should prefer it if you were not to owe anyone, particularly as it is within my gift to see that you do not." She paused. "Your new house is lovely, and I hope you and Matilda and the children have a very long and happy succession of summers there. And now, you may breathe a bit easier, because you can own it, outright, and do not owe anyone for its construction," she had told him.

To say that John had been shocked would have been an understatement, and he pestered his mother to tell him the source of the sudden windfall. However, remembering Bartholomew's final words, she reminded herself that John will 'make his own way,' but that she might 'help' him if she chose. And that is what she had done. So she just smiled mysteriously and John called her the 'American Mona Lisa' for her inscrutability.

In the summer of 1838, Matilda was stricken with a severe throat infection, although none of the rest of the family had it. After a couple of weeks, during which she ate only broth and water and stayed in bed, she appeared somewhat recovered. However, towards the end of July, new symptoms appeared, including a high fever and the complaint that her joints ached so badly she could barely move.

Her father, the doctor, almost certainly knew his daughter suffered from rheumatic fever, and correctly diagnosed her 'throat infection' as strep throat. The treatment of choice was salicylic acid. This eased the pain somewhat but did nothing for the actual infection. Weakened already by weeks of eating next to nothing, Matilda succumbed to the fever on August 5, 1838.

All the LaPorte children were devastated, although 15 year old Bart handled his mother's death in a very adult fashion, consoling his sister and trying to maintain his dignity, like his father.

John was in too much shock, at least at first, to grieve. His wonderful, clever, challenging Matilda could not possibly be dead! Sadly, as the days went by and the death notices went out, and the family prepared for Matilda's funeral, John did come to accept his wife's death.

It was then that the grief hit him. He kept to his room when he was at Azilum, not willing to set a foot inside Matilda's, and delegating the sorting and removal of her things to his mother, Elizabeth.

She, too, grieved for the loss of her daughter in law, but more than that she grieved to see her son so bereft. He cancelled the cases he'd been due to hear for the immediate future and spent most of his time in the second reception room, playing endless games of Patience at his father's old gaming table, and drinking: John nearly always had a tumbler of something in his hand for the first few weeks after Matilda's death. Elizabeth had asked him, once, if the liquor helped the pain.

'No, *Maman*, it does not make it less. But it makes me better able to bear it,' John had replied sorrowfully.

Little six year old Samuel was almost too young to understand that his 'Mama' was gone, but her absence left a sadness in his heart that it would take the rest of his childhood to understand, and deal with.

It was Lisette, whose world up until that point had been remarkably free from struggle of any kind, who took her mother's death the hardest. Now 13, she initially reacted by denying that her mother was dead and believing that Matilda had just 'gone visiting.'

It took Elizabeth, who had moved in to the LaPorte House to help out when Matilda had first become ill, to finally bring Lisette around to the point where she accepted that her mother was, indeed, dead.

Dully, the child helped Elizabeth make tokens of remembrance for all who attended the funeral of Matilda Chamberlain LaPorte: black bordered handkerchiefs, black hatbands and sprigs of rosemary from the Grand Maison's *potager*, with black silk ribbons, were fashioned in almost total silence in the foyer of the House.

Lisette, echoing her father's emotions, positively refused to work in the Ladies' Drawing Room, because it reminded her so much of her mother, and because that memory was too painful to be borne. In addition, it was the warmest part of the summer, so the grandmother and granddaughter sewed yard after yard of black ornaments with the front and back doors of the house wide open to catch the river breezes.

Elizabeth tried to cheer the child with Bible readings that spoke of the joys of Heaven, but it was too soon for Lisette to even think about that, and she took little comfort in the possibility that her Mother was better off now. The fact that she was no longer in Lisette's life was still too agonizing for the child to see beyond it.

When Matilda's personal items were disbursed, the lion's share naturally went to Lisette. But the child firmly refused to have any dresses made over from any of her mother's frocks. Instead, the dresses were given to the staff, and to Matilda's sisters.

Matilda's jewelry was likewise divvied up, although Lisette did keep her mother's pearls in their pretty velvet box. She would not wear them until she married some years later: by then, the memory of her mother would have softened to a sweet pang, and the pearls—a long strand of lustrous orbs that had been John's wedding gift to his bride—would bring a sad smile to her lips, but no tears to her eyes.

Elizabeth, who had always been a talented seamstress ever since she herself had been a young girl, taught by her mother Susanna, had taken to wearing only black once her husband Bartholomew had died. Now, of course, once Matilda died, everyone in the family had to wear black, for a full year and a day. Elizabeth got very busy fashioning black waist coats for the boys—John had a few already—and made two black matte bombazine frocks for Lisette.

Even their chemises were to be black, and Elizabeth made Lisette several. Oddly enough, Lisette did not seem to object to the dark colors. On the contrary, she embraced it and seemed to think that wearing black not only protected her somehow, but fit well with her new, solemn persona. She who had been so vivacious and outgoing now spoke very little, played very little and seemed to spend large portions of her days staring out a window, or down at her clasped hands. When Elizabeth asked Lisette what she was thinking about, the girl would merely shake her head, and resume whatever task she was supposed to have been engaged in.

Lisette now had another grave to visit in the family cemetery after Matilda was laid to rest there. Before the family left to return to Towanda for the autumn and winter, she gathered purple asters and goldenrod from Azilum's fields, and laid huge bouquets on all of the graves.

Elizabeth watched from an upstairs window as her granddaughter returned to the house, a slight, black figure against the green and gold tapestry of the field. She shook her head: of all her grandchildren, Lisette troubled her the most. Her son, John, had asked if she could possibly leave the Grand Maison to return with him and the children to Towanda.

'I don't know what to do, *Maman*,' he had begun. 'I mean, of course, Bart is all right: he's nearly a man,' he had said, sounding a bit gruff.

Elizabeth had smiled: yes, her oldest grandchild was stoic, but she knew he grieved for his mother nonetheless.

'I worry about little Sam, he is still young, and needs care beyond what his tutors can give him,' John had said.

Elizabeth had nodded.

'And Lisette—she is so quiet now! She, who was so —boisterous!' John had finished, frustrated. 'I had to command her to attend Matilda's funeral, you recall?' he had asked, bewildered. 'And she wouldn't stand with the family at the wake.'

That was true, Elizabeth had recalled. Lisette had not wanted to see her mother's body, and had almost thrown an infantile tantrum until Elizabeth had intervened and told her son that Lisette could perhaps be excused from that trial, if she would agree to attend the funeral service at chapel and gravesite. Her granddaughter's dark mood reminded Elizabeth sharply of her own after her many miscarriages, and after her beloved Bartholomew died. She understood Lisette, and understood her sadness, but Elizabeth did not want to think that her granddaughter might suffer the same lengthy depression that she had.

'I can only think that if you come with us to Towanda, they would do better,' John had coaxed. 'They need familiar faces around them, and I am gone so much of the time,' he had added.

This, of course, was true: John was now working full time as an Associate Judge of Bradford County, and so was gone most days except at week's end. But the few hours between Saturday noon and Monday morning were not enough to conscientiously raise a young family, and Elizabeth had known that John would need help.

Elizabeth thought that, as devoted as he had been to Matilda, John might never remarry. Although she could not be certain, Elizabeth suspected that John had always remained faithful to the woman he called his 'soul mate.'

So she had agreed to de-camp from her home at Azilum and, like Ruth, follow to the Towanda house at the corner of Main and Lombard Streets, where servants did almost everything.

Even with Elizabeth's steadying presence, however, Lisette faltered. She did less well in school, and no longer enjoyed playing her pianoforte. During the first two months of mourning, the LaPortes attended no balls or dinners or even informal dances, which was fine with Lisette, who kept to herself in one of the small family parlors unless she was needed for some activity, and went up to her bed chamber every night, bereft and silent.

Bart, as his father had suspected, brought himself around once he returned to Towanda and his friends at school, and his tutors and lessons.

Sam, too, was once more his cheerful self by the time winter began nipping at the family's heels in November: he had just begun school and had many new things to occupy his mind and new friends to occupy his time.

Every night, Elizabeth heard the children's prayers. Bart, of course, just whispered his, mostly under his breath as he knelt by his bed, and Elizabeth perched at his side on the down filled duvet.

Sam lisped for God to watch over his Mama and his Grand-Père in Heaven, and then painstakingly named each of the family's two dogs and three cats as well as the pony he was learning to ride and several of his school chums, and invoked health and happiness for them.

Elizabeth also sat on Lisette's bed each night, as the girl obediently folded her hands over her duvet once Elizabeth had 'tucked her in,' and silently said her prayers —or appeared to. One evening, Elizabeth asked her granddaughter if she, like everyone else, had said a special prayer for those who had died in a steamboat explosion the previous week, near Wilkes-Barre.

Steamships had begun plying the Susquehanna River a decade before, and men like John LaPorte as well as others engaged in commerce, hoped they would finally conquer the river's pesky tide and provide a reliable means of transport across northern Pennsylvania to the Great Lakes. However, steamboats had thus far proven more risky than reliable, and news of this most recent tragedy had been the regional headline for the past several days.

Now, Lisette gave her grandmother a long look as if assessing her trustworthiness, and then shook her head. "No, Grand-Mère," she whispered.

Elizabeth fought to keep her features calm in the light of Lisette's bedside candle. "And why do you not, *ma petite*?" Elizabeth asked gently, using the pet name for her granddaughter that Bartholomew had used for her for so many years.

"Because—because I do not think that God listens," Lisette finally said, so low that Elizabeth had to bend down to hear her properly.

"Why do you think that, Lisette?" Elizabeth asked, touching her granddaughter's smooth cheek gently. The girl had lost weight, and her face no longer bore the chubby outlines of childhood.

"Because if God listened to us, *Maman* would be here," Lisette replied stubbornly, but tears shimmered in her eyes. "I have asked and asked, every night since she died, and..." she broke off and pressed her lips firmly together.

Elizabeth took one of Lisette's slender hands in hers. "Do not be angry at God, Lisette. Your *Maman* was called to heaven and we may never know why. Just trust that she is there, and happy now, and watching over you and Sam and Bart and your father, just as she did when she was alive," she counselled. "God does listen, *ma petite*," she continued, nodding her head and smiling a bit. "But sometimes His answer is not the one we wish for."

Lisette had not seemed comforted, and Elizabeth watched her even more closely after that. To lose hope, and to be angry with God, while understandable, was something that needed to be dealt with, and dealt with quickly, before it could turn into a deep depression. And Elizabeth and depression were old friends: she saw the incipient signs in her granddaughter and knew she had to do something.

Elizabeth also knew that thirteen—which Lisette had turned at the end of November—was a tricky age. Not really a child but not yet a woman, it was an age when most young girls took refuge and found support with a gaggle of girlfriends. Elizabeth still treasured her friendship with Irene Gilbert Chamberlain, who had helped her during some very hard times in her own life, and wished Lisette could find that for herself.

At the moment, though, it seemed as though Lisette had cut herself off from everyone, preferring solitude, or the company of her many dolls. Elizabeth suspected the girl may have poured out her heart only to those dolls, whose bisque and porcelain faces never judged, and whose cloth bodies would always be available to be hugged.

And so, in the weeks before Christmas, Elizabeth hatched a plan. She went into town one day on a secret mission, and placed a special order at one of Towanda's finest mercantile stores. Then, about a week later, she began spending many hours after the children were in bed and the servants had banked the fires and trimmed the lamps, sewing by lamp light.

For Christmas that year, 1838, Elizabeth gave Lisette a new doll. It was a porcelain doll with a hand painted face and pretty hair made from a horse's mane. Elizabeth had special ordered it and had been making a wardrobe for it since its arrival. Lisette unwrapped the gift paper carefully, and gazed at the doll. It was beautiful, and she smiled, for she had always loved dolls, and this was by far the finest she owned.

Reverently she touched the cool, smooth cheek, and smiled again.

"You like her?" Elizabeth asked her granddaughter.

Lisette nodded.

The two of them were alone together in the room Elizabeth used at the Towanda house. Elizabeth, though she hoped for a positive reaction, had not been altogether sure that Lisette would respond favorably to the gift, and so had chosen to give it to her in private.

"Does her gown look familiar to you?" Elizabeth asked gently.

Lisette peered closely at the tiny garment, for the doll itself was no more than eighteen inches, its head the size of a lemon.

"It looks—like one that—*Maman* had?" she finally asked, choking a bit on the question.

Elizabeth nodded. "Yes. It was originally my gown, once upon a time: a beautiful deep fern green silk gown that I was wearing the day your Grand-Père asked me to be his wife," she explained, her voice soft with reminiscence.

Lisette's smile widened.

"When your Papa married your *Maman*, I knew I would never fit into the gown again," Elizabeth continued with a chuckle. Middle age had brought several extra pounds, particularly around her torso. "So I cut it down and re-fashioned it into a gown in what was then the new Empire style, for your *Maman*," she explained.

"I think I remember her wearing it," Lisette offered hesitantly.

Elizabeth thought for a moment. The gown had gone out of style by 1830 or so, but it was possible that Lisette had seen it, and remembered.

"I thought—I thought we gave away all of *Maman*'s clothing," Lisette whispered.

Elizabeth nodded. "Most of it. Well, except for this, and some chemises and petticoats that I've made over. But this, because it had been mine once, and had such happy associations for me, I saved this." She sighed, and pointed to the doll's dress. "I took the best part of it to make this little dress, for your doll. Something to have of your mother's," she explained. "I think you are ready, now, for that," she ventured, watching her granddaughter closely.

Lisette swallowed, hard, and touched the doll again. "It's almost—almost as though a little part of *Maman* is here," she whispered, fingering the silk of the doll's gown.

Elizabeth smiled hopefully. "I told you, *ma petite,* she will never really leave you: as long as you remember her, she lives on," she said gently.

The remainder of the deep fern green silk gown was carefully stored in a trunk in a far corner of the attic. With it was the rest of the bolt of silk that Bartholomew had gifted to the Franklins so long ago.

Elizabeth hoped that Lisette, or perhaps a future LaPorte, would once again re-make the dress in a current style, years in the future.

Now, Lisette raised shining eyes to her grandmother, and looked for the first time in months like the girl Elizabeth remembered. "Thank you, so much,

Grand-Mère," she whispered, clasping the doll to her chest, and then enveloping Elizabeth in a hug. "I love you, and I love her."

Chapter Forty-Eight

Fortunately, once a year had passed and the family shifted into half mourning, the lighter tones of grey, lavender and navy seemed to carry on the lightening of spirit that the doll had begun in Lisette. The successive traumas of her great-grandfather's death, and then her beloved grandfather's, followed by her mother's unexpected death, had forever tamed her youthful ebullience. But she grew into a contented, thoughtful, even-tempered and usually smiling young woman.

Her studies improved, and by the time the family marked the second anniversary of Matilda's death, in the late summer of 1840, Lisette had even gone back to playing the pianoforte, and found that it brought her much pleasure, as it had before.

She had grown close again to her father and brothers, but was especially close to her Grand-Mère. Elizabeth knew that in a way she had become a mother figure for the girl, but she felt that could do no real harm. She was only in her late fifties, and planned to live for many years and see Lisette safely into adulthood and, she hoped, a good marriage.

But before Lisette had even begun to think about beaus, the family dynamic was changed again by John's announcement that he and a woman he had come to know intended to marry.

Eliza Caldwell Brindle had herself come from a distinguished Pennsylvania family and had married into one of the first families of Lycoming Township when she married William Brindle on March 8, 1832. A few years younger than John, she had been widowed early and tragically when her husband, publisher of the *Lycoming Gazette,* drowned on May 15, 1833 while crossing the Muncy Creek near Clarkstown, PA.

For several years, Eliza had taken over her husband's work at the newspaper, although at the time such an occupation was not considered very 'seemly' for a woman. Still, as she told anyone who remonstrated her for her vocation, it gave her something to do, and it gave her a way to honor her late husband, and keep his good work alive.

The newspaper was the way in which she had become acquainted with John, a few years before Matilda died, when he had come into the newspaper's offices to discuss placing advertisements for his election to the U.S. House of Representatives for the 17th District of Pennsylvania. John had even told Matilda, always a champion of women, about the remarkable female editor of the newspaper, and Matilda had been glad.

'Some day, women will be able to be anything they want, John, just as men can do now,' she had remarked to him.

John had agreed with her, he recalled, although he also recalled that at the time of the conversation, Matilda had been breastfeeding the infant Samuel. And John had remarked that in his estimation, women already could do the most remarkable thing on earth: bring new life into the world.

John had continued to favor the *Gazette* with ads and notices whenever important things occurred and had of course sent in the notice of Matilda's death in the summer of 1838. He had been deeply touched by the condolence card sent by Eliza as well as the note she'd penned saying merely that she could uniquely understand his feelings, having suffered through the loss of a spouse herself.

Because he was retired from Congress, John had no reason now to visit Lycoming as he had when it had housed some of his constituents. So he had simply written back to Mrs. Brindle on the reverse of one of the printed cards the family had been using after Matilda's death, thanking her for her kind words.

It was late in 1839, at a Judges' Convocation in Williamsport to which all Judges from Lycoming, Bradford and Luzerne Counties were invited, that John once again met up with Mrs. Brindle. She was in attendance not only because the Convocation was newsworthy, but because a few select journalists and publishers had been invited as a thank you to them for their coverage and support of county judiciaries.

By early 1840, John was finding reasons to travel down to Lycoming a couple of times a month and in the spring, Elizabeth asked him about his trips—although she suspected.

"Are you certain this Mrs. Brindle is not just looking to find a good, solid man to support her?" Elizabeth asked, fearful that perhaps the widow's intentions were not as benign as her son seemed to think they were.

John shook his head. "Her late husband left his share of the *Gazette* to her, and 'tis a good living, a good income," he explained. "And you will see, when you meet her: Eliza is kind, and understanding. She has suffered, as I have, the loss of a spouse, although in her case I feel it has been even more tragic," he answered with a sad smile.

John and his mother were in the second reception room at the LaPorte House at Azilum. The family had just moved to the summer home for the warmer months, and Bart, Sam and Lisette were all still upstairs, unpacking and setting their bed chambers to rights while the servants scurried around, trying to make everything perfect. To ensure their privacy, John had shut the pocket doors as well as the single door that led to the downstairs hallway, and both he and his mother kept their voices low. It was late afternoon, and the sun slanted in the tall twelve over twelve windows through the lace curtains, and glinted off the rich fibers in the hand-loomed floral rug.

"Tragic?" Elizabeth echoed now, cocking her head. "How so?"

John explained that Eliza had lost her husband barely more than a year after they had been married.

"And she had no children?" Elizabeth asked, curious.

John shook his head. "No. She very much wants a family, though," he added, and gave his mother a hopeful look.

It was true that his romance with Eliza Brindle had taken off like a shot and after six months was still blazing. And while he had not yet proposed to her, John was certain that he wanted to, and equally certain that Eliza would accept. Both had found solace, as well as a renewed outlook on life, in each other's arms.

Elizabeth sat back and gave a delicate sort of snort before looking askance at her son and waggling a finger at him. At the very least, she thought, his companionship with Mrs. Brindle had brought a dramatic reduction in her son's drinking, so she could at least be grateful for that.

"You do not need my permission, John, if you want to marry this woman," she reminded him. "But you may wish to seek the blessing of your children. Their mother has not yet been dead for two full years, and Lisette, especially, has just begun to come out of her blue mood," Elizabeth continued, her voice a strident whisper. "How do you think she will feel if you bring a usurper into the family?" she finished bitingly.

"Eliza is no usurper," John replied, mild. "She would never wish to try and take Matilda's place with the children—or with me," he told his mother firmly. "Actually, *Maman,* I am very fond of Eliza, but I do not believe I could have what I had with Matilda with anyone else, ever," he added, very quietly. "But the children could do with…" before the words 'a mother figure' could make their way out of his mouth, John pressed his lips together and took a deep breath through his nose. He paused, then resumed: "they have been very fortunate to have you here, *Maman*. But you are no longer so very young, and I know you long to return to your own house," he said persuasively.

Elizabeth stood from the settee she'd been sitting on. "Perhaps that kind of coaxing works with your political friends but it is no inducement to me," she told him flatly.

"*Maman*!" He stood.

"I am prepared to stay with the children until the day I no longer draw breath, by which time, God willing, they will be adults with families of their own," Elizabeth said, her voice low but firm. "There is no reason for you to rush out and marry *une frippon*, merely to provide them with a mother. They have one. Me."

John was unfamiliar with the word his mother used, but knew from her tone that it was not a favorable term. He did not understand why his mother was being so negative towards Eliza. He bridled. "I shall marry whom I wish, and when I wish, *Maman*," he declared, his voice raised enough so that Elizabeth made a shushing motion with her hands.

"We do not need the staff overhearing this!" she remonstrated.

John looked down, but his face was implacable.

"Do as you wish, then, John, but heed my advice: speak to your children, before you speak to Mrs. Brindle."

He sighed. "Her name is Eliza, *Maman*. Will you not even meet her?" he asked sadly.

Elizabeth's face softened. "Of course, John, I shall meet her." She paused. "And perhaps then I will better understand why you wish to marry her, see a little bit of what you see in her," she added in a conciliatory voice.

She knew, of course, why John's news had upset her so. Although she had never resented Matilda, now that Bartholomew was gone, and Matilda as well, it had seemed to Elizabeth that she and John could carry on together in the family, bringing up the children and being each other's companion. It had worked well for almost two years, and John had never given any indication of wishing to find another wife. He had seemed content to live, loving only the memory of Matilda, and his children, and his mother.

But looking at her son's face, Elizabeth remembered how shattered he had been when Matilda had died, and realized that if this Eliza might keep her son happier than he had been recently, their wedding should be something that she would be glad of. For John's happiness meant more to her than her own.

John took his mother's advice and called the children together in that same second reception room, which he used informally as his parlor, a couple of weeks later. Elizabeth purposely absented herself: she donned a wide brimmed hat and shawl, and went out to see how the *potager* was progressing.

Bart seemed happy for his father: at sixteen he was only too familiar with the longing not having a woman in one's life could bring to a man of any age, and so was sympathetic to his father's plight, even though that was possibly one of the very last reasons John wanted to marry Eliza. Sam, at only seven, just seemed happy there would be another woman around besides his Grand-Mère. Maybe his father's new wife would spoil him, since his grandmother did not.

Lisette was quiet at her father's news, and only said that if he were happy, so was she.

"I know you are still grieving for your *Maman*," John told his daughter quietly once the boys had gone.

Lisette nodded.

"And so am I. I will always miss her, and I will also always love her, like I could love no one else, Lisette." He paused. "But Eliza—Mrs. Brindle—is not a replacement for your mother, not in any way. But you see little Sam, he needs a mother, and..."

"We have Grand-Mère," Lisette put in, her chin stubborn. Her eyes flashed at her father.

"Of course. And we are all so lucky that she has been well and able to live with us since your dear *Maman*..." He sighed. "But she will not live forever, Lisette," he murmured.

Lisette took a deep breath. "I know that, Papa, of course." She paused. "Do you—love—Mrs. Brindle?" she asked. She had only a vague idea of what 'love' really entailed, thinking it to be companionship but also a physical relationship, about which she knew very little. "You only said that you had been lonely since *Maman* died, and that now that you spend more time here at home than you did when you had to be in Washington, you found you needed a wife," she parroted his words almost perfectly. "But you did not say you loved her."

John gave his teenaged daughter a long look. What, indeed, was love? Matilda would always be the love of his life. But Eliza was sweet, and understanding, and not demanding. And she had wanted to have children. If they wed, he could provide her with that, as well as with a ready-made family of his own children, and would that not be a good thing? And, he thought, Eliza might be a good companion for him in his later years, since she was younger than he. Was all of that love? Of a kind, he supposed.

So he gave his daughter his answer. "I do not love her as I loved your *Maman*. I will never love anyone as I loved her. But I admire her, and respect her, and find her most pleasing to look at, and so yes, I suppose, I love her. Well enough," he finished.

Lisette frowned as though she found his reply dissatisfying, but did not challenge him further. She merely kissed his cheek and walked thoughtfully out of the room.

Chapter Forty-Nine

John and Eliza married on November 28, 1840, and moved into the Towanda house after a brief honeymoon at Niagara. John was most interested in seeing the waterwheels and factories that churned below the cascade, relying on their power to produce a multitude of products. Sadly, he thought to himself how much Matilda would have enjoyed seeing it too, and figuring out how everything worked.

Although Elizabeth remained in Towanda with the children until the couple's return, immediately after Christmas she moved back to the Grand Maison and left her son and his new wife to live in relative peace with the children. Elizabeth's view of Eliza had mellowed a bit since meeting the woman, who was, unquestionably, very polite and appeared kind and intelligent. However, she remained convinced that a co-publisher of a small newspaper would most surely look to trade that somewhat uncertain and only moderately lucrative life for one that aligned her to one of the most powerful and wealthy men in the area, and assured her a life of comfort and distinction.

Elizabeth's return to the Grand Maison was greeted with joy by the servants who had remained in the house year round to maintain it, and who by now considered it their home as much as it was Elizabeth's. Her friend Irene, Dr. Chamberlain's wife, was also overjoyed to have her great friend back where the two were close enough for daily chats and afternoon teas, customs they had begun decades before.

However, the Maison was in need of serious repairs by now, and Elizabeth had once again dipped into her diamond stash to obtain money for a new roof and repairs to several leaky windows. She hired local workers to help the now aging servants who had been with the Maison since it had been built, and gardens and gazebos flourished that spring. Elizabeth took great pride and pleasure in walking extensively whenever the weather was fine, and kept herself as trim as possible.

"I never liked the softness I acquired once John was born," she confided to Irene as the two walked one day along the river side path.

"You and Bartholomew tried so many times for more children, though, Elizabeth," Irene returned, placing a gentle hand on her friend's arm. "All those pregnancies, of course they wreaked havoc on your figure," she told her.

Elizabeth nodded. "Your husband says walking is a fine exercise and I intend to walk every day, now that I am here, and have no grandchildren's needs to see to," she commented.

Irene glanced at her out of the corners of her eyes. "But you miss them, surely?" she queried.

"Oh, I do," Elizabeth assured her. "But now that they have, erm, Eliza, they no longer need me, and so I am free to pursue my own interests," she finished, sounding both bitter and uncertain.

"You still feel as though John pushed you out when he married Mrs. Brindle?" Irene asked softly.

Elizabeth sighed. "Not so much pushed me out, as I wanted to leave once his new wife arrived. A house cannot have two mistresses," she added with a chuckle. "Although Matilda and I managed very well," she added thoughtfully. "But I had my own house and she hers, even if I did spend a great deal of time with them once the new house here was built"

Irene joined in with a light laugh, and allowed as that was very true. "Should they not be here for the summer by now?" she asked next. It was the end of May.

"They are usually here by the 15th at least," she added ruminatively.

Elizabeth nodded. "That is correct. But John wrote a month or so ago and said they would be delayed this year in their arrival. He did not say why, precisely, but I can guess," she added wryly.

Irene looked at her friend, puzzled. Then her brow cleared. "Already? But they were only married at the end of November!" she blurted out, surprised.

"I know..."

"You don't think—..." she left the thought unspoken.

Elizabeth sighed again. "I don't think, no," she answered firmly. "But I do think that she, especially, very much wanted to have children," she amended.

When the LaPortes arrived at the beginning of June, the reason for the delay was clear: Eliza Brindle LaPorte was pregnant, and just beginning to show. The fashions of the day demanded a natural waistline and corseting once again, after the freedoms of the Regency period in the 1810s through the early 1830s. This meant that although she employed the virtues of tight lacing, by June there was an obvious thickening at her middle.

John told his mother that his new wife was expected to deliver their child in late October, and Elizabeth, recalling her conversation with Irene several days prior, was relieved. At least the child had not been conceived out of wedlock!

Bart was now apprenticed at Towanda and so only came to Azilum at the end of the work week. But Lisette and Sam came along with John and Eliza, and both children were overjoyed to be back at their summer home —and to see their Grand-Mère. For Lisette in particular, the reunion with Elizabeth was very sweet, and the two lost no time in going off for a walk together after dinner the day the family arrived.

"She's resting," Lisette told Elizabeth with a giggle. At fifteen, Lisette had grown into a leggy but quite pretty young woman. She had her father's height, but Matilda's slender frame, and mentally, Elizabeth was reviewing young men in the area to see if any were tall enough to take on her granddaughter as a girlfriend.

"Well, she is *enceinte*, what, now, four months?" Elizabeth asked reasonably. "Not everyone is as hale as your mother was when carrying a child," Elizabeth counseled. Matilda had been exceptional, she thought, in that regard.

"Oh, Grand-Mère, I am sorry, I wasn't thinking," Lisette said quickly, touching her grandmother's arm. "I know you had a very hard time of it, and lost so many babies," she added in a small voice.

"Ah, *oui*, yes, but not with your father. When I was carrying your father I did everything: I rode, I walked, I danced: everything. It was only afterwards..." she trailed off, lost in recollection.

"Father calls it Eliza's 'delicate condition,'" Lisette continued, still giggling a bit.

Elizabeth remarked to herself that now Lisette called her father, 'Father,' not 'Papa' as she had before. She wondered if that were a mark of maturity, or a mark of distance. She also noted that Lisette called her step-mother, 'Eliza.'

"Really, I don't know why they need to have any more children: father has two sons, plus me!" Lisette declared.

Elizabeth just smiled. They walked on. Lisette chattered away, very much like her old self, about a couple of friends from school and about what diversions she intended to pursue that summer at Azilum.

"I want to do watercolors with you again, Grand-Mère, all right?" she asked, and Elizabeth was pleased.

"*Certainement!*" she agreed. "And you will ride as well? You're becoming an excellent horsewoman, if I recall?"

"Oh, yes, I will ride, of course. Father says the road to Wyalusing is very much improved, and I intend to see for myself, very soon!" she finished merrily.

The days passed quite quickly, even though, out of deference to Eliza's condition, John would not give any big receptions or dinners, either at his own House or at the Grand Maison.

He noted with pleasure the repairs his mother had made to the latter, although he did ask her where she had got the money for the new roof and all the landscaping.

Elizabeth reminded him that Bartholomew had left her well provided for, and once again he called her '*La Gioconda d'Amerique.*'

Lisette rode several times to Wyalusing on one of the family's sturdy horses, passing the new homes and farms that had sprung up along the way. One of the earliest homesteads, too, the one belonging to the Welles family, was of special interest to her, because it pre-dated even the Grand Maison, which to that point was the oldest house Lisette had ever seen.

The Welles house sat atop a knoll on the southern bank of the river, and looked down over acres and acres of fertile alluvial farmland belonging to the family. The view from the house was spectacular.

The Welles house had been built with the ubiquitous finished-edge planks as houses had been built at Azilum. However, visible white 'daub' between the planks reminded Lisette of frosting on a fancy layer cake. In her mind, as she rode by the house many times that summer, she came to call the Welles house, 'the cake house.'

She knew the family had settled along the Susquehanna several miles downriver from Azilum around the time of the Revolution. One of their neighbors, whose surname was Terry, had fought in the Revolution. She didn't know, however, if the house were that old, or had been built afterwards. But her grandmother had told her that her grandfather had reminisced about the very early days of Azilum, before anything had been built there, when only John King's house and the Welles house were bright spots of civilization in the wilderness.

One afternoon in August as she was returning from Wyalusing with the mail, which she had cheerfully volunteered to collect for her father, she spied a man outside the Welles house as she trotted up the road in that direction.

"Good afternoon!" she called as she drew near. Yes, it wasn't 'proper' for a woman to speak to a man she did not know, not until they had been introduced. It was probably even less proper for her to call out from the back of a horse she was riding, Lisette thought to herself with a chuckle.

Her deportment tutor, Madame LeFray, would probably rap her knuckles with a cane and haul her off by her hair if she could see her now. However, in Lisette's opinion, if one didn't ask questions, one never learned anything. And although she may have been a bit forward to hail the man as she rode by, he had been looking at her. Not to acknowledge him would have been rude, she thought.

"Good afternoon, Miss," the man replied, and tipped his hat. It was a wide brimmed leather work hat, not unlike the one Lisette's dear Grand-Père Bartholomew had worn, and it made her smile.

The man himself was not old, but not a teenager like herself. Lisette thought he was probably in his twenties. Judging from the breeches, suspenders and rolled up sleeves of his work shirt as well as his somewhat

342

worn boots, she suspected he had been out in the vast acreage that belonged to the family. Whether as worker or overseer, she could not determine.

"Fine day, isn't it?" Lisette said, slowing her horse and coming to a halt in front of the house's white picket fence. She looked admiringly at it.

"Indeed, it is, though I should like to see a little rain," the man answered. "For the crops, you see," he added.

"Of course. What do you grow?" Lisette asked then, nodding encouragingly.

The man's reply revealed that the family grew feed corn, flax and also raised hundreds of head of sheep. "Their wool, you see, quite valuable for making material," he commented.

Lisette, still atop her horse and feeling therefore quite secure even though the road was deserted and she was, in fact, alone with a strange man, nodded again. "I have a wool suit and a wool cape, and nothing is so warm in winter," she noted with a smile.

"True. But wool is the fabric of the army, Miss, if you'll pardon my saying so. Having an efficient, and large scale, wool production capability will set us up well should we have another war, you see."

Wisely, Lisette nodded slowly up and down. "I do see. Good planning on your part, for we shall surely have a war at some point, or so my father says," Lisette agreed, impressed with the man's foresightedness.

"And, forgive me, Miss, but your father is...? To whom do I have the honor of speaking?" he asked directly.

"I am Elizabeth Charlotte LaPorte," Lisette replied proudly, and gave a very small toss of her head that sent her chestnut curls flying out of their lacy snood. Yes, her father was one of the leading men in the county and indeed the region, as well as one of the wealthiest. But the

Welles family had been in this area far longer and were by all standards a very distinguished family. So no need for her to be uppity, as her father would say.

"Ah, Miss LaPorte!" the man replied, recognizing the name. And this time, he doffed his hat and gave a little bow. "Charles Welles, at your service," he introduced himself.

Chapter Fifty

Lisette learned that evening, when she told her father about her chance encounter, that Charles Welles was a son of Charles F. Welles, Sr. and his wife Ellen. They lived across the river in the village of Wyalusing, in a gracious Greek Revival clapboard home, painted red, with white trim.

"Oh, surely, I know the place!" Lisette had responded.

Her father had explained that the house she had noticed so often, on the south bank of the river, had actually belonged to the Welleses' grandfather.

"So he must be farming the family homestead," John had ruminated of Charles, Jr. "Odd, because his father is in business."

Lisette said nothing. She had deduced from Charles Welles' clothing that he had been engaged in some kind of manual labor, either directly or indirectly. This had made her curious, particularly coupled with what her father had just said, and she was now determined to find out more.

That summer, Lisette spent a lot of her free time when she was not painting or sewing or practicing her French with her Grand-Mère, riding throughout Azilum and beyond. She had been gifted by her father with a beautiful palomino horse for her most recent birthday. She had become an excellent horsewoman, much as her grandmother had been as a young girl. Also, John had thought the extra special gift might reinforce to his daughter the fact that he adored her, even if he now had another daughter to cherish. Lisette's birthday had been just a few weeks after Eliza's confinement, and little Matilda's birth.

Naturally, Lisette now made it her business to ride into Wyalusing at least once a week, looking with great interest at the gracious 'red house' owned by Charles Welles' parents. She also slowed as she approached the 'cake house' along the Wyalusing Road, in the hope of seeing Charles Welles again.

Several times he was in the field next to the house, and raised his hand to wave to her as she rode along. Lisette always returned the wave, but never stopped to wait for him: that would have been much too bold, she knew.

Fortunately for Lisette and surprisingly for the rest of the family, a letter arrived in late June inviting the entire family to a 'family supper and fireworks' the following Saturday at none other than Charles Welles, Jr.'s home along the river. The date of the event was July fourth, and the supper was to be followed by viewing the fireworks at Wyalusing, to celebrate the country's 64th anniversary of Independence.

The letter, addressed to John and signed by Charles, invited 'all the children' and mentioned that his 'great friend' Asa Packer would be his houseguest at that time, along with his own wife and young children. Hence, he explained, the little party and invitation.

John told his wife Eliza first about the letter, and her eyes lit up. "Why, John, he is quite an important man, Mr. Packer. He owns a canal boat company, and transports coal from the Wyoming Valley to Philadelphia," she said.

"Yes, I've heard the name," John replied.

"You've not met him?" Eliza inquired, curious.

"I think I did, once or twice, but only in passing," John answered, but his voice sounded intrigued. He looked at the letter again. "He says it will be a 'family evening,' and to bring the children," he repeated, reading the tidy handwriting. "Do you feel able to attend, my dear?" John asked solicitously. He was almost as delighted as Eliza about the new addition to their family, and respected the fact that pregnancy for her was not proving easy, as it had for Matilda. He remembered his own mother's struggles, and tried to be compassionate.

Now, Eliza nodded firmly and smiled. "I shall have a nap that afternoon...you said it is a supper and fireworks? So, in the evening?" she questioned.

John nodded affirmation.

"Well, then, we shall all go!" Eliza declared happily.

Bart made it his business to be at Azilum for a few days around July fourth, as it was a national holiday after all, and Eliza did have a good nap, so at about seven o'clock that evening, the entire LaPorte family, including Elizabeth, traveled in two carriages along the roadway down towards Wyalusing, to Charles Welles, Jr.'s home.

Lisette tried to behave as though the event were just another family outing, but inside, she felt as though a thousand buzzing bees were where her stomach ought to be. She remembered Charles as a good looking man, but since that first encounter she'd only had glimpses from afar. Would she still find him attractive and engaging? Would he seem as gregarious and quick when they had time for a more lengthy conversation? Would they even have time for a more lengthy conversation, she wondered, because clearly her father thought that Charles had issued the invitation to him, and imagined some kind of triumvirate pow wow with Welles and Packer. Maybe that was really all it was, Lisette thought, now feeling glum at the idea, as the carriages drew up to Welles' house.

They all got out of their conveyances and just as Lisette alighted, the front door of the house opened, and Charles stepped out. He came towards the LaPortes, who stood in a cluster in the front yard while two stable boys rushed over to tend to the horses and carriages.

"Welcome, neighbors!" Welles declared happily, and he extended a hand to John. His brown hair, slightly longer than was fashionable, and curling over his collar, was a stranger to any type of pomade it appeared.

"Thank you, Mr. Welles, it is a pleasure," John replied, shaking Charles' hand. He introduced his wife, then Elizabeth, and then Bart, then Lisette and finally Sam. The ladies curtsied and the boys shook hands with their host and Lisette was sure that Charles gave her a special smile when she rose from her curtsy and their eyes met.

"I have seen your daughter upon occasion when she is out riding, " Charles told John as he led them towards his house.

John looked at their host, and then looked beyond the house, at the spectacular view: one could see across the river, downriver to Wyalusing, and also all the way upriver to Azilum, because of its situation and the way the river curved. No wonder Charles had invited them to see the fireworks at Wyalusing: they would have a perfect view from here.

"Indeed, you may well see nearly all the comings and goings from our settlement," John declared now with a chuckle. He turned and gave Charles a shrewd, but not unfriendly look. "And I daresay you might have looked out for one particular traveller, on her distinctive palomino?" he queried in a voice low enough that only Charles could hear. He had caught the smile Charles had given his daughter upon greeting everyone, and had experienced a sudden realization.

Charles bit his lip, met John's eyes, and then gave a short nod. John noticed the younger man's color had risen. "Indeed, sir," he admitted. "'Tis a beautiful animal, that horse."

"'Twas a gift to Lisette, her last birthday," John informed him.

"Tell me, have you many horses? Those animals leading your carriages are fine specimens..." Charles continued, shifting the topic, and the conversation was all about horses for the next few minutes.

Charles' house was older than the LaPorte's and even older than the Grand Maison, and so had lower ceilings and exposed beams. Altogether more rustic, still, it was charming, Lisette thought, as they were ushered into the large parlor. Plank walls were painted a soft blue-green and the furniture was a blend of upholstered and much older, plain wood.

On a blue settee sat a woman who looked to be about thirty, dressed in a beige cotton dress with burgundy polkadots and several flounces at the bottom of the skirt. Lisette noticed the flounces, and thought she might like to copy the style when the time came to make her next dress.

Next to the woman was a little girl. A tall somewhat fierce looking man stood with them. Introductions were made between the LaPortes and Mr. Asa Packer, his wife Sarah and nine year old Lucy.

"Why you're the same age I am!" declared Sam to Lucy with a grin.

Lucy giggled shyly.

Sarah Packer explained that the baby, Malvina, who had been born that March, as well as their toddler, Mary, who was not quite two, were upstairs with their nanny.

"I don't think we shall bring them to the fireworks," Sarah noted with a soft smile. "But they will join us for supper, if you do not mind?" she asked.

"Why would we mind?" Eliza returned, sitting next to Sarah once Lucy had jumped up to go off and take Sam down to the river where she was very absorbed in hunting for frogs. "Families are the center of things, really," she said happily, adjusting a pillow behind her back so that her pretty green and pink patterned dress billowed out just so.

Sarah eyed the guest and leaned in. The men, along with Bart and Lisette, were busying themselves with glasses of lemonade in the far corner of the room. "I think your family will be increasing very soon?" Sarah asked Eliza, low.

Eliza blushed, and tried to look as though she'd been hiding her expanding shape even though she had been doing exactly the opposite. She was very proud to be carrying her husband's child: she felt it solidified her position in the family, and so did not mind if someone noticed her condition.

Although this was Eliza's second marriage, it was her first pregnancy, and she was no longer a young bride. Therefore, both she and John were being exceptionally cautious, to be sure that everything went well. The children, particularly Lisette, found the care and concern silly, perhaps, but they were unaware of all the reasons.

"In October, we believe, if the doctors are right," Eliza confirmed, putting a protective hand against her belly.

The conversation between the two women then turned to babies, and carried on as they were handed glasses of cool lemonade by a servant who had appeared. Charles brought John along with Asa, Bart and Lisette, on a short tour of the main floor of his house, explaining that it had been built in the late 1780s by his father's father, one of the first settlers to the area.

Upon their return to the parlor, another servant appeared and announced that if everyone would make their way into the dining room, dinner was ready.

Asa Packer held out his arm to his wife, and John did the same to Eliza, and the adults led the way into the dining room. As Lisette was preparing to follow along with Bart, Sam and Lucy, Charles surprised her by offering his arm to her and bringing her into the dining room of his house with the other adults.

Bart, left to shepherd the younger children, just grinned and shook his head: like his father, he'd observed the glances between their host and Lisette, and thought he knew at least one reason the LaPortes had been invited to Charles Welles' home.

The Nanny shortly appeared with Mary and Malvina. Mary had a little wooden high chair but Malvina's appearance was only for show, really, as she had already been fed and was sleeping. Not wanting the infant to wake, the Nanny merely handed the baby to Sarah Packer, who showed her around for admiring pets and coos, and then Nanny took her back upstairs.

Chapter Fifty-One

Lisette gazed with a feeling of heaviness in her heart at the landscape outside her window. Her room faced the river, and although it was only early September, the signs of approaching autumn and winter were unmistakable. Hay lay in tidy bales throughout the fields which themselves were now golden, not green. Leaves on the trees had begun to fall, carpeting the gravel pathway between Elizabeth's Grand Maison and their own summer home with specimens in brown and yellow and red. Birds formed long skeins against the deep blue of the sky, as they winged southward for the colder weather.

Every year, the LaPortes packed up and returned to Towanda for the winter, and this year, 1841, was no different. It was especially important, too, because Eliza and John's new baby was due in October: she would begin her *accouchement* almost as soon as the family got back to the brownstone in Towanda. Her doctor was, of course, in Towanda, so it all made sense. Still, Lisette always disliked leaving the house, and this summer the departure was especially distasteful.

She sighed, and turned from the view to gaze at her trunks, which were all packed. They were leaving later that morning, and in fact some of the larger trunks had been sent on ahead.

"I had so hoped to see Charlie, one more time," Lisette whispered to the doll her Grand-Mère had given her a few years before, when her *Maman* had died.

The doll's painted eyes looked back at Lisette, who imagined them full of sympathy.

"But he probably doesn't even know we are leaving today," Lisette finished, and tucked the doll into a large reticule that she herself would carry on the journey.

She had managed to 'run into' Charles Welles, Jr., or 'Charlie' as she called him in private, several times since the fireworks evening at his house. She thought it might be her imagination, but it seemed to her that he was more often near the roadway when she rode by, and although they sometimes did only wave, a couple of times she stopped and they chatted, and on one particularly hot August afternoon, he had brought her a cup of cool water.

Her Papa had told her—not intentionally, of course, for he had no idea of Lisette's distinct interest in their neighbor—in conversation that Charlie was managing the farm for the family now. It had fallen into neglect once his grandfather had died, and he had been tasked with getting it back into shape, and producing as it once had.

After that, her father had said, Charlie's brother and family were planning to move into the house and work the land themselves, with the crew of laborers that Charlie had developed and trained.

John LaPorte had said he was not sure what their neighbor would do at that point. He could possibly go into business of some kind with Asa Packer: he was experienced with canal boats and like Packer and LaPorte as well as some others, Charlie felt that a canal system along the North Branch of the Susquehanna was crucial to the area's development. Packer owned fleets of canal boats and even built locks for Lehigh Coal and Navigation, which plied the rivers from southeastern Pennsylvania all the way up to New York.

So Charlie, if he went in with Packer, could end up working anywhere.

Lisette had also heard her father mentioning Charlie to her stepmother, noting that their neighbor was nearly thirty years old, but had never married. Eliza had commented that she found this odd, and had asked John if he had any knowledge of why this should be.

Lisette, who had been coming downstairs and had heard the discussion between her father and stepmother where the two were seated in the Ladies' Drawing Room, had paused to listen, one hand on the graciously curving bannister of the stair.

But her father had merely said he hadn't a clue, and supposed that Charlie had just been busy, and then had ventured that thirty was not so very old to be unmarried, not for a man, at any rate.

The summer had been largely a pleasant one, although they did receive some sad news in late August, that little Malvina Packer had died. Eliza in particular had seemed to find this news extremely distressing, and had taken to her bed for three days to recover.

But now, Lisette heard the crunch of gravel beneath the wagon's wheels as it drew up to the front portico to wait for the family. Footsteps came from all corners of the house, and a servant came to the room a few moments later and removed her trunks. She heard her father call up the stairs for her another minute later.

Lisette took a last look around her room to be sure she hadn't forgotten anything, and then left, closing the door and walking listlessly down the staircase.

"What is it, pet? Sad to be leaving your Grand-Mère?" her father asked, noting her downcast expression.

Lisette seized on this and nodded.

"She will come visit, this time for a long time, probably until after Christmas, once the baby is born," John told his daughter. "And you may always write to her," he added with an indulgent smile.

Lisette tried to smile back, and sighed. She would miss Charlie, but more than that, she was afraid he would forget her. It was months and months until the following summer when they would return, and by then he could be off the farm and working who knew where. And by then he could also have met someone else.

"Oh, and speaking of writing, this came in the morning post: the last we shall receive here this year," John continued happily, producing a small, flat parcel from one pocket. "'Tis addressed to you," he told Lisette, handing it to her.

It was several minutes before Lisette had a chance to open her parcel, because first everyone had to climb into the carriage and get settled. Eliza, who was quite vast by this time, changed her seat twice before they set off, claiming that she had to sit in the shade or else she would be too hot, and wishing to be near an open window, for the breeze. It was clear that she was made extremely uncomfortable by her bulk, and Lisette sympathized.

In the end, the carriage was about two miles away from the house by the time Lisette slit the brown paper parcel open with a thumb nail, affecting only mild interest, but somehow feeling very excited.

Inside was a slender volume entitled, 'Poems,' by William Cullen Bryant. She opened to the flyleaf and saw, *'for Miss LaPorte, in the hope that she enjoys these works, as I have, your obedient servant, Charles Welles, Jr.'*

"What have you there, pet?" John asked, and held his hand out for the book.

Lisette handed it across the large carriage, but kept the folded note that had been with it in amongst the brown wrapping paper.

John opened the volume, scanned the first few pages, and handed it back to his daughter. "Seems a peculiar choice for a young lady, quite cerebral and a bit dull, but not inappropriate," he pronounced, smiling at Lisette.

"Mr. Welles and I both enjoy poetry," Lisette offered with a little smile. "He has told me that great subjects may benefit from a gentle treatment, and I suspect this book is meant to be an example of that," she finished.

Her father nodded, and looked out of the carriage window. Bart was already in Towanda. Sam was looking out of another window, and Eliza rested her head against a poufy pillow and turned closed eyes towards the breeze from a third.

Seizing the moment when no one was talking to or looking at her, Lisette opened the book, pretending to gaze at the poems, but stealthily slipped the note inside, and opened it.

'*My dear Miss LaPorte,*' the note began in Charles' tidy hand. '*I have much enjoyed our conversations this summer, and hope this little book will allow you to think of me from time to time, until we meet again next summer.*' And he'd signed it, '*Charles Welles.*'

It was hardly a declaration, Lisette knew, but to her it was a huge thing, for it meant that Charlie at the very least liked her, and was looking forward to seeing her again. She sighed happily, and tucked the little book, with its note, into her large reticule, next to her beloved doll.

Chapter Fifty-Two

When Eliza was safely delivered of a daughter on October 24 of that year, the fact that she insisted on naming the child Matilda after her husband's dead wife raised her stock in the family, and Bart, Sam and Lisette felt and acted more warmly towards her. John, of course, had been overcome with emotion when Eliza had announced her wishes. But he was also grateful when deeper harmony and genuine good will returned to his home.

Little Matilda was a good baby, pleasant and even tempered, with blue eyes and brown hair and rosy cheeks. She was almost seven months old when the LaPortes returned to Azilum and their summer home the following year.

In the intervening winter, Lisette had not heard from Charlie, but the volume of Bryant's poetry became well-thumbed from her handling it and reading it. Contrary to her father's opinion, Lisette had found the pieces intriguing, if somewhat beyond her ken at times. In these instances, she made notes of concepts she was unsure of, looked up words she did not yet know, and in general approached the poems as tools for stretching her mind.

The bonus of course was that reading the little book made her feel closer to Charlie, even though not a word had been exchanged between them for months.

Elizabeth had come in October to help with the new baby, and although Eliza seemed to come into her own and be far more settled and less insecure once she was up and around following the birth, the grandmother stayed until after the holidays. Thus, Lisette had ample time to talk to her Elizabeth, and finally confessed to her her feelings for Charlie.

They had been sitting in the small parlor at the Towanda house, Elizabeth sewing lace on a little cap for baby Matilda and Lisette reading her treasured poetry book when Elizabeth said, "you are very fond of Mr. Bryant's work, Lisette."

Blushing, Lisette had admitted that she liked the poems well enough although some were confusing to her, but that it was more because Charlie had given the book to her that she read it all the time.

"So you are more fond of Mr. Welles than Mr. Bryant," her grandmother teased.

"I am very fond of Mr. Welles, Grand-Mère," Lisette said honestly: prevarication had always been difficult for her, and she did not know how to be coy. "I do not know Mr. Bryant," she finished with a grin.

Eventually, the several encounters the previous summer between Lisette and Charlie were revealed to Elizabeth, even though most had been brief and out in the open along the road to Wyalusing.

"And so you find that you like this man, *hein, ma petite*?" Elizabeth asked with a smile. "Tell me, what do you like about him? Indeed, what do you know about him?" she asked with perspicacity.

"Well," Lisette thought for a moment. "I know he is a very hard worker, for he's whipped that farm into shape and he does not hesitate to work alongside his men if need be," she began. Charlie had told her during one of their roadside chats that if one of the men were ill, or if they were working to meet a deadline, he did not hesitate to join in with whatever task was on hand. She admired that.

Elizabeth nodded.

"And I know he is kind," Lisette continued, sharing with her grandmother information Charlie had given her on some of his workers. "He is concerned for his workers' welfare, not just because if they are ill, his work may fall behind, but because they are people, just like him," Lisette said quietly. But her eyes shone.

"Indeed, I have heard at church that some of his workers' families have benefitted from Mr. Welles giving them what he claimed were 'extra' provisions," Elizabeth agreed. "He seems both kind, and generous," she added.

"Yes. And he is very smart, Grand-Mère," Lisette continued, warming to her subject. "He's told me all sorts of interesting things about the river, and about crops, and about books he's read," she went on, gesturing to the volume of verse.

Again, Elizabeth nodded.

"And he's funny! He makes me laugh! Do you know what he said to me one day, when I told him you and I had been reading 'Macbeth?'" she asked with a giggle. "He asked me if I knew why Macbeth was the greatest chicken killer in Shakespeare!" Lisette said, still laughing.

Elizabeth looked bewildered. "There are no chickens in that play, Lisette," she began.

"No, of course not, Grand-Mère, but that's the joke, you see: it's Macbeth, because he commits 'murder most foul...fowl...foul...'" Her laughter rang out, and Elizabeth just had to join in: it was a clever pun.

"Well, ma petite, that is one of the best reasons to like a man, or anyone really," Elizabeth told her grand-daughter quietly, once their laughter had died down. She remembered her own darling Bartholomew with a pang that never really got any easier, no matter how many years passed. He had always made her smile, even during her darkest times. He also had been kind, and generous and intelligent. She looked over and met Lisette's questioning eyes. "Yes, my dearest granddaughter, if someone is kind and generous and intelligent and can also make you laugh, or at least smile, they are precious. Hold onto them," she advised, a catch in her throat.

Lisette beamed. "Oh, Grand-Mère, once we return to Azilum, I intend to!" she replied.

In early summer of 1842, Charles Welles met formally with John LaPorte, to ask permission to court Lisette. John, despite his surprise, could not help remembering his mother and father's tales of when Bartholomew had asked John Franklin for permission to court Elizabeth. John had objections now, just as Franklin had then. And just as before, the objections revolved around the youth of the female and the gap in age between her and the male.

"She is only sixteen," John told Charlie as the two men sat in the second reception room. John eased himself into a rocking chair while Charlie settled on an upholstered love seat.

"Ah, yes, and I am thirty, I realize that," Charlie replied: his birthday had been the month before, May 24. "But I wanted to first make my way in the world and have something to offer, some security, and a good future, a good life, before choosing a partner," he explained solemnly.

"Well, I should say you have that now, Mr. Welles," John replied genially. "Particularly with that new merchandising venture," he added approvingly.

Charlie had been operating a successful store near Sugar Run since 1835, and also was a partner in a second store in Quick's Bend. Both of these endeavors he had engaged in while still operating his grandfather's farm.

Now that the farm was being turned over to his brother, Charlie had acquired some land near Athens, and was planning to build a new home, and to open a dry goods store in the downtown district there. The burgeoning town needed one, as its current consumer goods store was very small. In addition, however, Charlie was looking to the future, and envisioning a chain of stores all along the North Branch of the Susquehanna and what he hoped would soon be a Canal.

Now, Charlie nodded in acknowledgement. "And to be honest, sir, no one has ever captivated me, on many levels, as does your daughter Lisette," he added with a smile. "She is beautiful, she is good, she is lively, she has a quick mind, and, well, what more could one ask?" he finished.

Charlie's delight in speaking of his beloved was so apparent on the young man's face that John could not find it within himself to deny permission. After all, it was 1842, not the middle ages. And if Lisette were in favor of it...

"Do you know my daughter's feelings in the matter?" John asked Charlie finally.

Charlie shook his head. "I am not certain," he admitted.

"Then, I shall ask her. And if she is agreeable, then, yes, Mr. Welles, you may court my daughter," John replied, and they shook on the agreement.

To say Lisette's reaction when her father spoke to her that evening was abundantly clear would be an understatement. She told him she was 'ever so fond' of Mr. Welles and could she ride over to his farm first thing the next morning?

John, with a chuckle, suggested that sending a note might be more ladylike, and Lisette spent about an hour later that night, seated at her grandmother's desk in the Ladies' Parlor, crafting a brief letter that was both polite and heartfelt.

Elizabeth sat nearby to give encouragement and weigh in on the final product.

'Dear Mr. Welles,' the note began. Lisette, who had no stationery of her own, had asked her stepmother if she might use one of the pale pink note cards she had. These were embossed with the initials 'ELP' for Eliza LaPorte, but since Lisette's given name was Elizabeth, the initials matched.

Thrilled that Lisette had asked, Eliza had of course given her permission and Lisette wrote carefully on the heavy, pretty stationery.

'My father has informed me of his agreement to your request that we begin courting,' the note continued. 'I am delighted to also give my agreement to this, and look forward to seeing you very soon.' She signed it, 'yours very truly, Elizabeth Charlotte LaPorte.'

That summer was possibly the best few months Lisette and Charlie had ever had in their lives. He called on her at least twice a week, usually took Sunday dinner with the family, and brought Lisette to Welles family functions, too. By the end of the summer, kisses had been exchanged as well as more ardent embraces, and Lisette thought privately that it was perhaps a good thing she and her family were de-camping back to Towanda for the cooler months.

"But you will miss him, of course?" Elizabeth asked her granddaughter as she watched the young woman pack her things in early September.

"I will, Grand-Mère, desperately," Lisette replied fervently, clutching a dress with elaborate smocking and ruffling on the sleeves in both hands, and looking up from the valise she was filling. "But I think, perhaps, a little time apart, to—to slow things down," she explained, hesitating, "might be good. Or we—..." she broke off, unsure of how to say what was on her mind.

"You are afraid of being carried away with your emotions?" Elizabeth asked softly. Oh, how she remembered feeling exactly that way!

"Yes, Grand-Mère, and I think he feels it too," Lisette asserted, blushing. "A couple of times I know it's been difficult for him to pull away."

"Well, you can write to each other, of course," Elizabeth consoled her granddaughter. "Every day, if you like."

Lisette nodded quietly.

Chapter Fifty-Three

The winter of 1842-43 was not quite as sad or lonely as Lisette had anticipated, for she and Charlie Welles did write frequently, letters flying from the brick house in Towanda up to Welles' new house in Athens, just a mile or so from the downtown business district where his store was due to open. Charlie's brother now owned and tenanted the family farm along the Susquehanna, and Charlie had had a new house, in the Queen Anne style, built right along Main Street.

Also, since the distance between Towanda and Athens was only fifteen miles, and served by two very fine roadways, Charlie was able to call in at the LaPorte townhouse from time to time during that winter. He attended Lisette's birthday party in November, as well as Christmas Dinner.

On the Sunday before Valentine's Day, February 12 of 1843, Charlie had been invited to dinner at the Towanda home of the LaPortes, as had become quite usual. Unusually, though, the weather had been bitingly cold and a blizzard had dumped nearly a foot of snow in the region the two days before. Even though by Sunday the snow had stopped, a fierce wind had sprung up, blowing any tracks made in the snow by horses or carriages shut with drifts that were hip high.

"Oh, I do not know if he will come!" Lisette said anxiously, peering out of the windows for any sign of a rider on horseback—which is how Charlie normally arrived at their house. He said since it was just himself, riding a single horse rather than driving a gig, or even one of the new cabriolets, was faster.

"We can hold dinner a little while," put in Eliza, who was doing some embroidery on a pair of socks for little Matilda. She was sitting, along with John, Bart and

Sam, in the main parlor of their home. A brisk fire burned in the big fireplace and gas lights made the room very cheerful and bright.

"But Mother, I am so hungry!" wheedled Sam, now ten. "Why do we have to wait for Charlie?" he asked truculently. "We see him all the time. Cook can keep a plate warm for him, surely?"

Eliza, who was especially fond of Sam because he was the only one who called her 'Mother,' tut-tutted at him and explained that Mr. Welles was an important friend of the family and that a half hour of hunger would not hurt anyone. "Think of the starving savages in Africa, or India," she admonished her younger step-son. "They know hunger all day, every day. Surely, you can wait a little bit." She glanced outside the windows that fronted on the main roadway: beyond the stately blue draperies she could see only white.

John exchanged a look with his wife. They had received a letter from Charlie Welles earlier that week, stating his intent to propose to Lisette, if they would give their blessing. John and Eliza had written back by return post that they were in favor of the marriage, if Charlie and Lisette would wait until she were eighteen. John had privately said to Eliza that although the two young people seemed very much in love and quite well suited, and although he had no qualms about Charlie's ability to be a good provider, he felt that waiting until his daughter had reached the age of majority and also the age at which most young women were considered to be 'marriageable' was wise.

'But why, John?' Eliza had questioned. Not that she wanted to get Lisette out of the house, for she had become quite fond of the girl and the two got on reasonably well— at least as well as many natural mothers and daughters. 'A summer wedding, at Azilum, would be so lovely!' she had continued with a smile.

John, however, had been adamant. 'Perhaps because I am a Judge, my dear, and I am held—and hold myself—to a higher standard. And so too, my family must be seen never to so much as put a toe in the pool of impropriety,' he had answered.

Eliza had still thought making Lisette and Charlie wait almost a year to get married was rather harsh, but it was her husband's decision, and she must abide by it.

As must Lisette.

Now, she glanced over at the young woman who still stood at the window, gazing forlornly out at the blowing, drifting snow. Then she gazed at the mantel clock as it chimed the quarter hour. They had been due to dine at one o'clock.

"We shall wait until half one," Eliza pronounced, with a firm look at Sam, who just made a face and went back to his book.

That same mantel clock was just striking the half hour, and John was checking it against his pocket watch as was Bart, in imitation of his father, when a jingling and jangling sort of noise, loud enough to be heard over the wind outside, became audible.

"What on earth is that?" Eliza asked.

Everyone stood up and went to the window, where a most unusual sight met their eyes. Through the still-blowing snow, they could make out four black horses in thick leather harnesses that were hung throughout with large silver bells. Behind them came a heavy sleigh, also black but with gold trim and more bells. It was being driven by none other than Charles Welles.

Lisette clapped her hands together and laughed.

Eliza gasped, then giggled in delight.

Bart stared out at the apparition in surprise, exclaiming, "well, I'll be! He's mad as hops, although bricky, I'll give him that!".

John muttered, *"mon Dieu, il est astucieux...et déterminé!*

And Sam, who had moments before so resented Charlie Welles' invitation to Sunday dinner, jumped up and down at the window and asked, "d'you think he'll give us a ride?"

Charlie himself appeared several minutes later, having brought his sleigh around to the stabling area behind the townhouse and been ushered inside through the kitchen and directly into the dining room. His snow-encrusted coat, muffler and hat were presently drying out, dripping on the hearth in front of the roaring kitchen fire.

Dinner was a happy one, with Charlie explaining that he had recently purchased the sled for use in just the kind of weather they were now experiencing. He told the eager Sam that yes, when the weather was better he would be happy to give him a ride on the sled. "Everyone could come, if they wished," he added, glancing around the table and giving Lisette a special smile.

"I remember my mother telling me that my father had a sled, over in Azilum, and when the roads were too bad for the carriages to manage, he would use the sled to make deliveries all throughout the settlement, and farther afield if need be," John put in at one point. They had eaten a savory oyster bisque, then roast pork and little red skinned potatoes fried in duck fat along with broccoli and carrots and were now enjoying a citrus ice as a palate cleanser before the rest of the meal.

"I may not need it often, but when I do, I shall have it," Charlie returned. "And I'll be the only merchant in these parts who does have one," he finished in satisfaction.

They discussed the blizzard, the speed of the sled vs. a carriage and the new government in the Oregon Country—which would become the Oregon Territory in 1846—over fresh rolls and butter along with jam and sweet pickles. Then came a six layer banana cake with cream frosting and raisins, followed by coffee and tea.

As they were dining *en famille*, Eliza did not withdraw with Lisette once dessert was finished. Rather, she and John together said they had 'something to see to' in the parlor, and excused both Bart and Sam to their afternoon activities.

"Lisette, you may visit with Charles in the Ladies' Parlor," Eliza said quietly as everyone preceded her in leaving the dining room.

Blushing, for it was not always the case that she and Charlie were allowed such privacy—even with the doors to the pretty parlor open—Lisette did as instructed. A few moments later she and Charlie joined the rest of the family in the main Parlor, where Lisette showed off the large, square cut diamond surrounded by smaller stones that now sparkled on her left hand.

"Papa, Charlie tells me you wish us to wait until I am eighteen," she said in an uncertain voice once congratulations had been expressed. John had rung for their butler and asked for the bottle of champagne he'd directed be put on ice to be brought up.

"Yes, that is true, Lisette," her father confirmed, looking every inch the Judge.

"But why, Papa?" she asked, much as Eliza had.

Again, John explained his rationale. Eliza, who still thought it overzealous of her husband to demand such a thing, stayed silent. Bart and Sam listened to the exchange, but did not seem terribly concerned.

"I told you, my dear, those are your father's terms," Charlie consoled her, taking her hand in his as they sat together on a love seat. "I shall be as anxious as you for the day to come, but it must be after your next birthday."

Lisette frowned.

The servant appeared and John opened and then poured out the champagne, even giving Sam a bit in a tall flute.

"To the happy couple," John toasted, and everyone echoed him and raised their glasses.

Lisette wiped the frown from her face and joined in the celebration. She would deal with her father's demands in her own way—as soon as the roads were clear.

Chapter Fifty-Four

Lisette and Charlie were married on November 29, 1843, just four days after her eighteenth birthday, at the little chapel at Azilum. When, just a week after becoming engaged, Lisette announced to her family that her wedding would be at Azilum, not Towanda, and furthermore that it would be the following November, John reacted with surprise. He felt some anger, as well, for Lisette's plans were clearly meant as retaliation for his dictate that she wait to wed.

"Don't you want to wait until summer?" Eliza asked persuasively. "All the flowers..."

Adamant, Lisette shook her head.

"Why not marry from our grand church here in Towanda?" John asked then.

Lisette thought that her father was probably planning to invite all his political friends and cronies, along with their wives, to what she thought should be a more private affair. She knew he loved her and was proud of her, and excited about her forthcoming marriage. He was very fond of Charlie, too, and had said many times that the uniting of the LaPorte and Welles families was 'dynastic.' So Lisette understood her father's desire to show her off, as it were, to all his friends and acquaintances.

But she did not want them all there: not at the ceremony, at least. However, she did not wish to say that to him. It might be true, but it would offend. So how to phrase it, she thought...

"Oh dearest Papa, you know Azilum has always been my real home, the place I love the most," Lisette had said sweetly. Well, that was true: she did not lie. She had chosen a family supper in the middle of the week when her father was tired from a day on the bench and likely to be less argumentative. "I've always dreamt of marrying in the little Azilum chapel, with just my family and my friends, and Charlie's, too, of course," she had added with another smile.

She had already told Charlie of her plan, and he had backed her completely, saying that he only wanted her to be happy. He was as unhappy about having to wait as she was, and although Lisette's determination to somehow let her father know how much his decision pained her had surprised her fiancé, he found himself admiring her spirit.

Lisette had then sent a letter to the priest who maintained the little church at Azilum. In her note, she had asked him if he would be available to perform a wedding ceremony at Azilum after November 25, 1843, and how soon afterwards.

His response had been that, because he only visited the little Azilum chapel to say Mass there every two weeks, he would have to coordinate her request with the demands and schedules of the other churches on his circuit. He had told her, following that explanation, that the first day he would be available would be the Wednesday following Lisette's birthday.

And so Wednesday, November 29, 1843 became Lisette and Charlie's wedding day.

Elizabeth had sewn the wedding gown for Lisette out of a thick ivory satin- striped silk, following the pattern of Queen Victoria's wedding gown just a few years before. The material, as well as the pearls that adorned the neckline, bouffant sleeves and hem, had cost a great deal and once the weather had broken that spring, Elizabeth had made a visit to the jeweler in Towanda and sold a couple more of the smaller stones Bartholomew had left to her.

'My son will be taking over the business,' the jeweler, now in his seventies, had told Elizabeth as they had concluded their transaction.

Elizabeth, who had met the younger man before, had nodded pleasantly at both father and son, and left the small shop, her bank account considerably fatter.

As a wedding present, Elizabeth gifted Lisette and Charlie with an ocean voyage to France for their honeymoon. This she had had to reveal to Charlie, who had intended to make his own plans for the traditional week or so away with his new bride.

'Can you leave your business for that long?' Elizabeth had asked shrewdly during one of the Sundays when both she and Charlie were at the LaPortes' townhouse for dinner. The trip would take about six weeks, with the Welleses first traveling to Boston, then boarding the ship that would take them to Liverpool, then traveling to London, across the Channel, and finally arriving in Paris. To return, they would reverse the process.

'I can—I have a good man in charge of the new store,' Charlie had agreed. His store had opened that summer and had been an immediate success.

Although he had no concerns about money, and could have afforded to take his bride to Europe himself, Charlie realized how important a trip to France, the LaPortes' ancestral land, meant to Elizabeth. And he was grateful to her for providing it, although he had also been surprised.

'She must have quite a bit of money in the bank,' he thought to himself with a chuckle once Elizabeth had told him of her scheme. The tickets she had booked for them the following April, both for the liner Britannia, and their hotels in London and Paris, were all first class.

Upon their return in June, Lisette and Charlie made their home at the gracious Queen Anne house that Charlie had built.

"I had you in mind when I built it," he confessed to Lisette their first night in their new dwelling. "And I am so happy, and quite relieved, that you like it."

"Oh, Charlie, I adore this house! Almost as much as I love Papa's summer home at Azilum!" she declared, snuggling close.

"You don't like the Towanda townhouse as well, then?" he teased her. He knew she had always found that house to be stuffy and somewhat confining. He theorized, rightly, that Lisette had also associated the Towanda townhouse with the loss of the freedom she experienced at Azilum.

He was correct.

Lisette shook her head against her new husband's bare chest. "No, Charlie, no."

Her grandmother—not her step-mother—had told her a little bit about what she called the 'delights of the marriage bed.' Lisette had found her grandmother's description to be quite tame, for nowhere had she mentioned the pounding heart, the breathless yearning and the joyous exuberance. At any rate, Lisette was quite satisfied in her choice of husband, and from his reactions she thought he was quite delighted with her as well.

Their honeymoon had brought them very close to each other, not only physically, but intellectually and emotionally. Experiencing the great Atlantic Ocean together, and then England, and then finally France, had been powerful for each of them. Sharing it had been profound.

Charlie's ancestry was English, so the few days they spent in Liverpool, going south, and then in London, understandably fascinated him. Lisette enjoyed England, too, although she was most anxious to see France, of course.

In London they visited art galleries and museums, boated on the Thames, saw the Tower of London,Westminster Abbey, St. Paul's Cathedral, Buckingham Palace, and marveled at the nearly completed building for the New Palace of Westminster, the Old Palace having been almost completely destroyed by fire a decade before. They also rode in the parks, shopped, and in general enjoyed themselves.

In Paris, they did similar things: visited museums, boated on the Seine, walked across the Pont Neuf, visited Notre Dame, and bought watercolor scenes from artists in the Rive Gauche. But Paris was shadowed by its history, a very personal history for Lisette, and now for Charlie.

Walking down the Champs-Elyseés or in the Tuileries Gardens, the shadow of the guillotine and what had happened to so many of Lisette's family's relatives and friends was never far. The Place de la Concorde, as it was now called, no longer held the horrendous guillotine, and Hittorff's statues and fountains gave the large square a gracious and lovely prospect. Lisette was brought to tears thinking of all that had passed in that place, but discovered, to her surprise, that the Place's new appearance, cleansed of its awful past and vibrant with art and artistry, somehow helped her heal.

'It is almost as though all the horrible things that happened here, and in France, have been cleansed— purified—or elevated, at least, in perpetual memorial to those who died,' Lisette had ventured.

Charlie had nodded agreement. 'Hittorff has done an excellent job re-fashioning this place,' he had confirmed.

A day trip to Versailles was equally emotional but equally healing: the glories of the palaces and the beauty of the gardens seemed to remind visitors, including

Lisette and Charlie, of the glories that were past, and that beauty and peace could somehow manage to live on.

Through all of this, Lisette found comfort and understanding in Charlie, and he discovered unexpected depths and strengths in his new wife.

Now, back in their beautiful Queen Anne home in Athens, right along Main Street in the Tioga Point section, Lisette and Charlie planned and dreamed of their own future together. His business was thriving, but he had heard of a scheme that he thought would make him even more successful. As for Lisette, she ardently hoped to shortly find herself pregnant, and start their own family.

Chapter Fifty-Five

The LaPortes and now the Welleses always summered at Azilum. The Chamberlains also generally spent several weeks there in the house they still owned, although winters were spent with their children elsewhere.

Bart married Emily Terry on July 31, 1845, a joyous occasion for both families, and the uniting, as John saw it, of his dynasty with yet another of the region. The timing of the wedding was unfortunate for Lisette, however, since two days before she had been safely delivered of a son, Frederick.

Although Lisette was quite well following the birth and recovered quickly, Frederick was a sickly and fractious infant who suffered from colic and who could only be soothed, it seemed by his great-grandmother's calming touch.

Elizabeth doted on her first great-grandchild and spent the rest of the summer that he was born caring for him. When time came for Lisette and the servants to pack up and return to Athens, where Charlie had been living during the work week, she impulsively asked her grandmother to come with her to the spacious Queen Anne home.

"You could see Frederick every day," she tempted, laughing. "And that roof needs to be repaired again," she added, pointing out the window in the Ladies' Parlor towards the Grand Maison.

The roof was sagging and leaking in more than one spot now, despite the repairs that had been made before. Elizabeth lived now out of a single room, with the rest of the great structure closed off and left to the mercies of whatever vermin might find their way in. She took all her meals at her son's house, and even slept there many nights, admitting that the Maison had become less than welcoming.

"And seriously, Grand-Mère, I should worry about you if you decided to live another winter here, in that old barn of a house," Lisette told her with a smile.

Elizabeth looked out the window, and sighed. She knew Lisette was right. But, "it has been my home since I married dear Bartholomew," she whispered. "Nearly half a century."

Lisette put an arm around her grandmother. "I know, Grand-Mère. But perhaps the time is right, now? To leave, I mean," she suggested.

Lisette said no more about it, but in a day or two Elizabeth told her that she would accompany her to Athens for the winter. "I shall take up residence at the Grand Maison next summer," she said bravely. "But my old bones find the winter along the river very harsh. I should enjoy being in a town, and mostly enjoy being with you and Charlie and little Frederick," she told Lisette.

Lisette for her part didn't mention that Athens was surrounded by water, so that if winters at waterside Azilum were harsh for Elizabeth, winters in Athens would likely be equally challenging, if not more. However, she was happy to have her grandmother join their family and happy to have her help with Frederick.

Meanwhile, John had become Surveyor General of Pennsylvania after leaving the bench. This job took him all across the Commonwealth and he was gone for long periods of time together. Eliza and Sam along with little Matilda lived in the Towanda townhouse in the winter, then joined everyone else at the house at Azilum in the summer.

The summer of 1846 when the families returned to Azilum, they realized that the Grand Maison was in even worse shape than they had imagined. Touring it before allowing his mother to resume her summer residence there, John and Eliza had deemed the Grand Maison unsafe, even though it was not much worse than it had been the year before.

"It must be razed, *Maman*," John told his mother gently the first afternoon they arrived, right after the tour. He, Eliza and Elizabeth were sitting in the little gazebo that was set in the now overgrown garden behind the Maison.

John gave his mother a long look: she was in her mid sixties, and becoming frail, although her spirit was still strong and her mind sharp.

Surprisingly, Elizabeth did not argue. "I know, John. I've known for a year or two that my days there were numbered," she answered him, smiling sadly.

Eliza reached out to put a comforting hand over her mother in law's.

"And it is not worth repairing, I do not think, not since you've built this lovely home," she gestured to the LaPorte House, which stood several yards away.

"Yes, and you spend most of your time with us, at any rate," John chimed in happily.

When he sounded like that, Elizabeth thought to herself, she was reminded of the way he'd been as a boy: ever optimistic.

"And you're very welcome, too," Eliza added with a smile. She remembered what it felt like to be an outcast, and never wanted anyone else to feel that way. "John is hardly able to come to Azilum now, with his schedule," she added encouragingly, "and Bart is with Emily, so it's just young Sam and Lisette and baby Frederick, so there is plenty of room for you!" she enthused.

Elizabeth agreed, but she asked that the demolition take place after they all left Azilum that autumn. "I may know it needs to be done," she sighed. "But I do not have to wish to be a witness to it."

With the razing of the Grand Maison, the last original structure from French Azilum disappeared. And, it seemed, some of the spark went out of life for those who still remained nearby, and who had known the settlement in its heyday. Although Elizabeth's life did not really change much from the way it had been for the previous couple of years, tears would still fill her eyes in the coming summers, every time she looked out of a window in her son's home, expecting to see her own, and did not.

Some of the timbers from the Maison were used to build a large barn near the rear entrance to the LaPorte House. Although there had always been the smaller carriage house, the expanding family and consequently increasing number of carriages, horses and the like, necessitated a larger place to accommodate them. Elizabeth gave her son money towards this endeavor, telling him truthfully that it would be a way that her old home the Maison might live on.

Meanwhile, Charlie had given over the operation of his stores to competent managers, thus providing jobs for the area. He himself became involved with the second segment of the North Branch Canal, something John LaPorte and even his father Bartholomew had dreamt of. In fact, Charlie invited John to become an investor, and the two grew close through this endeavor.

Once the fifty five mile segment called the Wyoming Extension had been finished in 1834, John and Charlie invested in the Northern Extension, ninety seven miles in length, from Pittston to the New York State line. Elizabeth became Charlie's 'silent partner' in this, too, as she handed him a wad of cash—the return on two more diamonds she had sold—that enabled him to buy more shares in the Canal venture. Her gift enabled him to become the majority stockholder and he was shortly thereafter named President of the North Branch Canal.

"But—this is too much!" he protested when Elizabeth caught him alone in the orchard that was to the west of the House. He had been checking on the early apple and pear crop from the trees that still survived, having been planted in 1793 when Azilum was first built.

She had given him the cash and told him what it was for.

Now, she smiled. "You know very well that a woman cannot make investments," she said quietly. "Consider it a gift—insurance that my grand-daughter will never want for anything," she finished.

Charlie looked at her in amazement. "But—where did you get the money, Madame?" he asked deferentially.

Elizabeth smiled her secret smile. "Ah, my child, you do not know all there is to know about me," she whispered. Then, with a chuckle, she turned away and waved, and made her way back to the house.

Chapter Fifty-Six

By 1850, John LaPorte was winding down his career as a Surveyor for the State and had gone into banking. He and Eliza lived principally in Towanda now, only visiting his House at Azilum briefly during the summers when his family was there. Bart with his family lived nearby, and Sam had chosen to go into business and so had also left the family townhouse. Matilda, of course, was still at home, and a bright, studious girl who brought much happiness to her parents.

Elizabeth lived with Lisette and Charlie in nearby Athens. Following Frederick's birth, the Welleses had welcomed a daughter, Anna, in May of 1847. Sadly, she had lived only 18 days. The following summer another baby girl had been born and had died in infancy. Frederick, although now two, was still sickly. But as Lisette consoled herself, at least he was alive.

Fearing that whatever had kept her from having more than one healthy child had visited itself upon her grand-daughter, Elizabeth watched over little 'Freddie' night and day.

But on August 14, 1850, another son was born to Lisette and Charlie. They called him John Charles after his grandfather and his father, and unlike his older brother, John was a lusty, healthy infant. Elizabeth breathed a sigh of relief: clearly, her grand-daughter's misfortune with her two little girls was not something that would haunt her the rest of her life. She had two sons now, and was still young enough to have many more children, and the Welles family was becoming one of the most prominent in the area.

Both John and Charlie were gratified to see the North Branch Canal finally in business, although it was not yet linked to New York State. In order to make that happen, the 'Junction Canal' only eighteen miles long, needed to be built to link the North Branch up to Elmira, NY. Here, it would connect with the Chemung Canal which led ultimately to the Erie Canal.

Meanwhile, railroads were beginning to criss cross the region and Charlie was asked to help build part of the New York and Erie Railroad near Hornellsville. This venture was successful and so in 1852, he built another section of track for the Buffalo and State Line Railroad.

It was while he was away on this project that Lisette's grandmother, Elizabeth Franklin LaPorte, caught a spring cold just before the family was to leave for Azilum. She took to her bed in the pretty Queen Anne house in Athens, initially assuring Lisette that she would be ready to travel after 'a few days of rest.'

Rest did not seem to help much, however, and on the evening of May 4, she called out to Lisette, who had not left her side except to attend to Frederick and little John.

"Yes, Grand-Mère, I am here," Lisette said gently, clasping her grandmother's hands in her own. "What do you need?"

"The doll," her grandmother said softly.

Lisette frowned. "The doll?" she echoed. What doll?

"The doll I gave you...made the dress..." Elizabeth explained, and she coughed, a dry raspy cough.

"Oh! Yes. Of course. Just a moment..." Lisette replied. She called for a maid to come and sit with her grandmother, then went to her own dressing room and dug in the back of her large armoire. There, carefully wrapped in tissue and put in a box, was the doll Elizabeth had given her when she'd been thirteen: fourteen years before.

When she returned, she dismissed the maid, and discovered her grandmother sitting up and looking, if not recovered, at least determined.

"Are you better, Grand-Mère?" she asked hopefully. "Shall I ring for some tea and toast?" she asked.

"Perhaps later," Elizabeth replied. She held out her hand for the doll.

Lisette handed it over.

Her grandmother smiled. "You've not looked at her recently," she said, but it was not a reproach. She knew Lisette was all grown up now, and had been busy with her children, and with Charlie, and with the house. She'd joined the Tioga Point Garden Club too, and had done much to beautify the property that their home occupied, as well as establish a park in the town, and see to the upkeep of the cemeteries.

"No, Grand-Mère," Lisette admitted simply.

"Look—..." and Elizabeth lifted the doll's skirt and held it out to her grand-daughter. "Feel that—..." she instructed. "Feel the hem."

Puzzled, Lisette fingered the hem of the dress. She had always thought it was smooth, but now, the hem felt as though part of it had lumps, hard little lumps, in it. With a frown she looked over at her grandmother.

"What's inside the hem?" she asked.

Wordlessly, Elizabeth took a small pair of sewing scissors and snipped a couple of threads. Then she reached inside and pulled out a long, thin roll of cloth.

Lisette held her breath.

"I put these in your doll's hem when they tore down the Grand Maison, and I came to live with you," Elizabeth said quietly. As she spoke, she began to unroll the cloth, which was about six inches long. "I knew they would be safe, because you had put your doll carefully away. And most importantly, they would be with you, for they are yours now. I shall have no further need of them."

Before Lisette could protest that surely, once she was over this cold Elizabeth could continue to use whatever it was inside the mysterious rolled up cloth,

Elizabeth took one hand, and poured several diamonds into her granddaughter's upturned palm.

Lisette gasped. "Grand-Mère!" she exclaimed.

Elizabeth chuckled, then coughed again. "Did you never wonder where I always found the money?" she asked. "Your father's political career to some extent—I helped a little when he was just starting out. The repairs to the Grand Maison and even the new roof on the Chamberlain house though they are sworn to secrecy. The LaPorte House at Azilum. Your wedding gown and your honeymoon. The new barn there, to re-purpose timbers from the Maison. Most recently, Charlie's investments, for I do believe in your husband, Lisette," she said, pausing in her enumeration. Had she forgotten any? Possibly. She couldn't recall them all, and she felt suddenly very tired, as though unburdening herself of the diamonds and their legacy had drained her.

"Charlie's investments?" Lisette echoed faintly, looking at the stones in her hand. It was impossible, by gas lamp, to tell their actual quality: a jeweler would have to do that. But if sparkle were any indication, these were worth quite a lot.

Elizabeth nodded, and explained the small ways in which she had helped Charlie in the past few years. "And he has produced a wonderful return on the investment," she finished.

"But where do they come from? How many were they?" Lisette pressed.

Elizabeth took the diamonds, then, and carefully rolled them back up in their sleeve of cotton, and handed it, and the little doll, back to her grand-daughter. "You will have to sew them back inside," she said. "And you will always have them, to use, to help the family," she told her.

And then, holding Lisette's hand, Elizabeth told her the story of how her grandfather Bartholomew had been given the diamonds by Antoine Talon, in payment for his assistance in smuggling him out of France.

"I remember Grand-Père wearing that funny little leather bag around his neck!" Lisette declared, smiling. "I always wondered what was in it." She paused. "And Papa does not know?"

Elizabeth shook her head. "No. Your grandfather was very proud of your father, his son. And he knew he would make his own way, and do well. He had the joy of seeing him serve in high government office, before he died, and for that I am grateful. But he told me, the night he died, when he gave me the diamonds, that I was to use them to help you. To help the family. And so I have. You may do with them what you wish: if you feel your brothers need assistance, by all means give it to them. But you have two sons now and god willing, more children to come. Charlie is a good provider: a wonderful man. But sometimes, everyone needs a little help. And now you have the means to give it."

After sharing the name of the jeweler in Towanda with whom she dealt, Elizabeth sent Lisette off to repair the doll's dress hem, and told her she felt very tired, and needed to rest.

Elizabeth did not wake up. She died the morning of May 5, 1852, age 72 years.

Chapter Fifty-Seven

Lisette was nearly undone with grief: her grandmother had been the bulwark and touchstone of her life, particularly since her mother's death. With Elizabeth, Lisette associated everything that was wonderful in her life, and most particularly her beloved Azilum.

She hastily sent word to Charlie, who left the job and rode night and day to make it back for Elizabeth's funeral, and her interment in the LaPorte family gravesite at Azilum.

"I cannot bear to think of going to Azilum for the summer," Lisette confessed to Charlie the night after the funeral. He was due to leave the next morning to return to the job site in New York, but for now they were together at their home in Athens. They were in their big bedroom with the huge four poster bed, in which their children had been conceived and born.

"But why, my dear?" he asked, concerned. "You love Azilum. You always look forward to spending the summer there. And you are supposed to be hostessing the Garden Club there, are you not, some time in July?" he queried.

"Oh, the Club, oh Charlie, I cannot think about anything like that just now!" Lisette replied crossly. "It's just that with Grand-Mère gone, Azilum will never be the same."

Charlie nodded. "I understand," he whispered into her hair. "But do you remember in Paris, how you found such comfort in the artwork and fountains of the Place de la Concorde?" he asked softly.

Elizabeth nodded against his shoulder. "Yes. I remember." She paused. "And it was the same at Versailles."

"Could you not do something like that—not on that scale, of course—..." he interjected with a smile for her. "But something to commemorate your Grand-Mère? At Azilum?"

"You mean...a fountain? Or a statue?" Lisette asked, puzzled.

"Well, perhaps," Charlie hedged. "What did she like most, at Azilum? Do you know? Was it the river? The trees? I know she loved the Grand Maison, but that is gone now," he murmured. "What else?"

Lisette sat up in bed, and stared at her husband, her eyes shining. "Her herb garden," she answered definitely. "We always had a *potager,* but Grand-Mère said that herbs should be grown by themselves, in their own dedicated plot." She paused. "But when la Grande Maison was torn down, the gardens were plowed over..." she said sadly.

Charlie looked at her, and smiled, and held out a hand for her to return to his embrace. "So, why not plant a new garden? An herb garden, near the house, where you and the children can tend to it, and see it from the windows. It would be a living memorial to your grand-mother, and one of which I think she would mightily approve."

Lisette took her husband's advice. She did return, albeit a little later in the summer than usual, to Azilum, and immediately began work on a small herb garden just west of the house, where it would get a lot of sunlight. Between choosing and planting the herbs for it, and tending to Frederick and little John, visits from her father and Eliza as well as other family and friends, and even a visit from her Garden Club who praised her flower beds and herb garden and brought cuttings from their own for her to use, the summer passed.

The following year, Charlie was home more, in between jobs with various railroads in the region, and by late summer, Lisette was pregnant once again. When on January 2, 1854, she was delivered of a healthy little girl, she could not help thinking that her grandmother was smiling down on her from heaven. She and Charlie named the girl Louise, and even as an infant, she seemed to share her mother's good nature and quick mind.

Although the personal tragedies of the family had been surmounted, challenges in Charlie's business life continued to confront him, although the stores he owned along the North Branch Canal were a good source of constant income. The bill to fund the Junction Canal that would link the North Branch with canals in New York and ultimately the Erie Canal was held up in Appropriations when Governor William Bigler blocked it.

"He doesn't understand!" railed Charlie after supper one evening when he was at home. Lisette listened sympathetically. "Without the Junction Canal, the North Branch is nothing...well, not nothing, perhaps, but not as great as it could be," he amended, calming somewhat.

"You say you think it's a political thing?" Lisette prompted.

Charlie agreed, adding that he believed the Pennsylvania Governor didn't want to do something that would benefit New York State, a neighbor, and also a rival.

"But it would surely benefit Pennsylvania as well," Lisette reasoned.

"Of course it would. But try to tell him that!" Charlie said hotly. "I've half a mind to build the damn thing myself."

Lisette smiled at this, and told him that perhaps he should do exactly that.

Angered by what he perceived as political reasons behind Bigler's denial, Charlie put together a group of his friends, including John, of course, along with Packer and others. They all funded the building of the Junction

Canal, and construction began, with the first section opening mid year in 1854.

Lisette had taken the carriage and gone into Towanda, visiting the jeweler her grandmother had specified, and selling a couple of the larger stones. This money she then gave to Charlie, telling him it had been a gift from her grand-mother and that he was to invest it in the Junction Canal.

Remembering Elizabeth's gift to him years before when he had wanted to invest in the North Branch Canal, a gift that made him the major shareholder and thus the President of the Canal, Charlie had accepted the money with a smile, still wondering where 'the old lady' had kept all her cash, but happy to have it in any case.

Some things, he reasoned, were only to be known in time.

The Junction Canal was built and survived for more than a decade, but its decline was hastened by natural disasters that damaged it and also by the rise of the railroads. Of course, Charlie continued his interests in the latter, and later in 1854, he built three more sections of railroads along the New York and Pennsylvania border.

Charles Welles, Jr., was becoming known as a transportation tycoon because of his ties to commerce and his involvement in both the canal system and the railroads. The Delaware Lackawanna and West Railroad contracted with Charlie to build an extension east of Scranton, followed by railroads in New Jersey.

In 1856 he was named President of the Lackawanna and Bloomsburg Railroad, and, still believing in diversification, joined in with his cousin Henry S. Welles in a water supply project. This included building reservoirs for New York City, and resulted in a payment to the Welles cousins of five million dollars, which they split. Some of the funding for the initial build came from three of the smallest diamonds in Lisette's doll's skirt hem.

Lisette did not tell her husband about the diamonds, not from any wish to be untruthful, but because of the delightful feeling she had when she could help him achieve his business goals and dreams. And so, their lives continued.

The following year the boom of the late 1840s and early 1850s made an about face with what is known as the 'Panic of 1857.' The international economy was declining and most investors had over extended themselves. Britain suffered a banking panic, and New York banks suffered when the SS Central America carrying tons of gold bound for their coffers, sank. The Ohio Life Insurance and Trust failed, and the large mortgage holdings it had defaulted.

Banks were affected, and by the end of the summer of 1857, the railroads had begun to lay off workers and stop expansion: with fewer and fewer goods to transport, they could not stay in business. This dealt a further blow to the banks, who worried about the falling value of railroad securities. Several railroads declared bankruptcy, and nearly all suffered heavy financial losses.

In such an economic climate, the two and a half million Charlie received for his share of the New York City reservoir project was a real boon, for it enabled him and his investments to keep their heads above water. Then, operating on credit which at the time was easy for someone like him to get, Charlie bought the North Branch Canal early in 1857. He did not tell Lisette until the ink was dry on the agreements and although she had no objections, for she thought her husband a shrewd and clever businessman, she did tell him that she wished she could have helped.

By summer of 1857, however, the North Branch Canal had closed, and Charlie confessed their ruin to his wife.

Epilogue

Elizabeth waited a beat, then took a breath. "Are we ruined, Charles?"

Her husband first looked down at the carpet, a Turkish one in now-faded shades of red and gold that had belonged to her father, and then back at her.

"Near enough, my dear. Near enough."

He sighed.

Lisette took his hand.

"Come upstairs a minute," Lisette said quietly.

"What? Why?" her husband responded, but he followed her nonetheless as she led him out of his study and up the graceful staircase at the LaPorte House. Quietly, they crept into the bedroom they shared and Lisette motioned for him to sit on the edge of their bed.

Then, she opened the closet door, rummaged for a moment, and retrieved her old doll.

"Do you remember this?" she asked him softly, handing him the doll.

"Yes. Your doll. Your grandmother gave it to you after your mother died." He fingered the green dress on the doll, now somewhat faded. "She made the dress from a dress she had been wearing when your grandfather proposed to her," he added.

"You remember!" Lisette said, very pleased.

"Of course. And that dress had meanwhile been made over for your mother, as well. It was precious to you because you thought all your mother's things had been thrown away. Having this doll, with this dress, was like having a bit of her back again, you told me," he finished.

He had no idea where his wife was going with this business about the doll, but he had learned in their years together to heed her.

"Exactly so!" Lisette was overcome with pleasure and gratitude that Charlie remembered all those details. He was a good and a thoughtful man. "And now that Grand-Mère is gone, it's like having a bit of her, too," Lisette said sweetly. "But there's more."

As her grandmother had a few years before, Lisette opened the seam of the doll's dress hem, and pulled out the roll of cloth, now somewhat shorter than before, for there were only a few diamonds left.

Wordessly, Lisette took her husband's hand, turned it palm up, and poured the few sparkling stones into it.

He gasped. "What is this?"

With a smile, she told him about Talon's payment to her grandfather, and the ways in which the diamonds had helped the LaPorte family over the decades, and her grandmother's gift of the remaining diamonds to her.

"So that's where you got the money to give me, to invest?" Charlie asked, smiling at Lisette in the moonlight.

She nodded. "I said it was a gift from Grand-Mère. And it was," she replied simply. "Now: use these to recover from the losses with the North Branch Canal, and to help fund your next investment, Charlie. My grandmother believed in you. And I do, too."

End Note

A short time after the conclusion of this story, Charles Welles joined with his good friend Asa Packer and established the Pennsylvania and New York Canal and Railroad Company. This was successful, and would ultimately bring the Welles family lasting security when he and Packer sold their company in 1865 to the Lehigh Valley Railroad Company.

About this same time, Lisette and Charlie sold the LaPorte House to their neighbors and friends, the Hagerman family, who had purchased a contiguous piece of property, one of many that the LaPortes and Welleses had sold off over the decades from the original acreage of Azilum.

Lisette and Charlie would have several more children: Robert on August 17, 1857, followed by Elizabeth in 1859, Henry in 1861 who died as an infant, Mamie in 1863 who sadly would die in 1868, and finally Jessie in 1866.

John LaPorte died in Philadelphia in 1862, and was buried in the family cemetery at Azilum. Lisette and Charlie located themselves full time in Athens after 1865. In 1872, Charlie would die, and Lisette, heartbroken, moved to New York City, where she died in 1885.

Their daughter Louise grew up to be a scholar and a writer, marrying into another great family from the area, the Murrays.

It is Louise who most likely made what is now known as The LaPorte Dress, of olive green silk. Its style suggests it was sewn in the 1880s or 1890s. Whether it was made from the same dress, or the same bolt of fabric from which Elizabeth's dress was made is not certain.

A handwritten note with the doll, purportedly from Louise, who appears to have initialed it, states that the doll's dress was made by Elizabeth Franklin LaPorte from her green silk gown, worn at Azilum in the 1820s, and the doll gifted to her granddaughter Elizabeth, whom I call 'Lisette' in the book to save confusion.

If we accept this as true, the only question remaining, aside from the remaking of the dress for Matilda, which is purely my invention, is whether or not the Victorian (1880-90) dress, known as The LaPorte Dress, was made from the same bolt of cloth as the original Elizabeth Franklin LaPorte dress. Given the luster and condition of the material of the former as well as its measurements, it is unlikely that it was made from the same dress itself. But it could have been cut from the same bolt of fabric, if that bolt had been stored away carefully.

Like so many other small but fascinating details, these have been lost to history and living memory and so, we are left with conjecture and imagination.

The LaPorte Dress, as well as the beautiful little doll in her now faded and slightly shattered green silk dress, are both on display at the House.

There are, of course, no diamonds—at least now—in the hem of the doll's dress.

The LaPorte family, the Welles family and Azilum itself along with other families who remained once the colony dissolved, have left a lasting legacy in northeastern Pennsylvania, affecting the landscape in ways far more enduring and far deeper than Bartholomew LaPorte could have ever imagined.

I do believe that he would be very proud.

FINIS

Made in the USA
Columbia, SC
14 October 2018